AMERICAN LIT

AMERICAN LIT

Jennifer Greidus

Querelle Books
New York, NY

Querelle Press
querellepress.com

American Lit
Copyright © 2025 by Jennifer Greidus

ISBN 979-8-9850341-8-9, paper edition
ISBN 979-8-9850341-9-6, e-book edition

Cover design by Linda Kosarin/The Art Department
Typeset by Raymond Luczak

First Published in the United States 2023

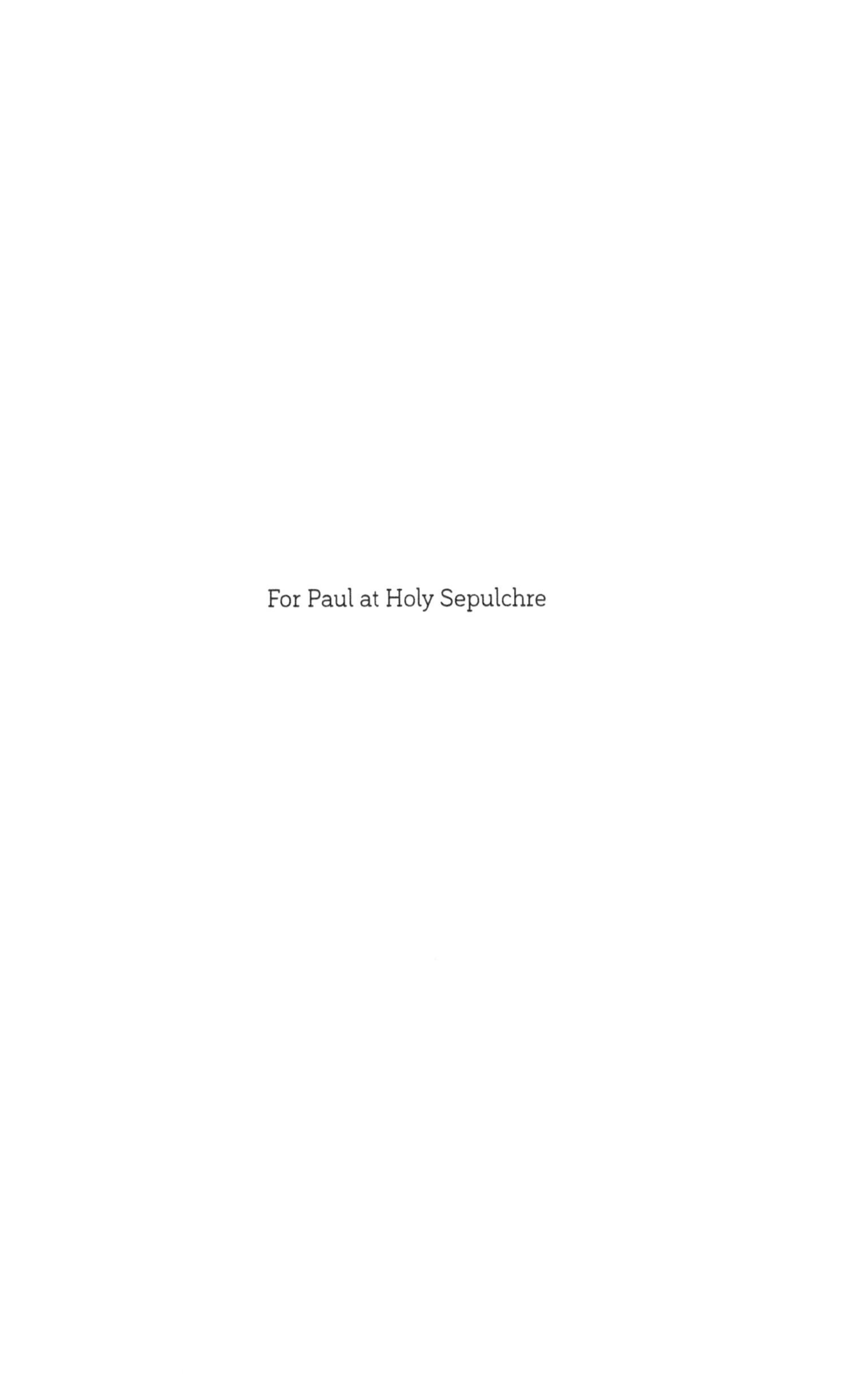

For Paul at Holy Sepulchre

*After you've banged about a bit,
you get used to your particular hole.*
—E. M. Forster, *Maurice*

While Ollie and I get stoned in his car every morning before school, I use my phone to take online career quizzes. I think in reverse, responding as I believe Mr. Stewart would. My mission is to find the amalgam of answers that triggers the "teacher" verdict. Only then will I know everything to say and do around him.

My favorite quiz—and the most thorough—was created by an Ivy League school to assist its undergrads. I log into that one about once a day. Among others, my hypothetical responses produced these career options: CPA, correctional officer, lawyer, architect, and copy editor. What a prospective correctional officer would be doing attending that school is beyond me. In any case, I have yet to see "twelfth-grade AP English teacher" pop up as the answer.

Always grumpy before the first bell of the day, Ollie broods and smokes between bites of a fast-food breakfast burrito. If I bother him with a question or to tell him he's dropped some hot sauce on his car's cheap upholstery, all I get are grunts or lazy hand signals; so, lately, I've been focusing on these quizzes.

You read the instructions before beginning any assembly. Yes.
You avoid arguing, even when you know you are right. No.
You always let someone know if she has a crumb on her face. Yes.

You are usually patient when someone is late to an appointment with you. No.

You don't mind getting your hands dirty. No idea.

That last one gets me every time. It might be the one that fucks up the algorithm.

During each class, if only for ten or our allotted forty-two minutes, Mr. Stewart, the thirty-something academic genius who corrects me with a verbal whip whenever I say *which* instead of *that*, lectures from a post directly in front of my desk.

The twenty square inches of zipper and fabric and subtle bumps and lumps inside his pants leave me overheated and dimwitted. If he's speaking, I don't know it. My interest lies only in his stretched fly, an ass of granite, and a minimalist leather belt that ties it all together.

Never has a single crease spoiled the light starch of his fitted dress shirts. His monthly haircut ensures every deep-brown strand is in place. Premature crow's feet appear when he squints or graces me with one of his infrequent smiles. From afar, I'd look twice. From this close, I can't look away.

"*Dan.*" Ollie tosses a wad of paper at my cheek. "Knock it off. You're sucking your pen like a dick."

Mr. Stewart's head jerks in our direction. "*Daniel. Oliver.* I can only imagine you're interrupting me because you have a question. Otherwise—"

"Hey, Mr. Stewart, I have a question."

Ollie and I both look to the right at Jesse, who yawns, his hand half-raised with an index finger pointed at our teacher. He wears the same jeans, hoodies, and T-shirts, sometimes three days in a row. He's consistently stoned, and he always has a fucking question.

"Says here," Jesse announces, "Mr. Hart Crane got drunk and fell off a boat." He taps his thumb against the back pages of the poetry anthology we've been reading.

Mr. Stewart stares him down. "What's your question, Jesse?"

"Well, yeah," he continues, slowly flipping one of his shoes onto its side with the big toe of a socked foot, "the bios are more interesting than the poems. Can we read those first?"

"We *can*," Mr. Stewart says, "but we will not."

Mr. Stewart believes grammar should be everyone's thing. When I think about him, I think, *me and him, him and I, he and I, fuck it, forget it*. He enjoys saying, "I do not understand why, on the verge of adulthood, none of you knows how to put together a sentence."

There's more to him than his obsession with grammar. We've spent a couple months in brief, after-class conversations concerning my future and books. We talk about tennis. Despite playing hungover, disliking the drills, and hating the parts where I need to run, I'm good at it.

Most days, he asks me, "Daniel, how did you fare at tennis practice yesterday?" And I always blather, "Good. Pretty good. Really good." It's tough gawking at a stashed but still conspicuous penis for almost an hour and then trying to keep pace in conversation with its owner after the bell.

All I want to do this year is have sex with him. It is my single goal. With a speck of effort, I'll conquer tennis at my club and on my school team, keep one sober eye on my handpicked senior schedule, and slide into one of the two schools of my choice in autumn. Having Mr. Stewart will be the sweetener. Audacity has been my stratagem for months—I've even flustered him a few times—but aside from some sideways glances and closed-lipped smiles, the flirting is meager, as difficult as trying to budge a piano with my pinkie.

After class, Ollie jostles me and kicks my shin. "Move it. You're like a girl with him." At six-foot-three, Ollie's body eclipses mine by four inches and forty pounds, and I take a second to regain composure before he shoves me again. "Why can't you want the corduroy Chemistry guy? The one with the brown fingernails? *English teacher*. Such a cliché, man."

Right on time, Mr. Stewart looks my way. "Daniel? A word."

"Unbelievable." Ollie snorts. "He asks you to stay like every day now. Hurry up."

Ollie heads for the exit as I pack up and amble to my teacher's desk. Rather than acknowledge me, Mr. Stewart contemplates whatever's on his laptop. I'm used to this delay; the silence Mr. Stewart and I share while I wait is the preamble to these afternoon one-acts. At the beginning of the year, I would fidget and cough, uncertain if I should speak while he wordlessly tidied his desk or erased the whiteboard.

Now I wait calmly and open a bag of homemade turkey jerky from my pocket. Drying meat on a rack for eight hours on a Sunday is the only way my mom knows how to show me she cares. Other than this gift economy, we are no more than roommates.

Mr. Stewart remains seated, and, as always, I stand across from him, the width of the desk keeping him three feet out of my reach. As I chew the dried meat, the aroma of the chalky cinnamon candies he enjoys hits me. I confuse his hold-on-a-moment smile for a speak-your-mind smile and forge ahead. "Great suit today."

He lifts his eyes. "How was tennis practice yesterday?"

"You know," I say, "instead of asking me all the time, you could come. See for yourself. Nobody else does."

"Your parents don't go?" The wheels of his chair squeak as he pushes back from the desk. He places both hands behind his head, stretching and expanding his chest until the shirt might as well be skin.

"My mother's in a world of her own, and my father—" I am distracted when he crosses his legs, resting an ankle on his knee. The landscape is crotch, all the crotch I could want. I force myself to look at his face. "And my father's dead."

"Oh." His hands drop to his lap. "I'm sorry. I didn't—"

My one-knuckled knock against his desk shuts him up. "Anyway. I only play tennis because he wanted me to stick with it. That and a partial scholarship. Really, I just want to sit around at home without pants, but it seems wrong to ditch it now."

"May I ask how he died?"

I tear at some more jerky with my teeth, and, as I've done every one of the last five-hundred times someone's asked me that, I grunt and huff. A crumb of jerky falls to his desk. When he winces at the morsel, I swipe it to the floor with my thumb. The smudge from my thumb causes a more pronounced wince, which I ignore. "Everyone knows how he died. Shot? Three years ago? Remember that?"

"That's—you're *that* Daniel." He sucks in a quick breath through pursed lips. "I apologize for being indelicate. Why have you never told me?"

I glance to the right as kids in the hallway rush past his open door. "It didn't come up."

"It must have," he insists, resting his elbows on his desk and craning his neck toward me, as if he's inviting me to tell him a secret.

I hope to put him onto the scent of a new topic. "So, what have you been reading lately?"

He drums his fingers on the desk, holding tight to the matter while pondering how he missed that gruesome part of my biography. "What about your mother? She can't manage to support you at a few matches?"

My mother can't manage much, except boyfriends, and barely even that. "My mom and I have this unspoken arrangement that lets us have almost nothing to do with each other." I hold up the plastic bag stuffed with jerky. "But she does make me this. So, you know, not all bad."

The crow's feet deepen with concern. "You understand you can talk to me about it anytime, right?"

"That is never going to happen. No offense." I'd rather not add my desire for Mr. Stewart to the existing tangled knot of emotions about my dad. For the past three years, I've chosen only guys who are nothing like my father. There's complicated shit there—I know it—and I'll save it for my twenties.

"I understand," Mr. Stewart says and opens his middle drawer. "On a lighter note, I brought you a book." He produces an inch-thick paperback, pristine, black with cubes of primary colors on its cover. "Please. Take it." When I hesitate, eyeing it like it might be homework, he shakes it once. "Take it. If you like Wilde, you'll like this."

With a tilt of my head, I acknowledge what we must both know: Oscar Wilde is the gateway drug to the entire gay canon. Although we talk about literature a lot, this is the first time he's given me something specific and extracurricular to read. I finger the edges of the book. "Who's Joe Orton?"

"Playwright. Give it a try. Let me know what you think." He lifts his laptop bag onto his desk, slips a hand into the side pocket, and comes up with a new tin of cinnamon candies. His manicured nails work open the plastic at its corner.

I quickly check out my hands. They are dirty and rough, the left one scarred from a battle I had with Ollie in fourth grade; he jammed a ballpoint into the meaty flesh between my thumb and forefinger, all over a bike.

"So," I say, slapping the book against my palm, "is this toilet reading or bedtime reading?"

The corner of his mouth twitches, as it does when he refuses to laugh, despite his obvious amusement. I suspect he wants to maintain a humorless teacher-pupil dynamic. This time, he gives in to a brief smile. "Daniel, I have to ask. Are you high right now?"

"Nope." I am.

"Just the same, some advice is in order. Use Visine. Get your hair out of your eyes. And whose shirt is that you're wearing? Who is Greg? Have you absconded with his work shirt? Is Greg a plumber?"

I touch the patch on my shirt as if this mysterious plumber is close to my heart. First, I know I'm not going to get eye drops; I've long since passed giving a shit if I seem baked. Second, it's been a few days since I looked in the mirror, and fuck that anyway. Last, this shirt has been my wingman so many times, I owe it a hand job.

"Mr. Stewart, do you run?"

"Why do you ask?"

"Because your body looks like you run."

The muscles of his jaw must ache from all the clenching he's doing right now. "Tenth period is calling you."

Students for his next class have begun to file in. I grin and turn on my heel. I'm not a foot out of the classroom before Ollie snatches my sleeve and drags me down the hallway. "You sounded like an asshole. Why don't you spend your time on something that can actually go somewhere?"

In a sinister, unlit section of the city, Ollie concentrates on the road and does his best not to drive us any further into the chasm of urban decay. His wipers flip-flap on high, and the fogged windows aren't helping matters.

I would rather have stayed home tonight, getting stoned and watching some nonsense videos. Instead, Ollie and I go to an "underage-night" at a club because he thinks he can fuck the girl who invited him. I go along because he'd do it for me. Also, Ollie gets easily heartbroken, and I'm here to talk him down if the night goes poorly.

After streets and streets of seedy row homes and containers overspilling with trash, we land on a main road. My phone calls out directions until we find what it reports is our destination. While searching for parking, we coast past the address.

The club's metal door, highlighted under the glow of a single, caged red bulb, is set back in a crumbling concrete wall. "Keep driving," I say. "That can't be it. Is that really it?"

"Yeah, that's it." Ollie pulls into a pricey public parking lot and finesses his mid-sized car between two that ignored the white lines. We share a joint. Tonight, being stoned is less recreational than it is the key to tolerating sweaty crowds that have no sense of acceptable proximity. When I get out of the passenger side, there is nowhere for me to step but in an inch-deep mud puddle.

Inside, I begrudgingly pull cash from my front pocket, handing it to a woman who has a toothy smile and a black eye. Paying to party is new to me—basements, back seats, and backyards are my usual chosen venues—and I make sure Ollie hears me grumble. We're frisked by a guy in a dark green suit and sneakers, and he waves us forward.

Once inside the club, we shake off the rain as my eyes adjust. Everything is red. The lights, the bar, the floor. The upholstery is velour, and red velour sofas butt against red velour walls. The lights equal headache. A flood of angry music rushes from the right side of the club, and it drowns out the angry music that's already playing to my left.

It's a sixteen-to-nineteen night. Older men have infiltrated and lurk in the corners; it's the perfect place to scope out adolescents. Girls with swept-up hair and slick lips sashay past us, their eyeballs white orbs in the center of dark makeup in this crimson light.

Everyone here pouts and casts smug glances at their competition or potential conquests.

Ollie sticks out like a sixth toe. His physique is more suited for chopping wood, not mincing in red strobes and wearing tight-fitting clothes. As if pulling a wet bathing suit away from an unexpected erection, he plucks his shirt away from his muscled torso a hundred times a minute. Until now, the tightest thing I've ever seen him wear is a T-shirt under his basketball jersey.

"Shit," he says. "I already want to leave. This place has a bad vibe. This is probably all pills and powder."

Two girls with fingertip glow-gloves walk past us, cursing while squeezing in between the bodies that don't step aside for them. One of the girls circles back and grabs Ollie's hand. He goes from slouched to shoulders-back in an instant, so I know she's the one.

Ollie rarely pulls girls from the giggling, superficial crowd, unless one of them is sloppy drunk, bored, or needs a ride home at four a.m. His poorly healed broken nose, a face that's too wide at the forehead and too narrow at the chin, and a cleft earlobe from birth might deter some. If anyone hangs around long enough, however, despite those perhaps undesirable physical qualities, panties will still be shucked. He's a seducer, funny and polite, and he has the musculature of a bull.

This girl likes him. She even touches that deformed ear and smiles. When I notice how she holds her bottom lip between her teeth and wipes the corners of her mouth, I hope Ollie remembered to pack a bushel of condoms.

For a twenty-minute loop of one song, he gets groped in an endless cock tease. The girl snuggles against him while I take a post next to them at the standing bar. The bartender wears a bunny suit, furry paws slipped off and hanging by strings from the bunny-suit sleeve. He pushes the bottle of water I requested toward me. "Six dollars."

"It's water," I say, digging out the money for what I thought would be free and from the tap.

"Yes," he agrees, "I know. And it's six dollars." After grabbing my cash off the bar, he winks. "It's fresh from the fjords of Delaware."

The wall calls me. I've been in this position dozens of times with

Ollie. Waiting for someone else to get laid is a tedious business. On front steps, on curbs under streetlights, in cars, waiting it out wherever necessary, this is what friends do. We lean against walls.

To my left, a hot guy—possibly a Pacific-Islander, slender, messy black hair grown to the collar line—takes the break shot in a game of nine-ball. His practiced frown and the red atmosphere accentuate his deep-set features. At least a dozen girls shift in their seats as they admire how his thin pants move against the skin beneath.

The way he sinks one ball at a time with a graceful poke of the stick and a modest smile belies his scowl and strut. As he lines up his next shot, leaning his torso over the black and red billiard table, he finally sees me.

I do the cost-benefit analysis: approach or stay here and enjoy my high? I'm still working out whether the effort I'll need to move my lethargic body is worth the chance of a hand job when a kid in burgundy velvet pants and a white T-shirt presses his back to the wall next to me. He touches his shoulder to mine. We say, "Hey."

Blond hair, smooth, pale face. New scars around his neck and old ones up his arms. The scars are the only thing that draw my second look; I've had blowjobs from two cutters and one burner, and they've all been fantastic.

Velvet Pants slides a few inches my way. "You here with someone?"

"Sort of."

"Boyfriend?"

I shake my head.

"Girlfriend?"

I shake my head.

"Any persons of interest?"

I shake my head but let myself smile.

"You want to dance?"

Of all the assumptions someone might make about me, I would have hoped that liking to dance would be close to last. A second's self-consciousness about it has me contemplating my posture, expression, and wardrobe. "Not really my thing."

"Want to fuck around?" His shoulder presses against mine.

I don't know exactly what "fuck around" holds in store for me, but if I consider the venue and the breakneck pace at which this is unfolding, I'm guessing we're on my preferred track. "Like what? Bathroom is probably super full."

Super full is not an issue. I leave my water bottle on the floor, and he pulls me by the hand into a hallway lined with girls waiting to pee. In the men's room, the light burns bright and white, an unwelcome contrast to the cherry-blaze of the rest of the club. The air is still, and the palpable stink of piss and ammonia sits at the back of my mouth like I swished with Pine-Sol.

Two stalls and all the urinals are occupied. An empty third stall waits for us. He pushes me into the tight space. It becomes clear why it's unoccupied. The toilet overspills with cigarette butts swimming in water the color of chicken broth. Condoms, baggies, every bodily fluid but blood coat the floor, most of it slick with urine and marked with footprints.

Regardless, the kid ruins his velvet pants by grabbing my hips and dropping to his knees. He unzips me, digging out my penis, up and over my shorts. The door to the bathroom squeaks open and closed like a metronome setting tempo. The faucets run. Guys piss and urinals flush. I steady myself with my hands on the walls, so my knees don't buckle. Someone says, "Hurry the fuck up."

Velvet Pants has target blindness. He licks my balls. He bites the inside of my leg. He swallows me whole. It is at this moment—two minutes into decent head and amidst the piss-stinking detritus—that my brain fixes itself on what it already has for months: Mr. Stewart, in his classroom after school, and a mutual, desperate, dirty grope-and-cum. I am ready to shoot already.

I wish I kept track of time. Hostages are supposed to do that. Or prisoners of war. Either way, I have failed. When it comes to the premature ejaculation minefield, my arsenal is well stocked with weapons of imagination. Torture involving eyeballs or kneecaps, breaking my ankle again, shit in my mouth, drowning. I focus on these scenarios three seconds too long, and my erection softens slightly.

"*Dan?*" Ollie's voice echoes throughout the bathroom. "Dan, you in here?"

My hand comes to rest on the top of the head bobbing on my cock. I hold Velvet Pants still and reply to Ollie. "Yeah?"

"Where are you? We need to go."

"Okay," I say, "give me a second." I step back from Velvet Pants, my hands immediately going to my jeans, which I yank up and zip.

The kid rights himself and grunts. Piss-water has darkened the knees of his pants. In a snit, he pulls open the stall door and is on his way, but not without flipping me off. "Thanks for nothing."

Ollie slowly pushes in the door and stares at me, mouth agape. "What are you doing?" Even when he sucks in his cheeks, he still can't suppress a chuckle. "Are you getting a blowjob in the fucking toilet?" He jerks his head to the side, as if I need reminding that there are about ten other people in the restroom with us.

I push past him, and he follows. I want to wash my hands—I want to wash more than my hands—but I keep moving out of the crowded room and into the club, where I backhand him in the chest. "I can't even count how many times you've done that to me."

"Eight." Ollie says. "And this one's my favorite."

My mom's wrapping up a work call when she enters the house. The presence of another person accentuates just how loud I have the TV. After a day's ration of weed, I am pot-deaf and not giving a fuck about much right now. Sunk into our doughy couch with my knees splayed and every muscle slack, save the ones I need to work the remote, has been my station for the past couple of hours.

Her perfume—a rich musk I associate with clinging to her neck each time she dropped me off at preschool—reaches me before she does. Right after she hangs up, she calls for me. "Danny? You didn't take your money for the week. It's still on the table—" She sees me in the living room and does a double take. "Holy Moses, what's wrong with you? You're white as a sheet."

I ignore her. Usually, her concern is fleeting, and she disappears into another room or out the front door before I respond. I am always a mix of relieved and hurt when she does that. Today, however, when she approaches and plants her petite body a few feet away from me on the couch, I'm unsure what to say or do.

Next to me, her white and navy striped skirt rises as her legs fall open too far. I've been taller than her since fifth grade, and whenever she sits on deep cushions, only her tiptoes keep contact with the floor.

I slide a few inches further away from her as she picks at the already flaking beige nail polish on her thumb. When she notices me watching her habit, she stops herself and feels for the frayed corner of the couch cushion, tugging on threads that barely hold the seam together. She sighs, gathering the energy to ask me to turn down the TV. "How can you hear yourself think?"

My finger puts forty pounds of pressure on the pause button. In the silence, I will my mother to leave, looking anywhere but at her: chipped glass coffee table that's gouged my calf dozens of times; velvety gold and burgundy chairs and chaise lounge, overstuffed dinosaurs worn from a decade of elbows and asses; faded golden curtains hiding the bay window and two dead potted plants; an ample living room she vacuums and dusts maybe four times a year.

We have cash from my dad's life insurance, and my mom kept her job as a real estate agent. Even with the means, however, we have reached the point at which bothering to replace a blown lightbulb seems like too much effort. My mom spends so little time here, upkeep is pointless.

I play with the buttons on the remote before exposing the batteries and rolling them under my thumb. My mom stills my hand with just an index finger between my second and third knuckles. "Danny, it hurts me to look at you sometimes. You look so much like your daddy in his twenties."

She says it a lot, and I never know what to say. Comparing my looks to his is the only father-son parallel my mother will allow herself to draw. It wasn't until a year after his death that she could say even a sentence or two about him, and when she did mention him to me, she spoke about how lonely, hopeless, or frustrated she felt without him.

I pull my hand from under her finger, and she *tsks*. "Okay. We'll talk about something else," she says, flatly. "The school called. You didn't go today? You've been absent a lot. What about college?"

"I've got early action for schools. I already told you that." I finally look at her. "Aren't you late for something? I don't feel like talking right now."

"Fine. I have to get ready anyway. I'm meeting Theodore for dinner. Oh—would you like me to bring you back something?"

I don't know who Theodore is. I assume a sampling from the large pool of men my mother dates. What I do know is her last question is a throwaway. "Why do you ask?" I say. "You always forget."

She tries to tuck a lock of her shoulder-length auburn hair behind her ear as she speaks, her voice stern. "So, we're going to argue now?"

"If you want." My grin dares her to start something, anything. "Go ahead."

"Don't be dramatic." She gives up on the stubborn, over-processed curl that won't stay in place. Scrunching up her nose, she waves her hand in front of her face. "Have you been smoking cigarettes?"

"No."

"I don't care about the rest, but I don't like cigarettes in the—"

"Yeah, I know."

"It sticks in the curtains."

"*I know.*"

My phone vibrates next to my leg. I let my head drop enough to see Ollie's message: *Get your lazy ass up and come over. Answer me motherfucker.*

My mom turns her attention toward the front door, her features fallen and inexpressive, a flush appearing on her neck and face. "Danny," she says, "I still get sad, too, you know. You're not the only one."

I stand and snatch my lighter and pipe from the end table. My legs collide with hers as I push past. "I'm not sad. I'm bored, and I'm tired, and I'm going to Ollie's."

After my mom and I were annihilated by the news of my father's death, she retreated to her bedroom, and I to mine. I was slayed, and she was slayed, but we were never slayed together.

I returned to school a week after his funeral, and I tiptoed around the house, making my own lunches, microwaving what I could find in the freezer or fridge, doing my homework. She stayed in her bedroom and didn't return to work for several months.

One quiet evening around the time she went back to work, we were about to pass each other in the dim upstairs hallway. I was just getting home, sweaty and tired from my tennis club, and was prepared, as usual, to move along wordlessly. Her cool hand fell upon my shoulder. I stopped and made eye contact. After a few seconds' hesitancy, she gave me a one-armed hug. For the first time since I could remember, she told me she loved me before quickly releasing me. Her bedroom door closed behind her.

Three years later, my mom and I still keep to ourselves and to our respective rooms, once in a while spilling over simultaneously into the kitchen or living room for an unintended and uncomfortable interaction, no sentiments proffered.

She and my father were loving toward one another. She worshipped and admired him, hanging on his words and anticipating his needs. But to the rest of the world, including me, she was distrusting and cold.

And her jealousy loomed, always. Any attention he paid me bothered her. Good report card? Winning my match? Tender moment? She was there, between us, interrupting our conversations, changing subjects, undermining any intimacy he and I shared.

The bathroom in school where Ollie steals a daily smoke is no secret to the seniors. Few teachers come this way, and there is no camera in the hallway, a musty corridor between two areas of disused classrooms that are hosts to broken chairs, wobbly desks, and permanently stained whiteboards. Most useful of all, any attempt by maintenance to install and regulate hard-wired smoke detectors is thwarted by the bathroom's frequent clients: burnouts who know how to disassemble them in twenty seconds.

By the time I finish squeezing out the little piss I have in me, Ollie's already lit up and sitting on a toilet. His eyes are closed in pleasure, the nicotine taking over muscle by muscle. His coaches would garrote him if they saw this, or at least strip him of his basketball jersey. I fill a one-hitter with my few remaining crumbs of weed and make the most of it.

Ollie titters at my desperation. "Your dealer sucks. He's got dirt weed, no weed, or overpriced weed."

When I'm done, I wait for him outside the bathroom, where the air is not so dank and sour, and chew on turkey jerky.

Sometime after my sixteenth birthday, my mother's proferrings of jerky started appearing in the kitchen. Suddenly there were warm strips of leathery turkey waiting for me on a cookie sheet next to a note with "Danny" on it.

Even impersonal instructions about what to do with the meat were conspicuously absent. Did this take the place of microwave dinners? Was it a snack? I would finish a batch, and another would show up. Over a year later, I'm still picking her offerings out of my teeth.

The double doors at the far end of the corridor swing open and grab my attention. Two figures of the suit-and-tie variety head my way. I turn and face the wall, examining my fingers and the bag of jerky crumbs.

Ms. Winter, a plump, ivory-skinned English teacher, walks alongside Mr. Stewart, who caught sight of me while I was gathering myself. He touches her shoulder as he slows and then stops in front of me. "I'll catch up with you in a minute, Maggie."

When she's out of earshot, he straightens the knot of his tie and speaks to me. "Did the bell ring? Why are you down here?"

"I don't know." I stuff the plastic bag of jerky into my pocket and suck my teeth clean. "Why are *you* down here?"

"Pardon?"

"Joking. Sorry."

Sniffing the air, he moves his nose nearer to my T-shirt. "I suppose roaming the halls is the least of your problems," he whispers. "You stink of marijuana."

I point toward the bathroom door. "Someone was smoking in there."

"Yes, and I think I know who the someone is. Where are you supposed to be when the bell rings?"

"A little piece of shit I like to call Fine Arts." I tuck my hands into the back pockets of my pants and grin. "But there's still, like, ten minutes left. You want to bond with me over jerky?"

"Are."

"Are?"

"There *are* ten minutes."

"You and the grammar." I wrinkle my nose. "Too much."

"I would have thought it would be second nature to you by this time."

The bathroom door squeaks. Out walks Ollie, who stutter-steps but realizes too late that he's been caught. His fingers go to his deformed earlobe, which he tugs until his startle response eases. Without a word, he takes off down the corridor.

Mr. Stewart ignores Ollie, but a moment's pause indicates he's made a mental note of the incident. He turns back to me. "You were sick yesterday? I see your empty chair more than I see you in it. What are you doing with all that free time?"

"I read some of that Orton book."

"Did you enjoy it?"

"Sort of." My eyes widen when I remember a gruesome bit from the author's bio. "Hey, you know he got killed with a hammer?"

"I did, yes."

I bounce on my heels, waiting for him to tell me to separate the art from the artist or explain why he suggested I read plays by a gay vandal with a jealous boyfriend. Instead, Mr. Stewart stretches his arm, lifts his cuff, and checks the time. "What else are you reading?" He gestures at my bag. "Anything in there?"

Weed crumbs, surplus turkey jerky, dirty tennis socks, and electronic devices. "Not books."

"In that case," he says, "would you like for me to bring you some other extracurricular works you might like?"

"Sure. Like what?"

The rhythm of our conversation snags, and I catch him staring at my body below the waist. My tongue tickles the corner of my mouth as I imagine slipping my hand in between the buttons of his shirt, feeling his ribs and the intercostal muscles firm beneath my touch.

"Perhaps," he says, puffing out his chest with a long inhale and exhaling his list of recommendations: "Borges, Chekhov, Brecht." He squints, his crow's feet deepening. "How do those sound?"

"I've read some Borges. Took me forever to get through."

Mr. Stewart quietly whistles. "His work is dense. Congratulations for tackling him."

"You think I'm home watching TV and smoking all night?"

"I'm impressed, not surprised." He slides his thumb up and down his lapel. The distracted repetition causes the lining of his jacket to shift against the creaseless, starched shirt. "You must know I already think highly of you. You're—" He stops, searching for the right word.

I stuff my hands in my pockets and lift my chin, inviting him to finish that sentence. *Smart? Special? Great?*

"Exceptional."

The compliment is thoughtful, serious. I expected a joke, or at least a lighter tone. I stay as serious as he is. "Thank you."

We nod in agreement, once, twice, before his eyes drop to my crotch. "Are those mechanics' pants?"

"Depends." I hold up one leg to examine the material. "Do you *need* a mechanic?" Our body types are similar, the same height, near the same weight, and I step a foot closer to him. When he doesn't retreat, I redouble my ambush. "You smell really good today."

He refuses to budge. Three unnerving seconds pass before I step back. He bows slightly, acknowledging my spineless withdrawal.

We stand in silence long enough for me to understand I should be on my way and he on his. He should know, though, that I'd do anything to drag this out.

I've attacked Mr. Stewart from a dozen directions, and we've plateaued at casual conversations and now a lending library. I know he has a tipping point, a place where desire outweighs ethics or fear, and I'll need to vary my approach to find it. I've not yet tried the savior angle.

"You're a senior advisor, right? What if I have a problem? Can I talk to you about it?"

"You have an advisor already," he reminds me. "Mrs. Valdez?"

"*Millie?* She's at least eighty. And she makes me call her 'Millie,' which is ridiculous."

"You underestimate her." He holds up his index finger. "She's experienced."

"Yeah, but I'd rather talk to you about the problem I'm having."

"Which is?"

"Home stuff."

He perks up; it's possible I'm not fucking around. "What in particular?"

Neglect is the crux of it. If I use that word, however, it implies I have either heard someone say it about me or I've done research about the concept. I'd rather he assigns the word to my claim. I offer only the facts. "My mom's never home. I mean, sometimes I don't see her for a week at a time. And she has a lot of guys around."

He studies me, one side of his mouth downturned. When he steps closer, not only does his cinnamon breath whispering across my cheek stir the hairs on the back of my neck, the nearness of his body to mine spikes my adrenaline.

"Daniel," he says in a quiet, compassionate tone, "I can do only one of two things here. I can let Mrs. Valdez know about your concerns, in which case, she will have to involve other parties and your mother. Or I can wait for you to tell me you're okay, that perhaps you were exaggerating, and that you will make it to graduation without child protective services visiting your home."

I situate my backpack and contemplate legging it before he can search my face for the embarrassment I feel. "Never mind," I mumble. "Just forget it."

"Wait." Mr. Stewart's warm hand encircles my wrist. He lets go as soon as he's sure I'm staying put. "I have to follow the rules. I'm sorry. You should tell me the truth. Are you okay? Yes or no?"

The idea of social workers visiting my mom amuses me. Her lifestyle would need to change. It would be a hassle; she'd need to keep her home cleaner, or she'd need to *be* home, at least. It would also mean no weed, no getting head on the couch, and no all-nighters. "Yeah, I'm fine."

As if the possibility that I am less than fine is absurd, he moves on without acknowledging my response. He consults his watch and tells me it's time we go. When it seems like he might wink, I turn away. Winking will pair poorly with my fantasies.

Alone, seconds before the bell, I stop at the end of the hallway and knock my forehead against the yellow paint of the cool cinder block wall. That interaction went sideways. It bordered on affectionate rather than carnal, and I don't need to feel cared for anywhere but in my pants.

It's a lazy blowjob type of night. This boy's been kissing and licking my cock for an hour. His name is Vincent, and he's so into it that he's in the fetal position on my bed with his head in my lap while I watch television. He's brought me to the edge a dozen times, moaning as he sups whatever oozes out of me, but I can just tell I'm not going to come.

I run my fingers over his velvety cheek and then through his chestnut hair, tugging once so he'll know to stop. Or at least to take a break while I dry off my balls. Even the mattress between my legs is wet. I've never had someone this stoned and this pretty, and his skin smells of peppermint.

I owe him something for sixty minutes of top-ranking head. "You want a hand job?"

"You fuck?"

"Nope." I change the channel to a documentary about bees. I move from bees to a man in a cow suit being tossed from a moving train. I go back to the bees. With my foot, I maneuver my blanket over my cold calves.

Vincent pokes my leg. "Suck me?"

"Nope."

Sometimes it's a surprise to guys when I tell them I don't suck dick. Other times, they sense it or don't bother asking. Regardless, most of them will drop their mouths on anything, and I'm happy to provide them with victuals.

Since eighth grade, I've upheld my truth that I would never be on my knees for anyone. It didn't seem like something my dad would want me to do, but not because he was a homophobe. It was more like he impressed upon me that there was going to be a power struggle in all interpersonal relationships, and it was shitty to be bottom dog.

When he caught me ogling James, our skater neighbor whose mother let him go up and down the street shirtless in summer, he slowly shook his head. "Always make them come to you. Your mother tried to pull me in with that coy bullshit. I stood my ground. And now," he said and opened a beer, "I can do whatever I want on a Sunday afternoon."

My dad was traditionally masculine: beer gut, bristled mustache that covered his entire top lip, a smile only for me, my mom, and anyone who worked for tips. Mid-winter, he'd tinker and labor in our driveway, assembling or repairing Indian motorcycles from the '50s. His rough, fat-fingered hands occasionally bled in the cold. He was a white-collar man by way of earned wealth but a blue-collar man at heart.

I move from the bees on the TV to a woman who, among squawks and screams and roars, machetes her way through dense rainforest, grunting with each slice. I glance down at Vincent. His head rests on my leg and I lift my knee, bumping him to get his attention. "So, do you want the hand job or not?"

"Yeah." Vincent unfastens his belt. "Pinch the inside of my legs while you make me come."

"What?"

"Jerk me off with one hand," he says impatiently, "and pinch the inside of my leg with the other. Hard."

"I have no idea why you want me to do that, but okay."

I guess it's not enough that it's midnight, and I'm jacking this guy in my bedroom so he can come and go. Now I have to involve thinking. *Too soft? Is this what he means? How long do I have to do this?* Also, because this job is more elaborate than the ones I prefer, I can't simply sit theater-style with my back against the headboard, continue to watch TV, and pump him until he shoots. I have to face him, and he stares into my eyes, which is the last thing I want.

I sigh and tilt my head back. As I contemplate the crown molding, I continue my mission. "Does it take you a long time to come like this?"

"Harder," Vincent insists and bucks his hips. "Talk to me. I like when you talk."

I know nothing about him, and I don't want him to know much about me. "Okay," I say, looking down at his pale legs for a second, "you read?"

"Huh? I don't know." He forces one eye open. "Yeah—faster."

"You know someone named Brecht?"

"I don't—I don't know."

"How about Chekov?"

"Jack off?"

"*Check. Chekov.*" I slow my stroke, gauging the swell, heat, and heft of his erection.

"I don't know." He shakes his head, trying to get his brain to move past the dense conversation. He tries to bring the discourse down a few levels, dirty talk for the everyman. "Talk—talk about something else."

I'm annoyed and I grunt, changing gears, moving my hand as fast as I can, pinching his skin enough to be sure blood vessels burst. I have a slight rush of renewed interest when he leans back, his left hand cradling his balls. I slow my pace once more and upgrade to fantasy. "What's the oldest guy you fucked?"

His hips stiffen and lift off the bed. "Mmmtwentymaybe."

"How about some thirty-year-old guy? Or forty. Like hot. You'd fuck him?"

"Mmmdunnomaybe."

The inside of his leg already glows an angry red. I give Vincent one last, nasty pinch and stand next to my bed. "Suck me again."

Before pushing him to the floor, I admire his angular face and farm-boy cowlick. He uses both hands and a sloppy mouth to get me off. I come in his throat while he kneels in front of me. He jerks himself off and shoots on his legs and my floor soon after.

I always stage the area so I can avoid the awkward moment-after junk; there is nothing within reach for the simultaneous clean-up. No bedside tissues for someone's sticky and spent body pressed against mine. No wiping down as we assess the event or lie about doing it again.

Just as is the case after any other sexual encounter I have, I don't want to talk, and I don't want to make eye contact. All I want him to do is leave. It's not that I dislike him. I only want him gone.

I pull up my shorts and head to the bathroom, mopping up my crotch before returning to Vincent with a wad of toilet paper.

He cleans off his legs and leaves the wet tissues on my bedside table. "What are you doing this weekend?"

Prepared excuses usually gush from my mouth without effort. Tonight, I don't need one. My tennis club has an away event. "I have a thing—tennis. An invitational. It's far away."

He pulls on his pants and studies me. "You're lying."

"I'm not."

With a smile, he says, "You don't play tennis."

I point to my open closet. Among piles of cotton and denim, on hooks where coats and belts might be, several jacketed rackets hang. "Have a peek on your way out."

Sitting on a bus for two hours to get to a tournament on a Sunday is vile, but the reward of winning my matches makes it worth it. During last month's invitational, I was hyper-focused. I didn't sweat or curse. I won, drank some water, had some fruit and protein, and got an unremarkable blowjob in the backseat of my competitor's car.

My dad first put a racket in my hand when I was nine, years before I'd play for school, and he never missed one of my club's matches. Of course, I'd trade the last three years of wins for only a few seconds of seeing my dad in the stands again, poking the stranger next to him and then pointing at me. I used to imagine him bragging about me during a tiebreak set. I was certain he experienced the same thrill I did after each point, after each triumph. Over sugary, convenience-store iced tea and soft pretzels on the way home, he confirmed as much. "No one is better than you out there. No one."

He and I usually traveled alone. I think my mother went to occasional matches only if he promised she could hit antique stores on the way home. In the car, she directed no conversation my way. My father was the translator in our relationship. She would ask, "Did Danny sort his laundry?" My dad would look at me in the rearview mirror and repeat, "Did you sort your laundry, Dan?" His wink would buffer the sting of her slight, but only sometimes.

I walk Vincent downstairs. The chill of the foyer's marble tile stings my bare feet as I wait with obligatory politeness for him to get in his car. When his car door closes, I shut out the night, falling back against the wall next to our painting by a Pakistani artist my dad liked. Camels and sand, a colorful but blurred bazaar in the distance, and one lonely dude bottom right, looking lost as fuck. For no reason at all, a muted laugh escapes my mouth.

"Danny?"

I jump. My mother's voice from the living room sets in motion what will be the joyless end to an otherwise okay day. I thought she was out. More and more, it feels like I own this house, and she's subletting.

I find her in my father's favorite chair. The TV glows with a cooking show, low volume. She makes no mention of the late hour, or my crumpled clothing and messy hair. Nor does she care that I just pushed some stranger out into the night. That she shuffles random men through our home like we're taking tickets at the door gives me license to do the same. I have sex in the house and stay out all night. So does she.

"Danny." She holds up a crystal tumbler. "Your daddy's good Scotch. Want a sip?"

When I decline, she wedges the glass between her leg and the arm of the behemoth of a chair. Her nightgown is too thin to protect her leg from the chill of the glass, and she flinches while motioning for me to take a seat in the chair next to her, the one she used while she and my dad watched TV.

Back then, before she would allow herself to relax, she nervously fluttered around him for an hour after dinner, bringing him soda, locating his remote, bumping the thermostat a couple of degrees to his liking. For every kind gesture she made, he always had a generous thank you.

I take a seat on the couch. Now her head rests on her shoulder as she drowses, the rise and fall of her chest barely perceptible. I'm hoping she's forgotten why she asked me to join her. Better yet, I hope she's done for the day, passed out, dreamless. I'm beat and just want to go to bed.

With some effort, I hoist myself off the couch and run a hand through my hair. Two steps, and the floor beneath the carpet squeaks. She shoots up, gripping the tatty arms of the chair. I stop mid-stride; the camouflage of my stillness might fool her into drifting off again.

"Why are you leaving?" she asks, offended.

"I don't know." I turn back to her. "Because I'm tired. You were asleep."

"I wasn't."

"Okay," I say, "you weren't. What did you want?"

With the glass, she motions to the kitchen. "I went shopping today. Eggs, the drinks you like, apples."

"That's what you wanted to tell me?" I know it's not; she starts every difficult or meaningful conversation—rare as they are—with an innocuous comment like that.

After clearing her throat, she tries to sit upright several times with no success. Her equilibrium returns and finally she's able to maneuver her ass center-cushion. She presses her shoulders against the back of the chair and burps quietly. "You know what day is coming up?"

"All of them." But of course I know. She drinks one week out of the year, and there's only one reason she would.

She opens her mouth wide, tilts the glass against her bottom lip, and takes a gulp of whiskey, spitting out the melting ice cube that snuck in with the amber liquid. A frown follows. "Your father's death day is coming up."

"Why can't we just remember his birthday or something? That's morbid."

Glass still in hand, she motions to the front door. "Was that your boyfriend?"

"No."

"Were you watching a movie with him?"

That's her shell game. The invitation to share is contingent on reciprocity. I often get the sense she wants me to consider her a friend, but if I show one smile too many, she interrupts with an unrelated topic, a chance to unpack her misery. She is my killjoy. "Mom. What's up? I'm tired."

"So, you're tired. The night ends because you're tired? Congratulations." She raises the near empty tumbler in a mock

　　　　　　　　　　　　　　　　　　　　　　　　JENNIFER GREIDUS

toast to me, her arm then sweeping through the air, the ice in her glass tinkling.

I don't want her to repulse me, but right now it's satisfying how much she does. Even from here, I can see the lipstick dried and caked in the creases of her mouth, how haggard she looks, and I revel in her fast-fading beauty.

"How's the boyfriend?" I ask. "Or haven't you narrowed it down to one?"

She wrinkles her nose. "Is that supposed to make me feel bad?"

"No." I deny it but quickly change my mind. "Maybe."

"Well, it doesn't," she lies, "and his name is Theodore."

I think about the men who settle for her—I suppose this Theodore, of late—and all the men she settles for. Her body and lifestyle accommodate each of them. She adapts and dovetails. At a breakneck pace, their respective broken parts create a single disgusting whole.

About five months after my dad's death, my mother began dating. It started with Bertram, a UPS driver who was missing a pinky. He knocked at our front door on a Friday night when I would have assumed my mother and I were still in mourning. I was on my way to answer the door, but she brushed past me in a tight pale pink dress and heels. "Go to your room, Danny. I've got it."

Since then, at least three nights a week, she goes out or has someone stay over. The offensive string of characters she chooses often hang around for weeks, seldom months.

A Newark native with no ass who liked to stare at the outline of my cock when I came down for breakfast in shorts. A hippie Jewish man who gave me a book on Buddhism and told me death was no big deal. Woodworker with a limp. Hirsute accountant. Bisexual barista. Unemployed. Self-employed. Married. Divorced. Alcoholic. In a band. In three bands. No socks. Manicures. Men who probably stole gum and men who seemed shady enough to embezzle thousands.

To me, at fourteen, her imperceptible period of mourning highlighted the gap between how much pain I felt and how readily she seemed to accept the loss; my interpretation was that she grieved too little. Nowadays, however, I understand this tactic of trying to smother grief; I do it every day with weed and blowjobs, and I am certain she would have killed herself had she not had the distraction of men.

On Saturday night, I drink room temperature beer and hide out in Theresa Keener's lavish downstairs hallway. Gilded mirrors everywhere. The marble dog statues might be greyhounds. Rumor is they have a Jackson Pollock in a locked bedroom.

I don't know Theresa Keener. It is a friend-of-a-friend invitation, and my friend-of-a-friend is Ollie. The entire night, all I've heard is someone screeching, "Don't smoke inside. Go *outside* if you want to smoke, fuckers." More than one of us has soured on this party.

Ollie sidles up to me. "Dan, you dick." He twists the top off two beers and hands one to me, taking my empty and placing it on the floor. "I thought you'd be near the door. You and your Irish exit bullshit."

"It's French exit."

"I don't think so." After a beat, he concedes, "Maybe it's both."

"Yeah, maybe it is," I say, cracking my neck. "I'm bored. I'm waiting for something to happen."

He elbows me in the side and juts his chin. "How is *he* fucking Jackie Floros?"

Jackie is kissing and hanging all over Jesse, the herald of Crane's nautical demise. His outfit is on day three of a three-day rotation. I gulp my beer while I try to figure that out. "Big dick," I joke.

Ollie shakes his head. "No way."

I grew up with Jackie. We've matriculated together since first grade and traipsed through the same parties since eighth. We have a few common conquests, those who may have miscalculated their preference on the first go-round, or those who shuttled between us for months or years. Jackie and I may not be friends, but we're friendly.

With little use for academics, sports, or female acquaintances, Jackie has plenty of time for guys. In truth, I admire her repertoire. There is nothing better than wanting cock and making no secret of it.

She tosses her long black hair, first over the right shoulder, then the left, exposing a small colorful tattoo of an octopus beneath her ear, one tentacle headed for her throat. She plays with the dozen necklaces around her neck, those chains her trademark. Everyone knows how she needs to throw them back when she gives head. An errant pubic hair caught in between links ruins the mood.

With a sly smile and a quick hand, Jackie slips a few bags of weed from the inside pocket of Jesse's coat. Ollie and I glance at each other. At the same time, we say, "Oh." If there's one thing Jackie and I like as much as dick, it's getting stoned, and it seems Jesse's dealing.

Jesse's all stoner. The hooded, red eyes and the thousand-yard stare, I know these are the badges of a pothead because I see them whenever I look in the mirror. Despite the chronic pull of euphoria, he gives anyone who wants it his sole attention with an earnestness that pairs perfectly with how he chain-smokes like an existentialist in crisis. He's cute—in a half-baked way—but Jackie Floros is easily six leagues out of his league.

A whale with a beer-breath blowhole, Ollie belches loudly and exhales the bad air ceilingward. I put my near-full bottle on the floor, and he snatches it up at once and drains it. "It takes you forever to finish yours."

"Because I'm not a glutton."

"Whatever," he says and pulls on his gnarly earlobe. "I know you'll get a blowjob at ten and be back for seconds by eleven. *That* is gluttony."

"No guy here tonight is sucking a dick. Believe me." I scan the room and renege on that, pointing to my prospective savior. "Except that one." Quentin, an overconfident junior varsity first baseman with thick lips and Southern Italian olive skin, sits alone on the floor in the corner, smiling at anyone who'll look at him. I am certain Quentin would love a cock in his mouth, and he's entranced by all the cocks now at his eye-level.

As I approach, I'm undecided if I'll make several passes or just drop next to him and ask if he wants to go to the bathroom with me. I decide on the latter. I'm about to squat and whisper when a wet belch rises in his throat. Vomit splatters down his T-shirt. I recoil at first but then pat his shoulder. Not knowing your limit sucks.

I spot Jackie and Jesse again. He palms off bags of weed and pockets the twenties he gets in exchange, and he does it in bare feet.

I've been using the same dealer for a couple of years, and ambivalence or laziness has kept me loyal to him, even when he went dry for a day or two. Tonight, I have weed, but I'm bored and curious about Jesse; so, I head his way as I fish a few bills out of my pocket, peeling a twenty off the remaining tens and fives.

When I tap his shoulder, he spins toward me, his face bright and relaxed. His brief smile is my invitation to continue. I hold up the twenty and raise an eyebrow.

Before Jesse can respond, Jackie squeezes between us and hangs off my neck. "Too tall," she says. "Come down." I lean forward, and she hugs me. Her bubble gum perfume irritates my nostrils as her tiny fist scrubs the center of my chest. "Stoned or tired?"

"Both." I touch her cheek with the back of my hand. "You look good. How are tricks?" Whenever she and I meet, Jackie brings with her a genuine and contagious enthusiasm about who she's with, what she's doing, and who or what is still to be done. Her lack of sarcasm refreshes me.

"Tricks is good, pumpkin, but I gotta go." Before she leaves us, she kicks back her heel, tugs on a piece of Jesse's neglected, sandy blond hair, and kisses him on the lips.

I point to Jesse's feet. "No shoes?"

"Yeah." He hides one bony foot under the other. "No shoes."

Both of us startle as Theresa speeds by us with a fire extinguisher, saying, "The curtains are fucking silk, dickhead." Theresa also wears no shoes, and her toenails are painted coral, which matches the wings of a poorly inked butterfly tattoo above her ankle.

Jesse says, "You think we should be nervous? Fire?"

I check over my shoulder, squinting to see to the end of a long, wide hallway down which she disappeared. "I don't think so. We're close enough to their pool."

"I don't swim." He mimes the breaststroke.

"Then, you're fucked."

I check out Jesse as he watches the hallway for flames. A comb would struggle to straighten the tufts of his thick hair, which is fucked-up and an inch past stylish. My fingers could hide in that wheat-colored thatch. His diagonal eyebrows rise at their tail ends. I zero in on lips that are fuller than mine, mostly creaseless, bubblegum pink.

When he laughs at Theresa, who can still be heard yelling from rooms away, his teeth show, all perfect except for his left canine, which protrudes slightly. His wire glasses are smudged.

I get his attention. "So, you and Jackie, huh?"

His cheeks pinken as he turns to me. "Yeah. I know her from her brother. I work with him."

"Where do you work?"

"Here." Jesse scans the room. "Anywhere."

"Oh. *Work.* Got it." I've only had one job—helping my dad before he died—but Jesse's line of business peddling gram bags of weed seems a hundred times easier and more fulfilling than counting screws, stocking light bulbs, and mixing paint. I hold up the twenty. "Can I?"

He takes my money and hands me a four-by-four zipped bag while scrunching up his nose. "What do you think of Jackie? She's kind of shallow, maybe."

I've never known Jackie to be shallow. Clever and goal-oriented, usually. Sexy, always. "I like her."

"I shouldn't have said that. I sounded like an asshole," Jesse hurries to say. "But I meant, like, we're not having any philosophical discussions or anything."

"Is that your thing? Philosophical discussions?"

"Not with Jackie." He hangs his head to hide his eyes. I get a whiff of his shampoo, something sweet, maybe vanilla. He watches his toes wiggle, and, to them, he says, "That wasn't supposed to come out like that."

"I know what you meant," I say. "Don't worry."

Two guys behind me wait impatiently to make a transaction with Jesse. He must be cleaning up tonight. I spot Ollie in the dining room. He's tilted a lamp and makes dirty shadow puppets on the wall, entertaining three girls. He sees me and does "the wave," which means he's pulled some pussy and I'm on my own.

I have a long walk home unless I find someone sober enough to give me a ride.

I push through the swarm of fucked up people and head outside. It's the sweet-spot time of year when frost one night fights the T-shirt weather of the next. I zip up my jacket and pull on one of my dad's beanies, out of style and with a few vertical threads missing from the navy blue knit. I sit on granite steps, avoiding the bodies of some of my tipsier acquaintances.

They all say, "Hey, Dan," when they use my shoulder to help themselves up the steps. Some of them were my friends before my dad died, but unless they've sucked my dick at least once in the past three years, they no longer know anything about me.

On my lap, I carefully roll a joint, afterwards searching for my lighter. It flickers, flickers, sparks. Nothing. I groan but then smile. My dad smoked a pack of cigarettes a day, never once remorseful, never once saying, "I should really quit." Each of his dead lighters ended up on my pillow with a note: *When we get to 100, I'll switch to lights.* The drawer of my bedside table is loaded with them. I add mine all the time.

Mr. Stewart assigns us to study groups of three. I end up with the two people in the class who are the least interesting to me, a couple of smart, humorless soccer players, and they're girls to boot. I grudgingly drag my chair to their corner, tossing my bag onto the floor.

We read Dickinson aloud to each other. Mr. Stewart said the metaphors would be clearer this way. They aren't, and I'm bored. Time drags for me, but for Ollie, Jesse, and Chris, the loudmouth of the class, the moments seem to be flying by as they giggle on the other side of the room. Mr. Stewart glares in their direction. That silences all three of them.

I sneak a look at Chris, a purportedly straight skater. His legs are spread, and the seam of his shorts splits his scrotum. Each testicle is trapped on its own lonely side. Shadows might be flattering the outline of his penis. I shift to get a look from a well-lit angle and smile. It's no illusion. I should have expected as much; Chris's limbs are king-size, and his elongated neck holds his head three inches too far above his shoulders.

Jesse, one shoe on, one shoe off, leans into Chris. At first, I'm envious of Jesse; I'd like to see what would happen if I pushed my knee against Chris's like that. But when Jesse's eyes meet mine, the breath I hold surprises me.

Until this class, I forgot about Jesse. Not a thought about him since he sold me weed over the weekend. Not a care about his bare feet with clean toenails and high arches. Not a memory of that shiny, crooked canine or his wish for deep conversation with a girl who does only one thing deep. I realize now, however, that our brief interaction has had a home in my subconscious since Theresa's party.

I look away and directly at Mr. Stewart, who grants me a rare smile, only for a second. He salvages the last fifteen minutes of class with a new direction: "Audre Lorde," he says. "Page seventy-nine."

Mr. Stewart wanders through the small groups of students, making quiet noises of approval or disapproval about pacing or pronunciation as Lorde is read aloud. When he nears me, his usual aftershave makes my cock twitch. He passes, brushing the back of my T-shirt with what feels like a fingertip. That's new. I track his movements throughout the room. He touches no one else.

By this time of day, through the dozen windows that line one wall of the classroom, the sun blinds us all. Mr. Stewart lowers one shade halfway, takes two steps sideways, lowers the next, meticulous about its alignment with the last. Over his shoulder, he glances at me, notes a beam still burning my eyeball, and lowers it another inch for my comfort.

Mr. Stewart's body language indicates the likelihood I'll be summoned to stay after class. The cue I hang on is his only tell; if he cracks his knuckles as I'm packing up, I am sure to hear my name called.

At the bell, though I haven't heard the crack, I am certain I'll be allowed to chat with him after class. That soft touch as he passed me earlier must mean I should stick around. When I linger, however, Mr. Stewart gives me no signal I should have. I keep moving, and it's not until I'm a few feet out the door that he calls me back inside.

Ollie blocks my way, but I sidestep him. "Don't be a such a dick."

"Don't be such a bitch," he says and laughs. "I'll see you later."

As I wait, I bounce my thighs against the front of Mr. Stewart's desk and have a long look at the body parts of his I want to think about tonight.

"One moment, Daniel." He gently shakes the pen in his hand, taps its tip against a blank paper to his right. "Please stop bumping the desk."

I do and mumble an apology. He scribbles some more. No ink appears, he swivels in his chair and drops the pen in the trashcan in front of the whiteboard. When he turns back, he squints at me. "You look high. Are you?"

By now, he might have learned to keep his disapproval to himself. Lying to him grew old months ago. If it were anyone else's inquiry, I'd doctor my reply with insolence. For him, I'm sincere. "When you ask, do you really want the truth?"

He frowns and pumps two globs of hand sanitizer on his palms, which he rubs together slowly. "Very well." He closes his lesson book. "There are parent-teacher conferences this evening. Can I expect to see your mother this time?"

"You *can*, but you shouldn't." My mom has never, not once, gone to a parent-teacher conference. My dad went, of course, but inevitably, she was always busy with a client those evenings.

"If I don't see her soon, I'm going to have to take my meeting on the road."

"Don't waste your gas. My dad was the one that did that shit."

Mr. Stewart straightens in his seat, pulling open his top desk drawer and removing a small green cloth. He unfolds it. The few tiny smudges on his laptop vanish as he wipes down the screen. "What sort of man was your father?" he asks, folding the material into its original perfect square. "If you could use only three sentences, how would you describe him?"

What a bizarre thing to ask. Three sentences.

There are a thousand things to say about my dad, and most of them have gone unsaid for years. As mundane as recounting someone's height, weight, and hair color should be, even describing his physical appearance gets me choked up. Digging deeper aches.

How he let me play my music on long car rides. How he helped me build my library with books I'd be years from appreciating. How he'd let me get out of going to Christmas at my grandmother's house if I felt like I wanted to be alone. All of these are all tender memories that will stay with me—and me alone—until I'm dead.

I stuff my hands in my pockets and shrug. "He was funny."

I don't know why I said that. He was rarely funny. He was affectionate, honest, and kind, but no one would have called him funny. "So," I say, changing the subject, "tennis was close yesterday. It's been forever since I've had a close match. All on me, though. I was dehydrated."

Mr. Stewart allows the conversation to go in the direction I want. After consulting his laptop, he goes to the whiteboard and chooses a marker from its ledge. His lesson takes shape on the shiny surface. "What else do you do with your free time?" he asks without turning. "Do you have any hobbies?"

"Hobbies?" I laugh. "I'm not retired."

"Then, what is it that you do with your free time?"

"I don't know. Watch TV. I work out. I read a lot."

While I like the view—his ass shakes as his hand works the pen against the white surface—I would love to see his face and make eye contact. I consider moving to the side of his desk, even closer, behind his desk, closer still, dropping into his seat, tapping his leg with the toe of my shoe before spinning in the chair.

He'd never permit any of that, of course. Even if he did, the clock on the wall tells me I have no time for an attempt; students will begin to arrive in a few minutes.

He turns, marker poised in the air. "What did you do when your father was alive? Did you have any other interests then, some you may have abandoned?"

I groan and throw my head back. "Is the dad thing going to come up a lot? You're ruining months of our great rapport." There's a baggie in my pocket with a lone strip of jerky. I pull it out and tear off a piece with my teeth.

He glances to the left as kids move swiftly past the open door. "We do have rapport. That doesn't need to change. I'm only concerned about your path."

"Path?" I pop the last bit of jerky into my mouth, crumple the baggie in my hand, and sink it in his trash can several feet away. I stuff my hands in my pockets.

Two students enter and take their seats without looking our way. I'm almost a staple here, between ninth and tenth periods, loitering at Mr. Stewart's desk. No longer does anyone seem surprised to see me or curious about what I'm doing here. I bet some of them think I'm the student who can't keep up, that I must be in receipt of consistent tutoring or in need of a stern talking-to.

Mr. Stewart takes his seat. "We can speak later. Good luck at tennis practice this afternoon."

I tap the desk to get his attention once more. When he looks me in the eye, I say, "I'm on a fine path. I promise."

I'm too fucked up to make conversation about the nonsense Ollie's had on my TV for two hours. He's asking me questions, my opinions on life hacks, podcasts, news, people dancing with their pet birds. I have nothing but grunts for him. As I fill another bowl, he throws an ice cube from a convenience store drink at me. "Let's go. You're lame when you're this stoned."

He texts a couple of people, groaning when he receives no reply. "No one's around tonight. What the fuck."

I remind him that Jackie Floros is always around, and she always has a place to party. Within thirty minutes of him reaching out, she's provided Ollie with an address: *Just come in!*

The address is that of her brother Brad. The house is in the middle of a string of neat ranchers with gardens, patriotic décor, and painted wooden mailboxes. Brad's place is the plainest on the block, off-white, neglected rust-colored shutters, a six-by-six-foot section of siding missing. Empty recycled containers lay horizontal, half on the street, half on his lawn. These neighbors must think he's the bruise on the polished fruit of their middle-class living.

Brad, who answers the door and mumbles an introduction, bears no resemblance to Jackie. His skin is pocked and picked-at; hers has been sheltered since birth: no sun, no scars, no need for makeup. He is the poor relation, and she is heir presumptive.

Brad swaggers around the house, scratching his balls and chin. No issue with showing his pasty potbelly, Brad's decided being shirtless serves him well. His scraggly chest hair is home to several crumbs, and the odd choice of skin-tight bike shorts that hug his thick legs and wide hips highlights either an admirable self-love or a dazzling degree of ignorance. He sips a thick, white liquid from a recycled sports-drink bottle.

In the kitchen, Jackie clutches a red cup in one hand and a pipe in the other. She raises her cup and winks when she notices us. We wave. I follow Ollie into the living room. He initiates conversation with three of the couple of dozen people here, and I keep my distance. I don't feel like moving my lips.

I help myself to four fingers of rum in an abandoned toddler's cup adorned with Pink Panthers and weave my way through noisy groups of classmates and college-aged bodies. I plop down on the nearest upholstered chair. The drink goes down in three gulps, followed by half a blunt. I smoke fast and squirm in the cushions until I'm snug. A tap on my shoulder gets my attention. "Right, Dan? Pussy and ass?"

I recognize his face—pug-nosed, untrimmed fingernails, scant mustache hairs—but I don't know his name. Two guys stand beside him and slap his shoulder, encouraging him to ask me again. One kid's face shines from skin too often scrubbed by acne wash. The other's eyes are too close together. Not ugly, but I remember reading something about that being a common physical characteristic of serial killers.

I curl my lip and look at the pug-nosed guy. "What?"

"Pussy and ass," he says and taps my shoulder. "They feel different."

My head falls against the wing of the chair. If I were sober, I would have a plan to extinguish the first flames of this conversation. Two fewer puffs, or two more, and I might be in the right state of mind to tackle questions about my apathetic stance on vagina.

The shiny kid says to his friend, "So, you go from the pussy to the ass and back again? Then what?"

"Then *what* what?" The pug nose wrinkles as he takes a sip from his cup and then wipes his negligible mustache with his entire hand.

"What's the point?" the shiny one persists.

"They feel different."

My peers continue. I've lost track of who's speaking.

"One's, like, meaty. The other's—I don't know—the ass is like this full squeeze on all your dick."

They all nod a lot, and one of them smacks my arm. "You know what I mean, Dan?"

Fielding inquiries like these from ignorant strangers is wearisome but doable. I have also mastered remaining unruffled by the inevitable follow-up questions when I am legless, woozy, and on the verge of passing out. Tonight, however, I'm squished under the leaden weight of sleepiness, ripped and inarticulate. For a pocketful of hundreds, I couldn't muster the strength to say anything more than I do: "I don't fuck pussy."

Struggling with what to say to whom, when to say it, and why the fuck I need to say it at all has not been my fight. My dad died before I put my penis in anyone. My mom is aware of what I'm doing on the couch or in my bedroom. The only person I ever had to come out to was Ollie, and all he said was, "Duh." I've understood myself for a long time, and I know I've had it relatively easy.

The pug-nose kid places another rum in my hand and says, "Too many people trying to get their dicks sucked and not enough people doing the sucking." I'm unsure if he's talking to me or his friends. I can't tell, either, if it's innocuous bellyaching or a hint. Is he smooth enough to pull off a tactical segue from the textural properties of pussy to an invitation to give or get head? I open one eye, see he's now alone, and decide it's a hint. I also decide it's a no.

Just in time, Ollie slides in next to me and shoos him away. "Are you over here talking about how much you like cock?"

I want to tell Ollie what a good friend he is, how I hope I'm a good friend, too, and how I'll be his best man and visit him at college in Houston. But I know maudlin confessions will only make him groan. I do, however, share what I think is big news, news he needs: "Olls? Olls?" I look around for eavesdroppers. "Did you know—pussy and ass feel different?" I press my forefinger against my lips. "*Shhhh.*" Then, my head falls forward into my chest.

"Sure, Dan." He slaps my knee. "You already look like you're gonna puke. I'll be back in a bit. Good luck."

When I wake up, the coconut stink of Ollie's plug-in air freshener makes me gag. Before I risk lifting one lid, I wipe my drool on a car seat infused with the odor of stale cigarettes and wet dog. In his backseat, I'm dry-eyed and nauseated. An unconscious body rests against mine. I click my tongue against the roof of my mouth. It sticks. "My breath is disgusting," I say to Ollie. "You have gum?"

"In a minute," he says. "You know where he lives?"

"Where who lives?"

"Him." In the rearview mirror, Ollie glances at me. "Jesse. He was passed out on the lawn. You wanted me to leave him there."

I squint to focus on the body next to mine. "You're bringing him home with us? He's not a stray cat." Bile rises in my throat. I swallow once and wait, making sure the sour mixture stays down.

Ollie drives at his usual pace: ten miles an hour below the speed limit. He could have had one beer or ten shots; his paranoia keeps his foot light on the accelerator. Even at this crawl, Jesse rolls around with each turn, stop, and start. After about the twentieth time he falls into me, I push him toward the door a bit too hard, and his cheek hits the window with a splat.

Ollie pulls into my driveway, and as I get out, the neighbor's dog stirs. A few soft howls and tired, pitiful barks. "Hey," Ollie calls out, "you know you gotta take Jesse. My dad will kill me if I bring him home."

Before I tackle the job, I throw up a sappy mix of mucus and bile in my front yard. Ollie opens the passenger side window and tosses a pack of gum onto the driveway.

It takes everything I have to haul Jesse out of the car. His head collides with the door. His glasses fall to the pavement. I scoop them up and put them in my coat pocket before accidentally dropping him on the asphalt.

I grab the gum and smack the side of Ollie's car to get his attention. "Where are his shoes?"

"I don't know. I gotta go," he says, already in reverse. "I'm sorry. You know I have to go."

I wave Ollie away and drag Jesse by his armpits onto the grass. I fall back next to him, my ass freezing, the back of my legs wet from the frozen dew. I pinch his ear; that always works on me. He doesn't moan or flinch. I remove my coat, lift his legs, and bundle his bare feet. "What a fucking idiot. No shoes." After struggling to my knees, I dry heave and then pinch him again. Nothing. One of his eyes is half open, the white showing.

I'm still fucked up, I know, but I still overreact and think he's dead. When I put my head to his chest to check for breathing, his body warms my face, and his heart beats against my ear. I sniff him. His sweet smell is at odds with every other untidy thing about him.

A good slap has worked a hundred times on Ollie. My hand catches more than Jesse's cheek and smacks his nose. He comes around quickly, but he's slow to place his whereabouts. "Dan?"

"Yeah," I say, struggling to my feet. "You have to be quiet." I grab the sleeve of my jacket and yank it from around his bare feet, which drop to the grass. "Can you be quiet?"

"Where are we?" He scans my neighborhood, closing his eyes when they catch the glare of my front porch light.

"My house."

We cross my front lawn, and Jesse stumbles and bumps into me. I finally grab his elbow to steady him. "Wait," he says, "where are my glasses?" He touches his face as though they might somehow be resting on his chin.

"I have them."

"And my coat?"

"You're wearing it."

My house key is buried deep in my pocket. I fish it out and usher him into the dimly lit foyer, where I drop my key, assorted bills, and his glasses. He holds his stomach before slumping on the stairs, gasping, and seizing my leg in alarm. "Oh, no."

"Hold it in." I am not cleaning up vomit tonight. If he loses it, I might lay him here next to it; he can mop it up in the morning.

I help Jesse climb the stairs, his arm slung around my shoulders and his head hanging heavily against his chest. When my mom's doorknob rattles and turns, I groan. She pops her head out of her bedroom, eyes watery, her hair tousled and in need of a root touch-up. The loose, shameless fit of her satin wrap shows too much skin, fuck-flushed and sweaty. If whoever's in there with her decides to show himself right now, I might puke again.

"Danny?" She yawns and with one hand shields her eyes from the glare of the hallway light.

"Go back to bed," I say, annoyed. "Everything's fine."

"Well, you're *usually* a lot quieter than this." She leans close to me and whispers, "Theodore is here. If you're going to make noise, do it in your room."

My mom asks nothing about the person hanging on me like a ragdoll. Whatever seedy enterprise I'm undertaking here, she has her own in the other room and would like to get back to it. She says, "I made your turkey jerky. Don't use the garbage disposal. It's broken. Goodnight."

I continue guiding Jesse to my bedroom, where I steer him through books and clothes on the floor. When I lower him to the bed, his arms hesitantly recoil from my neck, like he doubts he'll collide with the mattress when I drop him. He flops onto his back and covers his eyes with an arm. "*Jesus.* Way to toss me around."

I steady myself on the bedside table. "You want socks? Your feet are white."

"I'll live." He squirms, rubbing his temples and patting his inside pockets. "You know how much weed and cash I have in this coat? I would have been so fucked. Some of it's Brad's."

"Yeah, well, make sure you thank Ollie. He dragged you off the front yard." I kick a path through my scattered clothing on the floor. If he goes for a piss in the night, it will save him some broken bones.

"Jackie ditched me?"

"I guess." I consider what any of us does to get laid. I've never left anyone passed out in public, nor have I been left passed out in public. "So, you're still seeing Jackie, huh?"

"I am, yeah." Jesse burps. "But I don't think she ever sees the sun."

"You like nature girls?" I bend carefully, keeping nausea at bay and picking up a couple books that are in direct path to the door. On the way upright, I give Jesse the peace sign and a goofy face.

"Stop. I can't laugh. I'll throw up." He points to jam-packed shelving. "You have a lot of fucking books. It's like you took out a redwood with all these bastards. You read them all?"

"Most." I put away an unused bottle of lube, brought and forgotten by a guy who was pissed we didn't use it. After stuffing my overflowing T-shirts in a dresser drawer, I shelve some books, only to give up when the three I place on the shelf fall to the floor.

"Are you cleaning for me?"

I drop the last book in my hand. "I don't know what the fuck I'm doing. I'm tired."

"Hey, you know those circles?" Jesse slurs. "Venn puzzles?" He holds a finger in the air, drawing several lazy ovals.

"Diagrams?"

"Bingo," he blurts, beaming as if he figured it out himself. He interlocks his fingers in front of his face, fascinated by how they bend backwards, forwards, sideways. He wiggles a thumb at me, a miniature hello. "You, me."

I'm too fucked up to interpret clever parallels. I don't know what logical sets have to do with Jesse and me. I wipe my lips with the back of my hand, then cup my palm over my mouth to smell my breath. It will have to do.

"You and me," he persists, sighing and slapping his arm against the bed in frustration. "Think about it."

"I promise, I will." I extricate my blankets from under him. "Move over."

Instead of giving me some space, Jesse performs a Vitruvian Man stretch and looks me over as I slip off my sweatshirt. I leave my jeans and favorite green T-shirt in place. From my pocket, I pull a baggie that holds a comforting amount of weed. Candy cartoons dance across the plastic. Rockette donuts. Cakes with top hats. My dealer always sends me away with a cutesy parcel. I go deeper, digging out my pipe, lighter, and my phone.

"You've got big shoulders," Jesse says to my back.

I stop what I'm doing. "What?"

"You have wide shoulders," he says again, following it up with a casual sniff.

Immediately, Jesse has changed from some stoner who's hijacked my mattress to someone who's taking the long route to telling me he wants to fuck around. I never would have guessed the night would go in this direction.

I eye up the only free area on the bed. It's perfect, the corner that will have my dick closest to his mouth. I run a hand through my hair, resisting a smile before facing him. "The shoulders are from tennis," I explain, "and genetics."

Groaning, Jesse squirms and rolls, unable to get comfortable. "Genetics and Bio is the *worst*," he says once he finds a position on his side that suits him. "That class sucks so bad that I don't even know if I'm supposed to blame my father's mother or my mother's father or my maternal grandmother's second cousin for my skinny body."

I contemplate slipping out of my T-shirt but decide that's premature. His quick change in topic makes me think I read him wrong. "I meant *my* genetics. Not our class Genetics."

"Either way. It sucks to be narrow," Jesse laments. "I'm average. I mean, I'm absolutely fucking brilliant—but it would be nice to have bigger muscles. Like yours. And I'd like to have your face."

One hand lifts the bottom of my T-shirt—just above my belly button—as soon as I process what he said. "My face?" With one leg, I kneel on the edge of the bed, ready to retreat if this goes wrong. My timidity puzzles me; my zipper should be down by now.

"Yeah. I mean," he says, closing his eyes, embarrassed, "I always look like, I dunno, a beggar?"

"No," I say, studying him in earnest, "you don't."

"I do." Jesse cracks a red eye and grins. "You're a beauty queen." He yawns and sprawls on the bed once more, mouth hanging open with a complete lack of reserve. His focus falls on my hand, which has my shirt hitched up mid-torso. The small upturn of his lips divulges no confusion or repulsion, but neither is it an invitation for me to get my cock out. He's drunk and unaware. His goal is sleep, and so should mine be. I lower my T-shirt and lie down, turning off the light and staying near the edge.

Jesse rubs my arm with the back of his hand and keeps it there. His voice is deeper in the dark. "If you decide to feel me up in the middle of the night, I'll know you're stealing weed."

"I have plenty of weed. Guess again."

He laughs once—it's more of a hiccup—and his next breath is a snore.

Harry, my doubles partner at both school and my tennis club since ninth grade, has nothing in common with me but top seeding and a partial scholarship to our respective college of choice. Hot-tempered and petite, Harry uses his soprano voice and a raunchy vocabulary to splinter the egos of our opponents before, during, and after our matches.

This afternoon, on the high school courts, I sputter through warm-ups, pounding the little yellow ball to Harry in a rare display of incoordination. "Dan," he yells across the from the other side of the net, "wake the fuck *up*."

Despite the blinding sun, my sloppy play, and the occasional wind, I know I'll have my shit together in time to nail down the win. After I miss a lob, Harry joins me at the net and motions beyond the surrounding fence with fluttering hands. "You see that? More people here than usual. Play better. You're fucking embarrassing yourself."

I look where he points. In the small gathering, not thirty feet from me, stands my English teacher. I suck in a breath and hold it.

With a hooked finger, Mr. Stewart holds his navy suit jacket over his shoulder. He could be yachting, the sea breeze fucking up his hair and indifferent to his meticulous grooming habits. After months of asking, I'd given up on seeing him at a match or one of my practices.

He appears disinterested. It's difficult to tell if he's looking at me, the greenery, or another player. My nod at him goes unacknowledged. I now regret having skipped his class today and taking a nap in Ollie's car instead. My goal was a mix of wanting to get fucked up and a manipulative plea for my teacher's attention. Although it's obviously worked, I'm embarrassed about how childish it now seems.

Mr. Stewart catches me gazing at him. When he bows his head quickly, I bow back and smile. He's here for me. Whatever got him here doesn't matter.

Each of my teammates has had a parent or friend attend a match at least twice a season, and finally, someone is here to see me. Beneath my arousal lies something deeper. I'm proud. I feel worth showing up for.

I shake out my limbs and crack my neck. I grow bold and look his way again. We exchange smiles.

Each time I win a set, my focus switches from the game to Mr. Stewart. As I change court sides, I make eye contact. His nods are unmistakable signs of support. His chin dips lower, and he holds the nod longer. I counter with a bunch of smiles I try to vary. Broad, slight, close-lipped, lots of teeth. An ecstatic showcase. I could be doing headshots.

I haven't won with this fluidity in months. My opponent, a redhead with a severe overbite and impeccable skills, meets me at the net, and I shake his clammy hand. When I join Harry on the bench, he says, "Nice," and puts on sunglasses after smearing balm on his lips. Leaning forward, elbows on knees, he drops a red hand towel at his feet. "We're going to make States this year. We could do Regionals with one arm."

"Yeah, sure," I say, distracted, "I know." I cloak my hunt for Mr. Stewart in achy-neck camouflage and casually glance his way. The place where he stood is now empty. I blink and can still see his dark silhouette on my inner eyelids. I slap Harry on the arm. "I have to go, man. Tell Coach I couldn't stay for wrap-up."

I quickly hit the showers and get dressed. I find Ollie next to his locker. He's bright red, sweating like Swiss cheese at room temperature and pissed off from whatever happened today in basketball practice. I struggle to pull a T-shirt over my wet skin and speak to him through the fabric. "Hey. I'll be right back. Can you wait by your car? Five minutes. Unless I message you."

He throws his damp and dirty towel into his locker and slams the door. "Everybody's an asshole today."

I wave a hand in front of his face. "Five minutes. You hear me?"

"Yeah," he says, slapping my hand away. "You have five. *Just five.*"

I fly down two flights of stairs, racing to Mr. Stewart's classroom. After hopping the railing on the last three steps, I skid to a halt in the stale, desolate hallway. The mouthful of mints I chew burns my cheeks. Droplets of water trickle down my neck and darken the collar of my blue T-shirt. Before I cross the threshold, I drop my shoulders, crack my neck, and smooth out my shirt. It's eight steps from the door to Mr. Stewart's desk, and I take them without hesitation.

"Hello, Daniel," he says, while continuing to work. The pen in his lithe hand gallops across a thin stack of papers. "I will refrain from asking why you weren't in my class this afternoon."

When he glances at me, I wink. "Thanks."

"That was your invitation to be a gentleman about it."

"Okay. I had a headache."

"Headache? You'll make someone a fine wife."

"Ha." I bump his desk with my legs. "You should work on your delivery."

I've never seen him without a suit. That's all I can think when I take him in. He's wearing a zip-up, black track jacket, which hangs open, exposing a navy T-shirt underneath. The jacket's sleeves, unlike those of his suits, are not cut to fit. His wrist bones stick out. I didn't know I had a thing for bones, but those instigate what I know will be a full-on erection by the time I'm done here.

After a sharp inhale, he says, "What brings you here?"

"You were at my match."

"I needed some air." He looks at me. "Congratulations by the way."

"Thanks." I place my fingertips on his desk as though I'm about to type an essay. "Nice jacket. You run after school?"

"I do unless I have other obligations."

"Where do you run?" I despise running, but I could run for him. "The park? On Morgan?"

"Why?" The subtle tilt of his head indicates suspicion.

"Conversation." I fondle his sticky notes and pens and then double back a few beats. "What obligations? You're married or something?"

Mr. Stewart doesn't flinch at the shift in topic. "I'm not married, no," he says, flatly.

"I'm not married, either."

He puts down his pen, giving up on the work in front of him. "What can I do for you?"

"You think you could give me a ride?" One of his candy tins sits alongside his laptop. I tap it with my nail and rattle it once. "Maybe to the park?"

"No." He slides the candy out of my reach, next to a small stack of books from another class's syllabus.

"Come on," I say. "Nice day."

He stands, revealing matching track pants. I expected the T-shirt to be tucked in—I even think he could pull that off—but it's loose, the bottom of the worn cotton dangling just above a slight bulge in his pants. The shirt has been through the wash a hundred times, the words of the silkscreen no longer discernible. After a long day of the dry cleaner's heavy starch, I bet he luxuriates in its softness each time he slips it on.

He goes to the wall of windows. Three are open, and he tugs them closed. As the lock of the last clicks, he looks back at me. "I cannot give you a ride anywhere. You know that."

I wish I had the balls to weave through the desks and chairs and trap him against the back painted cinder block wall, right next to the poster of grammar rules from Strunk & White. But I fail to muster the courage to move.

He returns to his desk, and I persist. "Nowhere?"

"Nowhere."

He remains standing and packs up his stuff, gently closing his laptop and sliding his thumb back and forth over its edge.

"Not to my house?" I say, pulling at the collar of my still damp T-shirt, releasing a gust of heat and soap.

The noise he makes might be a laugh, a sound of disbelief, or just workaday disgust. "Not anywhere."

I clear my throat. "How about to *your* house?"

It's as if I graduated from the kiddie folding chair and table at Thanksgiving; I'm at the grown-up, solid oak motherfucker now, and I don't know which knife to use to butter my roll. I hold my breath.

"How about this, Daniel?" he says with a grimace. "You leave now, and we both forget you said that."

I exhale and try to salvage my bravado by returning to vague flirtation. "There's no way we can forget I said that." I tap my temple with an index finger. "The more you try to forget something, the more you remember it."

The stack of papers he struggles to straighten won't cooperate. He places them on the desk, sighs, and fixes his eyes on me. "I will have no problem with it, I assure you. Now it's time for you to get going."

"For instance," I announce, ignoring his dismissal and pointing to his tin of candies, "the next time you suck on one of those, you'll think of me."

When I smile, he doesn't. I know he expects me to look away first. Intimidating as he is, I refuse, biting my cheek as a reminder to remain steadfast. I walk backwards to the door. "You'll try to forget I just said that," I say, "but it will be in your brain forever." When I reach the doorway, he watches me exit. I immediately break into a sprint so I can catch a ride with Ollie.

It's Ollie's birthday dinner. He and I are on his lawn, on our backs, knees up, speaking in hushed tones about things he'd rather his parents didn't hear. Before we do the fun thing, which is a party at Jackie's brother's place, we need to do the obligatory family thing.

Although it's unseasonably warm enough to fall asleep outside on the grass, his parents have the fire pit raging. His older sister, Francie, who's home from college, insisted on roasting marshmallows. My asscrack is sweating. I blow my damp hair out of my eyes. "It's like we're in Ibiza," I say to Ollie.

For the third time, I discreetly redirect Gigi, one of Ollie's three German Shepherd Dogs, whose snout needs a search warrant. The canine trio has been trained to do everything but keep their faces out of any crotch within smelling distance.

"You know, I need a girlfriend," Ollie says, cracking his knuckles after telling Gigi to go lie down. "Like a real one. Not just a weekend one."

I push my hair off my sticky forehead. "Aren't you burning up out here? The fire pit could heat a small village. Fuck's sake."

"I always talk about this," he says, still wistful about no girlfriend, "I know."

I say nothing. We have this chat every week. I wish I had an example to set, some way to guide Ollie down the path to getting what he craves: love and not just sex. Although I operate in a different way, I've never teased him about it. He, however, harasses me constantly about how fast I've plowed through the student body.

"I really need someone," he repeats when I don't respond.

I put my hand against my phone in the front pocket of my jeans. If only I could record this conversation, we could avoid having it again.

The clouds in the night sky slowly cover the moon. I'm too sober to appreciate the passage or the few visible stars or the smell of burning wood from the fire, all things I'd enjoy after a joint.

Ollie's next step in this process is running down his list of contestants. "I like Daiana."

I roll my shoulders against the grass. "Too many vowels."

"Or Yui."

"Yeah, she's nice. Cute." I nudge Ollie with my foot, gesturing to his parents with a nod. "They're lighting candles. Blow the fuckers out before they invent a second chorus, yeah?"

Grunts and groans emerge from Ollie as he struggles to get off the ground. I jump up and punch his arm. "You're eighteen, not eighty, Grandpa."

He hangs his head, continuing his streak of ill humor. "At least there's cake, I guess."

"Olls," his sister calls, her pale, freckled skin glowing in the flames, "candles are burning. Hurry up. Dan, you blow, too."

A quip slips through his melodrama. "Yeah, Dan, you blow, too."

"*Oliver*," his dad snaps.

I've always been unsure if his parents like me. They are courteous, but I think it's because they tolerate rather than welcome the fact that I'm Ollie's best friend. If I said it could never be the gay thing that's an issue, then I'd be lying.

When I stay at Ollie's, we do nothing subversive. We don't smoke or drink. We don't even stay up late. I am the perfect young adult guest. But if we close his bedroom door, it warrants an emphatic knock from either parent about once an hour, followed by an inane inquiry. *Do you need more pillows? How about some cookies? Cheese and crackers? Is the heat on too high?*

Here, outside, they can keep an eye on us, and the atmosphere is comfortable, almost lighthearted, a rare ambiance in the company of this uptight family.

Ollie's mother, pale and freckled like her daughter, and his father, as tall and bulky as Ollie has been since ninth grade, clear their throats and prepare to sing. His dad holds up a hand and waves a pretend concert baton. As his family starts in unison, I cringe and turn away. My dad sang to me solo every year when he woke me up on my birthday. My mother never joined and avoided direct well-wishing by saying over breakfast, "Did your dad wish you a happy birthday, Danny?"

All of us watch as Ollie shovels in his second piece of yellow cake. I squirm in my seat. Each outdoor chair here is one of his parents' living room rejects, and the worn upholstery does nothing to pad the popped springs that would put the pikes of Traitor's Gate to shame. I've chosen the one I know to be most comfortable, and still, my ass is enduring an assault that will take a minute to walk off.

After his parents each squeeze his shoulder, they give me a curt wave and disappear through the sliding doors into the home. Francie circles us like a drunk beetle, offering water, milk, tea, coffee. Ollie tells her to give it a rest. The fire in the pit has burnt down to ash, and she churns what's left with an iron poker before dumping a bucket of water on the mix and saying goodnight.

Ollie polishes off the slice of cake and spills icing on his hoodie. After he changes, we leave, drive a few blocks, and pull over. He lights a cigarette first, puts it in the ashtray. Next, he lights a joint, puffs twice, and passes it to me. "Well," he says, "let's talk about the black hole before it sucks us in."

I hurry to exhale, needing to protest quickly, before he interprets any pause as a sign I need to talk. "Nope. It's your day. It really doesn't bother me."

"You're shit at lying."

"I swear," I say, "I don't care."

Ollie's birthday is also my father's death day, and this is the first year we've celebrated the birth instead of tiptoeing around the death. For the last couple of years, Ollie has commemorated his birthday with his family. He and I then met, with no mention of cake or gifts or balloons, and did whatever it was that we normally did. Smoking, playing video games, walking around the neighborhood. We talked about neither birth nor death. But this year, I am ready, and a day ago, I said as much: "What do you want to do for your birthday?"

Ollie holds out the joint and says, "Hey, you ever go to your dad's—what's it called?"

"Mausoleum."

"Fancy." Because he thinks the question will rouse unwelcome spirits, he whispers, "Have you ever gone there?"

"Not since we stuck him in it."

Ollie's shoulders fall. He regrets bringing it up—I know by how he tugs at his earlobe—but dropping the subject is out of the question now. He'll make me talk until he thinks I'm okay. "Your mom go there?" He relights the joint.

"I have no idea." If she does, I've never been asked to go along. I can't imagine what she'd do there. Sob? Complain? Bring a boyfriend?

He passes me the joint. "Shit, remember your aunt Brenda? It was like the pilgrimage to the Wailing Wall. How many fucking candles can you light?" He tries not to smile. "I only went so I could see your mom in a dress. Those legs."

My brief laugh gives him permission to relax. I hit the joint and pass it back. The smell of impending rain seeps into the car when I crack the window and blow out the smoke. He places the joint in the ashtray and chooses his cigarette instead. His lips clamp down on it, and he speaks around it. "If we went to the burial thingee— what's it called again?

"Mausoleum."

"Yeah. If you went there, would you cry?"

Would I? "I doubt it."

He's quiet for two pulls on his cigarette and then says, "Shit, I'd cry."

"That's because you're a pussy."

That gets me a backhand to the chest. I playfully shove him into the door. He shoves me back. He punches my thigh. I groan and shove him again. As he raises his fist, his cigarette slips from his lips. "*Watch, watch, watch,*" he cautions, frantically searching before finding it smoldering on the rubber mat under his feet. Settling now, we lean back in the seats. My leg kills.

The rain bypasses any warning drizzles and hits the windshield and roof fast and hard. Streams of water on our windows mixed with the outside lights of a few homes several car-lengths in front of us make Ollie's face look like it's melting.

When my dad died, Ollie was the only one I needed, the only one who could be sad with me or know when to distract me. On the evening of the interment, he stood next to me as my father's pastor said words I didn't care about while my extended and estranged family quietly questioned my mother about why I brought a guy in a cheap suit to what they thought was a sacred ceremony.

"Put that out," he says, motioning to what's left of the joint. "Are you ready?"

I'm suddenly concerned we're headed somewhere other than a party. "You do know that I don't want to go see my dad now, yeah? You're not—?"

Hands at ten and two, he squeezes the steering wheel, a mini ritual he performs just before he puts the car in gear. "I'm not an asshole all of the sudden. The only place we're going is to get me laid."

When Jackie agreed to host Ollie's birthday at her brother's house, she promised balloons, vodka, and that Brad would be gone. A couple gallons of bottom-shelf vodka are lined up on the kitchen counter. Red and yellow balloons swirl around the living room floor. The only letdown is Brad, unwelcoming and malodorous—I catch a subtle earthen whiff of root vegetables —scrutinizing each of us as we enter his house. He lets us in one at a time and, in between each admittance, pokes his head out his front door, glancing up and down his quiet street. "Hurry up, hurry up."

Jackie invited Ollie's basketball friends, too, and Brad sizes them up and cackles. "Really, Jackie? Who are these losers?" He holds his hand flat against the tallest one's chest and points at the door with the other. "No, no. None of that vape bullshit in here. You smoke bud or you don't smoke at all." Big talk until one of them feigns a threatening lunge in his direction. To regain composure, Brad straightens and says to Jackie, "No one goes in the basement. Got it?"

She breezes by me, hand trailing along my waist while griping at her brother. "Brad, you said you'd go out, so go. You're freaking everybody out, psycho."

"You hear me? No one in the basement," he warns her, slipping on a padded parka, suitable only for the Northwest Territories. "It stays locked."

"No shit," is her retort. They both glance over their shoulders at the three deadbolts and one keypad on the dilapidated interior door. The splintered wood around a hole in its center is evidence of a temper tantrum. One more punch would make those locks irrelevant.

Ollie is all about getting laid tonight. If a girlfriend seems unlikely, the happy-birthday lay will do. Once we got out of his car, he even cleaned up the backseat by tossing French fries and empty cigarette packs onto the street in front of Brad's home. He spots a potential gift and rushes to the dining room to get to her.

Across the cluttered living room, a barefooted Jesse lounges on a green and brown plaid couch. Since he passed out in my bed, I've only seen him in class, each time I replayed the facts of our drunken night. One, two, three: I brought Jesse inside my house; we slept in my bed; he left—with no shoes—before I woke up. I've assigned no meaning to the facts.

Jesse summons me with one wiggling finger and pats the sofa cushion next to him when I get there. "Looking for you. Is Paul your dealer?"

"Usually, yeah," I say, plopping down. "Why?"

"He got busted."

My head falls backwards. "Shit." Sobriety will crush my spirits like molars gnash hard candy.

"*So*," he says, showboating by buffing his fingernails on his T-shirt, "looks like I'm your man. But I don't sell that crumbly dirt-weed bullshit. You'll need to save your allowance." He offers me his pipe and lighter. "First one's free."

I take it and correct him. "You sold to me before."

"Really?" He looks at the ceiling, as if to recall. "Okay, second one's free. Your lucky night."

Before I can smoke up, a junior named Jaime approaches me and stops when his crotch is at my eye level. Although Jaime was teased and called *Hymen* for most of his school career, he has this year matured into someone fuckable: his acne failed to scar, and someone taught him hygiene and how to dress. Still, he's one of the sourest people I know. Muscled abs, ass, and arms go only so far when partnered with a perennial eyeroll.

He tries to tousle my hair, misses when I duck, and pouts. "Why do I only ever see you with *white* boys lately, Dan?" He curls his lip as he regards Jesse and then walks away.

"Who's that?" Jesse says.

"Just some asshole."

I take a couple of hits. The muscles in my neck and shoulders soften. I spread my legs and lean back. Jesse does the same, and his knee falls against mine. We stay like that—I am the only one who notices the knee—and the twitch in my pants makes me laugh. I need to come.

I've been smoking for years and have experienced nowhere near the nerve-ending crackle I do right now. My torso tilts forward in slow motion. With my head between my knees, I giggle and peer left. Only Jesse's bare feet and dirty pants are visible, the denim dappled with pen ink and a couple cigarette burns.

He leans forward and looks at me through his legs and mine, voice crawling at a pot-pace that pleases my ears. His lips move for a while before I catch what he's saying. "Dan's life is a horizontal fall."

It takes me a second to realize he's pinched a quote. "That's a fridge magnet."

"I see no fridge, and you aren't the only one who reads."

I sit up and get my shit together in time to catch Ollie's eye as he cruises by us. He does a double take and wiggles his eyebrows. Dropping my hand between my spread legs, I gesture for him to keep moving, but he backtracks just to fuck with me.

The empty beer bottles on the table in front of us clank and roll when he sits down. "Daniel's being extra social this year," he says to Jesse. "Usually, I find him in a corner reading dirty books on his phone. What's different tonight, Dan, huh? Anything different?"

Taking out a small black bottle from his pocket, Jesse tips a bud into his palm. He breaks it up with his thumb. The new green joins the old green residue under his nail. "Mark of an amateur." He holds up his dirty thumbnail. "Hey, Ollie, did you know Dan thinks he's smarter than all of us?"

"It's the dirty books," Ollie says, "I think he calls them *literature*."

I kick his foot. "Why don't you get us some drinks."

"I got it." Jesse bolts out of his seat, sways, and catches himself on my knee. The couch is so old, its foam holds the shape of his ass. He hands me the half-full bowl and purple lighter. "What do you want?"

"Beer," Ollie says.

"Red cup," I say. As Ollie slides in next to me on the couch, I shake my head. "Don't say it. Shut up."

He knocks his knee against mine. "Jesse, huh?"

I knock back. "No, not 'Jesse, huh.'"

I have always readily admitted my shameful taste. Intellect and sense of humor can get fucked; I only desire non-assholes who are nice to look at when I come.

Ollie doesn't give up. "Not in a hundred years would I have guessed Jesse." He retrieves a crushed pack of cigarettes from the pocket of his jeans, tips one out, and captures it between his lips. "He's not your usual type."

"I don't have a type."

He leans into me and whispers, "You totally do."

At the same time, we both notice Jesse working his way back to us through the crowd, holding two beers and the cup away from his body to avoid a spill. Ollie scooches forward on the couch and looks back at me. "You want me to go? Or stay?"

My shrug serves as a weak cover for how much I want him to fuck off. "I don't care."

Jesse's only several yards away when Ollie asks again. "Go? Or stay? Last chance or take what you get."

I hold out until I realize he might just stay. I shove his shoulder. "Go," I say under my breath. "*Go*."

Jesse reaches us as Ollie stands and takes the beer he's offered. "Thanks. Going to get my dick wet. See ya."

Jesse hands me the plastic cup. We sit in silence for a few minutes, watching Jackie dance in front of two shirtless boys who wear bowties and drink canned sodas from straws. Her shirt is bunched under her bra. The boys seem unaffected, so she tosses up her hands and heads our way.

"*Umph*." She falls in between us, squeezing both our legs just above the knee. I playfully slap away her hand as it slips up my shirt. "Oh, you're *grumpy*," Jackie says, dunking her finger in my cup and licking it. "If you're cranky and need a nap, Brad's bedroom is the one with the fish. You two want a Xanax?"

Jesse and I say no, although pocketing a few might save her from passing out in a corner somewhere. For such a tiny body, Jackie swallows, snorts, and smokes so much that, if she were anyone else, we would have had to call emergency services an hour ago.

When she wanders off, Jesse slides next to me and hands me the pipe again. I take a lungful, exhaling until my chest is concave. "Your weed is—"

"It's good, right?"

We are pleasantly lit, sunk into the couch, and everyone around us migrates to another room. The two people in sight are Ollie and the sophomore he wants to fuck, a sleek, blonde long-distance runner who's rubbing his hard-on through his pants.

Jesse leans against me. I turn, and we're almost nose-to-nose. I pull back, startled. "What are you doing?"

"You looked hot. Sweaty," he says and takes his pipe from my relaxed hold, putting it on the table. "No more for you."

My thoughts are no longer sluggish. He's either readying to kiss me or he wants to point out some otherwise unnoticed blemish on my face. He leans in closer and tips the mouth of his beer toward my cheek. "You're really—" he says and squints, "symmetrical."

Whether on purpose or because Jesse has only a drunken, loosening grip on the cold wet glass, the tip of the bottle touches the corner of my mouth. He slides it along my lower lip before pulling it away and downing some more of its contents. His gaze falls on the center of the room, and he nods his head to a few beats of far-off music. To himself, he laughs and says, "Beauty queen."

No one's ever called me beautiful. The closest I get to beautiful is an assessment of my features: nice cock, nice lips, nice arms. But beautiful denotes an appreciation that might have nothing to do with sex. Being hot leads to fucking around. I have no idea where *beautiful* is going.

I suppose I might be eye-catching, compared with Jesse, who's seemingly careless about his presentation. He has *something* though. A lot of unnamable something.

I blink, clear my head, look away. That jumped from simple observation to a turn-on way too fast. Besides sex, only two things usually cause a rise in my temperature like this are exertion and drunkenness. It's neither of those; I'm sedentary and my cup is only missing two sips.

I reach for the pipe he took from me and finally find my voice. "Your parents meet Jackie yet?"

"No." His head falls back, his eyes closing not long after.

"Yeah, she's—"

He perks up, smiling like we're sharing a secret. "Perfect, right?"

"I was going to say not parent-friendly, but okay."

"True. But they'll like her. They're always happy when I have a girlfriend."

A girlfriend, to his parents, could mean stability. Or maybe they're looking for grandchildren early. Perhaps Jesse mopes at home, and they just want him out of the house a few nights a week. Envy builds in me when I think about his family being happy for him, happy just because he's happy. Parental support: I barely remember it. "Why do they like it when you have a girlfriend?"

He takes a gulp and belches. "Who knows?"

But I think he does know, and I think it's something he'd rather not discuss. I wager smoking another bowl would uncork the truth.

I sneak looks at Jesse. I am too tired to continue the conversation. I let myself drift off in a pot-nap until his voice invades my rest: "... decide on school. You know what I mean?"

As Jesse speaks, his finger and thumb skate along the side of my pants, pinching the seam. His head rests on my shoulder. He absentmindedly pulls the material away from my leg, presses it back, his forefinger straying and exploring an ever-expanding tract of material. My penis awakens. I watch his movements and wait for what's next.

Chewed cuticles top off his ash-soiled fingers, all of which are now kneading the side of my leg. I accelerate the momentum of whatever's about to go down by shifting in my seat. Jesse jumps and yanks his hand away. "Shit, I'm sorry."

His apology seems earnest. Either that, or he's done this before. "It's fine," I say. "You're too stoned."

"I've never been *too* stoned."

"Of course not. Unprofessional."

"Exactly," Jesse says. "I'd be booted from the union."

I've never fucked around with any of my dealers, no matter how cute or willing. Should they want more when I don't, I'd lose my connection. Right now, however, I consider making an exception. I could push this, ease into a mutual grope in the bathroom or Ollie's car. If I put in the effort more than once, I might be able to get a discount out of it.

Jesse pulls his feet up onto the couch and tucks them beneath him, careful to avoid brushing them against any part of me. His torso twists awkwardly until he straightens and wedges his feet under my leg. "I'm sleepy now, Dan. You can finish the bowl." I take the paraphernalia he holds out to me. His decision saves me from having to make one of my own.

As a drunk chorus wishes Ollie a happy birthday, a guy stripped down to his underwear turns off lamps, meanwhile plugging in strands of dim white lights that are tossed and tangled on the floor of the living room. No one strings them anywhere.

Bodies line the hallway, spill out of the kitchen. Some people are fighting over the music. All familiar. Same drinks and drugs, smoky air, the same sounds of fucking and fighting, whether for only the night or as part of a tiresome narrative.

I light up once more and read some stuff on my phone. Little else is available to do. When I look at Jesse again, he's unconscious, mouth slack. He groans and shifts fitfully, annoyed at something in his sleep. The pink hues on his cheeks change as he sleeps, first blush, now the color of freshly slapped skin. One foot has loosened itself from the trap of my leg, and it fights to find room, ramming my thigh and pushing once, twice. His toes wiggle.

I've avoided making friends for years. Friends mean sharing history, if only facts, and I don't want to share history. If we could begin mid-friendship, no mention of my past, only the future in our minds, I'd be good with it. If I choose Jesse for this enterprise—I suspect he'd slide easily into the role—his bare feet quirk may soon irritate me. That, or endear me to him, and for no reason I can pinpoint right now, that's unpalatable.

Ollie and I head to our favorite school bathroom. He hurries me. "I need two cigarettes today. Fuck's sake with Calculus this morning. How are you passing these courses baked?"

"Yeah," I say and close the stall door, "it's how I function best."

"My lighter's dead. You have one?"

I open my backpack, pull out the baggie of turkey jerky, and hold it between my teeth while I dig in my bag. There are at least six lighters at the bottom, and I come up victorious with one in a camouflage motif that's been working without a stutter for a solid year. I hand it over. "I'm going out to the hallway to—you know." I make a jack-off gesture, referencing Mr. Stewart.

"You have no chance. Plus, he's old as fuck."

"He's not that old."

"How old do you think?"

"I don't know. Thirty?" I've never been able to tell. His skin is smooth and tight, there's no fat on him, and those crow's feet are probably premature. "Besides, I'm making progress. He knows I'm here, and all of the sudden he keeps showing up."

For me, if there's too much effort required for a routine orgasm, the line between horny and lazy is usually thin. There is no line with Mr. Stewart. It's all horny.

During my months of pursuit, he's grown more comfortable with me every week, our interactions coasting from banal to lighthearted. Finally, recently, more meaningful discussion has trespassed upon the dreary topics of a chaste teacher-student relationship. My tactics—repetition and frequency—have propelled me from an object of amusement to what I assume is an expected and enjoyable part of his day. Only a coward would abandon this now.

As I expected, Mr. Stewart enters the otherwise empty hallway. My eyes drift from the white shirt stretched across his chest to his fitted trousers. He ditched the suit jacket he wore between first and second periods when I spotted the back of his short, conservative haircut moving through clusters of first-year students at the end of the senior hallway. And that's a new belt he's sporting today. I imagine he considers me in the morning when he decides on his clothing for the day. *Will Daniel like this? Or this?*

"Hey," I say when he's several feet from me.

Chin up and shoulders back, Mr. Stewart nods but keeps moving. I watch him go while stammering a string of quiet *uhs* and *ums* to myself. Humiliation quickly snuffs out my initial surprise. He's never blown me off like this. If each of us is alone, he always has a few words for me.

He pauses before he turns the corner. His fingers curl and uncurl at his side. He rubs the back of his neck. I'd sooner expect a statue to blink than I would Mr. Stewart to fidget like that. He's having second thoughts, and they've manifested in these acute tics. I call his name. He turns on his heel and walks swiftly in my direction.

I'm denied eye contact until he stops a few feet in front of me. "You do understand," he says in a volume so low only reading his lips helps me fill in the blanks, "if you keep calling my attention to your—" he points to the door "—*habit*, I'm obligated to bring it to someone else's attention."

He would never do that. The frequency with which he lectures me about this habit is just shy of the perfunctory scolding he gives me about my truancy and sloth. My disobedience may annoy him at times, but he continues to pay more attention to my charm.

"You were just going to keep going?" I say. "No hello? No how are you?"

He nods at the bathroom door. A longer glance down the hallway follows. "Both of us cannot loiter here while you stink of marijuana."

"I wasn't smoking," I recall the hundred ways someone can tell if you're lying; I stare at his forehead, straining not to blink until my eyeballs are dry. "But still, I could use a mint."

"I have no mints," he says.

I point to his trouser pocket where an obvious rectangular outline proves him a liar. "What's that?"

Our attention turns to the shouting from within the smoky bathroom. An out of place soprano squeal follows a grunt several registers lower. Mr. Stewart watches the wooden door, expecting a subsequent problem. When nothing occurs, he sighs and looks at me. "Are you in need of anything else? Or was the mint your mission?"

"Yeah, I just thought you might like to know," I say and rap my knuckles against my backpack, "I found a hobby." I unzip my bag and pull out a small chess set, the hollow wooden board folded in half, the pieces tucked inside. "Chess. It's time-consuming. It's respectable in even the most discriminating circles. And, best yet, it's extra boring, so we know it must be worthwhile. Now I just need someone to teach me how to play."

"None of your unsavory friends could teach you?"

I flinch at his choice of adjective, and his use of the plural. Ollie is it for me, and he's far from unsavory. I hold up the board and shake it once. "Will you or not?"

He pulls his phone from his pocket and shakes it once. Several notifications show on his home screen. He checks the time. "I'll think about it."

"I knew you'd know how to play." The subtlest shuffle I can manage brings me an inch closer to him. Then another. "Besides chess, what else do you do? And you can't say reading because that's way too obvious."

He presses his lips together, carefully weighing what to share. "I write music, mostly for string instruments. I'm on a crew team with my alma mater."

I should have guessed rowing or swimming. The breadth of his shoulders and curve of his ass have always been my favorites. Of all the guys I've been with, no matter how hot, how fit, there will be nothing better than when I see Mr. Stewart naked.

"Okay, you row," I say, motioning with one hand, urging him for more. "And what else?"

"I have other more obscure interests."

"Name one," I dare him. "Nothing's that obscure. Whale watching? Fencing?"

Mr. Stewart waits a couple beats. "I'd like to see you doing either of those instead of sitting in front of the TV and smoking marijuana."

"How about magic? You like magic? No, wait. *Taxidermy.*"

Finally, he smiles. "Beekeeping? Ships in bottles?"

I take a step toward him and softly push his shoulder. "Wrestling."

After a glance up and down the hallway, he performs the trifecta of uneasiness: sniffle, shuffle, cough. "That's enough, Daniel."

Before I can speak, he tells me he'll see me in English. His long strides and a fast clip ferry him down the hallway and around the corner. I know that uptight walk, and it promises a humorless afternoon.

Several days of curt nods and no after-class visits crawl by before Mr. Stewart finally invites me to play chess after school. I accept with a chilly, "Sure," and save my smile until I'm in the hallway with Ollie, who calls me pathetic because I'm playing board games with an old man.

After school, each on our usual side of his desk, my spoken exchange with Mr. Stewart is minimal. He sets up my cheap board. I read the yellowed instructional insert and pick up on the basic rules of play before he has the pieces in line.

Several games later, I'm frustrated with my defeats and by how quiet he's remained. He makes no attempt to amuse or console me when I lose each game so quickly, no matter how many times I sigh or grumble.

"You need to give me some sort of handicap," I say, my hand hovering over a knight.

When I commit to the move, he immediately advances his rook. "A handicap will only let you ascend to mediocrity."

It's six p.m., and Mr. Stewart looks as though he's just stepped out of the shower, shiny and clean, and winked at himself in the mirror. The stillness of the school at this hour gives me butterflies in my stomach. We are alone, but not really. Occasionally, a teacher walks by, a leftover student. The janitors have begun their night's work. No one peeks in on us, and it seems like Mr. Stewart wouldn't give a fuck if they did.

"I don't think chess is for me." I slump forward on his desk, one arm stretched far enough to grab the edge of the other side. "This is going nowhere."

"Sit up. Pay attention to the board." He taps the corner.

I straighten my body, place my index finger on a pawn and lift it an inch. As I execute it, I sense it's a bad move, but I don't see anything better. Mr. Stewart shakes his head. I know I lost, even before he says, "Check mate."

As he picks up his queen to show me how his next move makes me a loser, I snatch the wooden piece out of his hand. "Nope. No, no, no, no."

The left side of his face puckers in a grin. "You wish to prolong the agony of defeat?"

'Don't be a dick." I hand him his queen. "We'll call it a rainout. This sucks."

"It takes practice. Were you good at tennis as soon as someone placed a racket in your hand?"

I lean back and puff out my chest. "Yeah, actually."

"A touch of modesty would go a long way." He sets up the board again, methodically working from left pawn to right. "Was your father a tennis player?"

"No," I say and mime a perfect serve. "That's all me."

Mr. Stewart leans forward, now hovering over the board, his face well within my reach should I want to feel the light stubble on his chin. I have only seconds to assess what his nearness means. Too bad his expression shows no sign of impending seduction. No cocked and curious eyebrows. No predator's sly smile. Only one sensible meaning remains: He wants me to confide in him.

The quiet between us has lasted too long. Just as I decide I'll tell a lame joke—Two deer walk out of a gay bar—he speaks. "Ever since you told me what happened to your father, I've talked myself in and out of sharing something with you, too. But I worry it will make you uncomfortable."

"Uncomfortable how?"

"Vulnerable."

My head drops forward. "If it's about my dad again—"

He cuts me off by touching the back of my hand. "My father died when I was nine."

For a moment, I'm thankful someone might understand what happened to me. Then I quickly decide I'm being conned. Counselors always have a common disaster to share. No ploy disgusts me more than that one; they search my eyes when they think they've struck a sympathy chord.

"You were right," I say. "Uncomfortable." The subject is as far from flirting as we could get. The dead-dad parallel shrivels what was left of my semi.

"You'd rather I hadn't told you?" he says.

The part of me that wants to continue our interaction knows there's only one way to do it. "No, it's fine. But when you were nine, did you want to talk about it all the time? Probably not."

The remainder of the chess pieces hold his attention. He arranges the bishops, the knights, the rooks. "If I had, I would have benefited from it."

I wish Mr. Stewart would look at me again. Right now, he concentrates too much on a game I already hate and not enough on me. I tug at the loose thread of conversation that will unravel more about who he is and how I can become a real part of his life. "How did he die?"

He responds instantly. "Suicide."

"Shit." That was more unexpected than if he told me his father spontaneously combusted.

I've never thought about killing myself, not even on my worst day. I'd bet anything my mom considered it, and I'd bet twice that she didn't think of what my life would be like if she did.

The subject feels taboo, and I whisper, "Was he depressed or something?"

"We had financial troubles."

"How did he do it?" I ask. "I mean, is that bad to ask? Everyone asks me how my dad died."

"Asphyxiation." Mr. Stewart finishes setting up the last line of pieces, never taking his eyes off the board while participating dispassionately in my Q&A.

"So," I say, wanting for him to open up more, "your mom raised you?"

He taps the board. "Go ahead. You can go first."

"It was just you and your mom?" I dip my head, leaning toward him, hoping he'll look at me.

"Play, Daniel."

I *tsk* and lean back in my chair. "You're the same as everyone else. Just because I'm younger than you doesn't mean you get to pry into my life when you won't talk about yours."

"It's your move. Start with a pawn." With his finger, he indicates the one I might consider. It must annoy him that I've made my first move with the knight every game.

I reach under my chair for my backpack. I pull it out and let it swing above his desk, right over his pile of Post-Its and six identical black fine-point pens, the only sort I've ever seen him use. "If you keep ignoring me," I threaten, "I'm gonna go home."

So he might see me, Mr. Stewart gently pushes my bag to one side. "It's not a matter of age. It's a matter of position."

I return my backpack to the floor and use my foot to shove it between the chair legs. "Position?"

I'm unsure how it's fair that I'm supposed to be answering a hundred questions about my father any time some authority figure wants, and yet, when I ask the same questions in return, I'm unworthy of answers.

"I only wanted you to know that we both lost our fathers early, that I might understand, if only a little. But it's inappropriate for me to tell you my life story," he says. "Teachers are here in service of their students and not the other way around."

A joke about servicing me is tough to pass up. I choose sincerity. "If you want to be, like, the last on a long list of people who've already said they were working in my service, forget it. Try a new tactic." I snatch the knight and drop it on its new home.

One side of his mouth turns down. "I suggested you consider a pawn." He makes the next move and rolls his shoulders. "My grandmother raised me."

I have little to say about grandmothers; my dad's mother is cruel and estranged, and my other grandmother died before I was born. Any comment of substance escapes me. "Was she nice?" The question is weak, and if I were using "nice" in class, he'd grimace and say, "Choose a better word."

After a deep breath, he says, "Yes." His response is weighted, solemn, more than a plain yes. With that yes, I know he thinks I would never be able to understand that level of *nice*, however impotent the word.

My index finger pushes one of my pawns forward as surreptitiously as possible. We've finally moved from silence to banter to significant conversation, and I don't want to distract him from our conversation.

My focus remains gentle and steady on his face. I speak softly. "What happened to your mom?"

"She killed herself a year after my father did," he says without inflection and pushes the rook two spaces toward my side. "To the day."

"They left you all alone?"

"Indeed, they did. But it was for the best. He was neglectful, a philanderer, and gambled away most of his paycheck. And she was," he says and pauses, "unfit." Under the desk, his foot taps several times, pauses, taps some more. He points to the piece I should move next and the square I should move it to. "Look, Daniel, I imagine you don't let yourself speak of your father often. But you can in here. It's safe. *I'm* safe."

We are quiet, the branch of an oak tree scratching at one of the higher windows to my left the only sound. I stare at my hands in my lap. I want to seem like an adult who has his shit together, not a child who snivels at some unresolved trauma and is certainly unready for sex with his English teacher.

A prickle in the corner of my eye tells me it's too late to prevent a rogue tear. Mr. Stewart says my name, and I look up and shake my head. With one finger, I try to massage the teardrop back into my eye. Useless. "It sucks. I miss him."

"I know." He stretches his arm and lays his hand on my side of the desk.

His hand. Palm down, not up. Am I supposed to touch it? If I do, this will devolve into a weird father-son thing, and I will never get my dick near him. I sit up straight and smooth out my T-shirt, blowing imaginary fuzz from the cotton.

"I've been meaning to ask," he says, removing his hand. "Would you like it if I came to a few of your matches?"

My answer is automatic. "No one comes. It's fine."

"Yes, but would it be okay if *I* did?"

I wish I could admit my interest with gratitude and ease. Of course, I do want that. But accepting anything from anyone who might take the offer away in the future feels excruciating. I muscle past my apprehension. "Yeah. It'd be okay."

He sits back and smiles. "It's okay to ask for things that make you feel good," he says delicately. "Not everyone will say yes, but not everyone will say no."

The manner with which he tries to soothe me feels worse than having admitted my desire for his attendance. I hate pity. I tip over my king, although I'm probably a few moves from losing. "Shouldn't you get going? Isn't anyone waiting for you? A cat?"

After sliding the chess board aside, he leans forward and puts his elbows on his desk, then lays one forearm atop the other. "After your father passed, did your mother find a therapist to help you navigate the loss?"

"I don't want to talk about this anymore." I stand and put the pieces back in their nooks and close the board before stuffing it into my pack, careful not to let any loose weed or paraphernalia spill out. "I don't need therapy. I got through it fine."

"You believe you're *through* it?"

"Shit, come on." Suddenly sluggish and heavy, almost rubbery, my body drops into the chair without having a choice. "I want to go home. You think anyone would really notice if you gave me a ride?"

"I'd notice." He stows his pens and notes inside his desk drawer, locking up with a key and a click. "If you're leaving, however, I'll walk with you."

"If you can *walk* with me, then you can drive with me. Or how about a bus? What if we happened to be on the same bus? Is it just the car that's off limits?"

After slipping into his suit jacket, he turns off the lights next to the door and motions for me to pass into the hallway. Outside the classroom, two of my teachers from tenth grade pass. They say hello. He only nods.

I follow Mr. Stewart down the hallway, staying a foot behind him. He walks fast, his shoes clicking against the school's old tiles. "Hey," I say while staring at the ruler-straight hairline above his collar, "I just remembered. Have you been thinking about me when you eat your mints?"

When he suddenly halts and turns, I stop short, losing my balance. I catch myself with one hand on the wall and straighten in a clumsy recovery.

His steadying grip on my arm draws my attention. I flex my biceps, trap his hand there, and step closer to him. I'm skeptical but hopeful that the hush we share is evidence of temptation.

He yanks his hand from the crook of my arm and shakes his head. "Why would you end a pleasant afternoon like this? My God, Daniel, you could be so much better than you are."

He walks away. I know to stay behind. Even if he apologized, it would take me more than a minute to regain my composure; after being curbed or ignored by him all school year, that rebuke hurts the worst.

I arrive home, feeling low enough to call it a night at 8 p.m., no sex or weed, just sleep. My mother is cleaning the upstairs bathroom. On the way to my room, I stop, watching her wipe down the sink. She's dressed in jeans and a gray T-shirt my father often wore while working in the garage. One of his blue handkerchiefs keeps her hair under wraps and out of her eyes.

I lean my shoulder against the wall across from the bathroom, next to a Picasso print of *The Old Guitarist* that my mother bought for him one Christmas. For several moments, she doesn't see me, or pretends that she doesn't. When she stops scrubbing, she sticks her nose in the air as if she smells something not quite right on the wind. I say hello, and she turns in my direction, wiping a trickle of sweat from her hairline and nods. "No match today?"

"No," I say, "just practice."

She takes another swipe at the sink with her cloth. We both speak at the same time. I am about to ask if she's home for the night, but she talks over me. "So, have you picked a school yet?" She gives me a second to respond, and when I don't, rushes to add, "Because I was thinking, maybe you should pick one out of state. I mean, don't you want to see more than here?"

Aside from high school, Ollie, and tennis, I have nothing here. In the fall, Ollie's going to college in Houston. I've never thought about why the college I choose matters to anyone but me. "I don't know. I'm still thinking about it."

After depositing the damp rag on the edge of the sink, she retrieves the toilet brush from the closet and tilts forward as if readying to disclose a secret. "Do you remember I told you about Theodore?" She waves the toilet brush back and forth in tempo with her words. "Well, his sister's husband is selling a house a few miles from here. If Theodore and I were to make a new start, it might be best if..."

There's no need for her to say anything else. I bow my shaking head, having finally figured out her angle. "You want me out of the house? You hardly even know I'm here. What's the difference?"

"Danny, don't give me that," she says with a sudden tenseness. "I give you your space. You'd rather I track your every move?"

"You know what? I don't even care. I would go to a two-year medical college in the Caribbean just to get the fuck out of here."

"Why do you always pick fights with me?"

My anger is fear; if she starts fresh without me, then I must start fresh without her. As hollow and unhealthy as our relationship is, she remains my anchor of discomfort. I squeeze my hands together until my knuckles are white. I'm only half committed to participating in a full-on fight, and I end up mumbling, "Because you say and do stupid shit."

"Danny," she says and sighs, "I'm—"

"*Don't* say you're sorry. You never mean it."

Immediately, she moves from prey to predator. It takes a

second before her features freeze in a scowl. "I wasn't going to," she says defiantly, throwing the toilet brush into the sink.

I disengage, then. When she starts to throw things, any rational conversation is over. I descend to our first floor. When I'm in the living room, the slam of the bathroom door upstairs startles me. She opens it, slams it again. When I hear it open once more, she is mid-scream, shifting pitches from a squeal to a howl and back. The shrieking stops, and she appears above me, hanging over to the edge of the staircase, yelling. "*I need to do what I need to do. It's not your decision, is it? It's mine.*" One last nebulous screech reaches me before she retreats and slams the door again.

My mother has had difficulty handling anger, resentment, or perceived feelings of neglect for as far back as I remember. When I was in elementary school, her episodes were milder but more regular. Growing up, I knew that if she was unhappy, noise was her way of communicating displeasure. Throwing a fork in the sink. Stomping up the stairs. Pushing hangers across the bar in her closet as she muscled a heavy row of clothing this way, then that.

My father handled these episodes well. He calmed her in minutes, often after a brief talk behind their closed bedroom door. She would then appear downstairs as if nothing had happened, coming between the TV and me, blocking the cartoons to ask me if I'd like a hot dog or carrot sticks.

The incidents became less frequent and more rageful after my father's death. If I am the cause of or witness to one of her outbursts, the silent treatment she inflicts upon me ensues immediately afterwards and lingers for days.

I leave the house and text Ollie. Although he just finished dinner and is enjoying a lazy night of video games, he agrees to come get me. "My mom," is all I say when I get in his car. He rolls his eyes, and I roll mine.

"Where do you want to go?"

"I'll give you gas money," I say. "Can we just drive?"

He reverses out of my driveway, and we end up taking a circuitous route to the city, returning to our suburbs by way of the highway. He listens to music, and I pull up some online tests on my phone, this time for someone other than Mr. Stewart. Instead of career placement quizzes, I take several psychiatric evaluations.

My mother is a clunky fit for the description of several psychopathologies, having only three of the eight required characteristics, for instance, or just missing the mark for any official disorder.

"You think my mom's a sociopath?" I ask Ollie.

He holds the wheel with one hand and lights a fourth cigarette with the other. "What? No."

I sink down in the seat. "She's something." I navigate away from a lengthy personality test with thirty multiple choice questions—*a) I like to look at myself in the mirror. b) I do not like to look at myself in the mirror*—because I don't know the answer to any of them.

Ollie turns off the music and makes a right turn onto my street. "She's definitely something."

During my middle school years, my father and I went into the city a lot and ate fish and chips served in newspapers at the pier. He would tear open packets of vinegar for me while we hung our legs over the wall that ran next to the river. The subject of my mom would come up. Then, no matter what we were doing or how we were positioned, my dad would make sure we made eye contact. "She can be—complicated. Her childhood, it's not something I can explain. Let's just offer her some grace."

Although my relationship with her now is more strained than ever, when I remember his words, the careful and tender way he spoke about her, I feel I should try harder, be more patient, love her anyway. But the feeling fades; I just have to replay the memory of what she did to me on the day he died, and all my sympathy for her curdles.

I've needed to keep myself numb and my schedule full all week. I can't stand to think about my last interaction with my mother, almost as much as I can't stand thinking of my last interaction with Mr. Stewart.

He and I have been ignoring each other. I do peek at him occasionally. I never catch him looking at me, though. The bell at the end of class gives me no joy, and I leave without receiving so much as a nod.

Last night, I woke up unsure of the time, unsure of my location. My body tingled as all the blood flowed back into the parts of me that had been twisted and squished when I fell asleep. The unfamiliar room was dim and smelled of honey sprinkled with ash, sweet but dirty. Shadows from a muted television danced on the ceiling and walls, between blinking blues and pinks and a dull flickering yellow. I believed myself safe and let my head fall back to the floor.

When I woke up for the second time, I was at home. I'd passed out on my stomach on top of the blankets—where Ollie must have dropped me—my right arm pinned under my torso, my ass in the air.

I ready myself for school, my brain still pickled with toxicity. I doze on the couch until Ollie pulls into my driveway, honking once. While he drives us to school, he chomps his breakfast burrito and makes it no secret he's ready to see the back of me. "You need someone else to entertain you tonight." He wants a decent night's sleep and to bypass yet another situation where he must drag me around as if I'm his alcoholic uncle on a bender.

That night, Ollie shows up at my front door, pushing past me when I answer. He tows Jesse behind him. "I brought him," he says, pointing with his thumb over his shoulder, "so you have company when I want to leave."

Within minutes, Ollie and Jesse are smoking weed and watching TV on the couch in my living room. I am wiped out from tennis, but my laptop has me in its clutches tonight. On the floor, I toil over a Hawthorne essay, for the second time.

My mom comes home with who I assume is Theodore, but it could be a new guy altogether. Despite her passion from the other night, Theo might be history. She ascends the stairs, saying to him, "I wish Danny would crack a window."

We catch the ass end of the boyfriend. Khakis too long, shoes too shiny. "New man?" Ollie says.

"Probably seasonal," I say.

Jesse pokes me with a toe. "I need a cigarette. Should I go outside?"

"It could be a fucking opium den in this place," Ollie says, "and his mom would still freak out about cigarette smoke."

Ollie has three grins. *I'm about to get laid; you're about to throw up; and I'm about to fuck with you.* When Jesse leaves, he shoots me that last one, and I shake my head, "Don't say something stupid."

"You know what we have here, Dan? For the first time in your life? A social triangle. Like, you've had a social straight line," he says, pointing to me and then himself, "and now you have a social triangle. By summer, who knows? Social square? Sky's the limit."

With fitting timing, the back door opens and closes, and Jesse returns.

Ollie knows when to stay, when to go, and how to do both without bringing much attention to himself or the situation he's squeezing in or out of. Now when he says he's going, he has his shoes and coat on and is out the front door within a minute.

Jesse seems not to notice Ollie's disappearance and sets up shop after collapsing onto my couch with a huff. He skillfully positions a bag of corn chips on his chest. I sit down in my father's overstuffed chair after tossing him the remote. He sticks out his tongue at my snack selection. "Are you eating cucumbers?"

"I am." I hold up a wobbly slice and shake it. "You want?"

"No, thanks. I don't combine suffering with sustenance."

Two hours of lazing around goes fast. After downing a liter of ginger ale, Jesse is the first to move. When he returns from the bathroom, he says. "Come outside with me. I need a smoke."

On the flagstone patio in my backyard, a covered and once cared-for grill has sat unused for three years. Empty terra cotta planters line the hip-high wall that separates the stone from the lawn. In the porch light, Jesse's lips have lost their usual high-gloss pink and are now the sticky, blue hue of a newly asphyxiated corpse.

Both of us spot a fallen bird's nest in a darkened corner. Leaning forward for inspection, Jesse says, "No eggs," and prods the bowl of twigs, dead grass, and random litter with his foot. He steps away, frowning like he tried and failed to collect and incubate.

His intensity portends an existential chat, which makes me uncomfortable. I sniff the air. "Smells like fire or something."

"Bonfire," he agrees.

He joins me in the center of the patio. Cracked stone from a decade of volatile freeze-thaw cycles crunches beneath his feet. We face each other, the distance between us a few inches too close for me to relax my shoulders. He pats the pockets of his coat, retrieving nothing. Not until he finds his cigarettes in his hoodie does the pinch of anxiety fade from his face.

Jesse's attention flits from his fingers to the sky and back. The blaze of the orange ashes flares once before he lets the cigarette hang by his side. "I smoke too much," he says self-consciously.

"I don't think so."

"I do. And I should be studying right now."

"Studying?"

I always figured Jesse's backpack was stuffed with anything but books. I'd seen him produce a few for English, but during Genetics/Bio, the only other class I have with him, he always has to slide across the aisle to share with someone. Rarely is his laptop open. I never see him on his phone unless he's texting, all business: on, off, back in his pocket.

"You're surprised I study?" he says.

"Kinda." I hope my brief smile snuffs out any offense.

"Good grades and weed money are the only way I'm going to college," he says. "My parents are not rich, like—are you rich?" Taking one step away from my house and looking up, he sniffs. "You're comfortable, at least."

"I guess. We have a little bit of money. From the life insurance."

How much time do I need to spend staring at the treetops before this topic dies on its own? I misjudge and face him too soon. Jesse clears his throat. "Your dad, he's—" He cringes at what we both know is the rest of that sentence. "I mean—Jackie told me a little bit."

I worry if I speak, my heartache will sully the rest of the night. I adhere to my minimalist approach. "Dead, yeah."

"I'm really sorry. What happened?"

Recounting the practiced, short sequence that led to my father's death is easy: an earworm, the worst song, its robot cadence never fades. "He owned a few hardware stores. Fired some guys that were stealing. They came back. One shot him in his throat. He died at

　　　　　　　　　　　　　　　　　　JENNIFER GREIDUS

the hospital. Or maybe on the way. No one ever told me exactly when."

As if holding back blood spilling from his own jugular, he clutches his neck with one hand. "How old were you?"

"Fourteen."

"I don't even know what to say," he admits after a pause.

"It's a conversation stopper. Just move on."

Owls hoot. Leaves rustle. I am about to call Jesse's attention to the owls, ask him if he notices how windy it is, maybe laugh about how loud we left the volume on the TV. Small talk, any small talk at all. But Jesse speaks before I figure out where to begin. "Is it okay if you tell me about him?" He picks a piece of tobacco off his tongue and flicks it into the night air. "Is that question weird or too much?"

Jesse is the only person who's asked if it was okay to ask. His consideration shifts my usual reaction from refusal to reticence. My teeth clamp down on a fingernail. "What do you want to know?"

The wind sweeps Jesse's hair into his eyes, then out. He drops his cigarette and flattens it with his shoe. "How about...how about the best memory you have?"

When Jesse asks, what comes to my mind are facts about my father, not memories of him. They are my standard responses. *He liked baseball. He knew a lot about motorcycles. He liked tea, not coffee. He worked a lot.* But that's not what Jesse wants. What he wants I never share with anyone, not even Ollie.

"I don't know," I say. "I guess I replay a lot of them. They're no big deal."

Jesse waits me out with the skill of an expert negotiator; his long silence compels me to fill the dead air. "We can talk about something else," I say. "I'd need to be completely fucked up to talk about this."

He fishes out a banged-up silver and red cigarette case from the pocket of his jeans, pulls out a blunt and hands it to me with his purple lighter. "Then let's get completely fucked up."

The breeze fights the flame, and he acts as my wind blocker, slipping in front of me and receding the few feet again. I take three hits instead of my normal two and hand it back.

"Go ahead," Jesse says, taking a hit. "Best memory."

"I don't know. We used to make pizza." I lower my head. I feel as though I've betrayed my father, sharing something that was just ours after years of holding my memories of him so tight inside me. "I can't think of much else to say right now."

"Like from-scratch pizza?"

"Yeah, the dough and all that. I'd get to pick the toppings. So, once I picked these chocolate caramel—candy—things." I choke on my words and step sideways, out of the back porch light. My eyes brew tears and burn. The memory itself is less painful than sharing it with someone. "And, you know, he let me put them on."

Instead of somber sympathy, Jesse reels back in exaggerated delight, like we're swapping family stories at a work picnic. "*Ha*. Gross. Did you eat it?"

My breath catches when he laughs. I'm used to people telling me I'll be okay, that it's a shame, I should be positive. They want to fix me. They urge me to heal faster, move on. Insincere well-wishers and guidance counselors did the head-tilt reserved for hurt animals and lost children, and they *never* laughed. Being amused about anything my dad used to do seemed impossible, before now.

"I didn't eat it," I say, allowing myself a smile, "but he did."

"That's so great." As he grows serious, his smile disappears. "It must be really hard to talk about this. Or maybe it feels good to talk about it?" His lips barely part when, having decided for me, he confirms his hypothesis: "Yeah."

I back up until my legs hit the short brick wall behind me. My ass bumps two of the clay flowerpots, which tumble onto the grass behind the barrier. I give them a second's attention and find them intact.

Being this vulnerable is dreadful. I would rather be naked, slicked up in oil, having my genitals mocked in public. I want to escape to my bedroom and be alone. I want to hug the perimeter of the patio, slip inside the sliding doors, and wave goodnight.

Jesse comes nearer. He grabs my shoulder to give it a quick shake. "Hey, I have a story. We can lighten this up a little." Smoke from the blunt swirls between us. He snatches it from his lips and holds it out to me. "You want any more?" I say nothing, nor do I reach for it. He stubs the blunt against the wall, tucking the rest back in the cigarette case.

"So," he says, "when I was thirteen, my brother—did I tell you about Pete at all? He's like four years older. Anyway, Pete went blind." The wind picks up, and Jesse pauses to look at the barren nest as it's blown several feet across the stone. "But just for eight weeks. No one knew exactly why. We still don't know why."

I barely register what he's saying. I'm eyeing those sliding doors. They seem so far away, and I am frozen, soles glued to the pavement. Jesse asks me if I'm listening. I utter, "Yeah, blind? Who's—?"

"Pete. My brother."

If I were telling this story to him, I'd be annoyed by his inattention. I would have said, "Never fucking mind." But Jesse, stubborn or oblivious, continues with a swift and spirited delivery. "Doctors and psychiatrists and shit. No one knew. After like two weeks into it, we were all sort of resigned to this new way he'd be. My dad was buying braille books. My mother was drinking tea and watching TV while she made specialist appointments in other states. Like, nothing rattled them. Even Pete seemed—I don't know—he was scared, but not like I was."

Jesse kicks my foot and pulls my attention again. "Anyway, both my mom and dad work, so they had to hire a nurse to hang out with him during the day until they could figure out what else to do."

The tale begins to interest me more than does going inside and passing out. I hold up my hands, so he'll pause. "Wait. Nurse? Is this a porn story?"

"That's *exactly* what my mom started to worry about. The nurse was pretty and nice. Maybe thirty. Every day when my mom came home from work, she'd knock on my door and ask me vague questions, like had I heard any noises coming from Pete's room that afternoon. So, like, not just for my mom, but for me—I'm curious myself—I decide to skip math club—"

"*Math* club?"

"Yeah, shut up. I skip *math club*," he continues, "and I sneak up to his room and crack open his door, and I see Pete was kneeling, and the nurse—the nurse was giving him some sort of communion with Triscuits and juice." Jesse reenacts laying a wafer on his brother's tongue, followed by a ceremonious bow, which I'm sure is absent from any church service.

"He was kneeling?" I say.

"It was a fucked-up scene, fucked up enough that I snitched and told my mom. She was so calm about Pete's blindness, but the communion thing made her lose it. Crying for days. I think she'd have been less disturbed if I told her he was fucking the nurse."

"That's crazy," I say.

Jesse agrees. "And, of course, we never had Triscuits again."

Every time Jesse's lips stretch into a smile, I find mine do, too. Aside from Ollie, Jesse's been the only life in this house for years. Boys on my couch or in my bedroom haven't been it. My mom is never it. I'm not it. We don't even have any living houseplants. Right now, Jesse is the lone lotus flower in this murky, inhospitable pond.

When he grows somber, he chews on a fingernail. "Hey, uh, I'm really sorry about your dad. I wish I knew what else to say."

"It's okay." I shake my head to clear the ugly thoughts. Rubbing my hands together, I turn toward my house. "Cold out here. You want to go in?"

He nods and follows me. I head for the living room, but Jesse stalls in front of my dining room sideboard. He snags my sleeve and pulls me back to the dusty display of my father's collections: kachina dolls, vintage brass ashtrays, antique Japanese cigarette cases, and a half-dozen authentic Bavarian beer steins.

"Is this your dad's stuff?" Jesse brushes two fingertips against one of the steins. He releases my sleeve and gets closer to admire the pewter filigree and hand-painting. "This is really—wow." His hand falls away from the enameled design. "Shit. I shouldn't have put my dirty fingers all over it."

I agree with him; he should have asked. I'd usually say it was fine, blow it off, stew silently. Before I respond with the truth, however, I consider what it meant for him to stop and pull me back; he noticed the pieces, assessed they weren't mine or my mom's, and asked me about them.

The collectibles were the only thing I ever heard my mom and dad bicker about. She insisted he keep those belongings in the basement, and for years, he did. The September before he died, after a few days of cool silence between them, the collectibles suddenly appeared here—main floor, main attraction—and were considered sacrosanct.

"No one has ever touched them," I say. "That's why it's weird, I guess."

"I'm sorry." Jesse hangs his head. "Shit."

"They're dusty." I swipe my finger over an ashtray in the shape of the Taj Mahal. "You see what I mean? You're the first."

"Your mom must really miss him, too, keeping all this stuff here."

Evidence of his life is all over the house. The three motorcycles my dad was rebuilding are still in the garage, parts, oil, and tools all exactly where they were on the day he was shot. There is food in our pantry that was here when he was alive, snacks only he liked: a plastic barrel of stale pretzels and several bags of cheese curls. In her master bath, a basket on the floor holds magazines he read on the toilet.

I guess an outsider *would* think she is a sentimental creature. I believe, however, the parts of him that are left lying around are less to remind her of how much she misses him and more to remind the rest of the world how much she misses him.

In the living room, Jesse sprawls on the couch. I sit on the floor in front of it. As a joke, he chooses a documentary on the business of soft porn, complete with clip after tacky clip, through which the producers chat about drug use, compensation, and suicide. "Look at this one," he says, nudging my shoulder with his socked foot. "They gave the prison wardens fake tits and kilts."

Jesse laughs and chokes on a piece of corn chip, which he coughs up into his hand and flicks at my head. I find myself on the receiving end of another prod—foot to shoulder—this time harder. He clears his throat. "Let me ask you something. The other night, I called you—I don't know—pretty or something. You remember?"

I remember his face close to mine that night. How he touched my leg. His head on my shoulder. And of course, *of course*, I know what he said. "The beauty queen thing?"

"Yeah, that," he says. "So, this whole time since then, have you been thinking I'm gay?"

As hard as it is not to jump on that and take what I want, I stay neutral. "I haven't really thought about it."

On the TV, three girls spread and grind on a cot behind prison bars. Overdone moans fill our silence until Jesse smacks his foot on the floor to get my attention again. "Jackie says sometimes I get embarrassing when I'm stoned."

We both have our eyes on the TV, but I keep us on task. "I wouldn't say embarrassing. But I do remember you touching me a lot, yeah."

His head swivels toward me in a panic. "I was wasted. And I probably seemed super gay."

"Super gay?" I flick his ankle. "Don't be an idiot."

He smacks the back of my head. I reach behind me, a handful of his hoodie all I need to haul him to the floor. A sophisticated plan is unnecessary; wrestling like a sixth grader is my way of pinning down Jesse's fluctuating sexuality. We grapple until it's clear I have the advantage with a headlock. "Take your time," I taunt, breathing hard into his ear. "I know you need to catch your breath."

The carpet muffles his obscenities until he pushes himself up with a grunt, swinging a leg over me, straddling my hips. He dips his torso until his face hangs over mine, messy hair falling forward. If he leans down just another couple inches, it will brush against my forehead. "You suck at this," he whispers, "and you've got, like, twenty pounds on me."

I slip my hand under his T-shirt and up his sides, tickling his ribs. He sucks in and holds his breath. As I'm about to slide my other hand down to the fly of his jeans, I whisper, "I don't suck at this. I'm letting you win, so you feel better about your super gay self."

He freezes before scrambling out of my grasp and bolting to his feet. He stumbles once, using my hip to steady himself. Jesse's eyebrows scrunch together as he straightens his glasses. "What? What the fuck does that mean?"

I prop myself up on my elbows, shocked by his sudden change of mood. "Wow. Take it easy. It was a joke."

Jesse paces and chews his fingers like they're dinner. His intellect works against me here. Unlike any other guy who felt his dick twitch in the middle of my living room, he won't fall for games or flirting. Blocking his exit and calling his bluff are out of the question. A rabbit under a hawk's shadow would feel safer than Jesse does right now.

"I should go. It's late." The search he does for his shoes beneath the couch is half-hearted; he makes one attempt at a grab and comes away with nothing. "I'm—I don't even know—man, this is messed up."

"Jesse, calm down. I like it."

"You like what?"

"Come on." I stop myself from teasing him. This is no time to make him feel foolish. "You have to know I like it."

"I—"

"And if you didn't," I say and smile wide, "surprise."

With his index finger still stuffed between the back of his shoe and his foot, he pauses as what I said sinks in. He falls onto the couch, as though the news just reached him that he's terminally ill. "Dan, uh, I'm—I already know who I am. Do you know what I mean?"

It sounds as if Jesse himself doesn't know what he means, like maybe he's asking me to fill in the blanks about why he has a semi right now. I'm more stoned than I thought, and I struggle to sit up. "I don't. But that's okay."

"I mean, I never—" He holds his lower lip between his teeth. "I'm not—"

"Hey, it's okay. I don't care. Pass me the bowl. Look," I say, gesturing to the TV, "you're missing important plot points."

The anticlimax deadens the room. The carpet is suddenly coarse against my skin. The smell of corn chips offends me. My tongue feels too big in my mouth and tastes of stale smoke. I keep my disenchantment to myself, and Jesse sticks around long enough to avoid seeming like a homophobic asshole.

Sticky seats, grease-smeared tables, and haggard servers who've mastered balancing three plates on an arm comfort me at eight p.m. on Sunday. In the diner's lobby, the host hunches over the stand, shifting uncomfortably in her brown poly dress that's ripped a few inches at the side seam. When Ollie holds up four fingers, she winks at him and says, "Big boy is back."

About twice a month, Ollie and I come here, and I order a combination of pancakes, fried eggs, and grapefruit juice. Fuck tennis, at least for those nights. This evening, we picked up Jesse and Jackie first, and the four of us drove around in Ollie's car, smoking weed and talking about horror movies and how the world will end. When Ollie extended the invitation, I was sure Jesse would decline. It seems gay-angst recovery time, however, is shorter than I imagined.

I'm forced to sit on Ollie's side of the booth. So unconcerned is he about my comfort, when he reaches across the table for syrup, he elbows me in the chin without apology. One of my legs sprawls in the aisle, and I must draw it in every time the server passes with a full tray.

Jackie and Jesse, on the other hand, could fit an additional person on their side of the booth. They press against each other like newlyweds in a rusty pickup. I have a mouthful of grapefruit juice when Jackie puts her heeled foot on my leg and simultaneously pets the side of Jesse's face. He pulls away from her. "That's really annoying." Her hand falls to his arm and continues its mission on his biceps. The pressure of her foot on my leg disappears.

When Ollie pushes my knee with his, it signals one of two things. Either he senses the possibility of a group sex scenario, or he wants to leave because he's miserably bored. When he relaxes in his seat, I assume it's the former. He has yet to be in a group sex scenario, and I'm unsure if he would know what to do with another penis in the picture, never mind two.

In my periphery, I spot a kid with whom I shared a bit of mutual masturbation. Not my top choice—the sex act or the guy—but it was probably late, and I accepted what was thrown my way.

For as random and carefree as all my sexual encounters have been, I'm usually not so much of an asshole that I've forgotten their names or how they made me come: the intensity of it, the skill level, and the idiosyncrasies of style. But as this guy raps his knuckles on our table, I reconsider. Maybe I am indeed an asshole because I can't remember his name.

Straight as a pin, clean fingernails, too many tattoos of celestial beings, and every hair purposely out of place, he's a three-in-the-morning choice. The only thing I remember about him is that he had a nice cock, uncircumcised and thick.

"Hey, Dan." The way he greets me, drawing out the *A* in my name, seems like he's daring me to admit I don't know him.

Ollie speaks up and saves me. "What's up, Mikos?"

Mikos glances at each of my cohorts and curls his upper lip. "Roughing it, Dan?"

"Almost always."

"You want to hang out later?"

I stuff more pancake in my mouth, hoping I won't have to answer that question. When he doesn't budge, I gesture to Jesse and Jackie with my lackluster, nicked-up diner knife, as if I'm a barbarian on a dais. "Doing stuff."

"How about after you *do stuff?*"

Annoyed that he won't take the hint, I sigh and say, "I'm probably doing more stuff."

"*I'm* free," Ollie says with a toothy smile.

Ollie can be such a motherfucker. The only thing that remark does is aggravate the awkwardness. For me, the lie comes effortlessly. "I'm seeing someone now."

Mikos clicks his tongue. "That's all you had to say, Dan. Be well, then." He touches my shoulder before strutting back to his friends, all of them with well-planned hair and sleeves of tattoos.

Since he shifts seamlessly from background to foreground only when he wishes to debate or be clever, after Jesse clears his throat, I'm prepared for an outcrop of witty banter. He raises his eyebrows and twists his lips. "Be well?"

"Yeah. Some of the pretty ones like poetry." I smile before shoveling in more pancakes.

My guess is that whatever Jesse's been holding in all night is about to surface. He absently chews his fingernails. When he notices me watching him, he drops his hand to his lap and stares at me, lips parted, his tongue buffing his left canine. As I've seen him do in English when he disagrees with some interpretation of text, he wrinkles his forehead and snorts dismissively. "*That's* your type?"

I lick a spot of syrup from the corner of my mouth before speaking. "My sometimes-type."

"But why?"

"Why what?"

"I mean—" He looks past me at Mikos. "He doesn't seem—"

All our attention snaps to Jackie, who groans. Her heavy head falls forward and rests on her arm, which stretches across the table. Syrup and crumbs stick to her skin. Jesse gently lifts her sprawling torso off the table and back into the seat. She is full of pills, and they've kicked in. "Danny?" she stage-whispers. "Hey, Danny? Danny?"

"Spit it out, woman." I wave my fork in the air. "I want to finish my fucking pancakes and get out of here."

"I can't believe," she says, struggling to express herself, "anyone would think—" she catches her drug-drowsy breath "—your pendulum isn't *glued* to the gay side of absolute gay." Jackie points at Jesse and attempts a wink, pulling off only a squint. "Jesse is cute *and* oblivious."

Jesse tears his paper napkin into long, thin strips before lining them up on his empty plate amidst the muffin crumbs. The water he dribbles from his straw onto the shredded napkin creates a waterlogged masterpiece.

Right now, he'd sooner dig out his eyeballs with his spoon than look at me. No matter how he feels right now, I have it worse. The vanilla is making me crazy. It's his skin. His clothing. I don't know what the fuck it is, exactly, but when I'm near him, it's always in the air.

She's wiggling her arm, and I am sure Jackie has her hand in Jesse's pants under the table. Either that, or she's struggling with the zipper. She kisses his ear. Her tongue darts out between shiny, coppery lips, drawing a wet circle on his cheek. "So innocent, aren't you?" she baby-talks.

Jesse pulls away and wipes his cheek on his shoulder. "No one wants to see you licking my face." She runs her hand through his hair. He's opposed to that too. "I'm ready to go," he says, pulling away from her. She won't relent, holding his chin between a thumb and forefinger, turning his face toward her.

I imagine having license to move Jesse's face any way I want, to tilt it, pull it out of the shadows, squeeze his cheeks until he has fish lips. I'd make him look at me.

When Jackie kisses him, I drop my fork. The noise startles them both. I force a smile and say that I'm ready to go, too.

Outside the diner, Ollie and Jesse share a smoke while Jackie snuggles against me, stomping her heels to keep warm. My phone buzzes in my coat pocket. I dig it out, hold it up, and the light illuminates her face.

It's Borys. He's in my Fine Arts class and likes silent films. Six months ago, Poland sent Borys here scrubbed up and ready to come out. He code-switches his native tongue and English and blushes when he does. The soccer shorts he wears almost every day beg to be dropped to the floor. Newly out, gorgeous, naive: If I don't hop on that fast, he'll be moving on to the next guy on his list.

I text him the location of the gas station across the street and slip the phone back in my pocket. "All right," I say and clap my hands, "I'm going. See ya."

Ollie grabs my jacket. "Where the fuck are you going? I'm not picking you up the next state over, motherfucker." He holds up his phone. "Forget my fucking number tonight. I'm tired and full. And you need to get a fucking car."

Ollie tells me to get a car every few months, just like my mom tells me she'll buy me a car every few months. A car makes me think of my age, a job, college. I sometimes worry that if I accepted my mother's offer to buy me a car, if I allowed myself the independence of being able to drive, I would never reach out to Ollie for anything. I would isolate more, and I'd be too lazy or inconsiderate to seek his company. Since my father died, things that once mattered no longer do, and I don't want Ollie to be one of them.

"Where are you going?" Jesse asks me.

Ollie shoves my shoulder. "Only two things motivate Dan. Weed and dick. And I'm sure he's got a pocketful of weed."

Jackie's eyes are almost closed, but she has enough energy to agree. "Priorities." Her shoulder knocks against my arm.

Only Ollie and Jackie say goodbye. Jesse takes about fifteen seconds to light another cigarette so he can avoid having to wave, nod, or speak.

I meet Borys at the gas station. I'm not in his Honda one minute before I regret it. I'm ready to head to his place, but he wants to kiss me in the car. He smells like he swallowed his gum a minute ago, which is considerate but pointless. I duck out of his lips' line of fire and say, "Let's just go back to your house."

"We can kiss," he says, scrunching his forehead. "Before we, uh, fuck *around*? We kiss now."

"I have a cold," I lie.

"Does not matter."

"I don't want to kiss. I like you, but it's not my thing. Anyone home at your house?"

We drive in silence. An addition to a family that already has four kids, Borys is an exchange student who moves through his host's home as if he's biologically theirs. He leaves his coat on the floor, removes his shoes in the kitchen, and slams the door to his room.

The blowjob is pedestrian and at one point turns bone-dry, but the way he waits for my approval each time he changes position or speed makes up for it. When a guy is embarrassed by his obvious inexperience, it's kind of sexy to me.

I let Borys shoot his load on my stomach. I'm fully dressed and yawning five minutes after that. "All right, can we go? I'm tired."

Tossing himself back onto his bed, fluffing his pillow, he asks me if I want to watch TV. He runs his hand through his short brown hair and scratches his abs. "Relax one minute."

I sigh. It is a good hour's walk to my house. "So, you're not going to give me a ride now?"

"We—relax, right?"

"I'm not the type to *relax*."

When Borys says nothing else, I text Ollie. *Come get me.*

No way. I told you. Tired.

Don't care. 911.

Nope.

911.

Fuck. Fine. Where are you?

I turn to Borys. "Where am I again? What road is this?"

"People say—they say you are sometimes...asshole. This, I agree."

"You came hard, right? No complaints?" I pull on my coat. "I'm gonna go."

"We will do again?"

"Maybe." I'm never going to see him again, and maybe the truth will keep Borys from haunting me. "Probably not."

The next day, Mr. Stewart arrives late to class, placing his bag and a couple of books on his desk with no apology for the unusual tardiness. Without greeting us, he says, "Open Joyce. Wendy, please pick up where we stopped." She sputters through the reading until he grimaces at her second botched pronunciation of Dedalus and has us read chapter one to ourselves in silence.

After a couple attempts at understanding page eight, I give up and put my head down. I'm stoned this afternoon. I smoked half of a blunt in Ollie's car at lunch. Right now, I don't care too much about Joyce or religious guilt or the Moocows. I'm fit for a nap.

"*Daniel.*"

The voice neutralizes my high. I force my eyelids apart and perk up. "Yeah?"

He slaps his copy of *Portrait* against the desk. "Do you need to go to the nurse's office?"

Although I accepted that I may forever go without it, I've been desiring his attention. If being dressed down in front of my peers is what I can expect, however, I'd rather be off his radar altogether. I clear my throat. "No."

"It's beyond me, then, why you'd be taking a nap during my class." He scans the room. "Does anyone else need a time out today?"

Eyes that were a moment ago on me are now all downcast. Jesse straightens in his seat and pulls his discarded shoes closer to his feet.

"Daniel, now that you're awake," Mr. Stewart says, "why don't you take us through page twenty."

As I read aloud, Mr. Stewart stops me several times to gather class opinions and poke around for comprehension. My lips are still working on weed time and become uncooperative when words with more than three syllables pop up.

Out of the corner of my eye, I notice Jesse's hand go up. As soon as I pause and take my next breath, he fills the gap. "If this is American Lit," he says to Mr. Stewart, "what's with the Irish?"

Ignoring Jesse, our teacher motions for me to continue reading. A minute before the bell rings, he asks me to stop, then addresses Jesse's question. "I want none of you to go to college without having first encountered Joyce."

Some kids nod, but I'm sure no one agrees with or understands Mr. Stewart's passion. Class ends, and Ollie sidles up to me. "When you read, you really do sound like you have a mouthful of balls." He looks over his shoulder and back at me. "Stewart's coming."

If Mr. Stewart were to touch anyone, I'd expect it to be me. Instead, he places an open hand on Ollie's shoulder when he speaks to both of us. "Are you gentlemen following the material?"

"I guess," Ollie says. "Is it true Joyce was a freak?"

Mr. Stewart cocks his head to the side. "How so?"

"Like, toilet stuff."

I elbow Ollie in the ribs. "Shut up. Let's go."

"Wait one moment, Daniel," Mr. Stewart says. "I need to speak with you."

Ollie leaves. Jesse, silent but smiling, brushes by me as he follows the rest of my classmates out of the room. Mr. Stewart closes his door. It's an unusual move; the door has always remained open.

The seat I choose squeaks as I slide in. I drop my backpack on the floor next to me and assume the cockiest position I can manage: slouched in the chair, arms on the desk, hands palm-up in loose fists, legs in the aisle and spread carelessly.

After adjusting his trousers for comfort and unbuttoning his suit jacket, he sits with one asscheek on the desk next to mine. His foot dangles between us, and he touches the tip of his shoe to the corner of my chair leg. "We haven't discussed this before," he says, "because I hoped it would improve. Am I losing you in class? I know we're tackling a lot of literature at once. It cultivates a good reader." He consults the clock on the painted cinder block wall. "I have some essays I need to grade, but for now, I want to know if you're getting a handle on Joyce."

I gather my legs and arms and sit straight. Literature is the last thing I want to talk about. "Joyce? Joyce is easy. Who cares about Joyce? You're not going to apologize for being a dick?"

He scours his eyebrow with a forefinger and then drags his hand down his cheek. "You're right. I am sorry for what I said."

"That's it?"

"What else would there be?"

"More groveling."

So he can talk softly, he leans closer to me. "To a degree, it's natural, this—this back and forth between us." He points at me and then to himself. "But for my sake and yours, it needs to stop. To you, it's flirting. To me, it's a potential suspension. Or worse."

"We get along," I say. "So what?"

"We do." He says it brightly--there's a half-smile--but he quickly becomes serious, eyebrows pinching together.

"Then, explain to me why getting along outside of school is so different than getting along inside of school."

"You don't need me to explain that to you any more than you need me to tell you how inappropriate your behavior was." When I begin to speak, he reaches for my mouth as if blocking whatever else is about to come out. He pulls back before he touches me. "I no longer need your input." When *input* makes me smile, his brow creases. "Let's just set some boundaries, okay?"

"Like?"

He sighs and continues. "How about this? If you want to speak with me about schoolwork, we'll meet in the library after school."

"Schoolwork? Look, I don't need help with essays. I have the Internet. If you want to help me, let's just do the chess thing."

"That's not a good idea."

"Why?"

"I just told you why. You *know* why."

The longer I stay here, the worse it gets. I need to leave before I'm cast out of AP English altogether.

My departure is less than nimble. I get up and trip on the leg of the desk. I wobble, almost falling against him. My bag gets caught on the chair in front of me.

I plan to stuff this interaction down, down, down, where I think I can lock it, at least until this evening when I'm stoned.

As I depart, Mr. Stewart says, "Please don't leave here with a sour taste in your mouth."

I exit and close the door behind me. Jesse is waiting right outside the room. He looks up from his phone. "You okay? What was that about?"

"Nothing. What are you doing here?"

"I don't know. Just loitering."

We begin the walk to tenth period Genetics/Bio. Jesse clears his throat four times. "How was your night with—what was his name? After the diner?"

My emotions are still back in Mr. Stewart's room, but I perk up and smile at Jesse. "It was average."

"What was his name?"

"It doesn't matter."

"What does that mean?"

I halt and turn to him. "Hey, Ollie has a game this weekend. I said I'd go. You want to come?"

I ask because I'm in a bad mood about Mr. Stewart. I ask because Jesse seems mildly nervous around me, and I like that. I ask because, if he says no, I can blow him off forever; and, if he says yes, I can probably get him to admit that he's been thinking about me nonstop since the scene in my living room.

"Yeah, sure," he says, the lilt in his voice excited and innocent. He walks backwards, beaming at me and blowing a chef's kiss. "I'll bring new weed. There are notes of blueberry in the bud. Perfection."

A half hour before tipoff, Ollie's basketball game is packed. I'm here on this bitter, moonless Saturday night with hundreds of high schoolers for two reasons: Ollie and Jesse.

Ollie's inside warming up, and I have Jesse to myself, happy and stoned in the unattended and darkened playground past the sports fields.

In my head, I'm running over a few proven schemes that will hasten a questioning guy to his knees in front of me. Usually, a few sympathetic words about how he's probably horny and hard up, if the boy is inclined at all, will lead to a hand job. It's my go-to.

Jesse and I stand close. He tips weed from his grinder in a small, green glass pipe and lets me smoke first. As I exhale, he says, "You can taste blueberry, right?" I don't taste anything except weed, but I tell him yes, anyway.

A hoodie, two flannels, and a cop coat do their best to protect him from the cold. He still shivers like he's stripped down to a T-shirt. The streetlamp at the three-way stop next to the playground illuminates Jesse's fair skin and reflects off his glasses. He taps the pipe against his bottom lip between hits and looks at the sky. "Freezing tonight."

"Yeah." I bunch my toes, trying to circulate some blood to the hypothermic bits. My choice of warmer shoes would have made this easier. For me, seduction has never been a cold weather sport. "How's it going with you and Jackie?"

He yawns between shivers and hops from one foot to the other. His automatic answer comes from between chattering teeth. "Good. Great. You?"

"What?" I laugh.

"Sorry. I mean, what's going on with you?"

"Tennis. Invitationals. Which are all kind of a pain in the ass."

"You don't seem like a tennis player." Jesse blows out a huge hit of smoke and passes the pipe to me. "I always picture angry, Eastern European dudes."

"You don't seem like a guy who would fuck Jackie," I say and tap his shoe with mine, "but you're doing it. We're blowing up stereotypes."

"Strange that she likes me, isn't it?"

I want to tell him that, no, it's not strange at all. He makes my cock hard; I'm sure Jackie is thrilled when he dips his dick in her. Instead, I say, "I think I taste the blueberry now, yeah."

When I hand the pipe back to him, our fingers touch. His are soft and cold, and he yanks them away at a speed anyone would interpret as fear or disgust. I rule out disgust. And if he's fearful of anything, it's the suspicions he has about himself.

With a tilt of his head, Jesse gestures in the direction of our school. "So, this is really not my thing. Sports. Crowds."

"Yeah, I'm the same. But, you know, Ollie asked."

"He comes to your matches?"

"Fuck no. He thinks it's boring. And it kinda is."

"Does anyone come?"

"Not really."

"What about your mom?"

Having to think about my mother in the fresh air with someone I like ratchets up my resentment toward her. Of all the possible events that might occur on, say, a Tuesday, *Mom comes to match* is somewhere beneath *Dad reanimates*. "Eh," I say, "she's busy a lot."

"How about a guy?" Jesse digs in the grass with the toe of his shoe. "Like a boyfriend or whatever."

"No." I push the word through a laugh.

"Have you ever had one?"

"No," I say with confidence and a curious swell of pride that surprises me. "Never."

"Never?"

"Never."

When he glances away, bashful, I allow myself to envision Jesse at one of my matches. I can't decide in what capacity he'd be there. Good fuck, friend, boyfriend? He doubtless blends all three roles well for anyone he chooses.

The usual disdain I have for "boyfriend" withers into a simple disinterest in the burden of responsibility. And then, because I let myself further imagine Jesse as the guy who always comes to my matches, my disinterest collapses, and I'm left with an unexpected feeling of shame about having desired him that way for even a moment.

With the end of his lighter, he taps the ash out of his pipe. "Wanna go?"

I reluctantly follow him as we duck and maneuver through the strip of thick, prickly bushes back toward the school. He pushes past a cluster of branches, one of which flies back and slaps me in the face. A thorn rips open my cheek. "*Tssss.* Watch what the fuck you're doing, man."

In the clearing, I stop to pick twigs and leaves off my coat. Jesse realizes he's pulled too far ahead and retraces his steps. Holding up the flame of his lighter for a couple seconds, he pulls a twig off my hat. The mist from our breath rises between us as his thumb sweeps across my forehead. "You're bleeding. Your chin, too." To me, the smear of my blood on his skin is more intimate than any blowjob I've ever had.

Right now, we should forget time and place. I shouldn't know my name. I might remember his. Attraction would lead us, keep things moving, and we would follow. We would forget our senses, or all five might fuse into a single smoldering core that savored only the other. No choices, barely any awareness.

I wish that were happening.

Instead, Jesse and I concentrate too hard. Neither one of us floats or dreams or gets carried away. Our discomfort harasses us. The less we act, the less chance there is to act. I stop myself from blinking, and he knows why. He chews his bottom lip, and I know why.

But I refuse to miss this. My torso tilts forward an inch, then two. I measure my volume and tone, and I don't dare move a limb. "Jesse?"

He quickly reaches for the strings of my hoodie, giving them a tentative tug before coiling them around his fingers. He looks up, leans in, and presses his mouth to mine. I freeze, and Jesse notices. His tongue barely touches my lips before he pulls away. The strings fall from his fingers. He stares at the dead grass. "Was that...not okay?"

I have never had my mouth on anyone else's mouth. Before this, I believed kissing was only a precursor to sex, and no one I ever wanted required much of a precursor. "No—I mean, yeah, it was more than okay. You just caught me off guard."

"Never mind." He pulls his jacket over his face like Dracula. "I was just seeing something anyway."

"It's just that no one's ever kissed me before," I say, amused with the situation. "I didn't know what to do."

"Is *that* how you're trying to make me feel better?"

My history is absurd; so many mouths on my dick and not one set of lips against mine. "I know you're waiting for the punchline," I say, "but I really have never kissed anyone before. Maybe that is the punchline."

The urge to get off with him now takes second place to my urge to kiss him again. My mind flashes not only on Jesse at my tennis matches, but on Jesse in my bedroom, Jesse rolling my joints, Jesse kissing me every day. I take a cautious step nearer with my left foot but don't commit with my right. "Did *you* like it?"

"I don't know. Maybe. Just don't say anything else right now. It'll make it worse. It's okay. Let's forget it."

Only one of us wishes we could return to a more wholesome time when Jesse was fucking girls, selling weed, and not kissing guys. I will never go backwards. Never. "Come on," I say, "try me again."

I slide my right foot forward a couple inches, and that is too close for Jesse's comfort. He takes a small step backwards. I reach for him but let my arm drop when he tilts further away from me. I try again. He bows out of contact. "This is just getting more and more fucked up in my mind," he says, pulling his lighter from his pocket. He flicks it over and over, never letting the flame thrive. "I want to go back to the game."

"If you think I'm letting you go back to the game," I say as I reach for him, "you're so wrong."

He backs away, appraising me as though he's seeing me for the first time. "Don't push me right now, okay? I have to figure this out." His cheeks puff out and deflate with a noisy exhale. I get no warning before he takes off across the field in a full-out sprint. I let loose a lone *ha*. I've never seen a pothead move so fast.

At lunch on Monday, Ollie and I sit across from each other in our usual seats at a table full of his teammates. He holds up a pizza roll, examining it before flicking whatever offends him off the pastry. "The cafeteria workers don't give a shit. Or maybe they even notice the fruit flies."

"I don't know why you eat that shit," I say, pulling out a baggie of carrot sticks.

"Because I'm not a fucking gerbil." He flicks the carrot I'm holding with his forefinger, and it lands underneath the table behind me. "Oh, yeah, Jesse asked if we wanted to go to Brad's tonight."

I reach for another stick, and my hand freezes mid-grab. "What? When?"

Ollie gives up on the pizza rolls and opens a package of powdered donuts. "I don't know. This morning?"

"What did he say, exactly?" I put my veggies aside. This needs my full attention. "Did he sound weird?"

"No," he says, rolling his eyes, "but you sound like an old lady. *That's* weird."

"Are you sure he said me? He wants *me* to come?" I need details. An analysis of tone. Was I just an afterthought? I want Ollie to recreate Jesse's facial expression at the time of the ask.

But Ollie is ignoring me and arguing with a vying power forward, smacking his hands against the lunch table like a dictator after ten espressos. This happens every few days. Leftover frustration from the previous day's practice, gearing up for games, the bitter swapping of girlfriends. It may soon get physical.

I get his attention by kicking him under the table. "How did Jesse sound when he asked?"

"What the fuck?' Ollie sputters and projects a few crumbs across the table at me. "He sounded like he always sounds. Jesus Christ." He gives me the finger and turns back to his friends.

I consume carrot after carrot, pushing them into my mouth and chomping fast, like I'm feeding logs into a woodchipper. I move on to some turkey jerky as I contemplate what I'll say to Jesse when I see him in English. Maybe I won't say anything. I'll just show up tonight with Ollie as if nothing happened, no kiss, no confession, no fleeing the scene.

The loudspeaker in the cafeteria squawks every few minutes, requesting a person report here, another to go there. I've been tuning it out for three years. Today, when I hear my name above the hum and rumble of conversation and the clanks of silverware and plates, I question whether I heard it correctly.

I look at Ollie for confirmation, and he pauses, mid-chew, a smear of white sugary paste in the corner of his mouth. "Was that for you? What's that about?"

"No idea." I pack up, in a hurry to find out.

Until college admission time hits, the guidance counselors'

offices go unnoticed by most of us in the school. Those with alcoholic parents, a history of petty theft, or sociopathic proclivities in general get to see what's beyond the heavy wooden door sooner.

In the tiny waiting room, I tell my name to the over-perfumed, over-kind receptionist. "Mmm, Daniel, yes. Door five." Leaning across the counter, I casually glance at her computer screen and ask what this is about. She only points down a hallway.

The row of closed doors. The worn center of low-pile carpeting. The discomfiting quiet and flickering fluorescent lights. An incubator for adults wasting their lives.

I take a few seconds to compose myself, swiping my forefinger along the bottom whorl of the plastic 5 screwed crookedly onto the door. I wipe the gray dust on my pants. I knock, and my muscles tense when I hear Mr. Stewart's voice. "Come."

He sits behind a desk that he shares with Millie, my legitimate counselor. It's littered with miscellany. A teal ceramic bowl filled with potpourri sits next to family photos taken poolside and a coffee mug full of pens whose colors represent every shade in the spectrum. The disorder must make him itch.

He's been waiting for me, his hands folded and head high. "Please, close the door," he says, inviting me to have a seat after I do.

I toss my bag with more attitude than intended. It bangs against one of the tan filing cabinets. My ass hits the chair with a thud. "This doesn't look like the library to me. And you look nothing like Millie."

"I smell marijuana," he says after a sniff. "Is that you?"

"Stop asking me."

"Instead, how about you—"

"So, why am I here?" I point to a band of teddies on the credenza. "And nice stuffed bears by the way."

He spots two used staples on the desk blotter and whisks them into his waiting palm before dropping them into the wastebasket. His face opens. His crow's feet disappear. "I'll just get right to it. I've been thinking about you—where you're heading—since we last spoke. You're sinking, Daniel, and I'm the only one who cares, or perhaps even notices."

I pick a dried rose petal out of the potpourri, crush it in my palm, and sprinkle the crumbs on the floor. The meddling and constant presumption are tiresome, but right now, appreciation outguns annoyance. To be cared for by someone other than myself hits me harder than tequila, a blunt, and a blowjob. I can't look at him. I'm embarrassed that I have no one.

Mr. Stewart rises slowly and comes to me. His ass rests against the desk, between the bucket of pens and the family photos. Instead of putting me at ease, his proximity makes me uncomfortable. He bumps my knee with his. I bump his in return, only harder. "Okay, Dad."

"That's not funny."

"No shit."

"I'm here for support, guidance. I care about your *education*. We cannot have an adversarial relationship. We aren't peers. I'm your teacher, not your friend."

"So, I like talking to you. Big deal. Who else am I going to talk to? My mom? And, I mean, Ollie's great, but all he thinks about is basketball and pussy—"

"Daniel."

"*Vagina*."

"You're affable. You're intelligent. Your sense of humor sometimes strikes the right note. All you need to do is aim higher when it comes to friends."

"I am. I just started hanging out with Jesse—"

"Higher than that, please."

"That leaves you, then."

He leans forward and whispers, "Is Jesse the one selling you marijuana?"

"No."

After challenging me with a stare, he sits back and says, "Very well. I'm not going to argue with you about the company you choose to keep. You need to learn, and I need to teach. It is as simple as that."

"I want to keep *your* company."

"Yes, you've made that obvious."

"If you really wanted to help me, you wouldn't be so half-assed about it. All I want to do is play chess and have someone to talk to. We can do that in your room or in the library if it makes you feel better."

"I'm unsure if that's a good idea," he says, shaking his head.

I scooch forward in my seat and whisper. "What will it take? If I promise not to smoke for, I don't know, seven days, will you play?"

It's a good five seconds until he yields. "In the library, perhaps, but—"

"Great." Before he can renege, I'm out of my seat with my bag over my shoulder. I extend a hand for a shake. His thoughtful pause before clasping it is for show; he wants to do this as much as I do. His dry grip and a single pump go right to my cock.

We both know my main objective is his company. Chess is the conduit. He will keep his word because he is the principled one here. To him, integrity may rate higher than even propriety.

Ollie, Jesse, and I are in Brad's windowless basement. It's where he keeps the "big TV." We smoke and sit on lawn chairs in the center of six grow cabinets and a cure closet. Two refrigerators hum in the corner. Dozens of crates of Mason jars line two walls. Jesse has a backpack full of restock.

Brad watches cartoons, ignoring us and belly-laughing with a gaping mouth full of cereal and milk. Jackie left for the store over an hour ago, on the hunt to satisfy her craving for bubble gum, Peanut Chews, and drinkable yogurt.

We've only been allowed down here because Jesse vouched for Ollie and me, like we're in some Dutch, milquetoast mafia. Were it not for a floor littered with sandwich crusts, withering orange peels, fast food wrappers, and several empty soda bottles, this basement would be cozier than Brad's main floor.

Along the wall next to the water heater, an exhibit of tactical knives, replica medieval crossbows and axes, and collectible katana swords decorate the cinder blocks. When Ollie and I descended the stairs and first clocked those weapons, he looked over his shoulder at me. "If he mentions the Messiah, go for a piss." The first ten minutes of the night included Ollie's incessant and uneasy tugging of his earlobe. After assessing Brad to be less of a menace and more of an enthusiast, we settled in.

I'm glad I brought Ollie. Jesse is probably still groaning internally about our kiss and how he ran away, but at least he seems at ease in a small group, rather than with me alone. If we stare at each other for too long, he looks at Ollie for relief.

"I have to read tonight," Jesse announces to the room, tossing his lighter to me. "Stewart is all over me lately. It's like he suddenly hates me."

"Stewart's all bark," Ollie says offhandedly.

"He keeps telling me I'm not participating enough," Jesse continues, picking at a now cold container of Chinese food Ollie and I brought with us. A piece of gnarly chicken escapes and lands on the floor next to one of Brad's moldy superhero mugs. Jesse leaves it there. "And he says I'm not serious enough about the texts. I don't even know what that means."

I know from the way Ollie shakes his leg that he's ready to go. "Extra practice tomorrow," he says before standing and stretching with a loud yawn. He slaps my shoulder. "Ride home?" He asks as a courtesy, but he knows to leave without me.

When he's gone, Jesse's attention drifts to his grades again. As he rambles about his GPA and how many months of school there are to go, I pinch his wrist. "Stop it. You're doing better in there than anyone else."

"Yeah, I'm paranoid."

Jesse's phone buzzes. His mom is wondering if he had a nice meal with Jackie's parents. "That is code," he says, "for where the fuck are you? She'd kick my ass if she knew what I was really doing, spending the night high in a basement with—" He cuts the sentence short and looks away from me.

What's unsaid must be about my company, or maybe about gay company in general. The only reason he would have censored himself is for my benefit or Brad's, and I don't think he gives much of a shit about what Brad finds insulting.

Brad yawns and places his cereal bowl on the floor among six others. The spoon falls out of it, clanking against the tile floor. "Right," he says and scratches his belly, "I'm going to bed. You staying down here? If you are, lock up after." A set of keys flies at Jesse, who snatches them out of the air.

When Brad stands, his testicles hang out of the bottom of one side of his boxers before he shakes his leg, freeing the material so it covers those hairy monsters. If he knows it occurred, he doesn't mind. Brad makes it up two stairs and comes back down. "Are you guys gonna fuck?"

My face burns, but not because he suspects we will; if for a second Brad held an image of Jesse and me together in this salmonella wasteland, I want to be sick. Jesse motions to the leftover foodstuffs. "Where? Should we make a bed out of the million pizza boxes?"

Brad guffaws. "If Jackie will bend over in this mess for you, I'm sure Dan has no problem with it."

My head spins to Brad. "*What?*"

"Damn," he says, obviously surprised by my reaction. "It was a joke. Besides, we all know Jesse's catching." He trots up the stairs after a chuckle, and the door slams behind him.

My desire to ask how recently Jesse had Jackie bent over in this shithole is a meal of misery; whereas, walking two miles home in the cold, losing a great high, and stewing all night comprise only a crumb.

"I'm gonna go," I say, standing. "I'm tired."

"Wait, and I'll go with you."

He struggles to get out of the lawn chair as I put in my coat. His plastic cup of ginger ale tips over at his feet, and he stands with a grunt, his foot tangling with one of Brad's grimy fleece blankets on the floor. The wall stops his fall. "Wait." As he tries to block my body with his, the blanket once again ensnares his bare foot. "Wait, wait. Dan. *Wait.* I'll drive you. Just wait a minute."

"You're too fucked up. I'll see you tomorrow."

I head upstairs. Jesse catches up to me in the hallway, which is strewn with used tissues, bottle caps, and candy wrappers.

Twice, he snatches my sleeve, and twice I shake him off. With his third attempt, he meets success and spins me around. "Dan. *Stop.*" When I do, he takes a step back and loosens his grip on my coat. "I wanted to say—" He catches his breath, words carried out in bursts of air. "I mean, what I wanted to say is that I'm sorry. I shouldn't have kissed you. I don't want you to think I'm using you. I'm just figuring stuff out."

My body tenses. "Using me? You think it's an accident that I had you alone in the pitch black in forty-degree weather? I invited you. You just needed to show up." I meant to say that last line in jest. Anger swelled inside me at the last second, however, and my delivery was cruel, bitter.

In this muted light of Brad's hallway, the slight change in his expression is difficult to read, and his reply is milder than I expected. "Dan, I like you," he says and shakes his head, "but you just made it super hard for me to keep liking you."

The slam of Brad's front door causes us both to freeze. The jingle of Jackie's necklaces announces her arrival. Immediately, I picture her as Brad said, bent over amidst pizza boxes, soiled blankets, and seeds and stems.

She rounds the corner and winks at me. "I was wondering who'd be naked." She holds up an open but full plastic bag of Peanut Chews. "Success. Who wants one?" Without acknowledging us further, she heads to the kitchen. The fridge door opens and closes, cabinet doors slam, and Jackie groans about whatever in there displeases her.

Jesse pushes a stray beer cap with his toe until it hits my foot. His body slumps. So does mine. Knowing what to do or say next escapes me.

The rush of the faucet stops, and Jackie is next to us in seconds. She leans on my shoulder and plants a wet kiss on my cheek. "What about now? What do you want to do?" She dangles a candy in front of Jesse's nose, the chocolate melted and smeared on her fingers. "I love these fucking things."

"I'm tired," I say. "I'm going to go home."

I nod at them both and leave without looking back. My usual route, four lanes of traffic and dozens of streetlights so everyone can see the deer and raccoons, seems unsuited for my mood tonight. Instead, I decide on the back roads, I light a joint, grumbling in the dark.

I don't get far. Behind me, there is the *click-flap-click-flap* of shoes hitting the asphalt. I smile to myself. I've never had a guy run after me before. The sound of panting grows nearer, and I pause for a dramatic moment before I turn and smile. When I do, I find it's Jackie who's pursuing me. Breathless when she reaches my side, she falls forward, hands on her knees. "Why do you—walk so fucking fast, Danny? Come back. We'll give you a ride."

Jackie, Jesse, and I go to my house. Jackie is immediately comfortable, made clear by her unsupervised journey to my kitchen and the subsequent catcalls about the contents of my fridge. She's difficult to ignore, and now she demands juice boxes. I hear the fridge door open, close, open again. "No juice boxes?" she yells.

On my living room floor, Jesse clutches the remote and focuses on an action movie set in Taiwan. He's spent minutes in that position and finally perks up. "I'm surprised she's not asleep. She took some pills. When she hits the juice phase, she's hard to keep upright."

Neither of us has said anything about the standoff in Brad's hallway from only an hour ago. My reward for hiding my annoyance, frustration, and horniness is that there is one person too many in my house. Jackie drove us here, and I'm unsure if she's sticking around to keep things friendly or to make things friendlier.

My mom is at dinner with Theodore, whom I've now met. The stocky Greek who wears too much jewelry and owns three Italian markets is much less shrouded in mystery than he is indifference. He shook my hand and asked if he could use the "terlet."

Jackie appears, wobbling and joyfully clutching a jar of applesauce. "I haven't had this in, like, four years. Okay if I eat it?"

She wiggles past me but then backtracks, leaning forward and bending at the waist for a friendly kiss. I oblige with a quick smack on her lips before she crams herself between me and the arm of the couch. She pulls a small enamel pillbox with daisies on its face from her hip pocket. The box holds six pale yellow pills, which she shakes against the sides. "Just let me know if you want one."

When Jesse goes to the bathroom, Jackie puts down the applesauce jar and closes in on me. Her fingers crawl up my leg.

She moves her hand a few inches closer to my balls. It's like Jackie has a map; she knows where I settle in my pants almost as well as I do. I politely take her hand off my crotch. "What are you doing?" I smack her ass as a joke. "Get off me."

"Please. We know what I'm doing. You like Jesse. And Jesse was too chickenshit to come on his own. *And* the only one here that loves cock more than me is you." Jackie's fingers walk over the fly of my jeans. "You want Jesse?"

I'm amused. "If I do?"

"If you do, you go through me." She pouts, poking me in the chest. "You sure you're not bi?"

"Surer than sure."

Grabbing a soft handful between my legs, she bites my neck, moves up, whispers in my ear. "Too bad. You have a big dick."

"Jackie, I—" I take her by the shoulders and push her back so I can see her face. "Is my dick really big, or are you just saying that?"

"*Ha*. No matter who you like to fuck, you all wanna know that, don't you?" She lunges and kisses me. When she pulls away, she wipes her lips with her wrist and studies me. "Why don't you open your mouth? You kiss weird."

"I don't usually kiss."

"What are you, a sex worker?" She laughs at me. "Give me a break."

Before I can respond, she suctions her mouth to mine again while trying to straddle my lap. I keep my lips tight, catch her leg, and push her away. "*Uff*. Jackie—" She tickles my armpits, and I squirm.

As she puts one hand between my legs and one hand on my neck, pulling me in for another tongue-assault, Jesse enters the room and clears his throat. "I'm having a cigarette. Try not to hurt yourselves."

He coasts past us, snatches his shoes, and walks out my front door. With Jackie still attached to me like a parasite, I stand and do a hard-target search for my shoes. I peel her off me and drop her on the couch. I hold up my palm. "Stay here. Don't move. Do not move."

I find Jesse on the side of my house, where he paces in the

moonlight. He chews a fingernail and pats himself down until he finds his purple lighter in the pocket of his jeans.

I lean against the retaining wall that surrounds the front of our property. He is unable to look at me. Instead, he offers me his pipe and lighter. I take them and place them on the wall next to me. "Are you okay?"

Jesse discovers a small ball of crumpled paper in the front pocket of his jeans and flings it into the grass. "What were you doing in there?"

"Nothing."

"It looked like something."

"Did it?" I laugh. "You know it didn't."

"*Psst*. Whatever. Just forget it."

I boost myself up on the wall and hook his leg with my foot, reeling him in. He trips forward and catches himself with his hands on my thighs.

My lips barely graze his before he leans into me hard, kissing me like he's afraid I might change my mind. His glasses press into my cheek. His hair is soft, and I alternate weaving my fingers through it and grabbing fists of it.

The gentle way I touch him is new to me. My hand slides down his arm, and his cold fingers tickle mine, recoil, and then brush against mine again.

When I guide his fingers to my zipper, he takes a quick step backwards. My leg yanks him closer. I entwine my fingers with his. The kisses I plant up his neck and behind his ear make him moan, but he twists out of my reach. "I'm thinking too much. I upset myself about stuff."

I hop off the wall and lift his chin with one finger. He resists at first, but his muscles loosen when I kiss him. He smashes his mouth against mine again, his blond stubble digging into my skin.

Up his back, over his shoulders, through his hair. I can't touch enough of him. Finally, I have more than I hoped for: his erection pressed against me. I groan and spin us, crushing him between my body and the wall. I thrust my hard cock against his, the front of our jeans creating more friction than he wants, more than he wants to want; he pushes me away and sucks in air as though he's been drowning.

"You want me to stop?" I say, breathless.

A nod follows a fast head shake. More nodding. "Yeah." He adjusts his dick. "I just need a minute. Or maybe—what about tomorrow? Can we get together tomorrow?"

"Tomorrow" is the coward's exit. When someone says tomorrow, it usually speeds up my game. The pursuit of victory becomes a sprint rather than a marathon.

With Jesse, however, I'm convinced that self-restraint will help rather than hinder. Although there's a hair-trigger in my pants about to trample compassion and patience, I calm myself and hatch a quick plan: jack off later and wait for a time when I can do whatever it is that he needs to hook him on repeats. "Tomorrow sounds good."

Inside, the scene in my living room has changed. Jackie's on the floor, slumped against my couch, chin on her chest. Beside her, tipped on its side, is the applesauce jar, which dribbles on the well-worn carpet. Jesse jostles her with his foot. Nothing. He prods her again, and then he jabs her in the hip. "Jesus. You'll help me carry her to the car?"

"You think she's breathing?"

"She is."

"You know where her shoes are?"

"Let's just carry her, and you find the shoes later."

"I'm not bringing her shoes to school."

We leave Jackie slumped over as we search for her belongings. I find her pillbox between the couch cushions and attempt to squeeze it into the front pocket of her skirt. Jesse snatches the tiny box out of my hand and tosses it on the couch, where pills scatter across the cushion. I pinch my brow. "What the fuck are you doing?"

"Move. Go." Clenching the back of my belt, he pushes me up the stairs and into my bedroom, closing the door behind him.

I smile and shake my head. "There's no lock on that."

"I don't care."

Within two paces, I'm unzipping his jeans and feeling inside. No underwear. Only Jesse, already stiff and a bit sticky. I push his pants to his knees and spit on my palm. Rubbing my hand along the bottom of his erection, I part my fingers at its base and roll his balls until he throws his head back. I press up the seam, and he sucks in a sharp breath.

His cool hands slide up my back as he tries to get as much of his body mashed against mine as he can. He makes fast work of uncovering my skin: my belt and buttons undone, followed by my pants and shorts in a pile around my ankles.

A whimper accompanies the thrust of his tongue in my mouth. Without letting go of my penis, he crushes me against the wall, getting a better grip on my cock. We jack each other off furiously, bulldozing into one another with no shame.

"*Come*," he demands when he pulls his mouth off mine. "*Just come.*"

I can barely mimic him. "You—come."

When he does, he hangs onto my neck with his free hand, pulling me down so my forehead hits his. "Fuck," he gasps as he ejaculates on the floor and my hand.

I fling an arm over his shoulder and maneuver my cock out of his grip, finishing myself off. His warm cum still dangles from my hand when I shoot all over his thighs.

The next night, Jesse and I sit in his car in his driveway and share a joint, sinking in the seat when we use the lighter. We're waiting for his living room light to go out—the sign his mom's gone to bed—before we go inside.

The second the living room is dark, we put out the joint and get out of the car, pressing the doors closed rather than slamming them.

On his porch, I wipe my dirty shoes on the brush doormat until I'm sure I'll track nothing inside. The outer door squeaks. His key sticks. He turns the knob of the wooden door and peers inside.

The only thing visible is a mustard-colored wall clock in the shape of an owl glowing in the corner of the room. It smells like a home-cooked meal—onions, maybe garlic—and it makes my mouth water.

I quietly close the door behind me. Jesse's the one who breaks the silence. "We look like we're here to steal electronics." His laughter cuts through the dark room, and I punch his arm, so he'll shut up.

By the light of his phone, he leads me by the hand up carpeted stairs and into the first room at the top of the landing. He shines the phone light on his face and invites me in farther with the tilt of his head.

Inside his room, he places the phone flashlight face up on the stack of vinyl records next to his bed that serves as a night table. "They sleep at the other end of the hall," he says and takes my coat from me, "but still be quiet, okay?" Jesse closes the door, and we have our own private universe.

In shadows that remind me of Halloween, I wander to each corner of his room. A swivel chair with the backrest torn off is tucked halfway under a wooden desk. An aloe plant flourishes under a switched-off artificial light. Laptop, deodorant, empty cans of ginger ale. A picture of Jesse with his arm around a shirtless, ripped, and Champagne-blond dude on the beach makes me curious—instantly jealous if I'm honest. "Who's this?"

Jesse beams and touches the photo. "That's Pete. Remember? My brother. He's in Cali with his girlfriend. Sucks."

I hope the gnat's life of my jealousy went unnoticed. I move on without eye contact.

In one corner of the room sits a chair with a pile of jeans and T-shirts draped over it. He sleeps in those, wakes and lives in those, and then comes home to do it again. They are the jeans he slips his dick out of when he jerks off. His bed is a double and unmade. I check out his stuff, and he lets me study everything as if I were at the art museum. "Take it all in. I'm fascinating."

I go to him, and he backs away from me. I step gently on his foot to keep him from getting any farther. I pull him in for a kiss. I bite his lips, and eventually, he bites me back.

His jeans hang low and loose on his hips, and I slip my hand in there only to find no underwear again. The glide of his skin against my fingers goes right to my penis, and it takes me only ten seconds to get him hard.

He turns his head to one side. "I just wanted to hang out. Smoke."

"No, you didn't," I say, my lips against his cheek.

I guide him to the bed, carefully lower him, and roll him around as I please. The view I want is easily had with him flat on his back, his head propped on a pillow. Legs and arms slack like a drunk's—and an inebriant smile to match—Jesse makes only one move: slipping out of his T-shirt. I trail my fingers along the bottom of his ribcage. His body stiffens. "Can you turn off my phone light?"

"No."

"It's too bright—"

"No."

"I'm nervous. It's not helping."

Kissing under his chin before I slide down his body, I unzip his jeans and yank them down to his calves. More than ever before—or for the first time—I care about giving someone pleasure. I don't want to get him off in a hurry just so I can have my turn and go home.

My perfunctory yet expert method won't do. I take my time. Every trembling, stiff inch of him begs my hand to find the compromise of fast and slow, hard and soft. I prolong it until the muscles in his abdomen twitch.

I concentrate on making him come. Within moments, he emits a helpless wheeze as his semen runs down my wrist.

I flop on my back next to him and wipe my hand on his blankets. He turns on his side, his breath hot and fast across my face. "Better than anything."

"Thanks."

"Maybe I'm gay."

I know I shouldn't, but I tease him. "I think it's just a testament to my dexterity." I roll over and face him. "Open your eyes." My nose bumps his. "Please."

The lid of his left eye slowly lifts. "I'm probably bi."

"It doesn't matter. You're you. Who cares?"

"No one." His forehead wrinkles. "Well, me, I guess."

I lay my arm across his waist and pull him closer to me. His limbs fidget. I toss my leg over him to still his body. "It's just a word, man."

"It's more than a word," he says after a few seconds of consideration. "You know it."

With a sigh, I nod against his shoulder. "Yeah."

In the past few years, my self-assuredness has only been shaken a few times. I questioned my lack of interest in a boyfriend, why post-sex eye contact and conversation freaked me out, how imagining someone's tongue in my mouth sparked my gag reflex. I knew something about how I related to people was fucked up. I dealt with those feelings alone.

I searched the Internet and found plenty: anecdotes, pop psychology evals, the separation of sex and intimacy, and plenty of others who felt as I did. But no one in my real life could validate my concerns, tell me which way of a hundred ways was healthy or normal; I plowed right through my discomfort and insecurity alone. Knowing what to say to Jesse now would be easier if someone kindhearted and informed helped me navigate my own trepidation.

I cup his cheek with my palm. The remaining smear of cum between my first and second fingers slimes his skin. I wipe his face dry with a corner of his sheet. "You want me to go?" That's all I can think of to say.

"No." Shifting to create a space between us. He gestures to my crotch with his chin. "I want to—you know. But I'm going to feel stupid if I do it wrong."

I rise and quickly strip out of my clothes. There's no chance I'm letting him backslide into timidity. "You can't do it wrong," I lie.

Being with Jesse naked by only the light of his phone thrills me more than the rough and unexpected encounter we had yesterday. I hold my breath as I look down and admire him, not because he's particularly fit or gorgeous, but because he's about to satisfy weeks of my desire for him.

Where I thought he'd be rawboned, almost skeletal, instead, his muscles pour into tendons, his tendons back into muscles, all of him smooth except the hair in his armpits and around his cock. His hipbones and collarbone are the only sharp parts of him.

I fall back on the mattress, and he settles between my legs. I'm hoping for no teeth. A grip, a lick, a stroke will get me close—at least so I can finish myself off—and would quell his worry about doing it wrong.

He holds my erection up and presses his closed lips against it, opening slowly and sucking the head. He exhales through his nose before his tongue sweeps along the silky underside and flicks back and forth over the tip. With a grunt, he jerks his head up, leaving me cool and longing. "Is this right?"

"Keep going." I raise my head off the pillow, propping myself up on my elbows. "It's good."

And it does get good. Jesse allows more of me into his mouth. I pant. "Yeah. Move your hand."

He quickly releases my dick and sits back on his heels. "What? Why?"

"No, I mean, move it," I say, doing the jerk-off motion with my loose fist. "A lot of spit. Then move it while you're sucking."

He groans, either embarrassed or frustrated. "Maybe you should just fuck me. Is that what you do?"

I purse my lips and muffle a laugh. That is a remarkable leap and a remarkable offer, but I want this to happen again. If we fuck now, I'm not sure it will. "Get on the floor. If you don't want me to choke you, use your hand to jerk me off at the bottom. Breathe through your nose."

On his knees before me, Jesse sucks with more confidence now. The light of the phone highlights the spit that hangs in translucent vines from the sides of his mouth. When I can no longer keep the burning in my balls under wraps, I mumble, "Jesse, now. I'm—jerk me off."

He doesn't pull off me, but he doesn't swallow, either. Cum pours out of his open mouth and down my leg. He tightens his lips around me until my last thrust. My fingers zigzag through his thick hair, a sensory experience that pleases me almost as much as the orgasm.

When I left his house last night, I was drained of semen, lips kissed and puffy, smiling wide, and smelling of Jesse. The walk home was cold and quick, otherwise unmemorable. I fell asleep on my couch, woke up five hours later, and resented having to take a shower. I still smelled like him.

In school, my mid-morning text to Jesse goes unanswered. I muster some restraint and refrain from texting him again in the afternoon. I ask for a bathroom pass during Fine Arts with no intention of returning to the class. While I linger in the bathroom, I stare at my phone and conceive of all the emotions keeping Jesse from replying. Regret ranks number one.

Minutes before the bell at the end of eighth period, my phone buzzes. My heart rate speeds up until I see it's just Ollie, asking if I saw his away jersey in his car this morning. I grit my teeth in frustration and stuff the phone deep in my pocket without answering.

On my way to AP English, irritability and insecurity have me grinding the single bud I have in a baggie against my leg with my thumbnail. I contemplate a bold detour out the front door next to the offices. I could go behind the sports fields to smoke. But when I see Mr. Stewart's open door, I change my mind. The attention he shows me—if I can provoke some—will serve as a distraction.

His other students clear out, and I stroll into the classroom, dropping into my seat like I'm collapsing onto the couch and readying to pack a bowl. I check my phone again. Still nothing from Jesse.

Mr. Stewart distributes a thin packet of paper to every desk. He is fond of paper; even when we work online, dead trees supplement the digital. He saves me for last and places the final packet entitled "McCarthyism and Miller's *The Crucible*" on my desk, standing next to me as I inspect the stapled pages.

"Ugh." I flip through the pages. "Prepare to be depressed."

"Good afternoon to you, too," he says.

Under my desk are chunks of dried mud in the shape of someone's shoe-tread. I crush the dirt with my foot. "I wouldn't call it *good*."

Mr. Stewart taps the back of my chair to get my attention. "Are you intoxicated?" He waves his hand in front of my face. "Has our deal fallen through already?"

"I'm sober," I say and quietly add, "since this morning anyway."

My comment makes him frown. "The deal—"

"I know," I say, frustrated. "Deal's off."

When I look up at him, his smile—vague, almost a question—softens my scowl. Mr. Stewart moves closer to me, his body inches from mine. "Weren't you looking forward to chess this week?"

"Sure. Not all the interrogations that go with it, though."

"Daniel, you don't fool me" he says softly, bumping his leg against my arm. "I am certain you enjoy the interrogations as much as the chess."

It seems like a long time between those words and when the back of his hand caresses my cheek. As his thumb traces the line of my jaw, his body leans more heavily against me, so much that my torso pitches sideways from the pressure. He lifts his warm hand from my face, pushes my hair behind my ear, and slides his fingers along my scalp.

My penis fills with blood faster than when I hit puberty. I sink a couple inches in my chair, nuzzling him like a cat. As soon as I push my shoulder into his thigh harder, he quickly takes a full step backward and pinches the bridge of his nose. "*Shit.*"

With no warning, he hurries to the back of the classroom. Meanwhile, an erection bordering on painful throbs against my leg. The warmth from his hand on my cheek remains. That moment was the link between my months of investment and the sought-after payout.

Rallying my nerves enough to unlock my joints, I glance over my shoulder. He's straightening desks and chairs, pacing, shaking his head, clearing his throat. I face forward, fondling the *Crucible* packet, bending the edges into neat triangles while my classmates trickle into the room.

The breeze Mr. Stewart brings with him as he treads past my desk to the front of the room tickles the back of my neck. He greets his other students, kindly, comfortably. I mumble hello to Ollie when he enters. Jesse never shows.

I realize five minutes have passed while I've been staring straight ahead, unfocused. My slightly open mouth is so arid I have trouble with my next swallow. The packet lies unopened on my desk, even as the other kids are flipping pages, following his direction.

I fumble with the zipper on my backpack and remove my

laptop. Straightening in my seat, I pay attention to the man who just touched more parts of me than he should have, parts of me I've spent months imagining him touching.

He doesn't twitch when I repeatedly cough or sniffle. I crinkle my pages, turning them too loudly. Nothing. The frequent scuffing of my shoes on the floor draws his attention not one bit. Even Ollie tells me in a whisper to stop acting like a palsy victim.

Mr. Stewart spends the class moving from the play to a brief history of witch hunts online and back. His lectures are seamless. As usual, poise and control are his sidekicks.

After the bell rings, without a glimpse in my direction, he sails out of the classroom, probably to his car, and then to the airport where he'll catch a flight to a country with a non-extradition policy.

I struggle to sit still in Genetics. I watch the clock and jump up the second the bell rings. When I return to Mr. Stewart's classroom, the lights are off and the door is locked.

I forecast a fucked-up tennis practice. I surprise myself, however, and Harry praises my precision and focus with embarrassing hoots and claps between sets. A few times, I check the perimeter of the courts, hoping but not expecting to see Mr. Stewart. No one except a few students mull around behind the fence.

After practice, before Ollie finishes his shower, I run to Mr. Stewart's, only to find his classroom is again empty and dark.

I assure myself that I will have plenty of chances to be alone with him again. Avoiding me for the rest of the year is impossible.

As soon as Ollie and I are settled in his car, I punch his arm. "You will never guess what happened to me today."

Jesse finally texts me at seven that evening. *What are you doing tonight?*

I waste no time being coy or petulant. *Nothing. Come over.*

As I brush my teeth, I notice my smug reflection in the bathroom mirror. Has my face been like this since English? Mr. Stewart's touch was exciting, yes, but also empowering. I feel like I could take anything I wanted from anyone.

I wait for Jesse in the living room. My nervousness surprises me; for several minutes now, thoughts of him have edged out fantasies of Mr. Stewart. I pick at my uneven cuticles and listen for a car in my driveway.

When Jesse enters my house fifteen minutes later, he looks relaxed but sober. He must have made up for the sleep he lost last night with a day's nap. His pink cheeks and plump lips bring back memories of kissing him.

We don't say much, and we don't touch. He slips out of his coat, kicks off his shoes, and asks if he can have something to drink.

In the kitchen, he slides across the tile in socked feet and goes right for the fridge, snatching two of the beers from the door. He hands me one. "Your mom buys you this?"

"No. She keeps it for men. You know, boyfriends. *Entertaining.*"

"Something about the way you talk about her gave me the idea she hangs out with brandy drinkers. *Cordials.*"

"There have been some of those mulling around this place at midnight, yeah. It's mostly craft beer men now," I say and tap the unopened bottle in my hand. "But she is rarely here lately."

"You're lucky. I never get to be alone in my house." Jesse's chewed-up fingernails tear at the top of the beer label. He points to the ceiling. "You have a lot of bulbs out."

"Yeah, we just don't—" I don't know how to finish that sentence. *Remember? Have time? Give a shit?*

What started three years ago as two full rows of illuminated track lighting, has now dwindled to ten blown bulbs and four that, despite all the time that's passed, still shine.

"You know," Jesse says, turning to me, "I've thought about being with guys before. But more like—sort of like I'd think about bondage or peeing on someone."

We've moved from lightbulbs to light fetish. "Peeing?"

"I mean, like I never thought I'd actually *pee* on anyone."

If it were anyone else in my kitchen comparing water sports to sex acts with me, I wouldn't be laughing like I am. "That's, like, the worst analogy ever."

"Well, alright, not peeing." He traces squares on the floor with his toe. "But maybe it's like eating chips when you're not a fan of potatoes. Or you didn't know you were." His foot moves faster now as the squares he makes with his toe become smaller. "And don't get me wrong. I like the chips. But I don't know if all I want to eat are chips."

"I get it."

He points the top of his beer at me. "You've liked chips forever. I can tell."

"Yeah, potatoes have always been my staple." I rest my foot on top of his. "Come upstairs."

I lead the way to my bedroom. Once we're inside, I close the door and pry the beer from his hand, placing it on the floor next to my bed. My body is itching to touch him. When I reach for him, he tilts away.

A couple piles of books sit bedside, and he picks the top one off the stack. "I've never even heard of this," he says, dropping the paperback on my mattress, reserving the seat he's too nervous to take. "You know," he says. "I'm not high right now. I didn't smoke. I wanted to be sure."

"About?"

"About you," he says. "Like, I've fucked a lot of awful girls when I was too high. And then, you know, I'd sober up, and they'd just be assholes?"

I know what he means. I want to tell him the trick is not to sober up. "I'm not going to be an asshole. I promise."

"Yesterday, Jackie told me some stuff about you. Like you're a bit of a...pro."

I relax my facial muscles, hoping my expression stays neutral. I'm more hurt that Jackie made the comment than I am about Jesse believing or repeating it. I was sure she and I had a tacit respect for one another's indulgences, that we would honor and defend our choices until we parted ways at graduation. I close the gap between Jesse and me. "I think you already knew that about me. What do you want me to say?"

While shifting his weight from one foot to the other, he removes his glasses and places them on the night table. He traces the slender scabs on my chin and forehead. "You still have some little scratches on your face."

When Jesse shuffles closer to me, I tug at his fly. "Will you take

off your pants? And all those shirts. How many are you wearing?"
I search through the layers. He pushes away my hands, insisting
he's cold.

I tell him I'll go slowly, and I pull off one shirt at a time until
I'm down to the last. I tug it over his head while getting a nose full
of him. His pants are tighter tonight, and still his hip bones show
above the beltline. My cock thickens. I remove all my clothes in
seconds and kick the pile at my feet across the room.

I lean in to kiss him, and he flinches. "I don't know. Maybe I
should go."

"No, don't go." I drag my thumb across his bottom lip and lift
his chin. "Don't go."

"I feel weird." He crosses his arms and rubs his bare skin, as if
to warm up. "I'm too skinny. And it's way too light in here."

It never occurred to me that Jesse, easygoing and temperate,
would be ashamed of his body. I've never had a shy boy. I've had
reluctant, aggressive, and clumsy boys. Inept college freshman.
I've partaken of the questioning crowd. I've had guys who knew
their way around a dick like they'd been sucking since birth. But I
have never had a shy boy.

I gently unfold his arms and admire him. "You look amazing.
My dick's hard, and I don't see anyone else around."

"At least close your eyes so I don't feel so bad," he says, crossing
one arm over his waist. "When you stare, I feel like I'm stripping or
something. Close your eyes."

I do and count to five. I reach blindly into the center of the
room. The warmth of his palm as it falls into mine makes me want
to haul him into bed. "Jesse," I say and tighten my grip on his hand,
"I like you. I like looking at you."

With the worst timing in the history of time, there's a single
knock on my door. Jesse shakes free of my grasp, and I grit my
teeth. "*What?*"

"Danny," my mom says through the door, "can I see you a
second?"

"Not now," I say.

"I need to talk to you."

"*Not now.*"

After several seconds, she says, "When you're—done."

The hallway floorboards creak, and I know she's back in her bedroom. Using the distraction to his advantage, Jesse crosses the room and flips off the light switch. In the dark, his silhouette is all I detect. As my eyes adjust, his pale skin shows. His lips come into focus, his hair.

We sit on the edge of my bed. "It's okay if I touch you?" He whispers yeah. I stroke him until he forgets his body is anything but a cock and then give my next directive. "Lie back. Turn over."

While Jesse settles, I think of Mr. Stewart for the first time in over an hour. The caress, what it meant, what it's leading to. Fantasies about my teacher are unwelcome right now. Jesse's here, a sure thing, and I like him.

I push the memory of Mr. Stewart's touch from my mind, making quick work of positioning Jesse on his stomach, face down in the center of my bed. I kiss his shoulder, his back. While sliding down his body, I stop to lick the nook where the slope of his back ends and his ass begins. Now I am thinking of nothing but this.

The sheets are tangled in his legs. He can't shake them loose. A shaky giggle follows the clenching of his asscheeks. "Dan." The blanket muffles my name. "What are you doing? Don't even think about whatever you're thinking about."

I don't know what I'm thinking about. A blowjob, a hand job? Nothing seems good enough. I straddle his hips, pressing my dick against his cool, bare skin as I work it into the crack of his ass. I lean forward and kiss the back of his neck. My mouth grazes his ear. "What am I thinking about?"

Into the pillow, Jesse squeaks before he speaks, "Is any of this going to hurt?"

I let a glob of saliva fall from my mouth. It lands a few centimeters left of his asscrack. By squeezing every muscle below his waist, Jesse has created a fortress around his asshole. I scoop up my spit and work my wet finger past the barrier. Finally, I'm permitted to circle the rim. He moans once, cuts himself short before another can escape, and clears his throat. "Dan?"

"Mmm?"

"Maybe don't fuck me."

I quickly roll him onto his back and climb on top of him, I press my erection against his. We are hot and sticky, too sticky for a pleasurable rub. I slick us up with spit, once, twice, three times. I start slowly, pressing our cocks together and jerking us off. His penis is pinker than mine. The head is larger. I have more veins. I'm thicker. Now we are both sloppy wet.

A bubble of precum balances on his slit and then trickles down to the ridge. I have never seen anything better than this, not in porn, not in person, not anywhere.

After a few strokes, he's frantic and tries to push my hand away. "I'll come now if you keep doing that."

"Yeah, let's—" I huff. "Me too."

A few more strokes and he comes. Gratification, confusion, a sprinkling of disquiet, whatever mix of emotion he rode out with that orgasm makes him giggle. The river of his cum running down my shaft supplies extra lube. I shoot all over him in seconds.

I fall to his side and reach for a T-shirt. I let him clean up first. For several minutes of silence, we stare at the ceiling. I worry that Jesse is uneasy; if he is, I don't know what to do or say about it. Our upper arms are the only parts of us that touch until he rolls over and swings a leg over mine. He says, "I guess I should go."

Those are the words I usually say a few minutes after I come. I turn and face him. "You feel weird?"

"No."

"Really?"

"Maybe."

I kiss his shoulder and put my nose to his skin. He still smells like vanilla, but it's a thicker, spicy, devilish vanilla. "Yeah, I get that. Believe me."

"I think I'm just trying to go before you tell me I have to go."

"I don't want you to go. You can stay here. You can leave. You can fall asleep. Whatever you want."

He grabs his phone from the bedside table. "It's close to nine."

"Does that mean you're going?"

"I think so, yeah."

I walk Jesse to my front door. I want him to stay. I never want anyone to stay. I think he wants to kiss me. I want to kiss him, too.

We lean toward each other. Instead of a kiss, though, he laughs and rolls his eyes. "*Potatoes*. What a stupid thing to say."

In my driveway, Jesse pulls open his car door, looks back at me, and smiles. I wave. I check to see if any neighbors are watching and wave again. I close my front door, anxious to get back to bed and have a smoke. When I turn, my mom is right behind me. I jump. "Jesus. How long have you been standing there?"

She wears a satin pajama set and stands on tiptoes as the skimpy shorts with lace trim ride up on her. She wiggles, trying to get the material out of her butt without digging. I say goodnight, but she blocks me by planting a hand on the wall as I try to pass. "Danny," she says, "your English teacher called me this afternoon."

My mind goes to the most unlikely reason for his call: his confession. I relax when I appreciate how ridiculous that is. "What did he want?"

"To see if you're okay. Here, at home." She puts her hands on her hips. Her eyebrows pinch together. "Did you do something bad that made him call?"

"No. He's just a nice person."

"He wasn't *nice*." She reaches behind her and pulls her shorts down a couple inches. "He asked me why I don't go to those meetings with your teachers and why I don't support you at tennis matches. He asked why you miss so much school."

Although a smile comes, I hide it from her by looking down. I don't want her to know anything about my relationship with Mr. Stewart. It would taint the excitement and slacken the tension for me.

If she's bringing it up like this, he must have rubbed it in well. She's had plenty of phone calls from other teachers these past four years, and I know my frequent absences in ninth grade had the Vice Principal leaving her messages at least once a month. She never brought up those calls except in passing and sometimes accompanied by a quick check-in: "Are you okay?" When I said I was, she moved on, relieved not to have a conversation about it.

I compose myself and look at her. "What did you say to him?"

"I didn't say much. What was I supposed to say?" She exhales through her nose, annoyed that she's still talking about this. "Look,

I let you roam around here doing what you want when you want. They're your decisions. But to be honest, Danny, I don't want to deal with the consequences of any of it."

She starts up the stairs but stops on the second step. Sighing, she turns back to me. "He did say you were doing well with the—I don't know what he said—some poetry thing?" I say nothing, but she quickly adds, "That's good," and disappears upstairs.

Instead of stoned memories of Jesse keeping me awake most of the night, I replayed Mr. Stewart's classroom caress until after 4 a.m. The more I smoked, the more the touch meant. The next move had to be mine. I devised a plan that still seemed viable by the time my alarm rang at six, so I told Ollie I was skipping school and went back to sleep.

At noon, I sat up in bed refreshed and tried to remember all the perfect things I should say to Mr. Stewart when I see him. I consider how close I should stand, how much I should smile, and what muscles I should occasionally flex.

In my quiet home, I eat a bowl of cereal on the couch. I grow impatient with time and decide a workout might make it move faster. I smoke a bowl and do a dozen pull-ups on the door frame. I work up a sweat doing crunches until I want to puke up bran flakes, almond milk, and bananas. While watching TV in my living room, I do thirty push-ups every fifteen minutes until my arms can no longer support my weight. I smoke another bowl.

At 3 p.m., I shower, dress, and start the walk to the only park within a reasonable driving distance of school. I arrive there just before 4 p.m. and find a picnic bench in the grass at the center of the winding running path. It has a good vantage point of the parking lot. If Mr. Stewart runs today, I will see him when he arrives. I now count eleven cars in the parking lot. It's too early for one of them to be his.

A few runners follow the asphalt path through trees and around a manufactured pond. I spy a few moms with toddlers and strollers by the swing set and slides. A power-walking woman with a husky passes me and smiles as I slip off my backpack. I sit on the table, and my jeans take the brunt of the splintered wood. Propping my feet on the bench next to my bag, I read on my phone and wait. My palms sweat. I chew this inside of my cheek. I'm surprised by my nervousness.

A few minutes past five, a black Lexus pulls into the parking lot. Mr. Stewart steps out, and while he does a few cursory hamstring stretches, I make tight fists, opening them so I can shake out my hands to steady them. By the time he takes off in a light jog, the apprehension I felt has waned. Now I only feel excitement.

My picnic bench sits about twenty yards from the main path on which he runs. There is a short curve that brings him nearer to me for about five seconds each lap. It's then I can see his facial features well. He stops once, shaking his left foot, as if moving a roving pebble to a better spot.

For three laps, I go unnoticed as he passes me. On his fourth lap, however, when he darts out of a grouping of trees, he spots me and does a double take. With his lips pressed together and a creased brow, he keeps running, completing another full circuit before slowing and veering off in my direction.

He avoids my eyes until he's in front of me. He's barely winded, but his skin shimmers with sweat. "Sometimes," he says, his hands coming to rest on his hips, "I have difficulty discerning whether you are altogether artless or *so* artful you throw me off the scent by acting like an imbecile. Why are you here?"

I pick up a twig from the bench, tapping it several times against my knuckles. "I needed to talk to you."

"This is not the place—"

"Why did you call my mom yesterday?"

His face pinches with impatience. "Because that's my job. We can discuss it tomorrow, *at school.*"

"Yeah, we could," I say, "except I bet you'll avoid me for the rest of the year, *at school.*"

"I'm going to finish my run," he says, turning away. "Go home."

"Wait," I say, reaching for his arm and snagging the sleeve of his T-shirt, stopping him. "First tell me why you touched me."

He glares at my fistful of T-shirt until I slowly release the damp material. The bulge in his clamped jaw disappears. He faces me.

"Because I made a mistake. It's as simple as that." The words and their hushed delivery suggest weariness and regret.

I take a step toward him and say quietly, "Do you want to make it again?"

Looking at the sky, Mr. Stewart shakes his head, baffled. "*Every time* I give you some leeway, you abuse my benevolence. Do you think I enjoy your constant harassment?"

I laugh. "Harassment? *You* touched *me.*"

"Yes, out of compassion." He calms himself with a deep breath. "It was nothing else, and I should have known you'd blow it out of proportion. I'm sorry you feel rejected—"

"I don't feel rejected," I rush to say. "I'm seventeen, but I'm not *that* seventeen. I know the difference between rejection and restraint."

His frustrated sigh turns into a groan. He widens his stance, lacing his fingers behind his head. "How are you this arrogant?"

"Good parenting." I expand my chest. "So, what happens next?"

"Nothing," he says, glaring at me. "Nothing happens next."

"What if I want something to happen next?"

"And what would that be? To further pester me every day until I'm forced to transfer you to another class? I'll see you tomorrow, Daniel."

He walks away. My desperation swells. By the time I've chosen my next words, he's far enough from me that I need to raise my voice to be heard. "I want to have sex with you."

Spinning around, mouth open, he rushes back to me. "Have you lost your *mind*?" His scowl makes me steel for throttling. At the last second, though, he darts to the other side of the picnic bench, lifting it several inches off the ground and letting it drop. His frenzy makes my asshole constrict.

Pointing at me, he talks through gritted teeth. "Listen to me. When we leave here today—*shit.*" He squeezes his temples. "After today, this is over. We don't joke. We don't laugh. Unless it's about classwork, we don't speak."

"That's dumb."

"Noted. Now get the fuck out of here." He paces, hands on his hips.

This is the only moment I'll have like this. I've pushed his patience to its limit. If I leave, we will never talk to each other again, much less talk about this incident. The alternative—and this feels more my speed—is standing my ground until he either has another fit or gives in.

As each of us waits for the other to move, the distant squeals from the children on the swings break the silence. When he opens his mouth, I beat him to it: "I want to have sex with you. That's it. That's all."

He grips the edge of the picnic table and hangs his head. "*Goddamnit*, shut up. Please. Just shut the fuck up."

"What's the big deal? I know you want it too."

His eyes meet mine, and he mocks me with a snort. "You don't have the balls you think you have."

"Try me."

Without taking his eyes off me, he unzips the side pocket of his track pants, pulling out a set of keys. He removes a fob from the ring before tossing the unneeded bunch across the picnic table. He comes to me, takes my hand, and slaps it in the middle of my sweaty palm. "You think this is what you want? Here you go. I'm going to finish my run. If you're still obstinate and naïve in ten minutes, it's the black Lexus." He flares his nostrils and gets in my face, speaking through a derisive smile. "Otherwise, leave the key on the front seat and go home where you belong."

I focus on the black and silver fob in my hand. When my fingers twitch but do not seize the key, Mr. Stewart reaches for it. I snatch my hand away and back up a couple feet. "No way." I grip the key in my fist. "Ten minutes."

His car is parked at the far side of the lot. An overhanging pin oak tree has dropped a few orange and yellow leaves on his otherwise shiny hood and windshield, and one gust of wind shoos them away.

The one-minute walk seems to take fifteen, and I check over my shoulder every few paces. I may not look as though I'm going off for a blowjob, but I'm sure I look like I'm about to smash and grab.

Once in the passenger's side, I dig through my pack and find an unwrapped mint. Fuzz-free with only a couple specks of dirt, the grubby sweet mint will still do its job. I chew it fast and swallow the jagged pieces. After tucking my backpack behind my legs, I sink down in the seat and explore.

I touch everything within reach: dust-free dash, immaculate leather, not a crumb, not a coffee stain, not even loose gravel on the floor mats. The glove compartment is locked. As I'm about to check the center console for traces of his personal life, Mr. Stewart opens the door and slips into the driver's seat. I open my mouth to speak, and he holds up a finger. "Not a word."

I've only been with one older guy—a grad student and aspiring pharmacist who had a serious dirty sock fetish he refrained from mentioning online—and he had his hard dick out before I could unbuckle my seatbelt. My sweaty socks lay across my balls while he blew me. This is nothing like that. This will be expert, no props or distractions, only Mr. Stewart and me, cocks out, relieving months of tension.

"So," I say, drumming against my knees with my fingers, "is your car new? It's really clean."

"What did I say? Be quiet."

The track pants glide along his muscled legs as he brakes and accelerates. He pulls out of the lot and into light traffic. His tires hum. The heat in his car is on its lowest setting but sweat beads on my upper lips and temples. "I'm hot." I reach for the temperature controls. "Aren't you hot?"

"Do not touch anything." His hand rests on top of mine for several seconds. The soft touch contrasts with his authoritative tone. "Be still."

"I can't talk?"

"Not unless you want me to drop you at the corner."

I stay silent for about five minutes until we pull into his driveway. "I should have guessed you lived out here. All quiet and neat and shit."

Mr. Stewart lives in a high-end townhome, an end unit, stone-faced and surrounded by a narrow garden. It's only a couple miles from my house. I plot the route I'd take to get here the next time I come. I peek out the windshield, straining to see in one of the front windows. All the blinds are drawn.

Once in the sanctuary of his tidy garage, I disentangle myself from the seat belt and turn to him. "Can I talk now?"

"If you must." His stare defies me to say something of interest. The concession was letting me come here; entertaining my amateurish chatter was no part of the deal. When I press my lips together, he mocks me with a grin. "You know you have nothing to say. Get out."

I exit the car, at first forgetting my backpack and then cracking my head on the door frame when I retrieve it. I almost bump my head on two black and yellow oars suspended from the ceiling. I walk so close behind him that I kick his heel. "No boat?" I ask, and he ignores me.

Inside, I dump my bag where he hangs his coat, and we take a flight of stairs up from the entrance hall to his kitchen. He drops his keys on the granite breakfast bar. The edge of the kitchen marks the end of the trail for me. I suddenly lose all the nerve I had this afternoon. My blood sugar drops, and my hands tremble. I wait there as would someone delivering a pizza, hoping for a tip. "What are you doing?" he says. "Come in."

I take two tentative steps. Another three. After that, my feet decide that's far enough. I'm anchored. I inhale a light citrus fragrance.

After I give the place the once over, the only impression I take away is how each surface represents another place to fuck: I will sit on the edge of the stone fireplace with his head between my thighs; he will lick my balls and blow me on the parquet floor; we will make each other come on the minimalist sofa.

Every piece of furniture in Mr. Stewart's home sits on stilts. There is no fluffy upholstery, no place for a shoe to be lost or a stain to be hidden. One would never say, "I don't know where it is. Check under the couch," because under the couch is visible from across the room.

There are few cabinets, no drawers, no knickknacks. Separating form and function is prohibited. He's chosen art for his walls, two paintings, Mondrian squares, one above his couch, the other on the wall that separates the living room and his kitchen. The bold primary colors help keep the cozy out.

Once I grow the courage to walk freely, I inspect a simple black photo frame on a chrome table, which is, in my opinion, where a television should be. In the picture, he stands in between two younger women, his arm wrapped around only one. "Who are they?"

Without explanation or invitation, he ascends another flight of stairs, calling back to me. "Don't touch anything."

His bag on the kitchen bar invites a snoop. His wallet, thin and pristine, holds a few credit cards, a local gym pass, and six, crisp twenties. I locate his driver's license. Awkward smile, but still great. His first name is Brett. Brett. It doesn't suit him, but I work it over on my tongue in silence. I stare at his birth date and grind my teeth while I calculate our age difference. Almost twenty years separate us. Events from the decade in which he was born were topics in my AP history class.

Reaching farther into the bag, past protein bars, folders, and his laptop, I pull out *Lady Windermere's Fan* by Oscar Wilde.

"Not only are you reckless and presumptuous, but your manners are also atrocious." Mr. Stewart plucks the book from my hands. "Had she attended, I would have shared this behavior with your mother at the parent-teacher conference."

Loose track pants and a navy T-shirt boasting *Hanover Soccer* have replaced the suit. His hair is wet from a shower so quick, I question its efficacy. The T-shirt hangs off his pecs, and not once does it cling to the rest of his torso. Bare feet with high arches. I look at his crotch, and he widens his stance a few inches, which pulls the material taut. All this flushes my jerk-off imagery down the toilet. This is the best he's looked.

I grin. "Your name's Brett?"

"Forget you know it."

"You want me to call out Mr. Stewart while you're sucking my dick?" I touch the Wilde book still in his hand and look in his eyes. "Can I use your bathroom?"

"No."

My confidence tanks. Mr. Stewart's "no" sounds like talks are closed, negotiations terminated. I'll have no time to crank up my tenacity. What's going to occur now is no longer mine to decide. Mollifying my sudden misgivings with soft skills and civility is no longer his aim.

Taking a piss is my only hope. "I really do have to go to the bathroom."

He guides me up the stairs. After ferrying me into the bathroom, he leans against the doorframe. "Go ahead."

"Close the door."

"No. You're not taking any souvenirs with you. Hurry up."

If I were inclined to nick something in quarters such as Mr. Stewart's, I'd be hard pressed to find any trophies to stuff in my pockets. Even the bathroom is conspicuously clear of sundries; only a white marble soap dispenser sits on the sink. No evidence here of whatever he uses in the morning to make himself look and smell so good.

"Suit yourself." I turn my back to him, and unzip. "The place is nice. You have a housekeeper?"

"Daniel, does anyone know you're here?"

I shake and zip up. "Like my *mom*?"

"Now's not the time to amuse yourself," he says flatly. "Anyone."

"No, no one knows. Relax."

Before I can check my hair and teeth in the mirror, he crushes his body against mine and pins me to the sink, stroking my cheek with the back of his hand. Until this caress, my dick was uncommitted, half ready, but also half ready to go home. In the mirror, his glower tells all: I'm his reward, not the other way around.

Over my jeans, his thumb presses against my erection, sliding up and down the shaft. Heat speeds from his fingertips and to my pulse points, a circuit of arteries made for him, for this experience. Mr. Stewart's warm lips brush against my ear. "After this happens," he says, "you need to forget that it did." He turns me around by the shoulders and points me toward the bedroom.

My daydreams about him never involved conversation, but if they had, I'm certain those words would have derailed the dream. It takes his hand in the middle of my back and a shove to get me moving.

Hospital rooms have more warmth than his sleeping space. Not a photo, not a book, not a wrinkle in the blankets. Bed, two bedside tables. Perfectly plumb doors, scuff-free paint job, flush molding for the baseboards.

A clean-lined, mahogany dresser sits against the wall opposite the bed. It's immense, spanning almost the entire side of the room, and it makes me wonder how many months of a teacher's salary that set him back. A bare valet stands near the closet door. There is a mid-century caramel leather chair in the corner.

Unless someone's tendencies and taste are as understated as Mr. Stewart's, there is no evidence of a lover or partner.

I step out of my shoes while Mr. Stewart patiently pulls off my hoodie. I study his manicured nails as they fiddle with the buttons of my father's too-big plaid shirt before he goes for my fly. The way he focuses on undressing me reminds me of my mom pulling off my snow boots. I step out of my pants. "I'm not five."

"Quiet."

Most of what's happening runs parallel to my hopes, which was simply fucking my English teacher. Now that I'm minutes and inches away from attaining my goal, I feel like I'm being shortchanged. I want more. Flirting. Conversation. Seduction.

He should be gushing about how he's been dying to do this for months, about how he thinks of me all the time. I need to hear how thankful he is that I finally pushed him this far. I want my cock sucked, of course; but the act would be ten times better if he first told me I am the only thing he desires.

While he removes my clothes, I wish his sentiments were also stripping me of my guard. I could use some reassurance. If I knew I was a valued conquest, I could relax after we came, perhaps even unmask some of my many insecurities. It would be the orgasm of my lifetime, a safe and sated afterglow, accompanied by a confessional, uncensored peek at my psycho-emotional toilet bowl of adolescence.

My arms hang at my side. "You think we could slow down?"

"Too late."

"What?" I laugh nervously.

Mr. Stewart remains deadpan, busying himself with the hem

of my T-shirt, which he yanks over my head. The material drags across my unclosed eyes, leaving me blinking and squinting.

"It's too late to slow down. You're here," he explains in the same tone he uses to lecture, "and this is what you wanted."

When he pushes my chest, I lose my balance. My back hits the cool, silken comforter. Considering this unexpected, almost frightening procession, my relentless erection is a testament to how much I've wanted him for months. With a hot hand on my leg, he rolls me onto my stomach in one motion.

Behind me, the rustle and swish of cotton against his skin mixes with an unmistakable racket: the frustrated rummage. I know this rummage well; I do it in the middle of the night when I want a lighter that works but am too lazy to turn on a light. I flip on my back. "What are you doing?"

The foraging stops, and he comes up empty-handed, staring at me as if he's trying to remember if he left the iron on. "Have you done this before?"

I scramble to sit up, but the comforter's bulk and silky material puts me flat on my back again. "Gotten fucked? No way. Is that what you're doing?"

"It is." He returns to the dig, eyes squinting when he finds the square box of treasures. "What did you expect?"

Just—not that.

Messing around a bit with a student a few months before he's legal might be almost harmless: a bit of rubbing, jerking, blowing, and a slap on the ass before sending him out in the world. Ass-fucking, however, seems more about taking pleasure than giving it.

To me, anal sex is the tipping point at which the public decides if a predator is a monster or just a shitty human being. Sure, any contact will get you prison time, but if you keep your cock out of your student's asshole, someone from your extended family might still send you a birthday card every year.

Mr. Stewart rolls the condom over his bouncing hard-on. He slicks it up with gunk from a black tube and coats three fingers of his other hand with another slimy blob. "Roll over."

"No way."

"Trust me, you want to roll over."

My cure-all arousal has withered, but I do as I'm told. After I settle into a comfortable position on my stomach, he spreads my ass until a cold, jelly-slimed finger presses against my asshole. The pressure is soon replaced by a pinch of pain when he stuffs it inside of me and moves it north, south, east, west. That single digit might as well be his whole dick in there. I squirm. He only digs deeper. "Push out."

I do. Some of the pain goes away. He puts in another finger—or maybe it's five, I don't know. When he asks me if I'm ready, I want to say that I am most certainly not ready. Several times, he pushes his dick against my asshole with no success. When his patience fades, he slaps my ass and tries another few times. "Relax."

"I *am* relaxing," I perjure myself, my face squished against the mattress.

"You're not."

Ashamed of my lack of experience, I arch my back, get to my knees, and crush my forehead against the bed. "Just go. I'm ready."

The sting and stretch of being spread as the head of his dick breaches the entrance provokes memories of sun poisoning, the summer of my twelfth year, how each time I moved, it was as if my tight, blistering skin were ripping open.

I blow out the breath I've been holding. I want to ask if this is as bad as it gets. Is this the worst of it? If the sensation is what people rave about, I don't fucking get it, but I can handle it. "Is it—*what the fuck*—in?"

He gives me unwelcome news while dragging a finger down my spine. "Halfway." His cock flexes, and he snickers. "Feel that?"

The pulse is the first hint of pleasure, although far from enough to dull the sense that I might shit myself. The latex, even with the lube, nips at my insides, trespassing in an orifice I swore I would never allow open.

I brace myself as he presses on. His grip on my hip serves as ballast when he shoves my torso down with a sturdy palm between my shoulder blades. He drops all his weight on me. No pumping, only pushing. His cock is in as far as I think it will go and then goes deeper still. He bites my shoulder, mumbling my name or some cursed version of it.

I wish I could see this from every angle. I want to see his balls pressed against me. I want to see his triceps and biceps working as he holds his body above mine. I want to see his ass flex when he finally decides it's time to fuck.

As my asshole adjusts to his cock, I breathe hard into the mattress, like I'm blowing out a hundred candles one at a time. My penis shows slight interest and thickens under me. "You could—probably move now." I regret the words a second after they come out of my mouth.

He pulls out halfway and eases back into me. Relief melts my body. This might be good. This could be amazing. My asshole relaxes a millimeter more.

He withdraws almost all the way, waits a moment, and then slams his hips against my ass on the plunge. When he pulls out, I am sure all my insides go with him. Several strokes later, the glide of the reentry makes me semi-hard again. Tip to balls. Balls to tip. As I clutch the comforter, I spread my legs, maneuvering so he can get into me further.

He shoves his open palm under my face. "Spit." I do. When he captures my erection with his slicked-up fist, I expect a fast hand job like one of the many I've had before this. Instead, he pulls on me slow and tight until an orgasm comes to a standstill at the base of my dick. I want to come, and I only need the few strokes he's withholding to do it.

"Is this how you imagined it would be?" Bucking against me, he teases the head of my dick with a slick thumb. "It's *exactly* how I imagined it would be." His body jostles mine. "You want to come, don't you?"

My whimper—my plea—precipitates a squeeze around my cock. I wince. One hand around my neck, the other stroking only enough to keep me on the edge, he whispers, "Beg me."

I try to fuck his hand. Nothing works. My dignity crumbles. It only takes one "please" before his violent thrusts are once again forcing sharp hiccups from my mouth. He strokes me perfectly. When I shoot semen all over his dry-clean-only comforter, Mr. Stewart finishes the fuck and rants until his words mutate into incomprehensible noises. After his last silent shudder, he pulls away, and his penis decamps with a squelchy plop.

I'm soaked. So many nerve endings are in play back there that I'm sure my asshole now has its own heartbeat. I flop onto my back, and although I land on the cum-sodden blanket, I remain there, unsure what to do next.

After the snap of shucked latex, he dangles the condom from his index finger. I search for blood, shit, and entrails, but there is only a clear, glossy sack with a pool of glue in the reservoir. He goes to the bathroom. Self-consciousness convinces me the entire room stinks like cum and sweat. I reach behind me, gently touching my asshole with my middle finger. I inspect my wet fingertip. The pale pink blush of the residual lube indicates blood.

My pre-fuck jitters have mutated into their formidable post-fuck anxiety. I am too naked. My bare skin makes me feel more vulnerable to what I know is coming: the talk, the putrid guts of all this, the end. Before he returns from disposing of the condom, I jump up, pull on my shorts, and sit back on the bed. When I look up, he's leaning against the doorjamb. His running pants are on again and hanging low on his hips. "Are you okay?"

"Just need some water." I rock side to side on my asscheeks. "Maybe an aspirin."

"Your instinct is for jokes, I know," Mr. Stewart says and sits next to me, the space between us narrower than I thought he'd allow now that we're done. "But we need to talk about what's going to happen moving forward."

I want to speak about none of it, ever. Not about my bleeding asshole. Not about how I just pleaded to come. Not about how it's over now, and I sense I'm more his subordinate than I was before we fucked.

I stretch out my leg and touch his foot with mine. "You have long toes."

"Daniel," he says, followed by a hesitant sigh that only bad news merits.

"Can we just—" I groan and fall back on the mattress, pulling a clean corner of the blanket over my face. "Why can't we just relax and not have to talk and shit all the time? Is there some equal ratio of fun to boring you're supposed to keep?"

Mr. Stewart tugs the blanket and exposes one of my eyes.

Instead of looking at him, I lift my head and spot my T-shirt hidden at the bottom of my pile of clothes. I push away from him, pop up off the bed, and snatch it. After shaking out the wrinkles, I pull it on, the cotton armor making me feel ten times safer than my bare, sweaty skin. The veneer of my semen on my back causes an itch I'm too self-conscious to scratch. Squirming in the soft material alleviates some of the discomfort.

I wander the room. Since orgasm, one question has been bubbling in me. I stop and turn to him. "Have you done this before?" No matter how I try to relax my face, I know I'm displaying the pout of a spoiled child.

It catches him off guard. He begins to stand but settles back on the mattress. "No, I haven't."

"Really?" I'm unsure if I ask out of disbelief or if I just want to hear him say it again.

"Yes."

"So, I'm either extraordinary, like you said, or I just wore you down."

He reaches out and places his hand on my hip. "Both." The hand reassures me, but the unfiltered intimacy becomes excruciating when it lingers for more than a second. He must sense the latter because he pulls it away, letting it rest on the mattress next to him.

"So," I say, "no boyfriend right now?"

"I don't think we should discuss this."

"You just had your cock in me. You can't say asking you shit's inappropriate now."

He smiles and bows his head. "Okay. I'm not involved with anyone right now, no."

"You usually like younger guys?"

"Age isn't a factor when I'm attracted to someone."

"What are the factors? What are *my* factors?"

My cock is half-hard again, competition for the anxiety churning up my insides like a potato farmer's rototiller. Before, Mr. Stewart saw me as a nuisance, albeit a turn-on. I was a kid with acceptable taste in literature, a passable sense of humor, and a moldable intellect. Grooming me got him off. Now am I groomed? Is that it?

I dig at the flesh on my forearms under the guise of scratching a fierce itch. He takes my wrist and pulls me between his spread legs. With his hands on my waist, he shakes me, as a parent would a child whose fall was more startling than painful. "Come on. You're okay. Are you happy we did that?"

"Yeah." I sneak a look at him, hoping I won't see the twist of regret on his face. "Are you?"

"Of course." He says it clearly, with certainty. His thumbs caress my waist, and he pulls me closer. The top of my knee brushes against his crotch. "I've always liked you. Your company, your charm."

"Charm?" I try to step out of his hold, but he pulls me back. I poke his shoulder. "Do better than *charm*."

"You have many excellent qualities."

"Name some."

His hands on my forearms push me backwards several inches so he can look me in the eye. "We have to kill this now. You understand that, correct?"

I step out of his reach. Although this echoes the directive he gave before we fucked, it still takes me by surprise that he meant it. "You want to go back to playing chess and bullshitting?"

"We may have to go further back than that." When I frown, he tries to soothe me with a sickly-sweet voice I've never heard him use before. "Set aside your emotional reaction for a minute and put yourself in my position."

I pace in front of him, trying to think of a reason to change the subject. "Hey," I say when I remember downstairs there is the book that is my windfall, "was that Wilde book in your bag for me?"

After a moment, he says, "It was. It is."

"That seems weird now that you fucked me."

"I disagree." He touches the spot on the mattress next to him. "Please, come here."

"Look," I say, "it would be pointless for us to stop now. Like, legally, one time is probably the same as a hundred times, right?"

His eyes narrow under a wrinkled brow. "Pardon me?"

"That wasn't a threat or something." I hold up my hands. "Take it easy. I just meant—it's the truth, isn't it?"

"I'm going to go downstairs and make us something to eat," he says and stands. "Why don't you get dressed, access your rational brain, and we can talk about this like adults?"

"Fine." I peer past him and into the hallway, wishing I was on the other side of his bathroom door. "Can I take a piss alone now? Maybe have a towel?"

"I'll put one out for you. Meet me downstairs when you're done. We'll talk."

There's not a person in the world who wants to have that talk. When he's gone, I snatch my pants off the hardwood floor and pull them on so fast I shove both legs in one hole. I slip on my shirt and skip half the buttons. My hoodie goes on inside-out, and I don't give a fuck. Socks, coat, shoes.

I inhale as though I've been allotted only one more breath for the next two minutes. I want to run—I want to take three steps at a time, maybe hurdle the whole flight—but my asshole is so torn up that much more than shuffling is painful. When I reach the bottom floor, where he runs water and clanks dishes in the kitchen around the corner, I keep going.

I tiptoe down the next flight of stairs to the entryway, grab my bag, and exit through the door to the garage. After feeling my way around his car, I locate the door behind it. I fumble with its simple lock until it gives, and I push through to the cool evening air.

Once I have my bearings, despite the pain that ransacks my ass, I take off across the patch of grass that's a stand-in for a real front lawn. My shoe slips off the heel of my left foot, and I slow only to tug it off completely. I grasp the shoe like I'm a running back, and I ditch that development, taking the shortest route to the back roads in case Mr. Brett Stewart takes chase.

The next day, Jesse, whose texts I've been blowing off for over a day, waits for me outside of Mr. Stewart's before class. "Hang out tonight?"

"Yeah," I say, hoping my smile gives him the reassurance he needs. If I'm required to quell his obvious anxiety with more, I doubt I could pull it off. My asshole aches. I wonder when it will heal completely. Maybe I have hemorrhoids now. This morning, I made a note in my phone to investigate all aberrations of a healthy anus.

Since leaving Mr. Stewart's place, instead of enjoying what he and I shared, I've been worrying and anticipating, trying to figure out ways to control what's going to happen next. If I can't have him again, I want reassurance, a promise that we won't backslide into how it was at the beginning of school, before I perforated the factory seal of his daily routine with my charm and intellect, my extraordinariness.

Inside the classroom, Mr. Stewart writes on the board, his back to us. Dark gray trousers and a crisp white shirt conceal all the muscles and skin I've seen bare. I remember what he did and said to me. We have a secret. *Beg me.*

The bell rings. Mr. Stewart asks us all to sit and be quiet, Jesse loiters by my desk and whispers, "So, Brad's house tonight?"

As I'm about to reply, Mr. Stewart says, "Jesse, sit." He turns his attention to me. "Daniel, I don't want you caterwauling across the aisle to speak about your social calendar. Why don't you give Jesse your answer now, and we can all get on with our afternoon?"

Only one student laughs. Mr. Stewart's head snaps in his direction. "Did I invite noise from you, Christopher?" He looks at me again. "Go ahead. What's the verdict? Any sordid ordeal you have planned for this evening?" When I don't respond, he says, "Very well," and starts his lesson, as Chris still snickers in the background.

My strategy for today is to stay low in my seat, contribute when Mr. Stewart asks, and try to get a sense of our new rapport. I want to know what my remaining days in ninth period have in store. I thought he'd be nervous or remorseful, and I counted on a bit of favoritism because of it. Needling me about my evening's plans reeks of overconfidence.

For thirty minutes, I try to find meaning in everything he does. If he walks close to my desk, he wants me to smell him. I'm certain his few smiles must be for me alone. Is he spending more time than usual facing the board rather than the class? That view is for my benefit.

My Stewart's zipper appears in my eyeline. "Daniel?"

Like we're sparring and I'm dodging blows, I tilt away from him before I quickly right myself. "Yeah?"

"Did you read the assignment last night?" When I don't answer, he pats my shoulder. "I'm happy you're awake, but I'll circle back to you."

Yesterday, I would have thought it impossible to have an erection while Mr. Stewart wound out the class with a few words about vellum and dried animal bladders. But here I am, an awkward delight. *Beg me.*

At the bell, Ollie and Jesse chatter while I try to decide if I should linger and talk to Mr. Stewart. "I'll go to Brad's," Ollie says to Jesse, "but only if it's not all dudes. His basement is starting to smell like my ballsack after a game. Dan knows what I mean. Right, Dan?"

When I rode with him to school this morning, Ollie asked me what I was going to do about Stewart. I told him I might drop it. He said I was full of shit. I nodded and turned up the music.

Telling Ollie the truth over breakfast seemed a bit much. Before it's a "good story," I need to extract and dissect the emotions I have about the event. A couple mornings from now, I'll light a joint on the way to school and share details about my ripped-open orifice. I will speak of the indignity of getting fucked after years of swearing I wouldn't. I'll confess to running away like a spooked eight-year-old, and just after I stub out the roach in his ashtray and he devours the last of his breakfast burrito, I'll quietly admit that I am dying to do it all again.

I walk by Mr. Stewart's desk as slowly as I can. He mouths, *After school*, and then turns to the board.

Jesse, Ollie, and I firm up plans for the night. Before we part, Jesse moves his hand an inch toward mine. He wants to touch me. Skin-on-skin with Jesse in the middle of the science wing means something, and I don't have time to think about what that something is.

Instead of reaching for him, I salute them both, my hand stiff against my forehead for two seconds before falling limply to my side. They stare at me like I puked feathers. Ollie's eyes roll back into his head. "*Aye aye.* What the fuck are you doing?" He walks away, saying, "So, so, soooooo dumb," under his breath.

Genetics drags its feet getting to *after school*. I replay the humiliating scene in my head all through class and all the way to Mr. Stewart's. I wait outside his classroom until it empties. I knock. "Can I—?"

He waves me inside. "Yes, come in. Close the door."

I go to him, keeping my focus on the subtle gray pinstripes on his tie. Its knot is as far north as I'll allow my eyes to go. My attention shifts to the right, to the snug fit of his sleeves and the hint of biceps underneath. I remember his chest, sweaty against my back, and his long fingers covering my mouth, how one fingernail dug into my cheek so hard I was surprised later when I found no scratch there.

When I finally look at his face, he's squinting, studying me as I was studying him. He slides *Lady Windermere's Fan* across his desk toward me. "You forgot this."

"Thanks." I pick up the book and put it in the front section of my backpack.

"Daniel."

"*Brett.*"

"Watch yourself," he warns and presses his lips together. "You left. What happened?"

"I don't know." I look over my shoulder and consider sitting at my desk. From there, the tremble in my voice would be harder to detect. "Do we have to talk about it?"

"I can't read your mind. Tell me, please."

My muscles relax for what seems like the first time since yesterday. His sincerity surprises me, and I decide to tell the truth. "I think I just didn't want to have an awkward conversation. Like the one we're having now."

The PA startles us—someone's missing laptop was found—and Mr. Stewart's body stiffens for a moment before he talks. "I've been concerned."

"Yeah, it was stupid that I left." I lean forward a few inches, so he can hear my whisper. "I'm not going to say anything if that's what you think."

"Daniel," he says with a tired sigh that makes me feel foolish, "it's just us. You don't need to whisper."

"It feels like we should be whispering."

We both smile. When he stands and comes to my side, I'm unsure of what to do or where to go. He leans his ass against the desk, motioning for me to make myself comfortable in the same fashion. I rest next to him and ensure there remains enough space between us to avoid incidental touching. Still, to whoever might come in without knocking, my proximity to Mr. Stewart would look like what is: two guys that fucked.

Side by side, we look out over the classroom. In my periphery, I notice Mr. Stewart crosses his arms. I cross mine, too. He stretches his legs and places one ankle over the other. I decide that's a terrible look for me.

Getting to view the empty room from this angle is uncommon. So much beige. The aisles seem longer than they do when I'm part of them. Someone spilled red nail polish down the front leg of the first desk on the left, and the janitors have a ton of muddy footprints to clean tonight.

I envisage myself as Mr. Stewart, sneaking glances at my favorite student—Daniel, stage left, two back—each time the class lowers their heads to read. I imagine fighting to resist that student. I'm curious, if I were indeed Mr. Stewart, how long would I have waited to do it?

I push away from the desk, laughing. "I can't do this. It's too fucking weird. Why are you standing over here?"

"Very well," he says, allowing himself a single laugh before returning to his desk chair. "Our usual, then."

I pretend to wipe sweat from my forehead. "I mean, that was just awful. Let's not do it again—."

"Listen, Daniel," he interrupts, serious once more. "I was callous and overhasty yesterday when I said we needed to change our dynamic. You have shouldered—*are* shouldering—a heartbreaking amount of trauma, and I won't be another source of neglect for you."

"Is this a dad thing again?"

"No. This is, I hope," he says, pausing and inhaling slowly, "an understanding."

My brain readies for debate. It's honing its arguments against potential lectures until it snags on the last thing Mr. Stewart said. My eyes dart to his face. "Wait, what understanding?"

He raises an eyebrow. "Rules."

My heart rate spikes as if I just spotted a cellophaned pound of weed on the side of the road. "Hold on, hold on. Understanding? What does that mean?" But I know what it means, even as I complain that I don't. My cock has already hitched itself to fantasies of the coming months: clandestine communications and a lot of fucking.

From his suit jacket, which hangs on the back of the chair, he digs out a tin of his cinnamon candies, placing one on his tongue. "First, in and out of class, I need you to be respectful, careful, quiet." He says this coolly, as if the words were rehearsed for me, for this, or perhaps they're rules he's laid down many times before.

I am ready to spit, shake, and bend over. "I can do that."

"Let me finish." He stands and straightens his tie, then lines up the placket of his zipper with the buttons of his shirt. He checks where his belt buckle sits and decides it's perfect before his focus falls on me. "Never use my first name. Not here, not anywhere. No slip-ups. If you have a problem, you speak with me—and only me—outside of school. Say nothing to anyone. Don't change your patterns. And this is the most important rule of all. No matter how you feel or what you want, you cannot come to my home unannounced."

My sexual activities, so far, have involved two rules: Both of us wanted to fuck around, and both of us knew that orgasm ended our adventure. Mr. Stewart's list is long—and I am confident it will get longer.

Although meant to restrict and control me, the list further spotlights his vulnerability. For the first time since we met, I feel like I have the power; unlike Mr. Stewart, who is risking everything, the only thing I stand to lose is dick.

He says, "Do you understand me?"

I want to stop smiling, but I can't get my mouth to do it. "Yeah, I understand."

"There's one more thing. Are you having sex with anyone else?"

I can't think fast enough about which answer he wants to hear. "No. I mean, yeah, but nothing—"

"You need to stop. It's a requirement. Not up for discussion."

It's the second time today that a salute seems appropriate. I hold back the urge. "Sure."

He counts off on his fingers, instructions one through five: "Finish tennis practice. Cancel your plans. Approach my home from the back and use the door to my garage to enter. Use *discretion*. Be there at seven."

I walk away from him backwards, adjusting my semi-hard cock, watching him watch me do it. "You could have just said you wanted to fuck again when I first got here. I'm uncomplicated."

I am weak-kneed from a combination of intense drills, little sleep the previous night, and the two-mile walk to Mr. Stewart's. As he said it would be, the back door to his garage is open. When I tiptoe inside, nerves worsen the wobbling.

A plug-in light reflects off his Lexus. Part of me expected him to be waiting in here. Instead, I'm greeted with cleaning products, and a tire pump. I want to know about him, but gleaning info from a set of unused gardening gloves sitting on spotless metal shelving is a lame place to start.

I tilt the side mirror of his car so I can check my look, pushing my hair out of my eyes, checking my teeth. I drop my pack, coat, and tennis gear in his entrance hall before creeping up the stairs.

To find him eating an apple in his kitchen both surprises and relieves me. I expected a quick strip-down, fuck, and bum-rush to the door. "Hey, *Brett*."

Unamused, he glances at his kitchen clock.

"Really?" I say. "I'm fifteen minutes late. Give me a break."

"How did you get here?"

"My mom." I kick off a shoe. "Just kidding. I walked."

He pauses mid-chew and comes out from behind the kitchen bar. He wears his fitted shirt from school, unbuttoned, but the clashing choice of track pants and bare feet lures me farther into his home. I trail behind him to the living room.

I only peeked in here yesterday. Today, what I find upon closer inspection is more of the same. Tightly upholstered ninety-degree angles, no patterns, achromatic pieces that are more art than furniture. He indulged in a black area rug.

The only furnishings interrupting the grayscale of the room are two throw pillows of solid Mondrian blue to match the paintings. Well, to anyone else they'd be called throw pillows; he likely calls them precisely placed pillows: *Don't touch.*

I'm curious about him. I want to look at photos and see what's in his drawers. Books and degrees. Old invoices. Herb garden. Childhood mementos. Liquors, liqueurs, wine. I want to see a detailed credit card statement. Some inkling about who he is besides a gifted English teacher who tips toward OCD and, if I were to take the thrill and shine off our relationship, an ephebophile. Despite what he told me yesterday, that last thing could be serial, or I could be his first. I flatter myself and decide it's the latter.

"There's no clue in this house about your life. Like, what do you do when you're not teaching?" I pull back the shade on the window that overlooks his backyard, a patch of grass only large enough for a dog to cover in shit in less than a week.

"Please, don't do that," he says as he pries my fingers away from the shade. "The only fabric in my home you may touch without first washing your hands is the bedding. And I'm uninterested in the neighbor knowing anything about me."

I cross the room and swipe my finger over the mantel. No dust. "I know teachers get paid shit," I say, investigating spotless chrome, shiny floorboards, a gas fireplace, "so, how are you affording this place?"

"Is conversation your aim this afternoon?" He looks me up and down, his gaze lingering on my crotch.

Yesterday, I was a kid, and that was okay. Now it seems important I act like an adult with a thorough understanding of sexual etiquette. Is assumption or hesitation more attractive?

Before I can decide, Mr. Stewart comes to me, slipping a hand inside my waistband, and unbuttoning my jeans with one finger and a thumb. His lips brush against my ear. "I want to see you naked again." He quickly shucks his pants, slips out of his shirt, and parks his bare ass on the couch. He's well on his way to an impressive erection. He strokes his cock and nods at me. "Go slow."

Remembering all the sexy ways to get out of my shirt and pants proves impossible. Graceless and uneasy, I peel off all my clothes and toss them in a pile on the parquet floor in front of his fireplace. My skin shines with a thin layer of sweat.

As I approach him, he admires my penis, my legs. My confidence peaks when he remains unblinking for longer than must be comfortable. He shifts in his seat and holds up a hand, his next command catching in his throat. "Stop. Stay there."

I shake my head and drift toward him. "Too late."

"Yes," he agrees, "too late." He slides forward on the couch, grabbing hold of my hips. My cock is heavy, not hard. He devours it. His tongue and some suction do all the work. When my erection fills his mouth and throat, I don't dare direct his pace or depth as I would with anyone else.

My cock goes from hot to cold when he pops off. He pulls my body to him. The cool leather of the couch warms quickly and sticks to my knees as I straddle his legs. The way he drags his nose up and down my skin, inhaling, inhaling, inhaling, he could be snorting lines of coke off my torso.

"You're a mess," he says and drags his tongue up my biceps. "High, hungover. Slovenly. And every day, *every day*—" He shakes his head, probably reveling in all my horrible but hot qualities and the erections they've been giving him. He clutches my asscheeks. With his lips wrapped around his teeth, he nips at my armpit and lats, moving across my clavicle and speaking against the hollow of my throat. "Every day, I've wanted to fuck the shit out of you."

His declaration surprises me so much it's impossible to hold back the odd sound that comes out of me, a single soprano syllable that rings in my ears, almost a laugh. It's not funny, though; it's sexy. "For how long? Since you met me?"

Mr. Stewart ignores my questions, pulling at my lower lip with his index finger until I open up. "Get it wet," his husky voice insists. "Wetter."

He pulls me closer to him until he gains easy access to my asshole, which he rims with that wet but determined finger. The contact stings. I remember him rough fucking me yesterday. I moan as his fingertip wiggles and my discomfort fades. He buries the finger deeper and then adds another. My cock jumps.

Mr. Stewart sucks on my pecs, bringing blood to the surface of my skin. He milks me until I pant. When I'm seconds from coming, he withdraws his fingers slowly. His erection, neglected and about to split down the middle, leaks a clear rivulet onto his taut abdomen. He cups my balls with one hand, jerks me off with the other, and we stare at my cum as it sprays his chest.

My forehead collides with his shoulder, and he holds me to him, all the slimy mess squished between our chests.

I'm allotted recovery time of less than a minute. He pushes me off his lap, spins me around to face the couch, and kicks my legs apart. I brace myself with my forearms on the leather cushions. A glob of cum drops from my chest and onto his otherwise unblemished sofa.

His penis pokes my asshole. He holds my hips with hot hands.

"Wait," I say. "Condom."

"*Fuck*," is followed by a frustrated groan. "They're in the bedroom."

I expect him to run upstairs and get what he needs. Instead, he says, "Stay still. I want to look at you."

Within seconds, my self-consciousness disappears. I lift my ass higher, open my legs wider. I look between my spread legs at his shins, muscled and sinewy like a runner's. He caresses my ass, my lower back, sliding around to my ribs with a touch firm enough to avoid tickling me. His fingers trail over my ass again before slipping off my body. The noise of his frantic masturbation fills the room.

Two muted grunts, and he steps sideways, away from the rug. I turn my head and watch him. His semen hits the fancy hardwood floor, two sprays, one big blob, then drip drip drip, the last dribbles of a faulty faucet. After a couple of seconds, he cracks his toes.

I stand up and turn toward him, but I catch him walking away. He leaves the room, and I'm unsure what to do with myself. There are no books to leaf through, no TV to turn on. I step closer to the Mondrian print and count some rectangles.

Mr. Stewart returns clad in black boxers and a charcoal-colored T-shirt. He holds two bath towels and two cold water bottles and hands me one of each. "Clean up, and then you can sit on the chair."

He spreads his towel on the fireplace hearth and takes a seat.

I have never seen legs spread so wide. Maybe that's what it means to be an adult. They take up space, no invitation, no apologies. They have the right to fill a room, like gas particles fully occupying a container.

I sit with my knees drawn to my chin while waiting for what he says happens next. It takes only seconds before I find out.

"In the future," he says, "I promise to plan my evenings around your visits."

This must be the fastest "get the fuck out" on record. I know it beats any of mine. Cum still dries on his couch, my dick's hanging damp and dead between my legs, and he's giving me the boot. I retrieve my jeans from the floor.

"What are you doing?" My sudden movement confuses him.

"Leaving." I extend my towel, its corner wet with cum. "Where do you want this?"

"Hold on a moment." He checks that the cap on the water bottle is closed before placing it on the hearth and coming to me. "Catch your breath."

"I know you want me to go, so I'm going."

"Daniel, nothing bad is happening here." His hands come to rest on my shoulders. "I have things I need to do tonight. The next time we see each other, I will have cleared my calendar." Mr. Stewart caresses my upper arm. "Stay right here. Do you promise not to abscond if I leave the room for a minute?"

A mandatory, official goodbye wasn't one of his rules. I want to leave as soon as he bounds up the stairs and consider the speed at which I'd need to do it before he returns. He thuds back down as I'm slipping on my shoes. "Here," he says, pulling something from his pants pocket and holding it out for me.

Immediately, I know what it is and why it's about to be mine. "Is that a *burner* phone?"

"I have one, too. Don't open it around anyone. Keep it on vibrate. If you call me or text me, use that phone only. If I see any other number, I won't respond. When I contact you, I expect a response as soon as it's feasible. My number's in there. I expect it to remain the only contact you keep in that phone."

"So, you do want me to come back," I say, waving the phone between us, "but on a schedule?"

"Yes. I'm a creature of habit." With one hand on my ass, he ushers me to the edge of his stairs that lead down to the small foyer, which adjoins his garage. "I like to keep order. It's how I live."

"I see. Eat dinner, wash dishes, fuck Daniel, lights out?" I slip the phone into my coat pocket and face him. "How long do you think we'll do this?"

"I suppose until it cloys." With his palm, he pats my back and then runs his fingernails between my shoulder blades, up, down, sideways. The withdrawal of his hand means it is time for me to go. Neither one of us says another word.

On my chilly walk home, I look up *cloy*. That's a shitty definition.

Almost every night the following week, I've waited until dusk and then begun the walk to Mr. Stewart's place, taking the same route I took the evening before and the evening before that. Between Mr. Stewart fucking me and the next time Mr. Stewart fucks me exist only mundane activities: sleep, school, tennis, meals, showers. Routine trundles me through the day.

I've cut my weed consumption in half. My adjustment is much less that I'm heeding Mr. Stewart's advice, which is what I tell him I'm doing, than it is my preoccupation with fucking my source of the advice.

After Ollie's initial interrogation, our communication has consisted mostly of sniggering and elbows in ribs, and never in class. The last thing he said about it was: "I can't believe anyone would risk prison just to touch your dick."

Jesse, on the other hand, has been more difficult to manage. I've grown tired of telling him I'm tired, and by the way his face falls when I say it, he's grown tired of hearing me say it. He must think I'm running marathons in my spare time.

When I'm near him, I can feel how much he wants to touch me. I want to touch him, too. What I want more, however, is to continue seeing Mr. Stewart.

Tonight is the seventh night I've been to Mr. Stewart's. I've missed a day because of an away match I was tempted to skip but, at his insistence, didn't.

I enter my usual way and drop my belongings in his tiled entrance way. I begin unbuttoning my clothes before I clear the landing to his main floor. He's emptying the dishwasher and looks over his shoulder to catch me bare-chested and going for my belt. When my fingers hover near my zipper, he says, "Keep going" and comes to me.

He leans down, his tongue tickling me as soon as I'm naked. He goes from nipple to nipple. It's my least favorite of all the places he licks me, and I twist out of his tongue's reach, wanting whatever else he has to offer. Manicured nails scratch and dig into my lats. He squeezes my ass, spits in his hand, jerks me off for a few seconds.

Kicking my feet out from under me, his grip on my arm helps slow my fall to his dining room floor. "Lie down." With his bare foot on my chest, he pushes me back and then strips off his clothes.

My shoulder blades press against the floorboards and what must be the thinnest rug in the history of textiles. A lemon stink itches my nostrils. His place always sparkles, but fruity sterility is bullshit. I want us to smell dirty. I want him to sweat, huff, and heave. I want to choke on the sweet, sour, and pungent parts of him.

"Spread your legs." He falls to his knees between my legs and massages my chest. "Put your hands above your head." The lift of my legs onto his and the firm nudge of his cock behind my balls bring out the coward in me; there's no lube next to the salt and pepper shakers. Too many nights getting my ass fucked have left me raw, and I doubt, too, that he's going to pull a condom from behind his ear.

"I'm way too sore to get fucked."

He hunches down, grabs my ankles, and pushes my legs up to my shoulders. The exposure leaves me wriggling and trying to right myself. My asshole contracts when he pokes his hot, silky tongue inside. I am one big pucker down there. When he laps at the back of my balls, my erection throbs.

"I take it this is new to you." His voice is soft, and so is his touch, as he returns my legs to the floor. "When you're alone and thinking about me," he says and licks the swollen head of my cock, "what do you think?"

I'm fucking my English teacher. That's exactly what I think. Every time. "Just—you."

He tongues the slit in my penis, deep throats me once. "I think about how you shake when you come." His uncharacteristic laugh fills the room. "I doubt you'd be able to hold a pen while I'm inside you."

With an expert's skill, he licks and sucks until my hips buck. I can't control my orgasm. My muscles constrict. A burgeoning cramp tightens my hamstring, and I push past it, dropping my head back. He gulps my semen like he's downing tequila shots on spring break. I throw my arm over my eyes and gasp for breath. I huff, breathless, and exhale his first name.

While I recover, he kisses my shaft, licks my balls. When my shivers stop, he tilts me on my side and seizes a handful of my ass. "All this," he growls and squeezes my flesh, "is mine."

His brutish claim to my body causes a shudder from the top of my spine to my pelvis. The words are sexy, thrilling, bordering on intimidating.

He springs to his feet, dick still thick and bobbing. Instead of disheveled and wanton, he is his usual professorial self: alert, staid, and dignified. He marches to the kitchen, his tight ass flexing with each step, and drains a bottle of water. After replacing the cap and tossing the plastic bottle into a bin under his sink, he says, "You said my name. What did I tell you about that? Keep your wits, even when you're having an orgasm."

I raise a weak arm to wave off his concern. "Eh, I won't mess up in school. Trust me."

"It was rule number one, and it has nothing to do with trust. People get sloppy. You cannot get sloppy."

I fake a yawn and motion for him to come back to me. "Do you want to keep going here or upstairs?" Now that my penis is no longer central to my senses, the rest of my body has permission to catch up. I notice a stinging sensation above my left asscheek. I lift my hips and feel around my skin. I find the spot—rug burn—and yank my finger away after it worsens the pain. "I'm going to need a first aid kit."

Mr. Stewart doesn't hear me. He's staring straight ahead at nothing with an index finger pressed against his pursed lips. He shakes himself out of his thoughts. "Do you enjoy performing oral sex?"

I turn on my side and try to find lint on this immaculate rug. "You can't just say blowjob like the rest of the world?"

"You can call it whatever you'd like. Do you enjoy it?"

Mr. Stewart has taught me how to appreciate celery and nut butter and how to hang my washcloths in the bathroom to avoid mildew. We've spoken of speed reading, *Arabian Nights*, and my parents. Over the past several days, I've learned a lot, we've fucked a lot, but his cock has never been near my mouth. For that, I've been thankful.

"It's not my thing," I say. "It's not you. It's just too—" I pull a face as if I'm being made to eat my cauliflower. "Can we do something else? Let's keep going."

"What if I said I'm uninterested in anything else?"

That this has devolved into a discussion and not more fucking annoys me. "Then, I guess we're done." I get up and pass him in the kitchen. He watches me move but keeps his hands to himself.

The routine he's designed for me is simple: orgasm, hydrate, snack, shower. I assume the orgasms are over for the evening, so I scour his fridge, taking several moments to see what he has for a quick bite. I poke at a bag of jicama slices. Earlier this week, my introduction to jicama slices didn't go well, and most of it ended up in a napkin.

I hide the bag behind the almond milk. "I just don't suck dick. Don't take it personally." I'm unsure how much deeper Mr. Stewart wants to get on this topic. I keep my head in the fridge; the fruits and veggies are non-confrontational.

When I hear him go upstairs, I snag a grape before I duck out of the fridge, my goosebumps soothed by the warmth of the kitchen. I wait in my shorts, reading on my phone at his dining room table. As soon as he leaves the bathroom, I can go clean myself up. Then, as far as I'm concerned, I've completed the cycle and can walk home.

He returns fully dressed, his hair wet from a shower, and tells me he put a towel out for me. I gather my clothes and go to the bathroom, thankful we've dropped the blowjob topic, at least for now.

My towel sits folded neatly next to the spotless sink basin. I move closer to the mirror and open my mouth, imagining a cock going in and out of there. I wrinkle my nose and look elsewhere.

His shower, also spotless, contains body wash, one bottle of shampoo, one of conditioner, brands I've never heard of. The minimalist beige and black bottles fit the rest of the house. I would be unsurprised if that's why he chose them. I use them all.

After my shower, I open the bathroom closet. Towels, toiletries, extra toilet paper, nothing interesting. Sex toys seem outside of Mr. Stewart's repertoire, but I look for them anyway. Evidence of his sexuality is conspicuously absent from his home. Clues must be in his office, the only room that's gone unexplored. I could ask—boyfriend, fetishes, masturbatory tools?—but it's a welcome challenge to find out without inquiring directly.

I return to the living room where he waits on the couch, typing on his phone. He places it face down next to his leg and points to his taupe leather chair in the corner. On it sits what I assume is a book, wrapped in plain white paper and tied with twine. "I got you a gift," he says. "When I spotted it, I thought of you."

My face warms. I can't think of the last time an adult gave me a gift. My mom leaves me extra cash for my birthday—maybe even a different flavor of turkey jerky—but topping off my usual weekly allowance is far from thoughtful.

I pick up the book, smiling. "Is it toilet reading or bedtime reading?"

"I had a feeling you'd need to make light of my gesture."

As Mr. Stewart approaches me, I handle the gift as if it's made of glass rather than pulp. The wrapping paper is stiff. I peel the clear tape away from one edge with care. A corner of the gray spine peeks out at me.

Mr. Stewart interrupts the reveal, laying his hand on top of mine before I tear too far. "I need you to do something for me, in exchange for the book."

I should have known it would come with an asterisk. I press the opened corner back in place and lay the book on the chair next to me. "Then it's not really a gift, is it?"

"In adult relationships," he explains, "there are activities one party might enjoy less than the other does. Compromise is key. Turning up your nose at experiences unfamiliar to you is the mark of a child or a coward."

"Consider me both," I say. "Look, sucking dick's not my thing. Cross it off the list."

"That's nonsense. Sex has no checklist."

"It does, and blowjobs aren't on it. You're allowed to have rules, so that's *my* rule. No kissing, either."

He turns away from me. "I'm disappointed."

I leave the gift and follow him to the kitchen, where he removes those fucking jicama sticks from the fridge. He fondles three avocados in a glass bowl on the counter and decides on the one that pleases him. "If you're averse to oral sex, I'm not sure what to do. I don't desire a partner who is close-minded."

"Take it or leave it."

He sets the avocado next to a mixing bowl. "Every once in a while, you say things that remind me how immature you are."

"I'm sure you'll get over it if I let you keep fucking me."

He hands me a knife and spoon, gesturing at the snack in progress. "Can you manage this?" He leaves before I can tell him that, no, I have no fucking idea what one does with an avocado.

Several minutes pass. I yell up the stairs. "Are you coming back or what?"

No answer. I eye up those starchy snacks on the kitchen bar and decide to split before he force-feeds me. I grab a bottle of water and a pear for the road before packing up the rest of my things. I shout again, telling him I'm leaving.

"That's fine," he calls down to me but stays out of sight. "Keep a low profile. Lock the door behind you. But Daniel?"

"What?"

"Consider what I said. I'm not giving to charity."

It takes me a moment to understand that I'm the charity. The speck of resentment I feel will stick with me, no matter how the rest of this plays out.

I cross to the living room and pick up the book, now less a gift than a swap for my mouth. I tug back the wrapping enough to see the title: *The Nature of Alexander*, a used paperback with cracks in the cover that remind me of a river and its hundreds of tributaries. Underneath those creases, a photo of a stone sculpture, a head with one nostril chipped away. I press the seam of the torn wrapping back in place, hoping it will be undetectable.

I set the book down on the chair, stare at it, and finally snatch it up, stuffing it in my backpack between my laptop and a couple dirty T-shirts. I rush down the stairs and through the garage door with no goodbye.

It's a cool night, a bright halfmoon. It rained, but the pavement is almost dry. I light a joint on the walk home and entertain the idea of Mr. Stewart's cock leaking cum on my tongue before spewing all that thick jizz in my mouth. It's a turn-off. I contemplate sucking any one of the dicks I've seen or felt in the past few months. I cringe as random yet memorable penises zip through my mind. There is only one cock I'd put in my mouth, and it belongs to Jesse.

Recognizing that ruffles me. Tapping into the feelings underneath bothers me even more. I would do that to him. I would in a second. If he has the only dick I'd suck, then why aren't I with him right now?

I'm beginning to feel comfortable in Mr. Stewart's home. I know where the extra paper towels are, how he loads the dishwasher, and that his office is the only place off limits. I've learned that he wipes down his shower tiles once either of us is done. I sense he's more comfortable with me there, too, since he no longer hides that he does it.

I'm allowed to adjust the thermostat, within reason. We both enjoy an environment conducive to my perpetual half-nakedness. Seventy-eight degrees is the sweet spot.

We share meals now. Today, it's Asian Mandarin salad. Mr. Stewart sips his sparkling water before setting it on the granite countertop of his kitchen bar. "Do you follow professional tennis?"

I take a break between mouthfuls. "Nope. I just play. I don't give a fuck about that."

"We're having a conversation," he says, putting down his fork. "Obscenities are unnecessary."

"Obscenity or no obscenity, tennis is boring to watch."

"Another topic, then. When you're with your friends, what do you do?"

I stab at a pecan with my fork, tugging it off the prongs with my teeth. "We hang out."

"While intoxicated?"

"Usually."

"That saddens me." He frowns to emphasize his disappointment. "You're remarkable, Daniel, but your friends are mediocre. It would be healthy for you to start down a fresh path by finding some new ones."

"Healthy sounds like a lot of work."

He dabs at the corner of his mouth with the napkin and shifts in his seat for several moments, as if he can't get comfortable. "What sort of history do you have with Ollie?"

The idea of messing around with Ollie is laughable. It's also somewhat repulsive. "Ollie? Are you kidding me?" After an exaggerated guffaw, I stretch my legs and rest my feet on the stool next to him.

"And Jesse? You and he seem close lately."

I push my salad around the plate and make a game of it: no sesame seeds must touch; cabbage to the right; oranges to the left. I don't want to talk about my friends, especially not Jesse, not now, not here. "We're friends."

"I have a feeling your interpretation and mine differ as to what constitutes a friend."

"Here's the thing. There doesn't need to be a big life lesson in this thing between you and me. Talk about something fun, or at least interesting."

"Very well. Why don't you carry the conversation now?" He clears our plates. "And I have no interest in speaking about marijuana, tequila, or video games."

I've been curious about his past, and fathers are the one thing I've been hesitant to bring up, mostly because it sets me up for counter-interrogation. Today, though, I feel strong enough to be interviewed. I'm ready to speak to my father's character and maybe tell an anecdote or two. "You said you didn't like your dad. Were you, I dunno, happy when he was gone?"

Mr. Stewart wipes down the bar, prodding my elbows from its surface so he can reach my crumbs and slime. "As a child, I was relieved. As a young adult, I was angry." He touches the rim of my water glass. "Would you like some more before I take this away?" A bottle of sparkling water appears, and he empties its last few ounces into my glass before I can answer. "I've only been thinking about my father lately because of you."

"That's weird."

"I assure you, it's not. Relationships are complex."

"Maybe when you get old, they are. Mine are pretty simple."

At the sink, he rinses his dishes, the water so hot steam rises from the faucet. The dishwasher is open, waiting for his precise lineup of lunch's remains; an extra space will separate each plate, and the forks will be segregated from the spoons in the silverware caddy. He looks over his shoulder at me. "I'd like to ask you something about your father now."

"Yeah, I was waiting for it. Go ahead."

"What happened on that day?"

"There's no way you've known me this long and haven't researched that shit. He was shot. He died. That's all."

"I'll rephrase that." He turns off the water and dries his hands on a dish towel, a wrinkle-free waffle weave of bright red, the accent color in his otherwise grayscale kitchen. "What happened to *you* on that day?"

"What, like, emotionally?"

"Where were you when it happened?"

I planned to tell the story about my father trading fifty pounds of twelve-penny nails for a single Cuban cigar. He let me sample it, one disgusting puff, our secret. I have no interest in recounting the events of his death day.

On the granite bar, an errant piece of cabbage sticks to the centimeter's smudge of dressing he missed. I poke it with my pinkie. "I was in school." I say, my voice unsteady.

Usually, if I allow myself to think about the day, I think about anyone's perspective but my own. My dad's point of view, of course: going to work with his large hot tea, laughing with his employees. Or my mom, driving the car he bought for Christmas. She was probably on her way to a house showing when she got the call.

I think about how Ollie was told by someone in authority, or maybe it was just a rumor that reached him. I think about his ruined birthday; we were supposed to play basketball after school. He planned to smoke a cigarette he stole from his sister. That night, instead of celebrating, he probably tugged his fucked-up earlobe for hours.

I visualize the cops, what they might have had for breakfast, or if they hated their jobs or cared about murdered people at all.

Although I've never known at what point en route my father died, I've always imagined he didn't kick it till he was admitted. I wondered how many hands tried to help save him, and, when he died despite those efforts, what the hands did right after.

I've tried to reenact what my father must have gone through. I have sliced my skin and hoped the hole in his throat hurt no worse. I've choked on water while imagining drowning in blood. Afterwards, I would hold my breath and slow my pulse to next to nothing.

I can review the day from anyone's angle but my own.

Until now, Mr. Stewart stayed on the other side of the kitchen, waiting patiently for me to continue, as if any movement on his part might call attention to how vulnerable I'm about to be. Now he comes to me and places his hand on top of mine. "They told you while you were in school?"

I slip my hand from underneath his. With one fingernail, I pick at the corner of my white paper napkin. "Not really. They just called me to the office."

I was in the cafeteria, eating turkey and Swiss, and Ollie was farting into his hand. My name came over the PA system, but the vice principal was at my side before I'd even stood up. She piled all my food trash on my tray for disposal and asked Ollie to throw it away when he was done. I slipped on my backpack and went with her to the office.

Mr. Stewart inches closer to me. His proximity becomes almost unbearable. He rubs my upper back.

If I share the day's details slowly, I'll cry; so, I spill it fast. "Like, in my gut, I knew he was dead. Not just hurt, but dead. Some random teacher waited with me in the carport. She wouldn't say anything except that my mom was on her way. We stood there for a long time. She finally took me inside. I remember sitting alone on this rust-colored vinyl couch thing in the principal's office forever. No one would talk to me. I don't know how long I waited. Maybe an hour. Then—I don't know—I just left. I got up and walked home."

Mr. Stewart rests a hand on my forearm as I continue. "I didn't walk fast. I thought there'd be some bad shit happening when I got home, and I was right. Police and neighbors, inside, outside. Some of my dad's family, a few of his employees." I look at Mr. Stewart and curl my upper lip. "And my mother."

I suddenly need space to breathe, and the bar stool teeters when I stand and shove it backwards with my legs. We both reach for it. He saves it from the fall. I try to walk around him, but he blocks me, placing his hands on my shoulders before bringing me in close for a hug. His breath moves the hair near my ear when he whispers, "Your fucking mother."

For a few moments, resting my head on his shoulder soothes me. Then, I conjure an image of how we must look, how I must look. Pathetic and ugly. I push away from him, breaking the hug and wiping my watery eyes with the back of my wrist. He pulls me back. I fight his embrace and lose. I slip my hands into the front of his shorts. I go for his cock, dodging pity by demanding sex. I need distraction, not affection.

Slowly and calmly, he extracts my hands from his clothing and lowers my arms to my sides. "We need to let this settle for a bit, or perhaps talk more about it. How about we play chess for a half hour, and if you feel like talking some more—"

"No." I go for his shorts again, getting a finger in the band. He steps out of my reach, and the elastic snaps against his skin. I click my tongue and groan. "Come on. You really think I want to play chess right now?"

"It will relax you."

"*Fucking* will relax me."

I make another grab for his T-shirt, then his waistband. He

grabs my forearms and forces them to be still by my side again. "Will you please listen to me?" he says. "Let me take the lead here, okay?"

Being told what to do sits uneasily with me; my obstinance is not the reason, however. Letting someone care for me and make decisions on my behalf, someone who has my welfare in mind, is a treat I've no desire to taste. If only bland canned fruits are on offer, and there will only ever *be* bland canned fruits on offer, I am uninterested in nibbling when someone teases me with the only fresh strawberry in existence. I doubt anyone after Mr. Stewart is going to care about my well-being, and I'd rather not spend the next sixty years pining for nurturing.

"Please?" he says. "Come upstairs with me."

I keep my hands to myself, say nothing, and follow him with my head hanging low. Upstairs, he turns up the heat. I strip naked— he stays in his T-shirt and shorts—and we sit cross-legged and play chess on his bed.

My mood improves when he teases me, asking me if he should let me win, just once, because I've had a bad day. I lose one game, then another. Before he can suggest a third round, I shove the board to one side and reach into his bedside table drawer for a condom. I hold it between us. With a smile, he reaches for it. I pull it away and tell him I liked how pissed off he looked when I told him what my mother did to me. "You're even hotter when you're angry. I'll remember that."

Ollie and I loiter on Brad's front lawn. The quiet residential street is oddly lifeless this Friday evening. For fifteen minutes, no cars have passed, and nobody has crossed their tiny parcel of well-manicured grass to get the mail. As I'm about to ask Ollie if he finds the lack of noise pollution as eerie as I do, a junker that's been keyed and duct-taped pulls slowly up the road. Two bungee cords secure its front bumper. Ollie says, "That's Brad. Finally."

Brad parks in his driveway, and Jackie steps out of the car and waves. When I don't see Jesse, my mood downshifts immediately. I flick my lighter and walk in small circles, kicking at the dirt patches on Brad's lawn. Ollie smacks my arm. "There's your boy."

"What boy?"

"Don't be an asshole." He shoves me and points. "That one."

Jesse climbs out of the passenger side, looking as though he just had a nap. This is the first time in weeks I've seen him outside of school. I'm surprised at how fast my heart beats.

Jackie pulls me down to kiss my cheek. She slaps Ollie's ass. "I'm going to put this stuff inside," she says, touching her purse, "and then we'll go."

Jesse sidles up to me, and Ollie leaves us alone, joining Brad in the front seat. After lighting a cigarette, Jesse inhales deeply before talking. "The invisible man."

"Yeah," I say, my face heating from his taunt. "I'm—"

"It's okay." The wind sweeps his hair into his eyes, then out. "You've been busy. I'm patient."

Brad's horn startles us. Jesse stubs out his cigarette on the cracked concrete of the walkway. Inside the car, he sits between Jackie and me in the backseat. Jesse slips his hand under my leg, and I trap it against the torn material of the seat. Jackie and Brad argue nonstop about directions, how long we're staying, who's driving home, who must sober up first.

A half-hour of highway driving passes. Jackie fills her pipe— the bowl of blown glass the colors of a pimento-stuffed olive—and passes it around the car. Ollie and Brad decline. We arrive at a warehouse apartment near the airport in the city, and Jackie tucks the empty apparatus in her purse, removing a zipped baggie with several colorful tablets. She passes us each a pill, takes two herself, and argues with Brad about their parents' anniversary gift. In the rearview mirror, Ollie gets my attention by miming a noose around his drooping head.

If I leave the pill in my palm any longer, it will disintegrate. I've never done anything but smoke weed. My biggest concern is that other drugs will make me foolish, overly friendly, sentimental. I put that out of my head and toss back the pill, swallowing several times before it goes down. I hope it makes the night spectacular, but worry that I will think too much and fuck that up.

Instead of entering through a front door, Brad guides us toward the back of the brick building, and we hike up three flights of metal stairs. We enter through a fire door and continue down a dirty, yellow-lit hallway, following the bass of a song unfamiliar to me.

Inside, it's so loud, we communicate with each other by reading lips and body language. A few dozen people, most college-aged or older, lean against walls lined with throw pillows. Other bodies are asleep or gathered cross-legged in small groups on five queen-sized air mattresses at the back left of the expansive room. Everyone in the center of the place is dancing, each person confident about or oblivious to their lack of grace and humility. I silently chant to myself: *No matter what happens tonight, don't do that shit. No matter what happens tonight, don't do that shit.*

The overhead fluorescent tube lights are off. Hundreds of icicle lights hang from the ceiling around the perimeter of the apartment. Crepe paper fish on strings dangle from the metal beams above.

Jackie has made it her mission to make sure we have a good time, and she leads the way to the far side of the apartment, nearer to the kitchen appliances, circa 1950 or at least designed to look that way.

We five sit against a wall as she rummages through her backpack and pulls out gum and juice boxes. She holds out a pack of gum to me. "You'll probably need this." I take it and don't ask why, because I know she knows.

Ollie wanders off. Within minutes, he's doing his dirty shadow puppet thing, using a lamp with no shade and on a bare patch of wall. College girls show enthusiasm.

Jackie is already rolling, or pretending to be, nuzzling Jesse's neck in between yoga stretches. She reaches across his body and rubs my chest. "You are fabulous, Danny." She holds one of my hands, stroking in between each finger. "Your hands are beautiful, Danny."

I upturn her hand in mine, dropping my head toward her palm so I can examine the wrinkles and lines and fingerprints. I become aware of my brain. It's comfortable and won't let me think it's not. I'm lightheaded in a good way and headed for something unknown but pleasant, or perhaps I'm there already.

The fridge next to me hums. On it, a series of magnets feature vintage advertising and food mascots. A jubilant bunch of purple grapes wears tights and snaps its fingers.

After an indeterminate amount of time, I say, "Your hands are beautiful, too, Jackie." They are silken, and I think about them around Jesse's dick.

"And look at Danny's face," she coos, bringing Jesse's hand to my cheek and moving it across my skin for him. "Feel that, Jesse?"

I'm unsure how much time they've been touching me and saying sweet words. My lips are tight with a wide smile I can't abandon. Jesse's hand slides down my neck before resting on my arm. "Try to relax your face." He caresses my ears and cheeks before unwrapping a piece of watermelon bubblegum and pushing it between my lips. "Everything's fine. Here. Chew. One. Two. Three. See? It's good."

Yes, it is good. My body gives me no warning when it switches gears. I am chewing gum like a fucking maniac. Crepe fish flutter in the breeze as people pass. The strategically placed fairy lights twinkle in the shape of large daisies. Jackie holds my hand. She's the only person in the room, but not really. I squeeze her hand and swirl my thumb in her palm.

Jackie and I keep squeezing each other's hand for a long time. "Thank you." I say it over and over. I know there's no reason for me to thank her, but I can't stop.

"You're welcome," she purrs every time, like she knows what I mean and could never get tired of the reply. "You want to dance with me."

"Not yet." I lie down with my head in her lap. She holds my cheek and runs her fingers through my hair. Her octopus tentacle tattoo goes up her neck for miles. Her necklaces slice the tentacle in two. The links, the herringbone, the metallic charms. A golden teacup dangles from the delicate chain that holds my attention the longest.

Jackie pokes a miniature straw into the apple juice box I'm fondling. "Sip."

"Are these juice boxes?"

"Of course, they are."

Two guys I don't know sit next to her on the floor. One draws an imaginary line with his finger from my forehead to her lips and says, "Of course, they are."

I have my phone in my hand. I fondle it, flip it over, bring it close to my face, pull it back. Then, I realize I have the wrong phone in my hand—Mr. Stewart's phone—and I've been staring at a message forever. *It's long since passed 7, Daniel.*

"What's that?" Jackie says, touching the phone once before I close it.

I put the phone in my pocket. "It's nothing."

"Is that a flip phone?" She giggles.

The short interaction disturbs me briefly, but we're so fucked up, both of us forget before we finish the thread. I squeeze Jackie's leg and tuck my hand down her boot, which is covered in dayglow alien heads. She is more muscular than I thought. Then, her muscles rebound against my touch like they are amazing rubber.

"Where's Jesse?" I say.

"I don't know," she says.

Soon, I notice Brad dancing alone next to us. His belly jiggles and sticks out of the bottom of his shirt. I want to touch it but somehow know better. A crowd of people dancing faster than he is surrounds him, and he disappears.

I don't know where Ollie is. I need to tell him everything. I think: *He is my favorite person.*

"Sip," Jackie whispers in my ear. "Your phone is buzzing again." I forget her words immediately and can only think enough to ask again where Jesse is. She says, "He's on you."

I don't know when he got there, but the top of his head rests underneath my chin. I slide my hand under his T-shirt. My thumb can't get enough of his vertebrae.

Then my back is to the wall, and Jesse's on top of me, kissing me without breathing for a long time. Then holding my face in his warm hands. Then saying, "Where have you been?"

My head fits perfectly in the curve of his neck. Jesse is so sweet I can taste the pink of him. *He is my favorite person.*

Ollie walks by us once. And again. He is one of those carnival target ducks. He squats beside me. "Why, hello, Daniel." His bright, wide smile startles me, and he holds an unlit cigarette between his teeth. "Do you know where your shirt is?"

"Why?"

"Brad's ready to go."

"Where's Jesse?" I can't remember when the pressure of his body against mine disappeared.

"I pried him off you, Romeo. He's in the car. Have you seen his shoes?"

Ollie helps me up, and I follow him out of the building. In the backseat of the car, I observe as Brad and Ollie talk in the front. I touch Ollie's shoulder. "You two are really something." His nostrils flare, and he tells me to shut up. We laugh.

Jackie and Jesse make out, and it's okay; he seems happy, and I like that. He climbs across her and into my lap. Brad says, "Uh-uh. No way. Everyone's ass in a seat." His words are rough edges. Jesse falls beside me and rests his head on my shoulder.

Ollie is asleep, snoring, his stomach growling so loudly I can hear it in the backseat. I ask Brad if he'll take me straight home. It's on the way, and I warn him that Ollie may be asleep in his car for the next six to eight hours. Brad follows my directions. In my driveway, I stumble out of the backseat. Jesse stops the door with his foot when I try to close it. Then he's in my room.

On my bed, Jesse and I are naked. We don't think about his home or why he should be there and not here. He's stroking my cock, and I'm stroking his, but I don't want to come. The tiny particles that make up his face become distinct. His face is close to mine, and the small pores in his skin are a billion pinpricks.

We turn off the lamp and make shadow puppets on the ceiling with the flashlight on my phone. "I don't know how Ollie does it," I say. "Did you see the goose fucking the turtle?"

"I think that was just a goose."

Jesse and I are in the shower next. We're in the bright light, and he doesn't care. He scratches my chin. He pushes my hair out of my eyes. Drops of water hang off his eyelashes and the peak of his nose. He lets me look at all of him. I'm lazy-stupid, heavy-lidded yet sober. He rubs his thumbs along my eyebrows. "Beauty queen." He is sober, too.

We're in my room again. We're rubbing against each other, kissing. His kisses adopt a pattern: forehead, chest, cheek, cheek, the sign of the cross. The chest becomes the diaphragm, which then becomes my navel; then he kisses where my dick meets the rest of me.

Jesse asks me if I'm able to pack a bowl. I say that I could pack one in my sleep. We sit side by side with our backs against my headboard and smoke. Being stoned again pushes us beyond the need for surface-only contact. One of us wants to get inside the other. He sits on top of me, leans forward, and puts his mouth against my ear. "I like you."

I turn my head, my voice gruff with the late hour, and say, "I like you, too."

We switch positions. Since I outweigh him, he's easy to flip and flatten against the mattress. I'm face to face with his erection, and I lick my lips and suck it into my mouth.

I could never have guessed how good this feels and tastes. While I don't regret that I've skipped the act until now, I sure as fuck am glad that I chose this instant to change years of intractable policy.

"Jesus Christ," he says, loosely holding a handful of my hair. I let him relax while I stockpile spit in my mouth, drizzling a single strand of saliva until it snaps and slithers down his erection. "Okay," he says, "that's worse. Just—just—a second. Wait a minute. Stop moving."

I don't stop. I don't want to stop. Despite my obvious lack of expertise, I make him come with a copycat style and a talented hand. I spit it into my T-shirt. My tongue remains slippery with a veneer of cum. It's slightly numb, as it is after the local anesthetic given for a cavity fill begins to fade.

We're quiet. The only sound is Jesse's heavy breathing as it slows and is topped off with a sigh. He climbs on top of me. "Hey, I want to ask you something. I know you said—you said you never—"

I caress his legs and listen as he tries to complete a thought. In my periphery, I spot Mr. Stewart's phone across the room. It sticks halfway out of the pocket of my jeans. Alarm saps all the blood from my erection, and Jesse's voice becomes hollow and unintelligible. He pushes my chin so I'm looking at him. "Are you okay?"

"Yeah." I can't stop thinking about the phone. "Go ahead."

"If we—if I—" His sigh turns into a grumble. "What are you looking at?"

I've been fucked up or happy for so long that I only now remember Mr. Stewart's message from hours ago. And I only now remember the phone vibrating against my hip several more times since then. In the car? Against the floor? In front of Jesse? All possibilities. I only know that I ignored it every time.

"Jesse?" I push his hips and try to tilt him off me. "Can we talk tomorrow?"

"What?" He's surprised, struggling to balance himself on one knee. "Why?"

His eyes follow mine. We both stare at my jeans on the floor until he frowns. I don't know what he thinks he sees—and maybe it's just my crumpled jeans—but it's obvious he believes he should be noticing *something*.

"Everything's okay," I say and gently touch his shoulder. "I'm just really beat."

"All of the sudden?"

"Yeah, I swear."

I try to keep it light, as if I am indeed tired and this is the natural and timely ending to a perfect night. As he dresses, I toe my jeans against the dresser, careful not to let the phone free itself from the pocket as I hide it beneath the material. "Are you going to call Jackie for a ride?"

"I'll walk," he says quietly.

"Let's call her."

"I'll walk." His one-second forced smile does little to counterbalance the weight of his sharp tone.

I don't argue. The sooner he's out, the sooner I can deal with Mr. Stewart. "Let me throw on some clothes." Other than the pair hiding the phone, the only pants within reach are dirty.

"It's fine, Dan. I know where the door is."

I have only one leg in my pants when he leaves my room, closing my door quietly with no goodbye.

I wait a minute until I hear the front door. I grab my jeans. With sweaty hands, I fumble to open the phone. The final message is time-stamped only an hour ago. *I can only imagine what you're doing.*

My think tank is not always in my trousers; I'm also lucky

enough to make some questionable choices motivated by some deep-seated emotional issues. I'm aware my parents should be playing the leads in my life. Instead, I've had to bring in Mr. Stewart, the understudy. He may not know all the lines, but at least he's in character.

There are a thousand reasons to run after Jesse right now, but the one, faulty psycho-emotional reason I choose Mr. Stewart eclipses them all.

Without any consideration for the flimsiness of my lie, I write back. *I fell asleep. I was tired from tennis.*

His reply reaches me in seconds: *You had no tennis today.*

I consider sticking to the lie, telling him he's wrong or that it was a last-minute practice; instead, I text the truth. *I just didn't feel like it. Maybe tomorrow.*

My response begs to be punished. At this moment, I would enjoy a dressing down or a lecture from Mr. Stewart, not because I blew him off, but because I deserve some punishment for what I just did to Jesse.

My Mr. Stewart phone doesn't buzz again until the next day when he writes: *7.*

I am exhausted, dehydrated, and depressed. Mr. Stewart seems to have noticed none of it. He retrieves a condom from his pocket. Two others fall to the floor. He pulls his cock over the elastic waistband of his running pants. That's all the flesh he shows.

We're in the small laundry room, his odd choice. I'm on my back on the sorting table next to the washer. We have never done it like this, with me on my back. I suppose being able to see his penis going into me means I have some control over the depth and pace. But when the initial thrusts are harder to take this way than any other position we've used, I ask to get down. All I get is a "no."

It's not an angry fuck, only inconsiderate. The rougher thrusts drive my head into the corner of the fuse box. We've toppled a bottle of fabric softener. A mini steamer crashed to the floor.

Each time I close my eyes, he demands I look at him. Lifting heavy lids, I give him what he wants for a second and then turn my attention to the ceiling. When he pulls me toward him, my skin stutters across the table. He presses my knees out and down. I am spread like a dead turkey's legs. He licks his sweaty upper lip and fucks some more. "I'm not one of your callow boyfriends, you understand?"

"I think I need a different way," I complain, "or more lube." My squirms and protests arouse him more; the splotches of red that began at his collar line are now covering his neck.

"You're worth more than a grope on your living room floor," he says between subdued grunts. "Where were you last night?"

I want relief. I want off this table. I want to go home and sleep some more, or at least go to the bathroom and compose an overdue text to Jesse. He's messaged me several times. I've been unsure how to reply, even to his innocuous, *What are you up to today?*

I need to trip Mr. Stewart's cum-wire.

After dozens of encounters, I've noticed no pattern or combination of movements or moans that spark an uninhibited or uncontrollable orgasm. Since I'm flaccid now, with no hopes of pleasure, I spend a few minutes distracting myself from discomfort by conceptualizing new approaches. What is his cum button? Struggling or clinging? Pleading? What does he want to hear?

This is the best.

I don't want anyone else.

You make me feel good.

Right now, all untrue, but I'd be happy to belt them out if it would get me off my back any sooner. Since his censure or some unimaginative critique of my character complements each of his orgasms—and there's always a brief lesson or lecture during the refractory period—I feed him something to fuss over. "I was in a warehouse. Fucked up. Doing drugs."

He slows. The strained bliss on his face gives way to a disappointed droop. The bliss returns once he finds his rhythm again. From there, it's the fastest fuck we've had. He pulls out, snaps off the condom, and shoots on my balls.

I let him finish before shoving him away and hopping off the table. Cum slides down my leg. I wipe it off with my hand and fling it onto the laundry room floor. "Fuck you for that, by the way. My back is ripped to shit."

Mr. Stewart snatches my hoodie from the floor and drops to his knees before me, using it as a cushion. I'm hard in thirty seconds and receive the most proficient blowjob ever. I come quickly. He finishes me off, wipes his mouth, and stands all at once. "I'm going to shower. Please, clean that up," he says and points to the splatter of his cum on the floor, "and then have a snack. There are grapes and some cottage cheese."

I clean up with paper towels. I'm supposed to put them in the laundry room trash can, but his rule about never tossing them in the kitchen trash deserves no observance, not when my asshole's bleeding and my skin's abraded. I toss the towels in the kitchen trash, cum side up. I imagine jicama sticks and avocado peels sticking to the slime.

The shower upstairs starts. I roam his place while naked, trying to think of something to do, something he would never allow me to do.

I run upstairs. I slowly turn the doorknob to his office. With one finger, I push open the door, ready to scatter should there be one squeak.

I understand now why this room is off-limits; I am delighted to have discovered the only place where one might consider him imperfect—or normal—the place where he keeps all his life stuff.

I've found the only television in his home, a modest size, mounted to the wall between bookshelves. A computer with a screen speckled with some dust sits on a monster of a desk, which is covered in tall stacks of disorganized paperwork. The carvings on each of the desk's foot-wide wooden legs remind me of a gothic cathedral my dad took me to when I was twelve.

I peruse the hundreds of books that line his walls. I know only an eighth of what's here. Three entire shelves of tomes written during or about the Middle Ages: saints, myths, legends. Lots of fiction. Rather than alphabetical by author, they are grouped by geography. English, Irish, Asian, Russian, American, South American. If I were familiar with all the works, I'm certain I'd notice the volumes were organized down to the region, province, oblast, or state.

A dozen or so books on fencing or rowing—both with shirtless hot guys alongside history and instruction. An eight-book set of comparative religions. The most interesting titles are on the top shelves, however, art and photography at my eye level. I slip one from the middle of a crowded row: *A Century of Gay Photography 1899-1999*. I carefully open the immaculate hardcover to a black and white of three hairy men naked next to a bird bath on someone's lawn.

That book is the first thing in his home—besides his overly neat, right-angle style—that would make an astute stranger think, "Huh. How about that. He's gay."

I sit down and look through his desk. There are very few personal effects. Some loose foreign coins, rubber-banded notecards for a presentation on Scandinavian fiction, a sketch of a black Labrador. In the bottom drawer, I find what must be a year's supply of those cinnamon candies.

In the center drawer, a neatly folded linen handkerchief hides photos of him as a kid—two grammar school portraits and another of him leaning against a woman I presume is his mom. His mom and he are blowing out a large, turquoise *8* candle that sits atop a chocolate-iced cake in the shape of a car. Neither one of them smiles.

Mr. Stewart looks about twenty in another picture, and he stands awkwardly next to an attractive salt-and-pepper-haired man at least thirty years his senior. The way the guy looks at him, I'm guessing that's not a relative.

In the last picture, he's playing in a pile of dead leaves with an older blonde woman who wears gold-rimmed glasses and a pale-yellow windbreaker. Bringing the photo so close it almost touches the tip of my nose, I try to discern whether that is, indeed, Mr. Stewart rolling around in those leaves. The kid is laughing, which is why I doubt it; in none of the other pictures does he look happy.

When I turn, Mr. Stewart is watching me from the doorway. His hair is wet from the shower, and he wears only a pair of dark gray track pants. "Which photograph is that?" Instead of coming to me and snatching it from my hand, he takes a seat in the only other chair in the room, an angular unit upholstered in velvety apricot material with polished brass legs.

"Is it the one of my grandmother?" he says, nodding when I

　　　　　　　　　

hold it up. "If there's something you want to know about me, please ask. Now's your chance."

Maybe Mr. Stewart is about to give up the facts and feelings I've been wanting, but the only thing that comes to my mind is: "Why is your TV in your office?"

"The bedroom is for sleeping. The living room is for reading. The kitchen is for cooking," he says. "Is there anything else?"

"I don't know. It's like you have no other life but the one I see when I'm with you. What else do you do? Or who do you see?" I approach him and give him the small stack of pictures, hating that my hand trembles when I do. I point to the photos. "Like, who's this guy?"

He moves the salt-and-pepper man to the top of the pile. "We lived together when my grandmother died."

"Like a boyfriend?"

"Something like that."

I take the photo from him and examine the picture. His shoulders were narrower then, his face even leaner. No crow's feet. "You were hot back then. I mean, you're hot now. Don't get me wrong."

He tugs my arm, indicating he wants me to plop down on his lap. I shake my head. That's too weird. Instead, I sit next to him on the thick arm of his chair, tapping the photo with my pinkie. "Was it...like us?"

"No," he says, shifting a few inches closer to me, "not like us."

And why not? What's different? Am I better or worse? I can't just be different; there's always a better than/worse than. "Were you in love with him? Have you ever been in love with someone?"

"Of course," he says in a tone that suggests I'm silly for asking.

"When was the last time you had a boyfriend?"

"A year or so ago. He moved to Holland."

"Holland?" I wrinkle my nose. "I know nothing about Holland. There's probably a reason for that."

"The reason is that you're seventeen. There is little of interest to you other than sex, marijuana, and parties."

"When you were seventeen, weren't those things on your mind?"

"I already felt thirty when I was seventeen. I had to grow up fast," he says and pats my leg. "Daniel, I want to ask you something."

I mimic him and pat his knee. "Sure."

"Your *episode* last night—the drugs, the disobedience. Do you understand it happened because you shared the story about your father with me? I assume it's a pattern, getting close and pulling away."

I stand and look down at him, raising my brow. "Disobedience?"

"I mean no offense," he says. "I only want you to think about it. Isn't it possible? And as we continue to grow closer, I expect you'll rebel occasionally."

I toss the photo onto his messy desk. "I have a life outside of coming here and getting fucked, you know?"

"Your life is off course. I want what's best for you."

I am uneasy about what was said and what remains to be said. *Disobedience?* "Look, I like coming here a lot, but—"

"It's okay. We don't need to talk about it now." He gets up, caresses my shoulder, and tugs on my arm so I'll follow him. On our way downstairs, he stops and looks back at me. "Does your mother notice when you don't come home at night?"

"I—my—what?" I squint at him, upset that he's asked a question he should know the answer to. "You know she doesn't. Don't grind it in, man."

"I only asked because I think it would be a good idea for you to sleep here tonight. It's late. It's a weekend. Would you like that?"

I admire his bare arm. The veins and lean muscles are sexy. I contemplate that limb draped over me all night while I sweat beneath it, dying to go to the bathroom but wanting to avoid waking him. I can picture the awkward moment when his alarm sounds, when we look at each other over the pillows, and I force a smile. I conjure up a tense breakfast and morning rituals and exactly what he thinks changes because I slept in his bed rather than only fucking in it.

Then, I imagine the long walk home in the cold before smoking myself to sleep at dawn, and I say, yes, sure, a sleepover sounds nice.

*

Mr. Stewart's routine is to turn it at eleven. It's quarter-till, and while I'm itching for weed, he's already shutting down: dishwasher cleared, thermostat lowered, doors locked. Fear strikes at this point. With any forethought, I would have realized this was a shit plan. I can't smoke or watch TV. What am I going to do while I wait for sleep?

"It's freezing in here," I say. "Can we turn the heat back up?" He ignores me, and I sigh, fidgeting in the high-thread-count hell. Another orgasm is the only thing between me and the long, lonely night. "I want to fuck again."

When I grope for his cock, he shifts out of my reach. "Calm yourself. It's unhealthy to use sex as a distraction. You're restless. Instead of what I assume is your ritual of passing out rather than *going to sleep*, let's try the natural method. I'm right here. You can wake me up if it's unbearable."

"Can I go watch TV?"

"I'd rather you didn't."

"Does that mean I can't, or is it just your preference?"

"Both. If you'd like to read, you can choose a book and bring it in here. I don't mind if you keep your light on."

My indecision outlasts his consciousness. His breathing becomes rhythmic and shallow. I read on my phone, browse the Internet, watch captioned videos and podcasts. Sleeping in someone else's bed sucks. Sleeping with someone else who likes to tuck himself in like a sausage in a roll, leaving me a scrap of blanket while keeping the room temperature at absolute zero is fucking impossible.

I go to his bathroom and jerk off. I try not to come for as long as possible, only so I don't have to be alone with my thoughts. Afterwards, I scroll through messages from Ollie, who never expects a response, and the three from Jesse, who was the subject of my fantasies a moment ago. It's late but not late enough to guarantee he's asleep. I write back: *Sorry. I slept all day. You?* Five minutes pass. No reply comes.

I am keen to see the sun. I check my phone too often; five minutes seem like an hour, and an hour feels like: *why the fuck isn't the sun out yet?*

Mr. Stewart keeps no alcohol. *It's poison.* Instead, I down two bottles of sparkling water and sit at his square dining room table, absorbing the surroundings and the way I fit into them.

I am the disobedient mutt at the dog show. I am tap water. I'd be best suited for his broom closet, and even then, I'd bring down the property value. I am too boorish to be here.

Perhaps I'm only "exceptional" because he's made an exception for a boy too crude and too disheveled to go with his tidy life. Despite my flaws, he allows me to come around. Of course, I draw a comparison between my father and Mr. Stewart. As any exceptional person would.

I stare at my backpack, jiggle my legs, bite my lip. I touch the zipper. An observer might say I'm *caressing* the zipper. If I smoke, he'll know. I could go outside, down the block, and he'll still know. If I sleep here again, I'm going to need edibles.

After some ho-humming, I snoop around his linen closet and bathroom cabinets. I've seen it all before. Not much of interest: no second toothbrush, unfamiliar cologne or deodorant, or mystery prescription bottles. No evidence of another person having ever been here. In my home, there's always a trail of offloaded crap from my mom's exes: Freddy's Paxil in the kitchen, Allen's paper bag of condoms in the guest bathroom, Dave's defunct keyboard in our garage. We still get mail addressed to *Mr. Justin Fallston*, who only stuck around a month or two.

When the first light comes through Mr. Stewart's window, I crawl under the sliver of sheet I was allotted. I poke his shoulder. I poke him again, and he shifts his legs, cracking his toes. I close my eyes and fake a gentle snore.

Without a good morning, Mr. Stewart leaves the bedroom and returns with mouthwash breath. In bed, he scoots close to me. His cool minty lips brush against my warm ear. "Wake up, Daniel." He eases the sheet down my body and digs my cock out my boxers.

I've never been woken up with a blowjob. I've never woken up with anyone at all. He teases and sucks me. My hand hovers over his head. Usually, I would never touch his daily tamed and tidy hair, but now I indulge myself, grabbing two fists of his slept-on mess. The sucking stops. He rolls my body to one side and slaps my ass decisively. "Stand up."

He's already hard but gives himself a couple strokes for show. His nostrils flare, and his forearms flex. He rolls a condom down his cock, lubes up, and spins me by my shoulder. Kicking my feet apart, he pushes me forward until my cheek hits the mattress. My lips are squished and open. I drool.

"Tell me about the other night," he says. "What drugs were you doing?"

I smile against the sheet. "All drugs."

"With Jesse?"

Jesse is that last thing I want to think about right now. I envision him watching me and cringe. "Can you not talk so much?"

Mr. Stewart pushes a wet finger into my asshole. "Have you had a lot of sexual partners?"

I feel ridiculous having a conversation while my ass is in the air. "What's a lot?"

"You tell me."

"I don't know Four. Maybe five?"

"Are you being truthful?"

People have been making me come for three years. It's closer to fifty-five. Or eighty-five. I have no idea. I nod and then turn my face into the mattress. Mr. Stewart grabs my ass, smacks it, and stuns me with what feels like a hard pinch where the slap still stings. With that, he guides his cock inside of me.

He comes quickly. "Don't move." I stay still while he catches his breath, his cock softening, his hand between my shoulder blades keeping me in place. With one step backwards, his penis falls out of my ass. The condom snaps, and he folds it in a tissue before placing it on the bedside table on top of another tissue.

I'm allowed to turn. I only need to wrap my hand around the shaft and give myself three of the slowest, shortest pulls I can manage before I start to leak. My abdominal muscles lurch like I'm already spilling my load.

"Don't come yet," he says and sits in front of me on the edge of the bed. He admires my legs and chest, never once looking at my face.

My cock, heavy with blood, pulses in my hand. If I squeeze more firmly or increase my speed, I will ejaculate. A thin line of clear cum drools out of me. "I can't last."

His hand covers mine and halts my stroke. *"Slow down."* I return to full speed as soon as his hand moves. Grabbing my wrist, he pries my hand off my swollen cock. "If you can't control yourself, I'll do it for you. Can you control yourself?" The pressure around my wrist eases, but I'm still restrained.

I drop my head and blow out a frustrated breath. Sweat tickles my scalp. "Could you do it, then? What the fuck."

"Tell me. If not Jesse, who else?"

"No one." My hand attempts a sneaky side approach to my dick. I wince when he knocks it away.

"Assure me." Holding both my arms at my side, he shakes me once. *"Tell me."* One more shake. Then another.

"Nothing—no one."

He strokes my cock. "Only me?"

"Yeah. You." My voice quakes as his fist works cum out of me.

"And Jesse?"

"No. Not—"

"Listen to me," he says as I shoot all over the hardwood floor between us. "If you touch him again, you'll find this is as forgiving as I get."

Naked, in the bathroom, I grab my hip, twisting my torso so I can see the source of discomfort. The bruise leftover from his pinch excites and disturbs me. If this is lenient, my curiosity about the range of his temper is piqued.

Since Jesse doesn't touch me at school, I have no trouble following Mr. Stewart's latest directive. I stifle conversation, too. Jesse says, "Hey, Dan." I say, "Hey, Jesse," or sometimes, "Hey, man," as though I hadn't sucked his dick and kissed him and told him how much I liked him.

Dentist appointments, tennis club meetings, and Calculus homework. A bank of excuses has me too busy in the evenings and on the weekends to make time for Jesse. He's not buying it at all. His kindness keeps him quiet. Ollie stays out of it, and Jesse has too much dignity to pester him anyway.

After a couple weeks of routine—school and tennis, getting

fucked and skipping parties—I decide to take a day off from some of it and skip school and tennis practice.

I wake up mid-afternoon. I shower and smoke a bowl. When I know school is over, I wait for Mr. Stewart's text, one of two words any dog would know. *Come* or *stay*. The longest message I've received from him was a week ago: *Do not come here. Go home.* His neighbor's pipes exploded.

Today's beats that, though: *Be sober when you get here at 7 or I'm sending you home.*

I walk there slowly because I am fucked up. I walk even more slowly because I'm unsure if this is what I want to be doing right now. By the time I arrive, a piece of gum, some eye drops, and my sweat camouflage any residual weed stink or bliss.

I pause in the garage and pull out my phone. I bring up Jesse's number. I want to text him. I want just a toe to remain in his water. I want him to be there when I'm ready, and I don't know what words will make that happen. I put away my phone and trudge up the stairs to Mr. Stewart's office.

He sits at the desk and uses a letter opener to tear through an envelope. He wears a dress shirt, and he's loosened his collar and tie. He speaks without looking up. "Where were you today?"

I move a pile of papers and sit on the apricot chair. "Home." My eyes do the rounds. Nothing's changed from when I last looked, including the remarkable mounds of paper on his desk.

"Your truancy is out of hand.," he says.

"If you keep nagging me about shit, I'm going to stop coming here."

"I doubt that." He sniffs and looks me up and down before tearing into another piece of mail, this time a large manila envelope. "I truly doubt that."

"You know," I say, defensive, "before you, I wasn't scrapping for sex. I got what I wanted."

He sits back and rubs his stubble, yawning. "Yes, I imagine no one else did, however."

"What's your problem today?" I throw my leg over the arm of the chair and touch the edge of his desk with my foot. He shakes his head once. I touch it again. The letter opener meets the sole of my shoe. One prod, and my foot falls off the desk. I laugh. "You want to fight or something?"

"I've had a long day," he says, cracking his neck. "Wait for me in the bedroom. Get undressed. Fold your clothes."

"Ask nicely."

He looks up suddenly and squints his eyes. "Are you high right now?"

I smile. "You do want to fight, don't you?"

"Jesus Christ, Daniel." He drops the letter opener. "Get in the bedroom. Take off your clothes. You know what you're good at."

It takes me several moments to decide that I will, indeed, go to his bedroom and not home like my first instinct tells me I should. As I hoist myself out of the chair, Mr. Stewart begins to backtrack, apologize, explain himself. It's the first time I've heard him stutter. He skips-starts several sentences, and I snap at him. "Shut up. You can't smooth that over."

I go to his bedroom. As I hear him close his office door and pad across the small hallway, I feel ambivalent about him coming after me. I'd be just as happy if he went downstairs. I would take a nap.

I'm sitting fully clothed on the edge of the bed when he enters. I know his body language well enough to recognize he's trying to pull off sexy or sorry with his slow glide across the room. He's accomplishing neither.

He stands in front of me, spreading my knees with his soft touch and wedging his body in between my opened legs. I look up at him. The lamp on the guest side of his bed sheds light on his crow's feet, the tendons in his neck, his full lips. He runs his hand through my hair, as he did on *The Crucible* day. I'm ambivalent about this, too.

He takes my chin in his hand. Instead of rekindling the thrill I felt that day, the gesture only makes me imagine Jackie's hand on Jesse's cheek that night at the diner, what feels like a decade ago. I push Mr. Stewart's hand away from my face. "I don't like that."

He clears his throat, stepping away from me, forgoing the niceties. "Very well. If you want to act like a child, why don't you hide that pout in the pillow." He snickers at his own joke. At his dresser, he removes his cufflinks, turning his head toward me, eyebrows raised. "Are you going to take off your clothes?"

As he unbuttons his shirt, I strip as fast as I can. I don't want him to watch me get undressed; it's one of his favorite things to do. I lie down in the middle of the bed and stroke my cock. I want to get hard, to show off an amazing erection, despite his comments, but I can't. I stay soft.

When he's naked, he flips on his ceiling fan, which whirrs at a lazy speed, kicking up a light breeze. He removes the black bottle of lube from the drawer and plants himself by the side of the bed. The pillow he shoves under my ass is firm and barely sinks with my weight. He crawls across the mattress and kneels before me, squirting some lube in his hand. Lifting my legs, he folds me in half until my knees are at my ears. I cover my dick with both hands.

"Maybe you can suck me," I say and motion to my plump but floppy penis. "I'm not really into it yet."

"You'll get into it." He opens me up with a couple of fingers, slides his cock in too quickly, and pumps. For a few minutes, I lie there, watching the fan. Should I let him finish or insist he stop? I tense and try to push him out of me. "No," he says. "Relax."

"Let's stop just for a minute. Is that okay?"

"I suggest we proceed," he says, pausing mid-stroke, "or I will be forced to believe you've been sated elsewhere."

I seize his forearms and squeeze. "Just wait. Stop."

He pushes off my knees and sits back on his haunches, his penis leaving my body. "You're tiresome today."

"So are you. I need water." I roll off the bed, pushing his shoulder. As I leave, he calls my name. Not an *I'm-sorry* call. More of a *now-you're-even-more-tiresome* call.

I head downstairs, naked, flaccid, and shaky. After I find my backpack, I roll a blunt, leaving the discarded cigar tobacco in his kitchen sink without rinsing it down the drain. Having a relaxing, rebellious smoke in his home feels good. I enjoy several puffs. My satisfaction diminishes when he doesn't come looking for me after ten minutes.

Upstairs, he's in bed, still naked, his hands behind his head, legs outspread, erection on display. He notices the blunt, and his mouth gapes.

I shake my lighter. "Smoke with me."

"Do not light that again," he warns. "It's disgusting, not to mention illegal, and this is my home."

Reporting me for weed pales in comparison for me turning over on him for fucking my ass. I light it and take a hit. A faint click-click sound follows every full rotation of the fan, and I count twelve click-clicks before I say something I hope will cause a fight. "Hey, didn't you tell me you were going to come to one of my matches? When are you going to do that?"

He points at the joint. "Extinguish that."

My penis is in his eye line, and his disapproval has brought it to life. I take another hit and blow smoke in his direction, pleased that he's fixated on my cock and no longer the weed. "Come to a match," I say. "You said you would. You gave your word."

"Things have changed. Don't be obtuse."

"How is that obtuse? No one's going to see you at my match and automatically think we're fucking." I cup my hand under the blunt. "Where do you want me to ash this?"

"I don't. Take it to the bathroom and drop it in the toilet."

I puff again and pace in front of his dresser. "You know what I don't know? What you think about me. I mean, really, what do you think about me? You always seem like you're so disappointed in everything I do."

"If you don't know what I think of you by now—"

"How would I know? Tell me. What *do* you think? Or feel? Or whatever."

He sighs, leaves, and returns within a minute, holding a glass of water and motioning to my bad habit. When I shake my head, he snatches the blunt from my fingers, dropping it in the water. "Usually, I am quite fond of you. Right now, however..."

"Fond? Fond sounds like a Victorian novel.'"

He plucks a tissue from the box and lays it across his nightstand, placing the cup of water on it. "How could you possibly expect me to have stronger feelings when you disrespect me by having sex with other people?"

"I'm not having sex with other people."

"You disrespect me further by lying about it?"

I do a dead fall onto his bed, pressing my shoulder blades into his mattress. "Jesus? Can we not—"

"Daniel, I know you're young, and I know this is an unusual situation." He sits next to me and tries to cover my body below the waist with his blanket. I roll out of his reach. He continues, "I'm not going to share you. You need to choose."

"There's nothing to choose between."

"Do you think I don't notice how Jesse looks at you in class?"

"Holy shit," I say, clapping my hand over my eyes. "I told you. We're just friends."

"I see no evidence of 'just friends' on his face."

"So, when I'm not here, what do you want me to do? Sit in my room and eat chicken and vegetables and go to bed at nine?"

"Yes," he says, "when you're not here, that's exactly what I want you to do. That's what a healthy person would do."

There's little about this situation that's healthy. If I were watching this movie, I'd be bored already, having guessed the trajectory, the downward spiral, the inevitable collapse. If I'm seeing it and he's not, I'm curious about what he predicts will happen.

Using my heels as an anchor on the end of the bed, I pull my body away from him and hop up. My heap of clothes in the corner seems far away. I would rather he not watch me retrieve them. It's the first step to getting out of here, though. "I need to go. I'm tired. You want me back tomorrow or not?"

"Yes, of course. I want to see you as much as I can."

"You're not acting like it."

His eyes stay on me as I dress. I put on my shorts and pants, muttering loudly enough so he will hear my complaints about his bad mood, his nonsense weed rules, and my soft cock. Instead of engaging me, he lies down, fishes a thin paperback from his night table drawer, and begins to read. After only a few seconds, he places the book beside him. I ready myself for a lecture; instead, he fluffs his pillow and picks up the book again.

I shower and dress and leave without saying goodbye.

Because Ollie told me Jesse would be in attendance, I take the night off from seeing Mr. Stewart and go to a party at Brad's. My heart beats faster when, on my way to the kitchen, I spot Jesse in the hallway. He's exchanging bills for bags.

Rather than the crowd I used to see every weekend, this place is full of kids who usually frown on mainstream events. Pastimes include pretending to be too good for everything, practicing the art of the vacant stare, and moping in corners.

Jesse is the hub of this shindig. For the sake of profit, he blends with the nihilists, anarchists, and Dadaists—I've been told what that means three times tonight—as if his parents hatched a full-blooded misanthrope.

Although we move in separate circles tonight, I enjoy watching Jesse make new contacts. His sincerity always invites a hand on his shoulder or a whisper in his ear. Some hands and whispers ignite my jealous side.

After an hour, Ollie and I sit on the couch. He's tipsy, depressed about a short-lived girlfriend who broke his heart. He motions impatiently for me to take the joint he pinches between thumb and forefinger. "I'm thinking about letting *you* suck my dick."

"And I'm thinking about a polite decline."

He points at Jesse, who's been cornered by a skittish black-clad group of girls. "Your boy's quite a capitalist." Scanning the room, Ollie shakes his head at the crowd. "Look at these fuckers."

"They're not bad," I say, stealing the joint from him. "I've had a few blowjobs from this bunch."

"Any fangs?"

"Like him." I gesture to one whose face is smooth and beautiful and who had the patience of a seeing-eye dog. Vincent. Great blowjob.

"He's on his way," Ollie says. "I think you just gave him the signal for another round."

Vincent bumps my leg with his and snatches the weed out of my hand. Pot makes me pliable, and he slips between my legs with ease, perching on my thigh. "You smoke too much, Dan." The puff he takes is quick and for show only. He sticks the joint back in my mouth. "What are you two doing here? This is not your usual rabble."

I shake my leg, but Vincent hangs on and stays put. Ollie's fist comes down lightly on my shoulder. "Good luck with all this. I'm going to see if there's a miserable chick in mourning that wants to suck on my balls."

When we're alone, Vincent swings around and straddles my lap. He grinds. I start to get hard. He is triumphant and thinks that earns him the right to lick my ear. "You with anyone tonight?"

One and one-half of my eyeballs are on Jesse. "I hope so."

His lips press against my ear. "Room full of talent."

"Yeah. Not one of your doomsayers, though." I point at Jesse, who's charming a small group of girls with an anecdote he peppers with full body animation. "Him."

Just then, Jesse sees me for the first time tonight. It's difficult to tell if he's more surprised by my entanglement, or if Vincent, who does a double take, is more awed by my disclosure. "The kid selling weed?"

I part my knees, and Vincent slips between them. "You need to get off me." He repositions himself and squeezes my legs together with his before dropping a hand between us and rubbing my penis. I shift and poke him in the shoulder. "Seriously, get up."

Rattled and resolute are states of being Jesse shuns, either on principle or because of sheer intoxication. I'm witnessing a watered-down version, though, as he walks toward us, his spine straighter than I've ever seen, his eyebrows raised mid-forehead. Vincent says, "I didn't know he had it in him. I'm not getting my ass beat over you. Later."

"Fuck off somewhere else," Jesse says to Vincent as he retreats. He kicks my shoe. "Do you have a fan club everywhere you go? How have you fucked around with so many people?" He stares at me in amazement. "Every time I see you in public, which is, like, *never* these days, there's some asshole who knows you."

"It's not like that." I reach up to him. He smacks my hand away. Not hard, but enough that it stings my skin. A few people look over at us.

"What's it like, then? That's either someone you fucked," he says and points to Vincent across the room, "or someone you were going to fuck."

Before I can speak, Jesse's gone.

Oh, to get off the couch in a fast and composed fashion. That hour has long since passed. I'm able to stand by hanging onto the belt of a guy in front of me who does not seem to mind. I trade the quarter joint for the kindness.

Front door, obviously. That's where I would have gone. Outside, Jesse leans against a car that's not his, inhaling a lungful of smoke with every breath he takes. When I'm near him, he says, "Let's just rewind about five minutes, okay?"

I lean against the car, too. The quick, unsteady pursuit has me dizzy. That he's upset has me queasy. I take his cigarette out of his mouth and toss it into the street. "We don't have to rewind."

"Yeah, Jesus," he says, embarrassed and staring at his feet. "Did everyone see that?"

I laugh. "I think everyone did."

"Really, though," he says and looks at me, "how many guys?"

"I don't know. A few. A lot. It's no big deal." My attention is drawn to a car creeping by the house. It's the second time it has, and I recognize it for a reason beyond that. Black Lexus. I'm sure it's a coincidence, but I tug on Jesse's coat anyway. "Let's go inside. It's cold."

He pulls his sleeve from my hand. "Jackie said you have two phones. Why do you have two phones? You don't deal. You're not a narc. Why do you have burner phones? Do you have one on you now?"

I twist away when he reached for my coat pocket. "No. It's my mom—"

"Yeah. Your mom. Ollie. Wrong numbers. How do you do it? You look good. I get it. But there's something—did you get me the way you got all the other guys you fucked?"

I give the question its due respect with a few moments of silence. "You make it sound like I'm some sort of predator."

"You make me feel like you are." He tilts his head to one side. "Can I see it? The phone?" When I take too long thinking of an excuse, Jesse pushes past me, his shoulder knocking my arm. "Forget it."

I trot after him. "Can we just go somewhere else? I want to talk, but just someplace else."

I follow him to Brad's backyard, a modest rectangle surrounded by a grayed wooden fence. Dead leaves from several autumns cover the lawn, a landscape of red cups and beer bottles for as far as I can see.

Jesse stops, turns, and shoves me against the house. My head hits the wall with a thump. The siding creaks while he fumbles inside my clothes and slides his hand down my pants. Just as I feel his fingers against my half hard penis, his eyes snap open. "What did you do when I left your place the other night?"

I want him to unzip me, maul me, kiss me, but there's no way I'm going to say the right thing to facilitate that. "Nothing. I was tired."

His disbelief is obvious. Despite that, he can't get enough of me. We rub against each other, and he lets me kiss him.

Light penetrates my eyelids. With my mouth still on Jesse's, I peek at the car coasting down the street. This is its third run. That the vehicle is a shiny black Lexus proves nothing. It's the frequency that's unsettling. It could only be a dealer, a pedophile, or a stalker. It's quite late for pedophiles, and Brad is the neighborhood dealer. The stalker might be mine.

I honor my suspicions by telling Jesse I want to be alone with him somewhere else. "Can we just go to your house?"

He laughs as if I asked him for a kidney. "Your balls, man. I can't believe you." When I try to kiss him again, he pulls away and sighs. "Fuck it. Fine. My house."

He drives in silence. I spend the entire ride wondering if we're going to fuck or fight when we get to his house. I follow him inside, and there are lights on in the dining room, off to the right side of the house. We listen. No voices. He signals with a tilt of his head that I should follow him upstairs.

Once we're in his bedroom, we undress quickly, still in silence. Jesse has never gone this long without smiling. He blows me like he's angry—sucking and squeezing, sometimes too hard—and we don't look at each other's face until after we come, me in his mouth, him in his hand.

Jesse's wet chin shines in the light of his phone. He wipes his mouth on my discarded T-shirt. After cracking the window, he comes to me on the bed. We are side-by-side and naked in the dark, our backs against the cold wall.

"I'm supposed to be grounded," he says. "Calculus test. I got a C." He lights a joint, takes a hit, and passes it to me.

"Your parents get torn up about a C?"

"They do."

On the floor next to his bed, my *everyday* phone—not the Mr. Stewart phone, which I left in my coat pocket—vibrates for a third time since we've been in his room. Jesse did well for the first two notifications, but now he clicks his tongue. "You want to get that? Maybe it's your *mom*. Or the guy you'd be with if you weren't here."

I pick up the phone, check it first, and find several messages from Ollie, two of which are about his athlete's foot, the other one about a new girl he'd like to fuck: *She's actually doing coke. Have you ever done coke?* I hand Jesse my phone. "See? Just bullshit."

"Yeah," he says, recalling the party we left, "everyone there likes to be jittery. I was making no money tonight." Jesse's leg shakes against mine like a rough motor. "So, what the fuck happened the other night?"

I free my phone from his grasp and place it face down next to his bed. "I told you. I was tired."

"Tired? For days and days? You barely even talk to me."

"It's not a big deal. Besides, I'm here now."

His disingenuous laugh is louder than any noise we've made in an hour. "Like you're doing me a favor?"

As much anxiety as I have over what this conversation will precipitate, I understand there's no way I can get around having it. "Look, I know what you're thinking, and even if I were fucking someone, you don't need to worry about it."

His mouth falls open. "What does that mean?"

"It means I'm always safe."

His eyebrows draw together. "Fuck you. I'm not fucking worried about that shit. Are you kidding me?"

I know turning the tables is a coward's move. I have no other defense, and I don't want to lie to him. "You're still seeing Jackie."

"That's different." Jesse shifts his body. Our skin unsticks. He moves again, and his heat disappears.

My cock is still out and wet. No one with his deflating penis swinging loose should start an argument, but I'm doing it anyway. "How is that fucking different?"

As if the foot we are apart is still too close for his liking, he drags his blanket between us. There's no chance our flesh will accidentally touch. "I sell weed with her brother," he says. "You know what she's like. We hooked up sometimes when we were bored. She knows people at parties. She gives me rides sometimes. Buys me food."

I scoff and get out of bed. "I'm glad she's such an asset."

Soon, I'll be dressed and out the door. None of this has gone well. I put on my pants and search for the rest of my clothes. When I can't find them, I turn on his lamp and catch a glimpse of his naked body before snatching my shoes from under his bed.

"Why don't you get what I'm saying here?" Jesse says. "I don't want to do that anymore. You need flash cards? Or some fucking flag signals? See me. Just see me. Whatever you're doing—endless hand jobs or blowjobs or whatever the fuck else—stop it and just see me."

Then, it sinks in. Jesse's exposed. He doesn't scurry to find his clothes. He doesn't dive to turn out the light. He doesn't cross his arms over his chest or turn toward the wall. He only frowns and watches me. His docile demeanor makes all the grumbling and huffing I'm doing seem absurd. I drop my shoes.

His attention darts from my eyes to the window to his aloe plant. While ignoring me, Jesse gnaws despondently on his fingernails. His other hand twitches and rests on his hip.

"Jesse," I say. "I like you a lot, but it's just—it's just bad timing. I can't."

My words undermine his obvious struggle to be as vulnerable as he's probably ever been. He crosses one arm over his body, turns off the light, and reaches for his T-shirt and jeans. When he flops back onto the bed and lights up, his face glows orange in the flame of the lighter. "You should go."

I dawdle, hoping he'll change his mind. When it's obvious he won't, I exit but linger in the hallway. The air is humid, like a bathroom after a shower. I listen for his movements as I place my hand on top of the doorknob. I twist it slowly, pushing open the door several inches. He's in the same position, taking a pull from the joint and focusing on the plume of smoke he exhales.

I'm scared to admit what I want, but I push the words out. "I don't want to leave with you angry."

He turns to me. I wait for his smile, a bit of rejoicing. Instead of an invitation back to his bed, Jesse yawns. "Do me a favor," he says. "If you pass my parents on the way out, try not to look like we just fucked."

I back out of the room. Once again, I am alone in the dark hallway. I make myself walk away. I am the sort of sad that makes it hard to swallow.

I lie in bed for hours, watching TV while composing confessional and regretful texts to Jesse. I send none of them. Instead I read, reread, and delete each, only to write another, more pathetic than the last. My body tenses while I write. I groan each time I erase. It is useless to pressure him, not until I'm unencumbered and can make a genuine overture.

I'm exhausted yet wired. I swap my phone for my pipe and smoke for the first time since I got home. Pulling up my blanket to my chin, I close my eyes and fantasize about ending things with Mr. Stewart. The idea of telling him the truth sours my stomach: *You're right about Jesse and me.* It will precipitate a lecture about my self-degradation and bad judgment.

I drift off but wake moments later, anxious, desperate for a plan. I smoke more, get too high, and consider texting Mr. Stewart a list of reasons why we should break up, all so I don't have to do it in person. But no assertion I can think of would be heartfelt or true.

I'm worried you'll get caught.

I think my mom might know something.

We should stop before I start to have feelings.

In a moment of lucidity, I put my phone back in the drawer. Texting him was a worse idea than sending Jesse all those mawkish messages.

It would be simple to stop going to Mr. Stewart's house. I consider this coward's tactic, disappearing while in plain sight. There is nothing Mr. Stewart could do. We would return to how things were the first week of school, before he took an initial interest in me, the day he asked me to stay behind to elaborate on my "compelling insight" about the Beat poets.

If my father were here—and, say, statutory rape wasn't part of the scenario—I know he would raise an eyebrow at my bloodless strategy. He would ask me if that was the sort of reputation I wanted, or would I rather be noble, direct, respectful?

I decide it will have to be a conversation. I also decide that it will go best if I do it quickly, after school.

The next day, although we argued, seeing Jesse gives me comfort. When we make eye contact in English and again in Genetics, he only raises his chin and walks by. I am thankful he bothers with any acknowledgment at all.

As planned, I go to Mr. Stewart's classroom after school. He's not there. I wait by my desk, feeling more nervous as time passes. Too bright, too lonely, and stinking too much of dust kicked up from the forced heat, the empty room warns me to turn tail and get an actual plan together. I only have one sentence rehearsed: "I don't want us to see each other anymore."

I'm still contemplating leaving when he appears in the doorway a minute later. Seeing me, he pauses. "Hello. Don't you have practice?" Without waiting for my answer, he closes the door and sits behind his desk. I approach, my posture straight and stiff, ready to state my business and then take off. I stuff my hand into my front right pocket, clutching the phone I will return to him. Just as I clear my throat, he speaks. "Did you receive my texts last night?"

Caught off guard, my stance softens with the shift in mood. "I—"

"No excuses," he interrupts. "You ignored them. And how absurd is it that you think humiliating yourself in the middle of the street with a drug addict is an acceptable way to spend an evening? Is that your usual routine?"

Dread runs through me as my queasy guts roll. "That was you?"

"Yes, of course." He leans back in his chair, folding his hands over his solar plexus. "You didn't respond to my messages. I wanted to make sure you were okay."

"How did you—" I shake my head. "No, never mind. I don't care. It just makes this easier." I roll my shoulders back to relax myself, making sure I speak clearly. "I don't think we should see each other anymore."

After a quiet laugh, he pulls a small protein bar out of his desk drawer, peeling back the wrapper. "I've been expecting this conversation for a couple of days. The closer we get, the more you push me away. Why don't you meet me at my place later, and we'll speak about it there?"

"No." I shake my head several times. "That's okay. Look, I really liked being with you, but I'm just not into it as much as I was." I take the phone he gave me out of my pocket and slide it across the desk.

He picks up a pen and, with it, slides the phone back to me. "No, thank you."

"Take it." I push the phone toward him again.

He cocks his head and brandishes the partially unwrapped protein bar at me. "Would you like some?" I curl my lip at his offer, and he shrugs before nodding at the phone. "Put that away. You're being a child. I'll speak to you about it tonight. Dinner is at seven."

"I'm not coming over."

He takes a small bite of his bar and chews slowly, his Adam's apple bobbing as the food goes down. "I've been meaning to ask you. Have you decided on Princeton? You know they discourage a downturn in performance, especially in the last semester."

I press my lips together, briefly wondering if he's headed for some sort of blackmail here. If he is, it's a bold and impressive move from someone who's fucking his student. He is too smart to tangle with me like that, unless he figures tossing extortion on the pile is no issue when you're racking up felonies.

After I broke it off, I figured we'd spend the rest of the year ignoring each other in class. I supposed he might glare at me in the halls. I knew there was even a chance he could call me to the guidance office several times and verbally abuse me. All that, but I never thought he'd fuck with my grades or my future.

I tilt my head, silently assessing the meaning of his last statement. When he grins, I think, yes, that is exactly where he's going with this. I return the grin and counter with my own threat. "Do you ever think about if anyone finds out? Like my mom. What if I tell her?"

He takes a bite of the bar, skipping the requisite twenty chews per side before he swallows hurriedly. "What do you think she'll do with that information? Call the police?" He chortles. "She's next to worthless. The dynamic between you both disturbs me."

"It's just the everyday dynamic. It's not the my-son's-getting-fucked-by-his-English-teacher dynamic."

"Lower your voice," he warns and tosses the uneaten half of the bar into the trash.

"Look," I say more quietly while circling his desk to be nearer to him. He quickly stands, meeting me halfway before pushing me backwards with his body and squaring off with me. "You're acting out right now," he says between gritted teeth, moving his face closer to mine. "I'll tolerate it because we're in school, but I suggest you go home and calm down before you come over."

I step back a foot, startled by his sudden aggression. He closes the gap between us, his forefinger pressing my breastbone. "You think you're in love with a boy whose name you'll forget in six months. Trust me. He'll forget you in three." His voice has grown too loud, and he reduces it to a harsh whisper. "God, you are unbelievably selfish. Do you enjoy hurting me?"

"Are you kidding?" I poke his chest as he does mine several times before he bats my hand away. "I'm here, being honest. I could have blown you off."

Mr. Stewart glances at the door and then grabs my chin with warm, slightly damp fingers. He pulls my face so close I could count his eyelashes. "Don't push this," he says, the smell of his breath tinged with the sweetness of the protein bar. "You understand? Pick up your fucking phone, finish your tantrum at home, and I will see you at seven."

He snaps my chin to the side as he releases it. After kicking his chair out from the desk, he drops into the seat while mumbling to himself. Several sticky notes serve as placeholders in his copy of *Leaves of Grass*. He strips them from each bookmarked page with a steady hand and tosses them in the trash can behind him before looking up at me. "Why are you still here?"

"I'm not coming over," I say, leaving my phone on his desk and heading for the door. "If you like me at all, you'll leave me alone."

"It's precisely because I like you that I will not do that."

"Fine. Wait for me. See what happens." I leave and slam the

door, precisely because I know it will piss him off. My hands shake. Before I head to tennis, I collect myself in the alcove of an empty classroom.

I hurry through tennis and shower. Ollie didn't have basketball practice today, so I have to walk home. I stop at the first intersection, believing I've figured out the perfect message to send to Jesse. I haven't.

On my phone, my fingers fly over the letters, the send button, and a string of texts speed Jesse's way.

Are you okay?

Just text back.

It was a dumb argument.

I walk to Ollie's. His front door is open, which is usual, and I let myself in. In the dining room, his three Shepherds lift their heads an inch before stretching out even more on the cool wood floor. The TV in Ollie's room is on. I push open his door, close it behind me, and flop down next to him on the bed.

He turns his head slightly in my direction, hesitant to look away from the woman on the screen, who's licking whatever phallic items are in sight, seeing how deep she can go. "I coulda been jerking off or something. Don't you knock?"

"Please," I say. "I know you do that shit in the bathroom. Remember when your mom asked me if you were constipated from all the mac and cheese?"

He kicks my shin. "Get off my bed. You're all sweaty." When I wipe my forehead with his blanket, he says, "Gross. Knock it off, motherfucker."

"What's gross is your blanket. Smells like a dirty aquarium." I shove the offensive blue material in his face, ducking his follow-up punch. "Hey, guess what. I broke up with Stewart."

He looks impressed. "Really? Is he on suicide watch?"

"He was more pissed than upset." I find the remote and turn off the TV. "You have any idea where Jesse's gonna be tonight?"

"Brad's probably."

"Can we go to Brad's?"

He gets up and looks in his dresser for a clean pair of jeans to slide over his red and green boxers. "Yeah, after dinner, we can go to Brad's. You want to stay? It's fish sticks."

Fish sticks, soggy green beans, and tater tots fill my plate; neither of Ollie's parents has ever made anything from scratch. I eat quickly, slipping my tater tots to the Shepherds underneath the table.

We get to Brad's house after nine. About twenty fucked up people have already planted themselves on the floor in the living room and plan to stay there until dawn.

I scan the home for Jesse. I peek in the kitchen. I check Brad's bedroom, where nothing but a guy blowing two others holds my attention for a few seconds. No Jesse. Since he slings weed everywhere for his college fund, I hoped he'd be slinging it here tonight.

I join Ollie and Brad at the kitchen table, a gouged and ravaged thrift-store find. As Brad picks at hardened smears of leftover food on its surface, he brags he paid only fifteen dollars for it and the three matching chairs.

Ollie scoffs. "Fourteen too much."

The three of us share a blunt, and Ollie drinks his beer too fast. He punctuates every sentence with a smelly burp, which he blows at me. They stink worse than Brad's house—a potent mix of bleu cheese, weed, and body odor—but I'm too stoned to care.

Brad wipes his mouth on his sleeve and complains. "Legalizing weed is going to fuck me so bad. What am I going to do then?" he says and slaps his hands against his big belly. "Get a day job?"

"Sales," Ollie says and opens another beer. "Anyone can do sales."

The napkins Brad's been blowing his nose in for the past fifteen minutes are crumpled and swimming in the leftover milk of his cereal bowl, one of three servings he's finished since we've been here.

As I'm studying his stained gray sweats, the generic sort one would buy at a farmer's market, my only lifeline to Jesse appears, and she tucks her skirt under her before sitting side-saddle on my lap. Jackie's necklaces are stuck in her bra and some wisps of hair have loosened from her ponytail, glued with sweat against her delicate neck.

"Danny," she says and kisses my temple, "you illustrious boy." Jerking her thumb over her shoulder, she motions vaguely down the hallway. "You know that guy Terrell Creston? I think he's a candidate for your collection. Just took me ten minutes to get him hard, and he didn't look at me once."

"Yeah," I say, "I think he's just uptight."

"You know him?"

"Tried to."

She pokes the corner of my mouth with a cool finger. "Does your face look like a mudslide because Jesse's not sitting where I am?"

"Yeah, maybe. Why isn't he with you?"

"We're not stapled together. I like Jesse," she says and flutters her eyelashes, "but I like a lot of people."

Brad's foot is barely covered by a white and threadbare sock, and he uses it to get my attention by poking my shin. He crunches down on a celery stick loaded with peanut butter and speaks with his mouth full. "Jesse was here. Somewhere. Maybe he left."

Pining for Jesse, the dispiriting conversation, and the dilapidated furnishings spur my desire to be alone. My motivation takes me only so far as the front yard. The faint noise from a busy road miles away and the thumping bass from the music in Brad's house are the only sounds in the night. I step through overgrown shrubs and knee-high weeds and lean against the small home's grimy siding.

I've never seen another soul on this street, although plenty of warm yellow lights show through windows up and down the block. Brad's told me not to smoke outside, but what will one joint in the bushes hurt, especially when inside there are pounds of weed, rigs, and underage drinking abound?

I take only one hit before the screen door flies open and Jackie yells. "Dan! The toilet! Help."

I extinguish the joint against the siding and tuck it back in its tin. I show myself and shush her. "Be quiet. What about the toilet?"

"There you are. Come here. Come here." She stomps her foot

and grabs me by the elbow, tugging me inside the warm home. As she pilots me down the hallway, she shoves me between my shoulder blades with every step. "*The toilet.*"

I brace myself on the wall. "Wait—stop. What happened?"

She huffs impatiently. "Jesse puked blood in the toilet. Go. Come on."

Jackie guides me through the hallway, swaying bodies ricocheting off us. The door to the hallway bathroom is ajar. The light over the sink is the brightest in the house right now.

Since my dad died, I have had no occasion to panic. There's been nothing left to panic about. What could leave me as raw and trembling as my dad's death? I am numb to personal upheaval; nothing worse can happen to me.

When I see Jesse slumped on the floor, however, I hide my alarm as I go to him and drop to my knees. I pluck his earlobe, shake him by the shoulders, pinch his cheek and arm. I remove his glasses, which sit crookedly on his nose. With my thumb, I lift an eyelid. He moans, and I exhale. "He's just super drunk."

"What if he had too many pills?" Jackie wrings her hands and shakes her head. "Look in the toilet. See?" She points and hops, with each jump dropping her index finger an inch closer to the water in the bowl.

I crawl over and look in. It is red, but it's not blood. I glance up at her. "Calm down. That's licorice. Did he eat licorice?"

"No."

"Did you see him puke that up?"

"*Yes.*"

"Then you saw him puke up licorice." I lean back against the tub. "Get me some soda or something. He's fine. It's no big deal."

But it is a big deal. My gut, head, and heart tell me it is. Jesse's a big deal to me.

Here on this urine-speckled bathroom floor, I suddenly remember the dormant parts of me that I liked, that someone else may like, too. Jesse has resurrected my better nature. I care about him.

Before my dad died, I used to laugh a lot. I used to give a fuck about some things. I was sincere, and I used to try. At this moment,

I want all those qualities back, and I want to share them with Jesse.

I search for a safe place for his glasses, finding one on the edge of the grimy tub, behind the mildewy vinyl shower curtain. I bunch up a towel behind his head and then lie next to him. Guys come in and piss. Girls come in, grumble, and go piss elsewhere. Jackie never returns. I toss my leg over Jesse's, sliding him to me across the dirty tile. The party outside the bathroom door eventually disperses, and the clanking of the baseboard heating competes with a few quiet voices from the other rooms.

I wiggle my hand under Jesse's shirt and place it on his heart. I find my heartbeat with my other hand. My breath synchronizes with his as I doze.

Brad wakes me. He sits on the toilet, eating a deli pickle. The juice dribbles down his arm each time he takes a bite. On the floor at his feet is a pile of crumpled tissues, and he rests the pickle on his knee so he can grab another one from the box behind the toilet. The juice has splattered his sweats. He blows his nose in the tissue before swiping it from elbow to hand. "What are y'all doing?"

"Nothing," I say. "He passed out."

The pickle crunches as he bites down and slurps. His belly jiggles. With a rub and a slap of his fat, he acknowledges his heft with pride. "I meant to ask. You and Jesse are boyfriends now?" When I don't answer, he says, "I always wondered what gay guys get up to."

"Maybe watch some porn?"

"He talks about you a lot." His big toe sticks out of his dirty, holey sock, and he raises his foot toward my face and wiggles it to get my attention. "*A lot.*"

I push Brad's foot away and rest my hand on Jesse's cheek, which holds heat like he's feverish. He wakes slowly and opens one eye, squinting in the light. "Twizzlers," he groans, at once noting his closeness to me, our lower bodies aligned, my hand now slipping off his face. He tries to shift away but is too tired to go far.

Standing and waving his pickle in the air, Brad announces, "That's my cue. Don't use my hand towels to clean up."

When Brad's gone, Jesse and I remain as we are. We look everywhere but at each other until he says, "If you want to be nice, you'd fuck off and leave, because I can't even get up."

     JENNIFER GREIDUS

"Jesse—"

He sighs impatiently. "Just leave me alone for a while. I was really high yesterday, and I didn't mean any of it. And now I'm embarrassed." He struggles to get on his hands and knees.

My touch tries for a truce; I finger his spine, up, down. He lets me. I pull him toward me, grabbing under his arms, and he sighs before crawling closer. I tug on his shirt. "Come here." With my help, he straddles my lap.

Worming my way across the floor with him on top of me so I can kick the door closed makes us giggle. He tips sideways a couple times and catches himself with his fingertips. "Stand up," I say, poking his hip. "Let's stand up."

After a full minute of sluggish effort, we're both upright. Jesse is no longer liquor-limp. My body pushes his against the sink. I grind my dick into his ass. Our eyes meet in the mirror.

Without him asking, I reach over and drop the light switch. A plastic night-light in the shape of a mushroom shines on our faces from below. In the mirror, the shadows make me appear hostile, or like I'm scheming. The notion that he sees this every time he looks at me, that he's seeing it now, disturbs me. I scrunch and stretch and wiggle my features, hoping they morph into an acceptable combination of happy, decent, and worthy of his affection.

Jesse lightly elbows me in the ribs. "What are you doing?"

I try for a smile. "I don't know."

"So, are you gonna tell me now?" he says. "Is it just one other person? Or a lot of people?"

"It was one."

"And now?"

"No one."

Reaching back, he caresses my thigh. I run my fingers through his hair and ease my other hand down the front of his pants. He's halfway hard. I recall how his cock feels in my mouth. "I want to make you feel better."

My hand slips out of his pants when he turns so that we're chest to chest. Chills run from the back of my neck to the tips of my extremities when he kisses me. He pulls away, a thread of saliva hanging and breaking between us. His readiness and vulnerability are his armor. He lifts his chin and says, "Okay, yeah. Do that."

*

The next night in my bedroom, Jesse tips some weed from his pocket grinder into his pipe, packs it in gently with his lighter, and places it on my table. We've already smoked a bowl. We lay side-by-side on my bed, my laptop open on his chest. Trash videos have been playing for over an hour while we laugh and complain about how tedious life is outside my bedroom.

He declares the wildlife videos pearls among the viral pebbles of the internet. "Can I switch to them now?" he says. His enchantment with elephants as they nuzzle rivals mine for him. A frenetic school of fish outpacing a shark receives his full attention for minutes. I study his profile while he stares at the screen. Now ants are problem-solving.

I tell Jesse I'm going to the kitchen for water. It's my third trip downstairs tonight. I perform a scan of the darkened neighborhood through the small window in my front door. This time, I check the back patio, too. Nothing but the grill and flowerpots.

Of course, it's unlikely that Mr. Stewart would show up here. What would he say to me or my mother, or the police if I called them? Still, I have an uneasy feeling I can't shake. If I'd thought this through better, I would have kept that burner phone. Receiving a hundred threatening or debasing texts from him would make me calmer than being ignorant about his state of mind. That I've heard nothing from him in over forty-eight hours unnerves me. In school, he seemed unfazed and even smiled at me once.

When I return to Jesse, the ants have moved the twig, and he closes the laptop and kneels beside me, bouncing on the mattress. "I feel really good right now. Do you?"

I want to tell him this is the best I've ever felt. That this blows everything away. That I want him with me all the time. How I feel when I'm with him is tenfold "really good." But I only find the balls to say, "I do feel really good, yeah."

He plants a quick kiss on my lips. "I brought condoms."

Grabbing his hand, I hold it as if we're about to arm wrestle. *Condoms.* Presumptuous but sexy. Still, I am unready to take his dick in my ass. I run my fingertips over the fine hair on Jesse's legs.

"I don't know if I feel like getting fucked right now."

Jesse, ever-bashful, murmurs, "I meant me."

The noise that comes from my mouth embarrasses me more than any emotional confession I could make. It's like, *huh-huh*, squeaky, before my voice changed. I stare at the ceiling, slack jawed. I am simply the luckiest fucker on the planet. "It might hurt."

"Okay. A lot?"

"Well, yeah. Actually, like a motherfucker. But just for a little while."

"You've done it?"

"Once or twice." Those stats make it seem as if I've entertained it, run a few experiments, not like I've been bending over left and right. I've lost count, anyway. After three, it was no longer a novelty.

I grab his hand. "Don't get me wrong. I want to fuck you. But I'd also like to see you again."

Pink creeps up Jesse's neck and colors his cheeks. He chews his lower lip as a soft smile unfolds. "You'll see me again. Use your skills."

How difficult could this be? Mr. Stewart rutted into me like a dog all the time. Release for us was equal parts physical and—I'm no fool—psychological. "Maybe," I say and point to his pipe on my bedside table, "hit that again."

Jesse pushes himself off the bed with a grunt and digs in his coat, tossing the condom box at me. Before returning, he flips the switch to the overhead light and turns off the lamp by my bed. He hurries to undress, and I do the same, throwing my clothes on top of his on the floor.

Light from the street shines through the slits in my blinds. The golden glow across Jesse's midsection shows his penis is heavy, half-interested. "So, is this like a spit thing or a lube thing? You have stuff to do this?" He feels his way onto the bed and swings a leg over me so he can park his ass on my thighs. "Hey, wait. Do I need to have an enema?"

"*What?*"

"I read that. Online."

"I don't know. I never have. Just don't shit on me."

We laugh while I fumble with the condom box, tearing through plastic and cardboard with my teeth. I toss the trash aside and spread six squares of foil on my belly. He holds up one to his face and sniffs. "Peaches. I didn't know they were flavored."

I wipe the rest of the condoms off my chest onto the floor. Jesse hands me his pipe and lights up for me. A weightlessness I've not felt in years takes over my body. I'd say it was the premium weed, but I know the company I keep. I'm already hard. My five senses care only about getting off and getting Jesse off. Right now, if he hadn't suggested getting fucked, I might be pressing for it anyway.

He exhales and opens his smoky mouth against mine. His voice echoes off the back of my throat. "I'm already wasted."

"Put the condom on me," I say.

He squirms down my body, fumbling with the slippery latex. The project seems like it takes half an hour, but I know only ten seconds have passed since he began sliding the condom down my erection. A swimming pool of lube has somehow filled my navel. I poke at the jelly and smear some on his leg when he straddles me again.

I hold up two fingers. "We should start small with these first."

He inhales through his nose so hard that his nostrils seal themselves. "No way. The more steps you add, the closer I'll be to telling you I left the oven on or something. Just let me—"

After a few unsuccessful, stoned attempts to position my dick and enter him hands-free, finally he reaches back and holds me steady. He tries to push me into him. Within two seconds, he freezes, fright ripping across his face. Eyes and mouth open wide, he falls forward on me, laughing so hard it shakes the bed. "I might not be the person for this job."

"We can stop."

"No," he insists. "If we don't do it now, I don't know if I'll try it again."

I understand first-hand what Jesse's about to endure. Meanwhile, I am so high, I'm sure an orgasm is about three hours away for me. The condom works against me, too. But then, after another minute of effort, I'm inside him, and I worry I'm going to come before he has a chance. He purrs every time he settles onto me another inch. His heat devours me, and I am enveloped in a mind-blowing squeeze that prevents speech. I'm unable to moan or do anything much but drop my jaw.

When he's sitting against me, squirming, grabbing my arms, breathing like he's trying to birth something, I slide my hands over his dick and roll his balls in my hand. His chest and abdomen are satiny. I bring him to life. My usual unpolished, greedy clutches, tugs, and grabs dissolve. I sense everything I'm doing to him as if I'm on the receiving end. His erection pulses in my hand.

He places his hands on either side of my chest and drops his forehead into my armpit before whipping his body upright again. The first full stroke of my cock inside him prompts a cringe and whimper; by the third, his eyes are squeezed closed. Determined, he rides me, moving erratically, undecided if fast or slow feels the best.

After one last deep breath and a dip of his head, Jesse arises, throat exposed, back arched, his nails digging into my chest. He moves as if we were meant to do this. When he can manage one, his kiss is brutal. He is erotic, shameless, almost savage.

I want to lick his neck, his armpits, his balls. I'd even eat his ass. I'd do all those things, but I'm so high and close to the edge right now, it's all I can do to check every couple of seconds to make sure I'm still stroking his dick. After I say his name, I'm unconvinced that I said anything. "Are you gonna come?"

"Yeah—I am, yeah."

He could have said "no" or "wait," and it wouldn't have mattered one fuck's worth. A natural disaster might occur at this very moment, I'm still going to come. I thrust into him and jack his cock until he makes a noise—almost a cackle—so incongruous with the experience, it somehow heightens my senses.

Instead of merely releasing my orgasm into the world, I am bringing his home with me. The crescent of his eyelashes, the anarchic clumps and twists of his knotted hair in my fist, his ragged breathing. I will always remember this.

He falls forward, his semen spreading between us as our chests heave together. I remain as still as I'm able to be. I want to stay inside him. Sweat has matted strands of his hair to his forehead, and I brush them away from his face. He shivers in waves as he searches for my hand with his.

*

Last night, Jesse slept pressed against me. I dozed on and off, and each time I woke, I was relieved to discover he was still there. When he stirred, I stirred. He'd nuzzle my neck, mumble, and then fall back to sleep.

I didn't need to smoke or watch TV. Peace edged out any concern I had about Mr. Stewart. While next to Jesse, my customary restlessness disappeared. I studied how many minutes until my alarm would sound. I calculated the hours until I'd get to be with him again. I estimated how many more days before I had to leave for college.

Although Mr. Stewart treats me no differently now than any other student, I remain vigilant about keeping my affection for Jesse to a minimum. I try to be inconspicuous. If I want to look at him, I put my head down on my desk and watch him crack his fingers, doodle, draw purposeless circles on his touchpad. Today, my focus falls on his legs, up his legs, between his legs. When he catches me staring, his body shakes with silent laughter. He shields his blushing face with a hand.

Jesse's pen teeters on the edge of his desk. It's mangled, covered in teeth marks. I daydream and try to recall what his teeth look like when he smiles. I close my eyes, contemplating—celebrating—how I made Jesse come two times last night. My arm is a poor excuse for a pillow but will do.

Mr. Stewart stops reading "Clef Poem" aloud mid-stanza. "Daniel, is Mr. Whitman boring you?"

I lift my head, wiping the drool at the corner of my mouth on my sleeve. "No, sorry. Long night."

"I'm sure the class is uninterested in your escapades. Sit up."

I move one muscle at a time, shifting slowly from recline to a drowsy droop to an unsteady upright. The bell rings. Jesse and I rise at the same sluggish pace. "What are you doing after school?" We both say it. Next to us, Ollie groans and tells us we're making him sick.

The back of Jesse's hand touches mine. An accident, I believe, but the second's contact sends a belt of shivers around my ribcage.

     JENNIFER GREIDUS

My five senses welcome anything he has on offer.

Mr. Stewart's voice startles us. "Jesse. Daniel. Stop by after school. I need to speak with both of you."

Ollie pokes my shoulder and whispers, "I bet he tries for a threesome." He wrinkles his nose. "Not a pretty picture."

The idea of Mr. Stewart violating Jesse deserves more than a wrinkled nose. I would never let that happen.

In Genetics, I am too nervous to flirt with Jesse, or at least too nervous to flirt well with Jesse. The elastic's gone from my face. It seems implausible Mr. Stewart should have the upper hand, but I worry that I've missed something, that somehow he does.

I stall. I tell Jesse I need to go to the bathroom first, and I pretend to piss. He leans against the wall of block windows, his legs and arms crossed. I flush the urinal. I take my time zipping up. As each tooth of my zipper connects with the next, I wish for Mr. Stewart's immediate if inexplicable decapitation, retrograde amnesia, sudden classroom sinkhole. Anything.

At my locker, I remove a book I don't need and replace it with one I should take home. Jesse and I smile at each other but remain quiet as we walk together. I enter the classroom first, and Mr. Stewart tells us to come in and close the door. When Jesse isn't looking, Mr. Stewart leers at me. I am being processed and prepped and dangled over the pot of whatever he has boiling.

Jesse and I station ourselves at the opposite corners of his desk, mirroring one another. I push my groin against the sharp angle. The painful distraction of self-harm might lessen the blast effect of this explosion.

"Jesse," Mr. Stewart says, "Daniel has done you a favor."

Jesse perks up. "What favor?"

"It may not seem like a favor, per se."

"What is it?" Jesse peeks at me, as though I might know.

"First," Mr. Stewart says, "understand that Daniel only did it because he cares about you and because he trusts me."

I don't know what this is. I shake my head at Mr. Stewart. I plead with wide eyes. When I'm ignored, I go to Jesse and tug on his sleeve. "Let's just go."

Jesse lifts his arm until the material slips out of my gasp. "Wait.

What favor?" His shoes scuffle against the dirty tile as he moves away from me.

Mr. Stewart folds his hands on the desk. From where I'm standing, I see his right leg bouncing up and down. He's excited about whatever it is he's about to tell us. "What happens at 2166 Lawnton Avenue, Jesse?"

Jesse's lips move, a dozen sentences blooming and dying. When his head falls forward, mine does, too. I close my eyes and blow out a long breath that announces my surrender.

The conversation could end here. From that one sentence, I know exactly how this is going to play out. There is nothing I can do or say; I am climbing a rope that's falling from the sky.

"Daniel and I are not trying to harm you," Mr. Stewart continues, taking advantage of Jesse's distraction to sneak me a wink. "Having the police haul you away because of your activities would be fruitless. I only want you to know that he told me, and we want to help you." He reaches into the inside pocket of his jacket and slides a business card across his desk. "On the off chance you'll need it. A lawyer friend. In case Brad Floros finds himself in prison and decides to link you to any of it."

Jesse hesitates before picking up the card. Spinning in my direction, he pokes me with the glossy card's corner. "What the fuck, Dan?"

My instinct is to reach for him. Physical contact can succeed where words will fail. "I swear," I say, fighting the impulse to grab his arm, "I didn't tell him anything. Nothing."

"Why does he know Brad's name, then? What the *fuck*, Dan?"

"Please don't blame Daniel," Mr. Stewart says, "He made the right choice. We only want you to make the right choices from now on, as well."

Jesse walks toward the door but circles back as if he has a hundred more questions. He pockets the card and scrubs his face with both hands. "What the *fuck*, Dan?" His head hangs as he turns back toward the exit. Flinging open the door so hard it hits the wall, he dashes out of the classroom.

The shouts and laughter of carefree kids roll from one end of the hallway to the other. Locker doors slam. Each click of the second hand on the overhead clock fortifies the silence of my standoff with Mr. Stewart.

I should be chasing after Jesse. However, I'm still here, stuck right here when I should be moving, moving fast. I don't know why I'm not moving.

Mr. Stewart rises and closes the door to the classroom, returning to me. As he passes, rounding his desk, I find my voice. "Do you want me to tell everyone about you and me?"

"I do not, and you will not," he says, taking a seat, calmer than I've ever seen him. He rolls his shoulders back, cracks his neck, hums contentedly. The only time I've seen him look this pleased with himself is after he comes. He takes a deep, satisfied breath. "You don't want to hurt me, Daniel, any more than I want to hurt you. Or Jesse, for that matter."

"You *are* hurting me."

"You may hurt," he explains, "but *I'm* not hurting you. I'm doing what needs to be done. I am, as always, supporting you, caring for you. And I will continue to support and care for you until you leave for college."

"I don't need your help."

"I know you don't recognize it because it's been absent from your life for so long, but this is what it feels like to be loved."

"Loved?" I'm shocked by his use of the word, too surprised by it to even laugh.

"Don't scoff at it. I think we both know the last person before me to love you was your father."

I think about that. Ollie loves me. I know he does. I'm inclined to defend myself but decide it's a waste of time. "This is stupid, arguing with you. I'm going to find Jesse."

Mr. Stewart dismisses me with a graceful hand shooing me out of his classroom. "Do what you need to do, this last time. Dinner, as usual, is at seven."

I leave, speeding through the halls, sideswiping a few kids on my way to Jesse's locker. I round the corners, almost slipping, hanging on to the walls for balance until I regain momentum.

Jesse is there. Relieved that I caught him, I push my way into his personal space as he removes papers from his bag and situates his laptop so the flap closes. I touch his shoulder. He shrugs me off, so I capture his hand. He pulls away as if I'm corrosive.

"I never told him that," I whisper. "He's just—he's in my business. You know what I mean?"

Jesse slams his locker closed, spinning the lock, and slips on his backpack. He pushes my chest. I stumble backwards. Before I can steady myself, he shoves me again with both hands. "Are you kidding? You want to pay for my fucking college, Dan? Because that's the least of the shit that's going to happen to me."

"I promise, nothing is going to happen to you."

"That's funny. Then why do I have a lawyer's business card in my fucking pocket?" His voice cracks twice. "What do *you* think's going to happen now?"

"Nothing. I promise. Let's just go," I say and tug on the strap of his backpack, "and I'll explain."

"*You.*" Jesse draws himself up to his full height and leans closer to me. "And *him.*"

My body recoils. I have no control over my surprise. I know immediately what he means, and I am too stunned to feign ignorance. My stutter lets me begin several sentences but keeps me from ending any.

Jesse tells me to shut up. "I'm not blind, man. When I said I wanted you to stop seeing other people, I meant him, too."

Well, that's it, then. There is nothing to look forward to except tepid blowjobs, endless nights of resentment and malaise, and a father figure who is the antithesis of everything a decent father should be.

Maybe I'll trudge through earning a Master's degree that will kick off a distaste for my chosen field of study. Maybe I'll defend a frivolous dissertation while I isolate myself and eat frozen burritos. If I'm lucky, I'll find humdrum employment working from home in my pajamas.

There are so many ways I can give up.

Right now, I should get the proper sort of fucked up not meant for company: a forget-the-past-present-future sort of fucked up, where I wake up mid-afternoon, half undressed with unidentifiable food and drink stains on my sheets, and the TV blaring a stream of cartoons.

At home, I skip the weed. Instead, I drink the last of my father's scotch. I get just drunk enough not to feel the bite of the cold wind during my walk to Mr. Stewart's, but not drunk enough that I have to stagger there.

The backdoor of his garage is locked. Unusual. I peek in, shielding the glare in the glass with my hand. His car is there. I know he's here, smug about his triumph today, eating nut butter and grading essays. I dash to the front of his place, finally understanding what necessitates ringing a doorbell a hundred times in a row.

As soon as he opens the door an inch, I force my way into his home and toss my bag across the entranceway. He reaches behind me and closes the door, taking my arm before I can get further into his home. I smack his hand away. "Don't touch me."

"You smell like liquor. Are you drunk?"

"Door's locked," I say. "Why?"

"You're late. I doubted you were coming."

The arches of his feet invite a stomping. Instead, I target the wall, losing my balance and falling against Mr. Stewart. A muddy mark remains after my foot meets the matte paint. I kick it again, this time maintaining my equilibrium and grinding the sole against the surface. He regards the smear. "Are you having another temper tantrum?"

A swish of scotch bile bubbles up in my esophagus. I swallow it down as I lace my fingers behind my head, pacing the tiny box of an entranceway. "You're a *nightmare*."

"Calm down. Come upstairs."

"You can't be serious." I sneer and slur my soft consonants. "I'm not going anywhere with you."

"If you want to talk about what happened today, I refuse to do it with my bare feet on the freezing tile. Please, come upstairs."

"Why would you do that today? I don't—" Defeated, I drop into a crouch and hold my face in my hands. As I let fall what I promise myself will be the last tears of the year, his hand on my back gives me the chills. I twist out of reach. "Don't touch me."

"Just come inside. We can talk."

"I don't want to talk to you anymore." I rise and strip off my coat and hoodie. My shoes hit the floor. I remove my socks and throw them against the wall. Pushing past him, I slog up the stairs. More clothing falls. T-shirt, fourth step. Jeans, fifth. He follows. I shake off his tentative touch on my lower back.

The soft light of a single table lamp in the dining room illuminates the unadorned furnishings. I push down my shorts and step out of them. Unlike the adrenaline that propelled me here, exhaustion rules now, and I've finally hit the wall.

"Brett," I say, exhausted.

Nothing.

"Brett." I'm unsure if he can hear me. "*Brett.*"

"Yes?"

"No matter what, I get to call you Brett now." I sink to my knees, contemplating laying here or crawling to the couch. "I'm drunk. And hungry. I haven't eaten."

Slipping his hand under my arm, he lifts me to my knees. I stand with only a slight falter. I'm aware of my nudity and that he's staring at my cock. Floppy flesh. Of no use to me. He can do what he likes with it.

"How about some water first?" he says. "You're flushed."

"Eggs. Just make me some eggs. I'll get my own water."

I trudge to the kitchen. The glasses, as always, are lined up with precision in the cabinet over his sink. Not a fingerprint on one of them. I drink some tap water and place the glass in the sink. That dirty glass will irk him; every dish must be cleaned and put in its proper place as soon as possible.

My legs open when I fall back on his couch, my flaccid cock on display. I scrunch my toes, close my eyes, and think about eggs. It's curious that I have any appetite at all.

When I wake up, I'm on my stomach with my skin pulling against the leather of the couch. Mr. Stewart is behind me, knees spreading my legs. The leather squeaks as he wriggles down the couch and buries his face in my crotch, lifting my hips slightly so he can lick the back of my balls and my asshole.

My limbs are as limp as my dick. My leg drops off the side of the couch. The only thing on my mind: *Will my sticky balls hurt when I need to peel them off this fucking leather?*

"Happy now?" I whisper it twice, in case he missed the first one.

His lips tickle my ass as he speaks. "No more Jesse, correct?"

I mumble into the cushion. "Yeah, don't worry about it."

"You're done?"

"I'm done," I mumble against the cushion. I have no interest in fighting with him anymore.

The familiar snap of latex and the farting sound of the last of the lube from his black bottle awakens a part of me that still gives a shit about him coming in my ass; the forlorn, fuck-it part of me doesn't care. If he skipped the condom, my indifference edges out mustering the strength to protest.

While he humps into me, I can't take my unblinking eyes off our warped reflection in the chrome of the chair. He's moving; I'm being shifted. He sits back, making sure all his cock stays in me, and he tries to pull me up to my knees by the hips. I hang like a dead ferret— "*Hmpf. Ungh*" —before falling back to the cushions.

"Get on your knees."

"Just fuck me this way."

The cushions pull away from the skin underneath me as he moves up my body until he's straddling my waist. His warm breath on my neck repulses me. He kisses just below my hairline, snuffles in my hair with his nose. "Are you okay?" I have no answer, and he wasn't waiting for one, anyway.

Unhurried, he enters me, as if he's doing me a favor by not tearing me up. He licks the back of neck. I remain a lump. His needs increase—or his frustration—and he fucks me harder, I suspect with the intention of punishing me for my disinterest.

He comes. He caresses my shoulder. After a moment, he tries to roll me onto my back. I'm a dead weight. "If you turn over, I'll make you come," he says.

I want to die. I choke on saliva and squeak, "Never mind."

"Later, then." He smacks my ass, and a satisfied sigh follows. "Would you still like some eggs?"

"Yes." The couch muffles my voice. "Scrambled. Dry. No goo."

His softening dick and the condom, heavy with a pool of cum, enter my line of vision. I liked Jesse's cum. Mr. Stewart's will never cross my lips. I'll get through these next months by offering up my ass, doing well in school, and dodging any hints at blowjobs. I'll wait for college, and I'll listen to Mr. Stewart's criticism. *You could be so much better than you are.*

The tinkle of ice cubes in glasses and the crack of several eggs are my reality for the next couple months. We are going to play house, more so than before.

From the kitchen, Mr. Stewart blathers for minutes. "... don't like that you've been drinking and..." I quickly tune him out. When I stand, lube leaks out of me, dribbling down my inner thigh. I wipe it on the back of his wool throw pillow. In the kitchen, a glass of sparkling water with three ice cubes waits for me. The eggs are whipped, and the pan heats on the stove.

Mr. Stewart hands me the water. I place the drink on the counter, yawn, and scratch my balls. "Can I watch TV?"

"Eggs first. Then, we'll see." They sizzle when he pours them into the pan. A drop of egg splashes outside the pan, and he quickly wipes it away with a dishrag. "You'll sleep here tonight."

"Okay."

I don't dress. The cold steel of the barstool stings my ass. We eat in silence. Occasionally, he smiles at me. I can't return the smiles. I put down my fork. "Can I watch TV now?"

"This one time. Don't touch anything else in my office. And why don't you change the sheets while you're up there? Linen closet, middle shelf."

I may withstand the resentment, shame, and heartache, but I doubt I'll handle the boredom all that well. "Yeah, okay. The gray ones?"

For a while, I don't need to make any decisions. It feels good to have my days and nights structured for me. I haven't had that in years. Almost every day, I receive a fuck, a meal, and an audit of my recent activities. *Was your mother home this weekend? Have you decided on a school? With whom did you speak today? Did you finish your essay?*

　　　　　　　　　　　　　　　　　JENNIFER GREIDUS

On the weekends, I sleep at Mr. Stewart's. I shower, brush my teeth, and I am either fucked or asleep by eleven, sometimes both.

On most weekdays, I leave through his backdoor when he readies for bed, about nine. I light a joint and make the walk. The night air on those walks is an hour in the yard of a prison camp.

At home, I'm supposed to study, stay sober, and read. "Limit your television and take care of your body." I do none of that. I eat sandwiches from the gas station, watch TV, get stoned blind, and fall asleep closer to dawn than to midnight.

At first, there were some surprise inspections. Both of us grew tired of the process: He would demand to check my phone, and I would give a token protest before handing it over. Finally, he requested the passcode, and I gave it. He checks my phone and my laptop. None of it matters; any sexual or affectionate messages have long since been deleted. I've wiped my emails, blocked almost all my contacts. I deleted photos.

I text only Ollie, and those messages contain insignificant info: *I'm going to be five minutes late. I'll pay for gas this week.* Every day, he says, "What's up with you?" I tell him I'm tired. He asks me to do stuff. I tell him I'm tired. When he tries to make me laugh, I tell him it's not personal, I'm just tired.

Jackie sells to me. She does so with a sad face. When she says Jesse's name, I shake my head, hand her money, and snatch my baggie. "Don't care."

My mom is the only one who triggers any feeling in me at all, and it's not a good one. I leave her a note on a Sunday: *No more turkey jerky.* When a new batch is ready for me the next weekend, I write another note: *Could you stop with the fucking turkey jerky already?*

In class, I stare at Jesse's feet. It's where my eyes fall when I have my head on the desk, since Mr. Stewart no longer cares when I have my head down.

Mr. Stewart is subject to Jesse's furtive scrutiny. He's trying to figure out what I like about our English teacher, or what we do, or if we're still doing it. Since we broke up, a wrinkled brow and a dismissive sniff are Jesse's hallmarks of disapproval.

As far as my grades, graduation, and quality of life, I only need to stop slapping the water and float until June.

What pleases me—and the pleasure is minimal—is stealing Mr. Stewart's cinnamon candies. When I go for a piss or to clean up his cum from my skin, I raid his desk drawer and pocket two or three tins of his five-hundred-tin collection. I calculate the number of days it will take him to notice the stock has diminished at an unusually fast rate.

I search *DNA evidence* on my phone and quickly clear the history. A batch of aged condoms will do me no good. I like to fantasize about collecting them from his trash and showing them to someone. My life is an exile in a Communist state, and I'm happy to engage in impotent subterfuge, having been stripped of any real choices.

All this grief, and when I'm fucked up, Mr. Stewart still makes my cock hard. If he's so inclined, he can suck my balls dry in under three minutes. I am sometimes able to forget who he is and who I am, but afterward, when I remember, I despise us both.

"How long," he whispers as he fucks me on my side, "was my lecture today?"

I don't care. "Dunno"

"It is one of my favorites, but I gave the abridged version," he says and stills his thrust. His arm encircles my waist, stroking my dick once, twice. "Do you know why?"

I don't care. "No."

"I found it more riveting to sit at my desk and watch you fidget." He tries to still my hips, but I push and pull against him. "Slow down, Daniel. *Slow—*" He gives up the fight and rocks with me. "Each time you look at me in class, you spread your legs. Even while you're pouting, you spread your legs for me."

It's untrue. If my legs are spread, it's because I don't have the energy or interest to close them. If my eyes are on him, I'm envisioning what nastiness nests inside of him. Bones. Gristle. Blood and guts.

"You tug your bottom lip when the text bores you. Always wasting time and—yes, keep doing that, yes," he pants, near orgasm, muscles rigid, faster strokes, ready for the payoff. "Always daydreaming. You're—barely there."

I am barely there.

All this talk, and his message is the same: *Daniel, you are inadequate. You are more than, less than, too much, too little. You are careless, argumentative, arrogant, stoned.*

"This situation with Jesse. What I did has nothing to do with us together," he says as he pulls out of me. "This is about your future. I'm stepping in because no one else will."

As I trudge to the bathroom to take a shower, I mumble to myself. "What would I do without you?"

He has heard me. From the bedroom, he calls, "Falter."

On a Friday night at Mr. Stewart's, I help myself to seltzer and handfuls of almonds in the kitchen. He does lesson plans on his laptop at his dining room table. He notices I've chosen Wittgenstein from the library upstairs. "That is far too advanced for you."

"I thought you said I was 'exceptional.'"

"Return it to the shelf and choose something else."

I pull off my socks and toss them in the corner. I crack the book's spine. I drum my fingers on the leather couch. I know dozens of ways to make him scowl.

Within a paragraph, I realize he's right. For show, I chuckle a couple times, like Wittgenstein and I are sharing tittie jokes at the bar. I continue with the charade until my eyelids get heavy. Then, I doze on his couch and wake up with a stiff neck. "Why don't you have comfortable furniture?"

"Sleeping on living room furniture is vulgar. I made an exception this once."

I notice my bag on his dining room table, its contents removed and lined up in order of offensiveness, least to worst: books, laptop, crumpled tennis roster and stats, dirty socks, dirty T-shirt, an empty pack of Ollie's cigarettes, rolling papers, pipe, tin with joints, a half-ounce of weed, and last, *The Nature of Alexander*, out of the wrapping paper but unread. My forgetfulness more than disinterest kept me from starting it.

Mr. Stewart says, "I don't like marijuana in my house. Your entire backpack stinks of it. And yes, I did notice my gift went missing some time ago. Here I find it, among your slop."

"You want it back?" I bite into a green apple. A trickle of juice slides from the corner of my mouth when I speak and chew. I wipe it away with my thumb. That bad habit of mine—failure to use a napkin—is on his list of daily grievances, second only to leaving the bath towel on the floor.

Mr. Stewart examines the front cover of the book, tracing over a new bend in the cover with his thumb. "You shouldn't have taken it in the first place."

"Yeah, okay, but do you want it back?"

"That's not the point." He sighs when I again wipe my mouth with my hand. "If you can't be bothered with a plate, please eat that over the sink."

"Why'd you pick that book for me, anyway?"

"I hoped you'd draw a comparison between his achievements and your potential."

"To conquer the world?" I extend my arm, the apple cupped in my palm. I toss it up, catch it, and take another bite.

"We're getting off topic. Where are you getting your marijuana?"

"Not Jesse," I say between chews. "Don't worry about it."

"What would your father say about your marijuana use? Do you think he'd be proud of you for it?"

My shoulders fall. I stop myself from throwing the apple at him. He acknowledges my disbelief with a curt nod I take to mean: *Yes, you heard me, and no, I'm not apologizing.*

My dad would be pissed that I smoke weed, and I hate that Mr. Stewart assumed it. I dislike, too, that he does any contemplating at all about my relationship with my father.

That low blow has parched my mouth; bits of unchewed apple skin sit on my tongue, and I work up some spit so I'm able to swallow before I talk. "You didn't know him. He'd be fine with it."

"If he were alive, it's not something you'd be doing, is it?"

"I don't know." I frown. "Maybe not."

"Then, one might assume his absence is the reason you get high."

"So what? Do you blame me?" I try to keep my voice steady, but its quaver reveals how much I'm rattled.

"You can't change the past, but you can change—"

"Look," I say, stopping him, "I smoke sometimes at night because I want to sleep better. That's all. I'm being good. I'm not doing anything, going anywhere, seeing anyone, and I don't want to."

But I do want to.

Today, we had oral presentations in English. Mr. Stewart scanned the room for the first victim. "Jesse. I assume you're prepared." Our classmates snickered, which is ridiculous, since Jesse could bury any one of us with his grades and intellect; last week, he explained to three-quarters of the class what the words *immure* and *dichotomy* meant.

As Jesse shuffled through some random papers tucked in his bag and tore a corner from one of the pages, he glanced at me twice. He gave a flawless presentation, only once referencing the scrap of paper, and I eventually had to look out the window while thinking of nothing but his mouth on mine.

Jesse has done his best to create a neutral environment in English. No smiling, but no obvious disdain. He will participate in class if asked. Distress has worsened his slouch. He wants to be invisible. To save myself some sorrow, I would be okay if he disappeared altogether.

Other boys have crossed my mind. In my head, I archived a shortlist for vengeance: a tenth-grader or two, somebody easy enough to forget after one orgasm. Random, covert blowjobs. A hand job after an away match. But why waste my time on antiseptic, spiritless orgasms? Nothing will scrub my mind of Jesse.

This morning, with his back pressed against his locker, Jesse made a trade with two freshmen, pocketing the cash inside jeans I've stripped off him. When he saw me coming, he looked up and down the hall, probably checking for the nearest exit.

Before he could flee, I got close enough to appreciate a few of my favorite parts, the parts I imagine when I'm alone. The avian wingspan of his clavicle, and how his top, pale pink lip emulates the curve. The major veins on his forearms twisted like my first-grade, pipe-cleaner creations. Those blue branches, art for art's sake.

I shake myself out of the fantasy and finish Mr. Stewart's apple.

In the fridge, after picking through a few platters of leftovers with my fingers, I decide on some grilled chicken and roasted asparagus, devouring them in less than a minute. I wash my hands, dry them on my pants, and crack my neck.

"Okay. I'm still beat. You want to fuck, or do you just want me to continue napping?"

He dismisses me with a quick wave. "Nap. I'll be an hour or so."

I grunt and save the luxury of sadness until I hit his mattress upstairs. I soothe myself by tracing the letters of the alphabet on my arm with my index finger. My dad used to do that when I couldn't fall asleep, spell out words on my skin that I'd say to him until I finally passed out.

How regular this is. If I could have predicted this all those months ago—the upshot, not the path to it—would I have wanted it? If Jesse was uninvolved in the whole affair, would napping on Mr. Stewart's bed while he grades papers and I wait to get my asshole rimmed seem appealing?

I drift off to sleep on my belly, my top lip flipped up, drooling on the silk comforter, several times marred with my cum stain. Mr. Stewart wakes me by caressing my back. "You know what?" he says and sits next to me, brushing the hair from my face. "If your father were to see you last September, my guess is that he would have been disappointed. Now, if we could just break you of your marijuana habit, I believe he'd have some hope for your future."

I don't have the energy to take a deep breath about anything anymore. "Why do you say stuff like that?"

"We both know it's true."

"It's not. But even if it was, you can keep it to yourself."

Broken Daniel.

He undresses. I unbutton my pants and shove them down my legs with my feet, kicking free of the now inside-out material. My socks always stay on these days. He hangs his belt in the closet, and I glare at his muscular back. "Can I fuck you?" I've never asked before.

His shoulders flex. "No."

"Why not?"

"There is no reason other than my lack of desire to be fucked."

"Yeah, well, maybe I have a lack of desire to be fucked, too, Brett."

Naked, he approaches the bed. "Is that true?"

I shrug and sigh. "I really don't care."

Like he's adhering to an agenda, every one of my favorites is executed. Licking the soft flesh inside my legs, a nibble behind my balls, a few flicks of his tongue against my asshole, kisses-slash-bites on my nipples. Then, one finger, two, half of three, and he's pushing his dick into me. Soon will be the dénouement, coming on my balls, abdomen, or in the condom.

But tonight, I slow him down. I roll on top of him and ride him well, hard. My upstrokes bring the tip of his penis to the very edge of my asshole, and a harsh slap of our skin meeting accompanies each of my downstrokes.

For the first time in weeks, the muscles I use to smile are put to work. I sit up straight, sneer at him, and then lunge. Every pound of pressure I can muster falls on his neck as I choke him with a hatred that I didn't know I had in me anymore.

Each of my thoughts rises slowly, receding, making room for the next. "You should be nicer to me." I say it five times in my head before I let him hear it.

I marvel at how much easier it would be to kill him than to explain to anyone why I continue to participate, consensually, in this relationship. How could I not have extricated myself from this by now? Explaining to a jury my motives for murdering him seems less complicated, somehow, than explaining this to the police, my mother, the world. I do not know why I am still here.

Should I kill him, I would call the police mere seconds after his last breath. Then Ollie. I would call Ollie second simply because no remorseful person would call the police second.

I would speak calmly to the arresting officers. After explaining the nature of my involvement with my teacher, who could blame me for crushing his trachea? Mental distress. Grief. Poor parenting. Anal sex. Neglect no one noticed in time. A jury will love and pity me.

Beneath me, Mr. Stewart grapples to pull my fingers away from his neck, but I squeeze, I squeeze, I squeeze. His eyes pop open, and his face distorts as his lips darken to a medium purple. His Adam's apple rattles against my palm as he growls and panics. The strangle-snort noises are just the spice this coupling needed.

"Beg me," I say, while fighting against him to sustain the throttle. "Beg me, Brett."

I grimace when he seizes my hips, digging his thumbs into the ligaments over my pelvis, but I am undeterred. Eyeballs red and bulging, he wheezes, chokes, and drools. Specks of spit shoot from between swollen lips and land on his cheeks.

Then, he wilts. He concedes. His fingers slip from my skin. His face slackens, as if for good. I freeze—mid-strangle, mid-stroke, mid-choke—straining to spot any evidence of consciousness.

I couldn't have.

My thighs grip a body that continues to rise and fall beneath me.

I haven't.

I lift up and slide my ass down his cock. He resurrects, bucking his hips, fucking up into me harder, angrier. His expression zooms from pleasure to rage and back. He manages a bloated smile while I struggle to remain on my perch, tightening my clutch on his throat for balance, the pressure nowhere near my earlier crush.

I've been trying to get him to lose control for months with no luck. Now, finally, he snarls, a dog protecting his food dish. When his body stiffens and he comes, I'm stunned, impressed, turned on. I release my grip on his neck and scramble to jerk off. I'm a second away from orgasm when Mr. Brett Stewart smacks me in the face so hard that I can't see out of one eye until breakfast.

This twist in our relationship makes me think back to those career quizzes I used to take in Ollie's car before school, to a time when I was still trying to figure out Mr. Stewart, what I could do to possess him or make him want to possess me. I decide to take my favorite assessment one last time, now that I'm sure I know how he would answer each question.

You read the instructions before beginning any assembly. Yes.

You avoid arguing, even when you know you are right. No.

You would always let someone know if he had a crumb on his face. Yes.

You are usually patient when someone is late to an appointment with you. No.

You don't mind getting your hands dirty. Turns out, Mr. Stewart does not mind at all.

The results still say that the quiz-taker should be a CPA or a lawyer, no mention anywhere of teacher.

Since I strangled him, his fastidious nature remains inviolable in every aspect of his life except sex. The best part: How we fuck has him possessed, and lectures escape him. No more mid- or post-jizz critiques of my character.

After I smack his face, bite his inner arm or nipple, or grip at the roots of his hair when he has his head between my legs, his lag time is nil. He responds in kind, dragging his teeth up my erection, pulling on my balls too hard, and fish hooking my mouth or stuffing three or four fingers in there at once. We spit on each other. He insults me, and, only during sex, he allows me to insult him.

There remain several lines I'm not to cross. I can't fuck him. I can't leave any marks that are visible above the collar line or on his hands. I still can't watch his television.

We agreed that should I incur any visible injuries, I'm to claim an altercation with a peer. We try to avoid any marks on my face, because that story will only work for so long.

Abrasions of the skin-to-skin variety ensue when his frustration peaks. Last night, minutes after we came, we stood naked at the fridge. He swiped a finger across the back of my neck. "Hmm. That one might show." The spot stung when I touched it, too. The chafe fell well short of a flaying but did need peroxide and a day of sympathy. I assured him it was okay and below the collar line.

I've been fucked sideways and upside down, in every room. We've squished our skin against every appliance, spilled semen on every wipeable, scrubbable, or washable surface. I believe the only reason he still uses condoms with me is that ten percent of him believes that ninety percent of me is unstable, that I am one sober, cranky day away from demanding a rape kit.

After we clean up, we do normal stuff. Over broiled cod and

a tube of antibiotic cream, he'll speak of someday taking me to MoMA. I'll ice my arm with a frozen bag of raspberries and ask him to pour me more seltzer. He'll suppose my ass can "take more than three fingers" while he opens a new pack of toothbrushes for me.

We have done everything I can tolerate, and every few days, he pesters me to do the one thing I won't. "Nope. Stop asking."

He fires demands at me. "Suck my cock."

"Leave me alone."

He prods my chin with his erection. "I know you can do it."

"Get it out of my face."

This, my last vestige of autonomy, amuses him. My refusal implies a power we both know I don't have. The illusion: He'll continue to request blowjobs while I'll continue to deny them. The reality: At any moment, he will decide to take what he wants, regardless.

He snatches a book from my hand and tosses it on the floor next to his bed. He unzips and takes out his cock. A fistful of my hair. Yank, snarl, release. "Stand up. Undress. Turn around. Spread your legs."

I bend over the bed, resting my cheek on the cool skin of my forearm. Behind me, his belt buckle clinks. As his trousers fall to the floor, they tickle the back of my legs. The lube makes its first appearance of the evening. A quart-sized pump bottle suits our needs nowadays. His cold, slick fingers swipe a silky line from my balls to my asshole.

I reach behind me and drag my nails across whatever flesh is within reach. I do no real damage. My asscheeks ignite when he slaps me—*one-two-three* on each side. Incensed, I grope around between his legs and grab a testicle. He backs away after pinching the sensitive skin under my arm. "You want the belt, Daniel? I suggest you stop."

I suppose I do want the belt. What else is there? I pull harder, this time on the delicate set.

If I had a stronger vocabulary, high-brow insults might bring his wrath. As it is, I can only muster, "Cocksucker." My vulgarity shakes out a fatigued snigger before he bends and slips his leather belt from the loops of the trousers pooled at his feet.

Like a dozen times before this, he threatens a few first-warning strikes against the back of my legs or on my ass, promising no more should I apologize. I never apologize, and the strikes are never warning shots. Each one is more severe than the next, and four strikes constitute the minimum penalty.

The pain and humiliation mid-act nourish me, but the real feast lies within the residual welts. I find and fondle them, pressing flat their swell as I absently watch TV or enjoy a snack. I squish, pick, and pinch those howling lumps and bumps until the pain steals my breath.

Tonight, the blows start low and move high, higher on my body than usual. I get two lashes across my lower back. I fall forward in agony but refuse to call out. Another two. He drops the belt. "Be good."

The crinkling of the condom wrapper: I widen my stance. The sticky unrolling of the latex: I brace myself on the mattress. Mr. Stewart's staggered, almost unmanageable breathing: My cock jumps.

When I hear only one gummy pump of the lube, I hold my breath. By some act of mercy, there is a second, then a third squish. I exhale. His hand crawls up my chest and claws at my abdomen, my nipples, and my armpits. He tweaks and twists my skin. "I'll go slowly," he says.

"Yeah," I say under my breath while waiting for the catch.

"For about twenty seconds. Enjoy them."

He takes ten seconds of my allotted time to push in and three seconds pulling out. Then, I'm just fucked, plain and simple. I bite my arm. He slaps my ass, hamstrings, torso, any part within reach.

I go for my erection but falter when he hooks me by the armpits, pulling me up and against his chest. The awkward angle prevents his full thrust, which hatches his annoyance. I fall forward, and he fucks me so hard that I need to tiptoe to keep contact with the floor.

When he comes, he slumps on top of me, cradling me with his arm around my waist. I arch my back, allotting myself enough room to work my fist and grind out a resentful orgasm.

His sweat stings the fresh slices on my back. "Get off me," I huff. His weight shifts then lifts. I roll onto my back and grimace. "Not so far up next time. Legs and ass. That's it. What the fuck."

If with every spurt of cum I also expelled some resentment, I might get through the rest of the year without hating myself for wanting out and, at the same time, enjoying this more than I should.

I skipped school yesterday, luxuriating in bed until one p.m. and celebrating the coming day and night to myself. By three, however, I wondered how I was going to fill all the remaining hours of sunlight. In the evening, I kept myself stoned and watched TV until four in the morning, full of self-pity and some old peanut butter crackers from the pantry.

I don't usually drink coffee, but this morning, after only a couple hours of sleep, I need some help. I head to the kitchen to see if I can remember how to use the coffee maker. I'm surprised to find my mom sitting at the table, legs crossed, immersed in something on her phone. Her nose is an inch from the screen. She jumps when she hears me. "Danny. I didn't know you were home."

She stands and places her phone face down next to her coffee and a self-help book called *When It's Love, You'll Know*. "Well, I guess," she says, flitting from the sink to the table and back to the sink with no clear objective, "since we're both here, do you want eggs? Toast?"

"No, thanks." I eye up her cooling cup of coffee. "Maybe coffee. Is there—?"

"Oh. Absolutely. Coffee."

We circle each other as I move toward the corner, and she heads for the cabinets. I suspect being this nice is as awkward for her as it is for me. We remain well outside each other's personal space. She points to the ceiling and says, "Another bulb is out."

I look at the ceiling. "One left."

She sorts through the mugs. Several of them end up on the counter while she digs and digs. Red, no. Design, no. If she thinks there is one that's special to me, she's wrong. They're all vacation collectibles and freebies. "Where have you been these last few weeks? It's a boyfriend?"

"No. I don't know. Not really."

Because I consider most of my life none of my mom's business, I usually ignore that question. This time, however, I want to share, and I want three things to happen when I do: She should care enough to be outraged. She should acknowledge how famously bad we are at picking proper partners since my father's death. She should call the police.

"Mom," I begin, "I think there's something—"

She ignores me and opens the fridge. "Milk? Sugar?"

"Mom?"

"Hmm?" She adds sugar before I can decline. The last of the milk I never said I wanted dribbles from the carton. "Oh, shoot. I thought I had enough. Did you see the work they're doing on the bridge? It takes me twenty extra minutes to get to the store."

"*Mom.*"

When I go to her, she flinches, her shoulders rising a few inches. The coffee steams, and the teaspoon she uses to stir it tinkles, tinkles, tinkles for about five seconds more than needed. She slides the mug to me. She's toed the line, and that's as close as I should get. "Here's your coffee. Do you want something else?"

I do want something else. I haven't in so long, but today I do.

I want her to make me eat a meal at our dining room table, a tradition we discontinued when my father died. I want her to stick around tonight and do mother-things while I do fucked-up things so she can take away a privilege, any privilege at all. Or maybe, all I want is a hug.

I decide to vary my approach. Perhaps I should warm her up first, a tactic I have never tried. There is one memory I'm certain will thaw her.

My father and she used to dance in front of me, when she was in a rare, playful mood. *Bumps*, she called it, hip-to-hip, and my father would tell me with a wink that she couldn't dance her way out of a bag. "Now," he would add, holding up a finger, "that's not to say she doesn't have rhythm." I was nine and had no idea what that meant at the time.

Gently turning her toward me, I take her soft hands in mine. I hold them loosely, hoping she will tighten the grip, so I know it's okay to tighten mine. Our arms are a bridge between us. I whisper, "You remember? Bumps?"

A smile, an admission, that's all I want. She can stay or go afterwards, but I want to know she remembers something good about us as a family. For years, I've taken what little she's given—cash and autonomy—and I've always been too pained or numb to ask for anything more. Until now. I admit to myself that I want something more than weed money and the run of the house.

"*Bumps*," I say and shake her hands once. "The dance? Dad used to—"

The flicker of recognition: a twitch of her top lip, the minute lift of her brow, an exhale that comes not from her lungs but from her whole being. She remembers, and the flashback is unwelcome. She drops my hands. "I can't do that, Danny. Please don't do that. I just—cannot."

I step back. When her eyes fill with tears, I hurt a little less; but by the time a tear trickles down my own cheek and side-winds to the corner of my mouth, she's composed herself. She sets her dirty dishes in the sink. "Okay, well, I need to head out. I'll be back late tonight. If you leave, would you turn on the porch light?"

My heart takes the quickest path back to its cave before it slows to its usual tempo of exile.

When I am alone, my first scramble is for the remote, my second for my one-hitter. But before I turn on the TV and reach for my lighter, I force myself to be comfortable with the silence.

I park my ass on the edge of the couch cushion, elbows on knees, head in hands. Without the noise of the TV or the brain-static of the weed, I notice the toilet upstairs that runs, the hum of appliances doing their job. I notice the house creaking. Creaking is the loneliest sound.

I sit with the creaks. I sit with my mom's refusal. I sit with losing Jesse, getting abused and fucked by Mr. Stewart, and the insignificance of well over fifty sex partners. I sit with how I'm scared to go to college, how I'm exceptional here but how I will be average there, both in academics and tennis.

I am a tidy box of sorrow, sealed tight, with a bit of saline seeping out the corners. Asking for help frightens me. Ignoring my pain has proven detrimental. Having to address it alone seems unmanageable. I will tote my little box with me everywhere, forever.

"Hey."

I jump. "*Jesus*. What the fuck?"

"Are you fucking meditating? I've been knocking for, like, a minute." Ollie drops a new pipe that's shaped like dick in my lap. A berry-scented car air freshener with a cheap Christmas bow on it follows. "Happy birthday. Get a car."

I try to remember the date, or even the month. "Thanks," I say and fondle the penis pipe before sniffing the air freshener. I am too embarrassed to admit I forgot it's my birthday, even more embarrassed to admit my mother did. I know I'm blushing, and I hope Ollie overlooks it.

"Got you a coffee, too. It's time to be a man. No more seltzer." He hands it to me and then points at the ligature marks on my wrists. "What's up with that shit on your arms?"

"Nothing." I leave my wounds exposed. I'm too tired to hide them or offer an explanation for the burns. I sip my second cup of coffee this year, wincing when another syrupy concoction of extra milk and sugar hits my tongue.

Ollie says, "What do you do with him, anyway?"

"What do you mean?"

His entire catalog of don't-bullshit-me faces flashes in seconds. "You know what I fucking mean."

"I don't know." I blow on my coffee. "Normal stuff."

"Yeah, real normal," he says, nodding at my arms. "He's so old. You watch the news together while you cuddle?"

"Shut up."

Ollie disappears into my kitchen and returns with an opened and clipped bag of pretzels that must be a year old. "Are you coming to school today, or what?"

"Oll?"

He grunts and stuffs another handful in his mouth. "Rrhutt?"

"How's Jesse?"

He dry-swallows some pretzel, hacking up a piece before speaking. "You fucked that up, boy."

"I really did." I hang my head.

He allows me a moment of self-pity before punching my shoulder. "Stop being a pussy. Get up. Get out of your fucking pajamas. Let's go to school."

Removing my pajama bottoms and sliding on clothes that make me look like I give a fuck about myself exhausts me. I sit on the floor of my closet until Ollie throws a dirty T-shirt at me. "You know," he says, "I get that you'll put your cock in anything, but Jesse really likes you, man. And I like him. You're a real dick."

"I know." I look at Ollie. "Please don't tell him I asked about him."

I have one more invitational this year, a charity match for the blind, called the "Spring Classic," to which I've already committed to go with my partner, Harry. As usual, no matter how I position my leg over the whole of the bus seat, Harry shoos it away and plops down. The worst conversationalist, he tells me more about eczema and fireworks than any person should know.

"Please, man. Just *please*," I say and cover my ears, "shut the fuck up for five minutes."

I'm drowsy from the bus ride and standing at sign-in, and I slog up two flights of metal outdoor stairs to our motel room with my bag and gear.

As I choose the bed I want, I realize I can't take my shirt off in front of Harry. All the scars I've developed over the past month are on my back, upper legs, and ass. I go to the bathroom to change for dinner.

"Who taught you manners all of the sudden?" Harry calls. "You're shy now, Dan?"

When I piss, my urine contains a curl of blood, which mushrooms until it disappears. With my back to the mirror, I look over my shoulder and note the bruise over my kidney. "That seems like a problem," I whisper. The four, half-moon scabs on my shoulder could be nothing other than the marks of a violent encounter, and I touch them one at a time with my pinky.

When I return to the room, Harry's already on his bed, lying down, legs crossed, messing with his tablet. "It stinks in here," I say as I prop open the door to our musty room. "Are you reading about tennis? I know you are."

"So what? You ready?" He's gruff, always annoyed with my lack of enthusiasm. "You sign-in for tomorrow?"

"Try not to be a crazy person all night. Take it easy." I kick off my shoes and flop back on the bed. "We've done this, like, eight million times."

My phone buzzes. *When you finish on Sunday, please come over for supper. I'll be thinking about you until then.*

The "please" surprises me almost more than Mr. Stewart's sentiment.

Could be this is some sort of sting operation. Someone has his phone, has him in custody, and I'm getting groomed to come home like everything's normal. I'll be testifying in court instead of on my way to freshman orientation.

I write back, leaving it neutral. *Probably 8 or after.*

He replies: *Good luck. I wish you were here.*

I read that again and smile to myself. What he expects as a response confounds me. He's rarely demonstrative, and never by text. I'm used to instructions and requests for check-ins.

Upon my third read of the message, I begin to dislike myself more than I do him. I hate how I cling to the scraps of his kindness, that the most watered-down show of affection made me happy. I spit and rub it into the concrete walkway with the toe of my shoe while staring at his words. I write, *Thanks,* and stuff the phone into my pocket.

Inside, I throw a sock at Harry. "You getting food?"

"No way. I'm not risking food poisoning on the night before a seven-a.m. call. I brought my own."

"I'll bring you back some cod."

"Don't."

"I'm kidding."

"I never know when you're kidding, Dan. Your sense of humor is nonexistent."

Dinner is a buffet—a putrid mess of food that is either overcooked or underripe—and there must be a hundred people here. A boy named Caleb eyes me up at the salad station. I recognize him from all over the state, all over the courts. According to my stats and the bracket, there's a good chance he and I could play each other before tomorrow evening.

I look him over. When he's not in tennis whites, I am certain

Caleb is working at his family's roadside farmer's market. Blonde, freckles, memorizes scripture.

Boys like Caleb are why I used to like traveling for matches. I was able to see a cross section of guys I hadn't chewed through, considered, or rejected. Dozens of wins, dozens of orgasms, and once a dry hump, which is something I'll never do again. The burn I sustained from a horny, overzealous Dominican kid pulled my focus at the next day's match, and an aggressive baseliner kicked my ass up and down the court.

When he speaks, I ready myself for what I'm sure will be small talk. "Hey." He checks me out over the salad bar's sneeze-guard. "You have an early call?"

"Yeah. Don't you?"

"Seven."

"Same."

"You want to hang out tonight?"

"I can't."

Caleb licks his lips and pouts. "How about tomorrow, after we're done? I haven't come for a week. I shouldn't do it now, anyway."

"That trick doesn't work." I rap on my tray with my fingers. "Better to be relaxed."

"It's always worked for me," he insists.

"If you say so. I'll be the one with the trophy when your pent-up plan backfires."

Caleb ignores my quip and remains determined. "What's your name?"

My phone vibrates in my pocket. It's Ollie: *Can you talk?*

I am sure I have not spoken to Ollie on the phone...ever. He calls before I can reply. I hold up a finger to Caleb, whisper my name, and leave my half-prepared salad plate in the queue. "Special occasion?" I ask Ollie "Are you on fire?"

"Man." It's more of an exhale than a word. I know he's smoking. I picture him with his eyes closed and a foot kicked up on his tire. "It's Jesse. His brother died."

I don't think. "Come get me."

*

The scene in Jesse's house is much like I remember in my own home after my father was shot. Standing room only amidst throngs of women, too much food, and a lot of stiff upper lips on tear-stained faces. With a meek series of apologetic mumbles, I weave sideways through a living room filled with middle-aged people as I try to avoid hitting anyone with my backpack.

In the kitchen, where it's also wall-to-wall people, I stand in the corner unnoticed for several minutes. Three men pick through a vegetable tray. When I'm finally granted eye contact from a too-tan mom in a cream-colored pantsuit, I say, "Is Jesse here?"

Before the too-tan mom replies, a woman with eyes and a nose that are unmistakably Jesse's looks up from arranging sandwich condiments. "Daniel?" She comes to me, taking my face in her hands and kissing my forehead. She smells of onions and soft florals. "I knew it. I knew you were Daniel. Jesse told me all about you. I'm his mom, Annie."

I want to ask what he said about me, but I follow the consolation script. "Sorry for your loss."

She holds back tears. Those eyelashes couldn't blink faster, but her expression sets itself to neutral again, her willpower rebellious. She pats the shoulder of the man pulling the plastic wrap off cold cuts. "Trev, this is Daniel, Jesse's friend."

I assume Trev is Jesse's dad, although they look nothing alike. Trev has olive skin, a round face, and the bags under his eyes are the color of a new bruise. At first, his smile seems sincere. When it wilts, however, like the rest of his face, he grimaces, pissed off that manners are of any importance on a day like this.

Jesse's mom rests two fingertips on my forearm. "Does he know you're here?" When I shake my head, she says, "He said no visitors. I'm so sorry."

I can't tell whether she's protecting him from only me or from everyone else in the world too. She may be the type of mom Jesse could share stuff with. Maybe she knew of a person named Daniel who was a dick and broke Jesse's heart and should never, ever, under any circumstance be allowed through the gate. But there is no way I'm leaving. I have to see him. "Just five minutes. Please."

She slowly shakes her head. "I don't think it's a good—"

"Annie," Trev interrupts, barely the breath to release the words, "just let him go up for a minute. Jesse hasn't moved in a day."

Before anyone else can tell me no, I push through the kitchen crowd, the tightly packed groups of adults in the living room, and the band of children at the foot of the stairs. On the second floor, I rush down the hallway, stopping in front of Jesse's door. I have no right to be here, and my timid knock agrees. I try again, this time with a rap he'd have to be obliterated by weed and beer not to hear. "Jesse?"

I turn the knob. His room shows itself different in the light, a pale yellow that is more outworn than cozy. When I sniff the air, all I get is the stink of musty pillows, unwashed clothes, stale smoke. Underneath, I detect air freshener where his mom must have tried to get a leg up on cleanliness, just for company.

There he is, a lump under blankets, not a toe or strand of hair visible. His blinds are down. A plate of cheese and crackers sits untouched on the floor next to his bed. I close the door. The further I can get into the room, the closer to his bed, I hope the less chance I'll be asked to leave. I'm already in. Why bother telling me to get out?

I stand next to the bed, analyzing the tempo of his breath. He might be waiting for a touch, a word, anticipating more cheese and crackers that will go to waste. He could be sleeping, escaping in slow, steady respiration. I gently touch the spot—one second, one finger—where his shoulder might be. The blanket muffles his murmur. I whisper, "Jesse?"

"Mmm."

It's all he says as I pull off my shoes, lift his blanket, and climb into bed beside him. I don't presume so much as to press against him, so I lie on my back and listen to him breathe.

I fall asleep with him for less than an hour and wake to find him returning from the hallway. His hands are nestled in the pockets of a hoodie I left at his house long ago. He crawls back into bed without looking at me and faces the windows. "Mmm."

Again, remaining quiet might be the only way he'll forget I'm here, keeping him unbothered just enough to let me stay. I am a weight on his bed, though, an indentation in his mattress. I know not to ask how he's doing, if it's okay that I'm here, if I can get him anything. When my father died, I didn't want to talk for weeks. If someone tried to speak to me, I didn't hear it anyway.

Within minutes, his gentle snores put me at ease. I fall asleep next to him again, wanting to put my hand on his heart like I did in the bathroom with the Twizzlers.

At midnight, Jesse's mom knocks and opens the door without waiting for a response. She remains in the doorway, trying to see if he's awake. I shake my head. We exchange a look, and she smiles, like she knows I have this watch. "We're going to bed," she whispers. "Help yourself to anything in the kitchen."

My mom rarely acknowledged me in the days after my father's death. She never peeked into my room, and no one brought me cheese and crackers. How his mom, who must be in shock and inconsolable, can still be caring so fully for her living child amazes me.

As soon as the door closes, Jesse rests his hand on my arm. "Go home."

It's not cruel or angry. It's half-assed. I push back to see how much he means it. "I don't want to go home."

"Go home. You've been here forever."

"If you really want me to leave, I'll leave."

"Mmm." He turns over again, but this time he presses his ass into my leg and sighs. "Will you put something on my laptop?"

In the dark, I feel my way to his desk, unplug it, and bring it to the bed. I put on what he loves: an endless stream of nature shows: wombats, flamingoes, coral, wolves. I lie back again and sit the laptop on my stomach. When the first video begins, the narrator says, "This Patagonian cavy can jump up to six feet in the air."

Jesse snuffles in his pillow. "That's good."

I've been holding in piss for hours. Each sentence I speak or any movement I make brings me closer to getting the boot, I'm certain of it. I can't wait any longer, though. "Is it weird for me to go to your bathroom?"

"No." Jesse turns on his back. In the light of the laptop, his face is swollen, the puffiness under his eyes obscuring his vision more than heavy lids on his most stoned day ever could. Without looking at me, he says, "Will you bring me water?"

At last, I can be of service. "I'll bring you whatever you want."

Jesse tosses and fidgets in annoyance. "I want water."

In the hallway, I run into a couple of elderly people in their pajamas. Their pleasant smiles make me feel welcomed. Downstairs, the only light is the glow of the owl clock and the digital timer on the oven. I search for food in a house full of hushed or sleeping mourners.

Before I hunt for the glasses, I use my alone time to check my Mr. Stewart phone. Time-stamped several hours after what should have been dinnertime, his text is to-the-point. *Where are you?*

I find the glasses to the left of the wall oven and fill two of them with water from a pitcher in the fridge. I fix a plate.

"Daniel?"

I jump. My grip on the plate loosens, and some of my finger sandwiches slide onto the counter.

Annie sits in the darkest corner of the dining room. The tilt of her body keeps her out of the moonlight, the streetlights, the glow of the owl clock. She moves her head into the light for me. Her wet face glistens in the moonlight. "I couldn't go to bed. I just want to look at him." She cradles her phone in her palms, swiping with her thumb through photo after photo of Pete.

For a moment, she reminds me of my mother, who sat for a day and night in my father's living room chair after he died, before she retired permanently to her bedroom. She had the same absent stare, and she clutched his last used scotch tumbler, occasionally dipping her finger in the amber liquid and rubbing it across her lower lip. My father's wallet lay open next to her, and she looked down longingly at the clear sleeve that held his driver's license.

I don't know what to say to Annie, so I busy myself returning the few small sandwiches to the plate. When I'm done, I speak to her softly. "I cleaned up the mess. I hope it's okay."

"Yes." She keeps her eyes on the phone and the photos. "Daniel? Get Jesse to eat."

"I will, yes."

Upstairs, Jesse now wears his glasses, which seems like a sign he's going to be conscious for a while. He faces me for the first time since I've been here. "Did you go to your dad's funeral?"

"I had to." I hand him a glass. "I was too young to choose."

Next to him in bed, I balance the plate on my leg. I remain still, waiting for him to go for a piece. I'm a birdwatcher hoping for the sighting of the decade. After a few minutes, Jesse selects a piece of cheese. He chews slowly and moves the mush around in his mouth as if it has no taste. It probably doesn't; for weeks, every sensory experience was either too much or too little. Jesse tries with a carrot. Same thing.

He touches the plate, shoving it an inch with his finger. "Move this." I do, and he puts his head on my thigh. It seems like permission to touch him. I place my fingers on his cheek, but when he flinches, I pull them back and hold my breath until I recover from the backfire.

The short videos have gone through a peculiar maze; the one that plays now features a documentary about the prospect of Chinese world domination. I find some chimps to reset the loop. We watch so many videos about deep sea life I feel like I'm in a submarine. We occasionally touch—bumps knees, knock elbows, conk heads—but it's never on purpose. Once, he rolls into me, distractedly tugging on the strings of my hoodie, and says, "I'm numb."

I can't touch him, and my words will fall short of comfort, too. I only say, "I know."

He pauses the videos. "Are you going to leave soon?"

I don't want to ask him what he wants anymore. "No."

"What about—clothes?"

"I grabbed stuff before I came here."

"Funeral clothes?"

"Yes." I thought I was being presumptuous when I packed anything other than jeans and a T-shirt. I don't have much to wear for a funeral, but I at least have a shirt with a collar, pants, and shoes that I use for tennis banquets. If Jesse refused me at the door yesterday, I would have gone home, ashamed and with only myself as witness, and returned the clothes to their hangers.

Jesse says, "I wish you had known him. Pete. Then, I could talk about him more, and you could get it."

"I still want to know. I could still get it."

"They never found his body." Jesse chews his bottom lip. "He was surfing. They looked for five days."

With Jesse, I discovered a way to touch out of affection. After being with him, I could boast that my every human contact was no longer wholly sexual. Now when I hug him, his body stiffens until he finally collapses into me.

I should be thinking about only him, if I'm hugging too hard or too long, if this is what he needs. Instead, I'm thinking about how I haven't touched anyone like this—without motive—since before my dad left for work that day.

When I wake, I find Jesse facing away from me. I know he's crying. He makes no noise, but the bed trembles along with his shoulders. He says, "How long does this suck for?"

My cool hand against warm skin startles him. I'm relieved he doesn't shrug me off. "It will always suck."

He writhes against me until he flips on his back, kicking off the covers, revealing dirty sweats barely pulled to his hips. He nails my shin twice with his foot. The kicks—calculated and well-aimed but meant to seem incidental to his repositioning—deserve retaliation, or they would at any time but this. His body rolls into mine. With an acid whisper, he buries his face in my armpit and denounces everything. "I hate everyone, every motherfucking one and every fucking thing."

"I know—"

"You don't know anything." His voice quavers. "You lie. Probably all the time." He drapes himself over me to capture his T-shirt from the floor. After pulling it on in a hurry, he stumbles to a stand and leaves the room with no word.

Alone, I can mope, exhale, and let my eyes water. I calm myself and take a few moments to wake up further under a gentler circumstance. His insistence that I leave could come at any moment. I dress and wait on the edge of his bed.

The door opens. No one enters. From the hallway, a huff, a moan, and a deep breath herald Jesse's return. He comes in and avoids looking at me, instead going to his closet and selecting a pair of dark gray pants. "We need to go soon," he says, holding out the pants for inspection. "I can't be bothered with much."

"I know—"

"Dan," he says and sighs, "I know you know. You don't have to tell me you know. All I want is for you to be here and not tell me how much you know." He tosses the pants on the bed beside me and returns with a white button-down shirt, still wrapped in the plastic from the cleaners.

As if it's me he's shredding, he eviscerates the dry-cleaning plastic, ignoring its perforated seam. "Anyway, you had an invitational this weekend?"

"Yeah." I am unsure whether to expound upon why I'm here and not there. "How did you know?"

"Because I'm stupid and still thinking about you." He drops his sweats to the floor and stands in front of me, naked from the waist down. Over his T-shirt, he slips on and buttons his dress shirt, which barely covers his dick. "I figured it out about you and Stewart a long time ago." He watches me cautiously. "And I still liked you."

"I've always liked you. So much. More than—" I decide not to finish that thought and instead reach for his hand. He sneers at me and leaves my offer untouched, midair until I drop it, disappointed.

He suddenly sucks in a breath and holds it, searching my eyes for an explanation about why I hurt him. His fingers disappear into the cuffs of his shirt. "You're still with him?"

"No," I say, "I'm not with him."

"Since?"

I lower my eyes. "Since...Saturday."

His toes curl against the carpet. "Okay."

His languor makes him vulnerable and permissive. Before I can touch him—and I think I telegraph that I'm going to touch him—he steps away and glares at me. "Actually, it's not really okay."

He pulls on his pants, still no underwear, and straightens, stiffening his posture and throwing his shoulders back. "Why are you here, Dan? You show up, digging into me because you know I'm too beat up to tell you to fuck off. And you were still with him *Saturday*?"

There's only *I know*, which I'm forbidden to say, or *I'm sorry*, which was always ineffectual when people said it to me.

After a low moan, Jesse takes a seat beside me. "You know how tired I am right now? I honestly don't give a fuck about anything, least of all this. Get your shit together. We need to go."

I expect to be uncomfortable riding with Jesse in the back of his parents' car, but everyone moves ahead as though that was the plan all along. I fuss over a toothpaste stain on my shirt, which looks like cum, and Jesse rides with his head against the window. When his parents get out of the car, Jesse turns to me. "Don't leave me in there alone."

"I won't."

"You better not leave."

"I won't."

Pete's circle of friends and family is extensive, so the funeral home has monitors for the way-back rows, like the ones in macro-churches or stadiums, but normal TV size. Risers for flowers, sitting rooms, podiums, and the appropriate but disconcerting hush. And as at my father's funeral, the directors try so hard yet fail to be unobtrusive; their every move is eye-catching.

"I have to stand over there." Jesse points to the receiving line where his parents stand, twitchy, gray, with faces sunken around the eyes. "This is going to be so long."

I know.

He digs into his pants pocket and hands me two joints. "Here, I don't want any today. I thought I would, but you can take them. I have to go."

In case anyone might want to stop me for a chat about Pete, only to find me at a loss for a memory to share, I avert my eyes as I move through the influx of funeral-goers. Finding a seat early seems like the best option, away from the sniffles and stories and sobs. No sooner has my ass hit the bench than Jesse appears next to me. "I changed my mind. Where can we smoke?"

"This place is huge," I say, recalling how my mother and I wandered into the wrong memorial twice. "Like a hundred bathrooms too."

We stand in a stall together, passing the joint back and forth. The silence is comfortable. This couldn't be more different from the last time I stood in a stall with a guy.

Jesse stares at the floor. "I'm not getting back in that creepy line."

"Then, just sit. People will come to you, though. It's going to happen."

"That's fine. I'm just on display up there. And everyone's thinking, *Well, let's see if this one can fill his shoes.*"

"No one's thinking that."

"You know they are."

I nod and change the subject. "How does your mom know me?"

"Because she's omniscient." He tosses the roach in the toilet. "How the fuck do you think she knows you?"

"You talked about me?"

"Don't get full of yourself. She's nosy." He examines his fingernails, picking at an already reddened cuticle. "My house is going to be filled with a ton of these people after this. You should go home."

"If you think I'm leaving, you're so wrong."

I haven't seen his smile in a long time. I touch the corner of his upturned mouth with my thumb. When I pull my hand away, I tilt my head, silently asking permission. He reaches past me and turns the lock on the door. "I don't want you to touch me like that anymore."

I hold my breath. To keep things moving normally, as if I don't care about that, I dig out mints from the pocket of my pants, offering one to him before we return to the hall. I follow Jesse to the third row. He sits on the end, so no older relatives need to reach too far to squeeze him against their hip or shake his hand or kiss the top of his head.

Ollie, Brad, and Jackie come together. No auxiliary friends, customers, or contacts come; Jackie and Brad made sure of that. Each time there's a rumble at the back of the hall—new arrivals who sob or console—I check over my shoulder to see the grievers. The word is out, and some teachers have come to pay their respects, singly or in clusters, but Mr. Stewart has stayed away.

Ollie's himself, in a suit that is one size too small. Brad wears flip-flops and socks and eats crackers from his coat pocket. Jackie knows how to dress for a funeral; her modest black dress falls below her knees, the curls of her shiny hair fall over the octopus tattoo, and her shoes give off nothing near a fuck-me vibe. Sitting next to me, she leans her head on my shoulder. "I was so happy to see you here."

Just as his friends are seated, Jesse rises. "Grandma." A hunched and broad woman with a complexion that matches his pulls him into her arms. He buries his face in her neck. When he steps back, his face is wet, his cheeks bright pink.

She wipes his cheek with an arthritic-looking finger. "Oh, my love. We've been worried about you. You wouldn't come out of your room."

He glances over his shoulder and points down the line at us. "That's Jackie, Brad, Ollie." His focus falls on me. "This is Dan."

When he reaches for my hand, it takes me a second to figure out what he's doing. He clasps it, and I follow his lead, holding his hand tightly enough to let him know I want to keep holding it. I tell myself that it's his nervous response to the surroundings and, of course, the circumstance. All the bustling, mumbling, and weeping, all the perfumes, body odors, and unexpected and sometimes unwanted hugs and kisses. Add even a smidgen of strong weed to that mix, and you've got yourself a festival of paranoia and an urge to flee.

His grandma hugs him again and sniffs his shirt. "Have you been smoking marijuana?" When he nods once, she says, "Oh, goodness. Don't let your father smell you like that. He'll ground you for good."

While Jesse soaks up his grandma's love, his grip on my hand tightens and loosens, tightens and loosens. Although we are not boyfriends—his stance about the terms of our relationship couldn't have flip-flopped within the hour—we are boyfriends for all to see. Hand-holding boyfriends. If ever there was a place to crack and admit I wanted a boyfriend, at a funeral in the middle of three hundred-plus people is the last place I would have chosen.

Jesse receives two loud, wet grandma-kisses on his cheek before she moves along, up the aisle, to one of the best seats in the house. Only a beat passes before Jesse looks at me, looks at my hand, and then lets it go.

*

　　　　　JENNIFER GREIDUS

After the funeral, Jesse's house is teeming with people, and I do my best to navigate, with some semblance of lucidity, the rooms of lamenters, abandoned cups of coffee, and appetizer plates. Fielding the question "How did you know Pete?" gets no easier each time I repeat the answer.

Every guest wants to help. They move in and out of the kitchen, trying to keep up with the selection of snacks, replacing cookies, crackers, meats, and cheeses as soon as they're snatched from the platters.

Jesse sits on the corner of the couch, hunched forward, his head in his hands. His position remains that way no matter who speaks to or touches him. I stand in the corner of the room, drinking flat soda and wanting to shelter him, to scoop him up to his room for more vapid videos about guinea pig gestation or cows lying down.

My phone vibrates against my hip. I startle, check that no one noticed my jump, and return to my flat soda. It vibrates again. I'm surprised it's taken Mr. Stewart this long. Usually, I'm chastised if I respond too slowly to a text, let alone skip dinner with no notice. I look at the time. I am a few hours away from missing another balanced meal.

I find the bathroom and read his messages. Instead of demands and degradation, there are only two innocuous sentences in the first message—*I'm worried about you. You weren't in school today*—and one request in the second: *Please let me know you're okay.*

It is Monday. Mr. Stewart knows about Jesse's brother by now. In the teachers' lounge this morning, the death must have been the headline. And in ninth period AP English, my empty seat next to Jesse's empty seat must have given the news some subtext.

It seems equally vital and frivolous that I keep in contact with Mr. Stewart over the next day or two. Deciding what to write requires some thought, but I have only a moment. There are two paths and choosing the one that buys me the most time with Jesse seems obvious.

I think I have the flu. Stomach stuff. I don't want to get you sick.

I flush nothing and exit the bathroom, fussing with the seam on my pants while I get my shit together.

Jesse is no longer on the couch; he's climbing the stairs to the second floor. I follow him. He begins to close his bedroom door behind him, but I stop it with my foot. "Hey. You okay?"

He waves me in with a limp hand as he kicks off his shoes and pulls off his socks. "I wasn't keeping you out. Just everyone else."

Inside, I lean against the door while he pulls his shirt over his head. Every move he looks like a burden. The sleeve gets stuck on his arm until he steps on the rest of the shirt and yanks it free. His glasses fall to the floor. He pushes them under the bed with his toe.

When he notices I'm watching him, he unbuttons his pants, pushing apart the placket so I can see the top of his pubic hair.

If it were another day, I'd say the show was a dare or an invitation. Today, it's apathy and exhaustion. He has the pained, resolute countenance that accompanies how one mistakenly believes he is, right then, experiencing the worst parts of grief, when what is true is that there is so much more to go.

"Jesse," I say and gesture vaguely to the door behind me, "I'm not going to ask you every day how you feel about this. I won't. I'll assume today is the watermark. If it gets lower, then you let me know, okay?" I take a breath and ponder if I'm saying this for Jesse, who seems unaffected, or for me, because it's what I would have wanted to hear at age fourteen.

I drop my head and quietly continue. "I can't take it away, but all I want is to make you comfortable while you're sad. That's all I want." It's the best I can do; I hope the words will help him feel supported, comforted, less alone.

When I look up, Jesse sneers. "Oh, is that all you want, Dan? You want me to feel good about that? How many guys have sucked your dick since me? Fuck you." He undresses fully, gets in bed, and turns away from me. "Whatever. Stay or go. I don't care. I'm going to sleep."

I wish my bag was by the door so I could take it and go. Instead, it lays open on the opposite side of the room, clothes spilling out of it, and my laptop wires are tangled with his. I remember I had another bag, a shopping bag for my dress clothes. I scan the room and don't see it. Packing will take too long, anyway, when all I want to do is turn and leg it—still an option. My mom can buy me a new laptop, and the clothes mean nothing to me.

Of course, I'm not going anywhere. If I leave, if *this* doesn't matter to me, then what could possibly matter to me, ever?

My clothes stay on. I remain near the edge of the bed. I recall when Jesse was in my bedroom for the first time, in this same position. Unlike then, I risk a touch. His arm, the curve of his waist, his leg. No objections present themselves; he is still and quiet, his breath slowing. My hand finds a home on his hip when I slip under the covers beside him.

I wake to Jesse twitching—and then full-on flailing—against my body in the bed. I shake him out of it. He sobs. I remember the sobs, the bawling that began before consciousness. Jesse cleans the tears off his face with the sheet. Unembarrassed, he watches the ceiling until his despair ebbs.

"That won't last too long," I say, pulling his head to my chest. With my thumb, I wipe a tear away from his cheek just before it rolls into his ear.

"How long?" he says.

"It's probably different for every—"

"*How long?*"

"A year. Maybe a year."

"When did you go back to school?"

Everyone gives a mourner a grace period. When my dad died, life paused, but it insisted too soon that I'd let enough time pass. People expected things again. School wanted me back. I was told staying busy would help. "A week, I think."

"No way. I can't."

"So, then, you won't."

When I touch his leg, he squeezes his eyes closed, shaking his head so much I fear whiplash. "Goddamn, man. It sucks I feel this way about you. I *just* got over you." While his thumbnail falls victim to his insistent oral fixation, he checks me out through puffy, red lids. "If you liked me so much, why did you choose him?"

"I had to," I say, "for you and Brad."

We sit up at the same time, scuttling to opposite ends of the bed, both knowing what I said is untrue and perhaps readying to fight about it. But Jesse is too exhausted to call me on it with more than a frown, and I'm too embarrassed to admit the scenario posed no threat to anyone. I could have turned that situation around in an hour.

He gets up, paces naked, looks for something to wear and finds a crumpled pair of boxers near the closet. Their proximity to him matters more than their cleanliness. Jesse hops on one leg then the other as he struggles to get into his shorts.

I stand, going to my unpacked bag, wishing I'd packed it hours ago. I shove my clothing inside and make room for my laptop. When it won't zip, I contemplate what things I won't miss if I leave here.

Jesse stomps the ground to get my attention. "What's the real reason?"

I should think the reasons for staying with Mr. Stewart are clear, even to Jesse: sex, novelty, bragging rights, a good fucking story. But those aren't my reasons. Neither are the handful of character flaws that I might use as excuses: lazy, selfish, disloyal, and compulsive. I say what feels true and maybe is true. "I think I just wanted to be told what to do." A tennis ball falls out of my bag, and I snatch it before it rolls under his desk.

When I straighten, Jesse is on me before I see him coming. Fierce and determined, he grabs my face and kisses me so hard my teeth gnash the flesh behind my lips. Pushing me away, pulling me back, pushing me away again, he growls and shoves me toward the bed. He fumbles with the buttons at my waist, shoves my pants and shorts to my knees, and pushes them to the floor with his bare foot so I can step out of them.

I don't fight it when he spins me around and presses my face into the mattress. I spread my legs and back up into him. I want him to know what I want. I hear him spit, and he swipes his wet fingers up the crack of my ass. My shirttail is in the way, and he pushes it up my back. I moan. I spread a little more.

What should happen next is obvious. But nothing's happening. I look over my shoulder. Jesse's lips are parted, his face pale. "Dan. What's—" His thumb traces two horizontal lines just above my waistline. A smooth palm follows the curve of my ass. His touch babies the slowly healing welts there, wounds I've not thought about for days. I jump up and turn around.

I look at his walls, the floor, and the aloe plant, at anything but him. With a warm hand, he inches up my shirt along the left side of my torso. I glance down at my skin, so I know exactly what he sees and how freaked out or repulsed he will be.

Up close, Jesse can examine every scab, bruise, and soon-to-be scar. One step back, and he can appreciate the full effect of the landscape: I am a masterpiece, the ubiquitous Seurat with all the bustles and top-hat guys at the river.

He unbuttons the shirt and slowly slides it down my arms. He carefully pulls my T-shirt over my head. My hair falls in my eyes. I leave it there, even when a strand pokes me in the tear duct.

Jesse touches a long, thin scab in its late stage. Its origins escape me. I picked at it for weeks. The manila crust will soon separate from the healthy skin underneath, and I will have a dying star, pink to brown to white. My skin will remain discolored for months, maybe forever.

I shake my head. *Don't acknowledge it.* I shake it again. *Please acknowledge it.* My skin tingles when he touches my back. He finds another telltale lump. "He did this shit to you?"

"No," I say right away, wishing it were so; but with all the chances I've had to tell Jesse the truth and haven't, now I want to start. "Yeah." The word stings worse than a belt.

"Shit." His fingers graze another scar.

In the morning, I smell myself. "I need a shower."

"You really fucking do." He laughs for the first time since I arrived. "You can go ahead. Just don't scare my grandma."

As soon as I step into the hot steam of the shower and close the door, it is a sweatbox of vanilla. Three soaps, and I squish a glob from a beige and brown bottle on my palm: Jesse's. Although I'm tempted to use it, I only ever want to smell it on his skin. I let the water rinse it off my hand and choose another soap.

In the bathroom, I check both of my phones. On the legit phone, Ollie just wants to check in. On Mr. Stewart's phone: 7.

Jesse has removed himself from seclusion. I find him sitting on his couch with sleepless relatives. He's squished between the arm and a middle-aged woman with her head on his shoulder. He's in sweats, no glasses, bare feet on the cushions, knees at his chin.

Everyone succumbed to sadness except his mom, who fakes it well as she ushers me farther into the room, her face brightening. "Daniel. Have a seat. We're having some breakfast. There's coffee on. Jesse told me he wasn't sure if you liked waffles, but," she says and points at what I assume are her sisters and sisters-in-law, "these piggies will gobble them up fast, so I saved you a few in the oven."

Sleeping or exhausted children, ages five to twelve, sit at the feet of the couch and in the corners of the room. The family is engrossed in a film. Something explodes every minute; no one reacts. Heads roll, guts spill, and no one can be bothered to change the channel.

I'm unsure where to sit, until Jesse's aunt reaches for my hand from the couch. "Help me up, sweetie. You can sit here. I need to stretch my legs."

I pull her out of the seat and squeeze between Jesse and another aunt, a pear-shaped woman in a rust-colored jumpsuit with a gold zipper running from pelvis to neck. As if waking from a pleasant but disorienting dream, Jesse swivels his head in my direction. "Do you eat waffles?"

"Sometimes."

He smiles. His eyes get into the smile, too, and I haven't seen that since we were fucked up and unhurriedly touching each other in my bedroom. Jesse pulls my hand into his lap, upturns my palm, and draws circles with his finger. He entwines his fingers with mine.

When his dad rounds the corner, carrying a box of keepsakes—I presume they're from Pete's childhood because a finger-painting on newsprint sticks out of the top—he slows and glances at my hand in Jesse's lap. He seems to say, "Oh," to himself and then continues to the kitchen.

Jesse wants to go upstairs, and I follow. His mom pulls me aside. "Make him eat, Daniel. Please." She hands me a stained melamine platter holding mini pastries.

I think twice about the selection. "Mrs.—"

"Annie."

"Annie," I say, "do you have any...corn chips?"

"Corn—?" She smiles and holds up a finger. "I do. Wait here. I do."

"And maybe ginger ale," I call after her.

Annie has both. She places the corn chips on the platter, and I tuck the ginger ale under my arm.

Upstairs, sweaty and pale, Jesse sits and rocks on the edge of the bed. I want to hold up the bag, celebrate my find, but rejoicing in snack chips won't alter the gloom. With just two tugs, I slip his hoodie over his head. I suggest he lie back, but he resists and groans. A hand on his shoulder works better than my proposal. When he's settled, I pull the sheet up to his chest and sit next to him.

I hope to entice him with the carbonated eruption of ginger ale. When I twist the top, the whisper of flat soda fails me, but the crinkle of the bag opening captures Jesse's attention. The familiar fried corn stink makes me salivate. Manners keep me from taking one before he does.

"Do you want to talk about Pete?" I say.

"Too tired."

"Okay. You want any food. A drink?"

His mouth moves—*no*—but nothing comes out.

I find a video of jungle birds on his laptop and hit play. Jesse pauses it right away. "We were really close. Until he got this one girlfriend. She was super uptight, controlling. And he sort of changed a little."

I eat one chip. He eats one. I take another. He follows. Single chips become handfuls. Soon, half the bag is gone. I will do this until one of us has a stomachache.

He motions for the warm ginger ale, which he swigs out of the bottle. "You know what?" he says, wiping his mouth on his wrist. "He rescued me from drowning. When I was eight. Public pool. I'm serious. Isn't that fucking funny?" Jesse sniffs and gives me a tired half-smile. "Now he's gone, and I can't believe it."

"I'm sorry."

Feeling under his sheets, Jesse comes up with his purple

lighter and pokes me in the rib. "The first time I was at your house, I noticed your drawer full of lighters," he says, "and I thought, 'This guy is really paranoid about not having a lighter.'"

"They're my dad's."

"I figured. I mean, after I got to know you, then I figured." He moves the bag of chips to the floor and slides closer to me. When he touches my back, he finds a welt, then another. He hums a single note in a pitch that makes him seem worried or sad. "You have any evidence or whatever? Like, I don't know, *stuff*. Anything."

My body.

"Besides your—" Jesse nods at my torso. "Besides your body."

"Maybe. Probably. The phone. Other stuff."

"You want me to go with you?"

In the middle of Jesse's anguish, saying yes would be the most shameful request I've ever made. I look around us for some sign of normalcy, some indication that it would be okay for me to say yes. *Yes, I do want that.* But grief saturates his room. Piles of clothing, funeral suit, shoes. He couldn't care less now if anyone sees his weed, papers, a pipe on his desk. Corn chips, the only thing he's eaten for days, are now spilled on his carpet.

And next door, a shuttered bedroom filled with Pete's belongings, thousands of items to sort through. Jesse will need to decide what to keep to hold on to Pete for as long as he can. He will snatch something from his brother's leftovers, the tiniest piece of the most treasured memory. It may fit in Jesse's pocket, and he may carry it around for decades.

Although I have waited too long for the refusal to seem genuine, I still shake my head no. The bed creaks as he moves closer to me, his leg pressed against mine. "It's gonna suck for you. I want to go."

Police. Principal. Millie. I dread telling the story to any one of them. Someone will ask, "How did it start?" and I will have to say, "I started it." I consider keeping all of it to myself, telling no one anything.

Jesse's finger pushes my hair behind my ear. He traces my eyebrows, touches my bottom lip. "Is it okay to touch you?"

We undress, watching and mirroring one another as we shed our clothing. His T-shirt, mine. My boxers, his. Socks together. I lay back, and my thighs part. He knows where to go, and I wrap my legs around him when he gets there. Jesse drops his gaze in between our bodies. His lips move like he's praying.

I smile. "What are you doing?"

"Nothing." He looks away, bashful.

I know what he wants to say, and I want to beat him to it.

ACKNOWLEDGMENTS

Thank you to Susan Strecker for the biggest push, to Don Weise for his editing expertise and patience, and to Laura Strachan for her persistence in finding the perfect home for a book that made most publishers queasy and nervous. I am grateful to everyone in my small world of support and love, past and present, especially Serena, Michael, Suzanne, and Chris.

ABOUT THE AUTHOR

Jennifer Greidus lives in Phoenix with her boyfriend and her sweet dogs. She is the Founding Editor of *X-R-A-Y Literary Magazine*. This is her first novel.